Rachel's Contrition

Rachel's Contrition

A Novel

MICHELLE BUCKMAN

A Chisel & Cross Book
from SOPHIA INSTITUTE PRESS®

This book is a work of fiction. Names, characters, places, and events are either the product of the author's imagination or are used fictiously, and any resemblance to actual persons, living or dead, is entirely coincidental. The work was written for entertainment purposes.

The author is not responsible for any comments, blogs, or websites that appear as a result of this work.

Library of Congress Cataloging-in-Publication Data
Buckman, Michelle.
    Rachel's contrition : a novel / Michelle Buckman.
      p. cm.
    ISBN 978-1-933184-72-2 (pbk. : alk. paper) 1. Single women —
    Fiction. 2. Domestic fiction. I. Title.
    PS3602.U28R33 2010
    813'.6 — dc22

                                  2010023416

10 11 12 13 14 15 10 9 8 7 6 5 4 3 2 1

In memory of
Durelle, Logan, Jason, and Joshua,
cradled in the arms of heaven

Rachel's Contrition

CHAPTER ONE

I have to act civil when I see him. That was part of the *agreement*. So, I plaster a fake smile on my face and bat my eyelashes at him. "Hello, Sinclair. I hope you had a nice weekend."

"Rachel." He says it as if my name is an answer.

His real name is Joseph Sinclair Winters, Jr., but his daddy goes by Joe, so he was stuck with Sinclair, which suits him better anyway with the highfalutin family he comes from. It also suits his sophisticated looks — his soft face and thick black hair, with serious eyes staring out behind those thin gold spectacles of his. Not ruggedly handsome like a guy in a women's magazine, but the kind you'd look for in *Forbes;* the kind voted Most Likely to Succeed in high school.

He has an IQ off the charts. *Intelligent but no common sense*, his mother says. She knew what I was at first glance. He probably agrees with her nowadays.

I agree with his mom about his lack of common sense. How else could he forget about our baby? He remembers now. He forgot only once. But that was enough to change our lives forever, and enough to end hers. Me, I'll never forget our baby, ever. Just thinking of her sends a shooting pain through my gut.

The parking lot is full of cars, but we're the only people standing out in the midday sun. We could be open with each other right now. No one would witness our conversation and pass it on during some social tête-à-tête. We could say what's really on our minds, we could come to terms with the truth, but we don't. We used to have so much to say to each other that we could stay up till the wee hours and not run out of words until our lips found better ways to communicate, but lately Sinclair doesn't even answer my polite questions. I think of all we've been to each other and wither inside.

The day has offered respite from the cold weather in the Blue Ridge Mountains. The breeze has stilled, and the midday sun is beating down on us, evaporating early-morning rain off the black pavement so that everything below my chin wavers slightly as if I'm looking through water, making me feel dizzy. I braved the cold and wore my short navy dress to impress Sinclair, to remind him why he fell in love with me, but it doesn't matter. He looks down at me emotionless behind his gold-rimmed glasses. "Did everything go all right?"

"Sure. Fine."

He nods. No more words. No small talk or anything personal to show we were married for years. I don't think that's very civil, but I'm not as fussy about the rules as he is, so I don't complain.

I push our son Seth toward him. Seth could cry and cling to my leg because he doesn't have to obey any rules about being civil. The *agreement* is about him, but not for him. Very confusing. Seth doesn't scream, or yell *Mommy* or anything, though. He walks silently to his father and places his perfect tiny hand in his father's large smooth one. Just looking at them, I can feel Seth's baby flesh as it used to clutch at my skin when I breastfed him, his sharp baby nails leaving red lines on my pale flesh, and Sinclair's doctoring hands, so well guarded against rough work, reaching for me with equal urgency. Men take and take.

I raise my eyes to Sinclair's, and we stare at each other. He shifts his weight, uncomfortable with the memories he reads in my eyes, and says nothing. We were never this silent when we lived in the same house.

I wish Seth would cry so I could hug him and tell him how much I love him, because I only get to keep him every other weekend. Every visit, we become more like strangers. I want to hold him, to make him love me, but I don't want to reach for him here in the open. I tried it once, and he shrank away into his father.

The *agreement* confuses me. I should have ended up with Seth. Dr. Arick says Sinclair got him because I need to rest, to get over the anxiety. He may be right because I do get anxious. A lot of things don't make sense anymore. I have to work very hard to think straight. But that's not the real reason. I know why they gave him to Sinclair.

Sinclair turns to go. "We'll see you in two weeks, Rachel. I'll bring him to your house."

Two weeks. I'm not worried about remembering the date because he'll call before he comes. He's very careful about remembering everything nowadays, while I'm no longer expected to remember anything at all anymore.

I stand in Applebee's parking lot and watch them go in to lunch. We used to eat at restaurants together. I used to fluff up my blond hair and curl the ends under. I'd rub blush into my cheeks, paint my lips a deep red, and file my nails to perfection. I had new outfits every week; I was never caught wearing the same outfit twice to anywhere we frequented. Sinclair loved to parade me to a reserved table, past his associates, past friends from the club, even past the women who flirted with him, showing me off to all of them. And I loved it. I loved being the one he chose against the prejudice of his family, his fair lady, the mutt who married a pedigree.

Now I'm left out here.

He said this meeting place was convenient for him. I might be blond, but I'm not stupid. He doesn't want me to know where he's moved. Dumb him. I already know. I watch him and Seth whenever I want.

I don't like standing in the parking lot alone. People are probably staring at me out the windows, and some media shark is likely to snap a photo and plaster it on the Internet. Once upon a time, it was about our Cinderella marriage, but dirt sells even better.

I stare at the ground, thinking about where I should go. At my feet, I see a picture. Not a photograph, but a little card with a colorized sketch of a nun on it, and with a flash I remember the nun in the graveyard standing off to one side by herself. Why was she there? I stoop down and pick up the picture. It might be the same nun, but probably not. The card says *Saint Thérèse of Lisieux* across the top. I doubt a saint would get caught anywhere near me. I smooth the dirt off it and slide it into my pocketbook to look at later. I don't want to look at it too closely here because I might start thinking about it all. I might cry and fall apart with everyone in the restaurant staring at me out the window. With Sinclair and Seth staring at me.

Nervous heat washes over me. I wish I could melt away into the pavement.

I need to go somewhere.

I can't go see my mother. She lives two hundred miles away. Even if she were ten miles away, I wouldn't visit her, because she doesn't want anything to do with me. She never liked Sinclair or Seth. She thinks Sinclair is stuck up. It's his manners. She thinks they're put-on airs because she's never been around anything but beer-swilling jerks. She wouldn't know a Chardonnay from a Grenache. Her idea of a three-course meal is chips and dip before the entrée and ice cream afterward.

I used to be just like her. I grew up in her shadow in a decrepit apartment in downtown Raleigh. I don't know who my father was. He could have been any of the guys who wandered in and out of our lives, but she never pointed to one of them and said, "There's your father." She never said anything to me about any of them. She'd tell me to get them a beer out of the fridge and to go to my room to get out of her hair. I was twelve before I realized I didn't have to lie in the dark listening to her bed thump against the wall. I didn't have to listen to the whispers and moans and feel so useless, so unwanted, so set apart and in the way. I could crawl out my bedroom window, and leave for the night and she wouldn't care a bit.

I found my own comforts.

I was a waif of a thing, with gold spun hair that hung down my back as long and thin as my pale limbs, far from a beauty at that point, but it didn't matter. I quickly learned there were men aplenty waiting to comfort a young girl with empty eyes and a heart as unformed as her body.

I'd planned to spend my first escape night with my girlfriend Jennifer, but I never got there. I met Kenny Sprat on the way. He was walking home from a ball game. Kenny wasn't the best-looking guy in school, but he was fourteen and worked out at the Y a lot, so most girls thought he was pretty hot. He fell in step beside me. Asked me where I was going. Turned out his dad worked the night shift. That night I learned all about thumping beds.

Kenny got bored with me after a few months, but I'd learned the ropes by then, and there was a little more fire in my eyes. With each guy, I learned about the power I held, and unlike my mother, I learned control. I learned how to make a man want me, and I learned to make them wait. By the time I was a freshman in high school, I realized I wanted more than guys with a little pocket money. I knew the money-makers were all headed to college, and that's where I had to go to set my future straight. I managed to pull my grades up enough to get accepted to the University of North Carolina, and with my mother's lack of income, I was given all the financial aid I asked for. I preferred art to science, but I put my major down as pre-med, thinking that, to catch a doctor, I ought to play in his field. I didn't care about the degree or a trail of distinguished letters; I wanted a gilded *Mrs.* in front of my name. My plan worked.

I played my cards carefully during my first year, dating only selectively. The back alleys had taught me that no one held on to an easy catch. I became the beauty regarded as a rare prize. A date with me was something boys hollered about in the halls of their sweat-laden dorms. After years of sleeping with the worst scum, the best of Carolina rejoiced over a kiss from me at the end of the night.

I moved into better circles. I dated the brother of Susan Chance, president of a sorority that mingled with grad students, until I was pledged. I studied those rich girls until I knew their every mannerism. I moved lithely among their eager boyfriends, searching for the right one, one with the smarts to make it big in a cosmopolitan practice, one with class and culture. When I saw Sinclair walk in one Sunday on Susan Chance's arm, I knew he was the one. He reeked of money. He walked with class. Over champagne punch, I listened to his confident drawl, more restrained and cultured than most of my companions. He regaled our lunch crowd with tales of his last trip to Europe, dropping names of people and places that had others nodding in recognition. His tale wound its way into my head, interspersed as it was with long words and philosophical ideals. I became determined his next trip would include me.

He wasn't a student. He was finishing up his internal-medicine residency. In May, he would be ready to pack his bags for home to join his daddy's well-established practice. As he spoke, I caressed him with my eyes and deliberately turned away when he fastened his gaze on me. As the gathering wandered off to the dessert buffet, he settled at my side. After that, he was putty in my palm.

If I'd kept everything on that level, if I'd remembered I wanted him for position and power, for financial security and a place in society, I would have been fine. But I fell in love with him, and that was my undoing.

Love wasn't a sudden thing. It wove its way into my being like a fine, stray thread of silk in a tapestry. In some ways, my love for Sinclair began years before I knew him, in the formation of who I became because of my stumbling course through life, so that when we crossed paths, everything was in place; I'd become who I needed to be. If we had met any earlier, I wouldn't have been ready for him.

But there was a moment I realized he had accepted me despite my past. We were at the club, and I was being introduced around as his fiancée. Jed, one of the boys from my early years, happened to be sitting at a table. I hadn't noticed him, but he noticed me. He kept staring at me, waiting for a chance to destroy me. Finally his moment came. He put out his foot as I passed him on the dance floor, and I tripped. He was right there, breathing on my neck, pulling me up, sneering at me. "That's what happens when you get above yourself. You fall. Watch your step." Then Sinclair stepped up. He was so serious, so heroic. He took my arm and glared at Jed. "No fear. It's my job to catch her. She'll never fall farther than my arms." And there in his arms, within the fold of his hands with his eyes blazing in my defense, I knew he loved me no matter my past. My original station in life hadn't bothered him back then.

Nevertheless, I couldn't possibly have taken him to see my mother — he wasn't so saintly he would overlook her slop of a hovel — so we invited her out to dinner for introductions before our marriage. We made reservations at The Pines, the most expensive restaurant in Chapel Hill. She showed up in black stretch pants and a leopard-print velour shirt. If he'd had any doubts about where I'd come from, I could tell by his face he knew as soon as she arrived. But he laughed it off.

Who I had been didn't matter at that point.

Sinclair settled into his daddy's practice, and I settled into being a full-time wife. I got pregnant almost immediately, and there I was, living the perfect life — rich, pampered, with husband and child. Everything sailed along blissfully until Seth was three and Caroline was born.

Inside the restaurant, I see Sinclair and Seth being led between tables to a window seat. I don't want them to look out and see me still standing in the open like a discarded person. So I leave.

I drive around awhile to waste time. I can't go home and stare at the television. The cable guy has been working on it for two days, and it still wasn't fixed when I left. I head to the bookstore and spend an hour picking out a new stack of books to read, then drive over to the mall to buy some jewelry, a couple of toys for Seth, eat Chinese food alone in the food court, and buy a couple of outfits. I stop at the park to go for a walk as the sun turns to a glowing globe behind the trees. I pick up a milkshake and drink it in the car as I listen to the radio before I finally decide to head home to visit my friend Colette. I live on her estate, now, right beside her sprawling Tudor. She's renting me the unused servants' quarters out by her pool, a little thing originally built as a pool house, supposedly converted to an apartment by the second owners because they disliked having their maid living in the upper quarters. My living in the pool house doesn't bother Colette; she doesn't swim. In fact, other than wearing short sleeves, I don't think she has bared her heavyset body to the world in over a decade.

I don't care for the pool house. It's too small, but it suited the *agreement*, so I gave in. It's hard to go backward in life after getting used to the Ritz.

It's usually a twenty-minute drive back to Colette's, but I take the scenic route through the park to watch the sunset and then through town to the drug store, the grocery store, and the car wash, wasting time. I can't get there too early, or Colette will still be eating or something. If I wait until nine or ten, her husband, Henry, will have gone to bed, and she'll be ready to kick back, offer me a gin and tonic, a smoke, and a hand of cards. Colette is like that — down home. She's perfectly proper in public, but alone with me, she's different. We lay out our real selves in private. Colette would rather have liquor than wine any day, and prefers poker to bridge, but if I said so to the crowd at the club, she'd laugh me under the table. And I would do the same to her, except I don't go to the club anymore.

When I get to her house, what I see are blue lights and orange lights flashing all over the place. Police are swarming over the property.

The lights make me dizzy. They bring tears to my eyes. My throat feels thick and clogged. I've been here before, surrounded by police and lights and cameras — a time warp, but different. It can't be happening again. It wasn't at night. And it wasn't this house.

My body twists and spins and I know I'm fainting, but I force myself to stand. I swallow the bile rising in my throat. I remind myself that this house is Colette's, not mine. I have to put one foot in front of the other. I have to find out what's happened.

Cameras flash at me as I cross the driveway, hungry photographers hoping there is more money to be made from the saga of my sorry life.

I ignore the orange streamers around the perimeter and stride across the yard to the front door.

CHAPTER TWO

※※

I walk past the policeman without even thinking it inappropriate, but he steps forward and grabs my arm. "Where do you think you're going?"

"I live here."

"What's your name?"

"Rachel Winters."

A skinny cop steps out of the shadows and stares at me. "Let her through."

I smile indulgently as I pass him — *Remember manners at all times,* says the voice in my head. *Be a lady.* Then I hear the skinny guy whispering behind my back. "That's the chick with the kid in the car, remember? She's loony-tunes."

His words sear my heart with their sarcasm. *My baby!* Followed by a flare of anger toward Sinclair. *How could he forget her?* Everyone thinks I ought to have gotten beyond it by now. I may never get beyond it.

"You mean this chick really does live here?"

"In the pool house. If they're looking for suspects . . ."

I glance back at them. Suspects? So it can't be an accident. I pick up my pace. My heels clack against the cement patio like horseshoes as I trot up to the door and rush into the house. My body flushes, one minute hot, the next cold. I call out, "Colette? Colette? Where are you? What's happened?"

Another officer is stationed inside the door. I ignore his startled snatch at me and progress through the open foyer, past the parlor and study to the main living area. Three more men are posted at various points around the room. A man in a suit is hunched on the couch, tape recorder on the coffee table, while a square, homely woman assistant with long brunette hair pulled into a ponytail sits beside him scrawling notes. He's leaning forward, staring at Colette and her husband, Henry, until I walk in. They turn and look at me in unison.

"Rachel Winters. We meet again," says the man as he rises and waves me to a seat.

I hesitate, narrow my eyes at him and force my brain to work. Who is he? He smirks, and I remember. Detective Brown. His name says it all: brown hair, brown eyes, brown suit, brown shoes. The only remarkable thing about him is his tie, which is emblazoned with the Tasmanian Devil from Bugs Bunny cartoons. I'm sure he intends it to symbolize something about his ability to devour bad guys, but I think it's more a caricature of his fat, round face and body, and lack of a neck. A self-portrait.

"Come in and join us," he says to me.

Colette has dropped her face into her plump hands, so I can't read her expression. Henry, pale and stoic, is staring at the wall like a zombie. I know the spot in Nowhere that Henry has found on the wall. My heart pounds in rhythm to the throb in my dizzy head. I think of Caroline, of seeing my baby dead and not believing it. He has the look; I know with certainty someone is dead. There's no way to plug the endless hole. There's no way to patch it, to make it go away. I feel the sharp blades of a blender eating into my gut. How does life continue after such tragedy? Another tragedy, and still we have to go forward.

I force myself to work my way around Colette's prized antique cabinet, past the grand piano (even in agony, my fingers caress the rich mahogany surface and I have to stop them from trailing across the ivory keys), to the two sage-green sofas nestled by the marble fireplace. I crouch in front of Colette, choked with fear. I can barely see out of the watery depths of my tears. "What happened?"

She looks up. Her makeup is a bit overdone, but perfect except for one streak of mascara smeared across her temple. Her narrow, dark eyes are watering, but her fleshy, round cheeks are dry. She's in control. I wonder for a mere split second how she manages it; my armpits are soaking wet, and I haven't a clue what's going on yet.

She looks past me toward her stepdaughter, Lilly, who is scrunched up on an armchair in the reading corner with her head buried between her knees, which isn't unusual. Lilly isn't a child to be coddled. She's a wiry, elusive adolescent, blond and pale as a moonbeam draped in black clothing, known to peer out watchfully from the oddest places like a frightened deer.

As Colette's vision focuses on me, anger stiffens her face. "It's Steven."

My gut lurches. Steven . . . I can still hear his voice ringing in my ears, see him, smell him . . . he can't be gone.

Steven is her son, seventeen, outgoing, handsome. If Seth could grow up like anyone, I'd want him to be like Steven. I don't want to hear what she's going to say, but my mouth asks before I can stop it. "Is he dead?"

Detective Brown answers for her. "Found in the pool house, stabbed six times and knocked on the head. Or maybe you already knew that?"

I turn at his voice and wish my eyes could annihilate him. "Why would I know that?"

"Just looking for options," he says dryly. "After all, you live there."

"You have the compassion of a housefly."

"I have a lot in common with houseflies. I see a lot of crap in my job. Have a seat, Ms. Winters."

I lay my hand on Henry's leg, but he doesn't respond, so I pat Colette's shoulder and move to the piano bench, away from Detective Brown's line of fire.

"So, he didn't come home after his ball game," says the detective.

Colette sighs. "I've told you already. He came home. Betts, our maid, she fed him. She said so. Then he changed clothes and went out the back door."

"So, you saw him change and leave?"

"No. Betts said he went upstairs. His school clothes are in a pile on his floor, so obviously he changed."

"No one saw him change."

"We don't normally watch each other change around here." Her sarcasm melts into tears and her fists ball up. "What is this? Why aren't you looking for fingerprints or something and putting out an APB?"

"We have people taking care of those things." He fixes his sights on Henry. "Mr. Gordin, did you see your stepson today? Mr. Gordin?"

Henry turns his blank eyes to the detective. His eyeballs twitch back and forth but don't focus on anything real. I feel just like him. Everything is unreal.

Normally, Henry is a very professional sort of guy, tall and lean with a strong handshake and unwavering steel gray eyes. He learned to exude confidence and public appeal in politics, which he dabbled in until his previous wife divorced him. Asheville is a fair-size town, but small enough that Marge's version of their parting followed by her un-timely death hurt his public image, so he receded into something he had a penchant for: playing with money. Prior to the divorce, he'd played with Marge's money in the stock market, or so I'm told. After the divorce, he fed his urge by becoming a financial advisor so he could play with other people's money. Some say his wealth came from investing well, but Colette insinuated one day that the money is hers, which would explain why he married her.

She's the opposite of him: big-boned and fleshy with a brash per-sonality that she doesn't bother to glaze with Southern manners when she's alone with me. I would never have pegged her as Henry's type. They don't seem to have much in common except a mutual apprecia-tion of money. But I could be wrong. Could be he really loves her. There's no accounting for why certain people fall in love.

I can see why she loves him. Not only is he good-looking; he also has a sense of superiority that anyone would respect, an uncanny ability to look people steadily in the eye throughout a conversation.

Whenever he turns those steel-gray eyes on me, I feel inferior, as if he has the ability to read all the secrets hidden within me.

But for once, he seems whipped. His voice whispers out from his dream zone. "He wanted me to go to the game today. I should have. I should have. It's my fault. I should have."

"How would that have helped, Mr. Gordin?"

"He would have been with me, right? No one would have touched him if he'd been with me at the game."

Detective Brown glances at Colette and back to Henry. "I thought he went to the game anyway. I thought we determined he came home fine after the game."

Colette eyes Henry and throws up her hands. "We did. He went to the game. Betts saw him come home."

"What's that?" The detective asks.

"Betts saw him come home."

"From school, right?"

"Yes, from school. Betts saw him come home from school."

"We need someone to verify he was at the game," the detective replies, and I see what he's doing, turning them in circles upon themselves, trying to trap them in a lie.

Colette pokes Henry, but he doesn't respond. She pokes him again, then twists in her seat a moment before flailing her hands toward her stepdaughter. "Lilly! Why won't you speak up?" She turns back to Detective Brown. "We have a witness. Steven took Lilly to the game. Ask her. Ask her! What has the game got to do with it anyway? It had to have happened after the game. He obviously came home from the game."

Detective Brown turns to Lilly. "How about it, Miss Gordin? Did you go to the game with your brother?"

Lilly raises just her eyes, red and swollen, and filled with lakes of water. "No, he didn't go with me. And he wasn't my brother. He was my *step*brother." She turns and buries her face in the back of the chair and covers her ears with her hands. "Can I go upstairs to my room? I don't want to talk about this."

Detective Brown nods to a policeman, who approaches and taps Lilly's shoulder and escorts her upstairs.

"How about you, Rachel Winters? Did you go to the game?" he asks.

I watch Lilly cross the catwalk above us and wish I could join her. My mind falters for moment, as if there's a chasm there and gone again like the negative charge of a lightning bolt slashing through the order of my thoughts, through logic. Is there something I'm not remembering? Did I go to the game? I feel myself spinning for a moment, trying to grasp where I fit in the picture, and then the whirling stops, and I find the answer in the black cavern of my brain. I went to the mall. "I ate at Chow Ling's. I ate an egg roll and wonton soup."

I don't want to say anything else.

CHAPTER THREE

⚕

The interrogation takes hours, eventually with all of us split into separate rooms. They ask me over and over what I did with my day. The skinny cop comes in to listen. Barney-boy, I dub him, wondering if he carries a bullet in his shirt pocket. He leans his bony elbows on the table and cocks one eyebrow at me the whole time in some practiced macho look. I know he thinks I'm a loser, hanging out at the mall like some teenager and eating alone at the food court, but at least I've got money to spend. At least I have, well . . . I've got money. And I'm still hot. His eyes are bugging out with a story all their own.

Listening to them trying to solve who murdered Steven makes me think of the Borg from *Star Trek*. I've been a Trekkie since I was a kid. I watched every old *Star Trek* rerun. The Borg was a huge computer-like cube full of beings collected from a zillion planets all networked into one Queen Borg. I was fascinated by the idea of all those minds being tied together. Everyone knew what everyone was thinking all the time without saying a word. It would solve so many problems in society. No one could lie. No one would have to pretend to be something they weren't. No one would have to keep up appearances or make excuses.

Everyone would know who killed Steven.

If I were part of the Borg, everything in my life would disappear because it's all made up; it's all built on lies. I created who I am by disowning my past and creating a new me. But if I were part of the Borg, I would be linked to everyone else. They would know my secrets.

Everyone would know everything about me and not care. I could quit reinventing my life.

But then I think about funny things, like how they'd all know when somebody was taking a crap or had gas or pulled their underwear out of their cracks. Borg never had babies; they only assimilated people from other planets, so I wonder if that means they never had sex. If they didn't have sex, did anyone ever think about having it? If one Borg thought about it, it would flash down the line like twinkling Christmas lights. Alvin Studler, a guy I met in a bar one night, told me the average guy thinks about sex every ninety seconds. How do they ever get any work done? It would be like trying to think with a strobe light flashing in their eyes. Alvin had a little-boy face with more freckles than an English setter, and pale blue eyes that made me think of melted ice. He seemed too sweet to think about sex that much. I bet his mother thought he was a saint.

Barney-boy, bullet in pocket, isn't at all sweet-looking. He looks more like a fox with his long, skinny nose and beady eyes. I don't need to be a Borg to read Barney-boy's mind. He's definitely on the same track as Alvin Studler but without the ninety-second breaks.

Finally I stand up. "I've had enough. I did nothing today. No one can vouch for me except the clerks. Hey, that's it." I pull my pocketbook off the floor and pull out my receipts, date and time stamped by the store computers. "See?"

Barney-boy frowns. He doesn't bother to look at them. He knows I'm innocent.

"My signature on the charge forms, too, see?"

"Sure. Well, don't go too far, Rachel Winters. I'm going to have more questions for you."

I can imagine the questions he has for me, and none of them have to do with a murder.

It occurs to me I'm supposed to go home, now, but I can't. My pool-house apartment is a crime scene surrounded by flapping orange streamers, and some madman murderer is on the loose. I find Colette gulping down sleeping pills in the kitchen.

"You're still here?" she says.

"I can't go home . . ."

She shakes her head. "You can't stay here. Not tonight. You understand."

Like she'd notice I was there; she has three spare bedrooms. "Sure. Where am I supposed to go?"

"I'll call Sinclair for you."

"That'll fly like a fat lady on a broomstick."

Her weary eyes pass over me to the phone, and she stabs in Sinclair's number. He's heard the news, of course. She hangs up. "He's sending a taxi."

As I stumble from the taxi to Sinclair's front door, I'm nervous. I am so disconnected that it feels like a week instead of just half a day has passed since I dropped Seth off at Applebee's. Besides, Sinclair and I haven't had a real conversation in months.

I step into his new house, more modern than the period home we shared. Huge plate-glass windows overlook the mountainside. The furnishings we so painstakingly chose together stare at me like a foreigner. The rooms are silent. Only two lamps are lit: the foyer chandelier and a new pewter lamp hanging over my favorite easy chair — burgundy brocade woven with golden ferns — where he's left a book open. I strain to see the title, but it's too far away.

Among other things, Sinclair and I both love to read. Escaping into books filled many of my lonely high school nights — at first, trash, books with women's bosoms busting loose from old-fashioned peasant blouses. But when I started hanging out with Jennifer Mayer full time, when I decided to remake my life and get an education, she got me reading better stuff, like *Wuthering Heights, The Old Curiosity Shop, Out of the Silent Planet,* stuff we could discuss, stuff that taught us how misfits overcame adversity. I developed a love for books that make me think, books that examine deeper meanings in life. It paid off later by having filled me with knowledge to spout during philosophical chats at the sorority house and table talk after that. Sinclair and I loved rousing literary discussions on quiet evenings. We shared a love of words, of prose that read like poetry, old tomes with knee-deep descriptions, and novels revolving around controversy. We argued over Golding's *Lord of the Flies* and its supposition that evil would rise to the top. Sinclair was of the Ballantyne's *Coral Island* variety; he hadn't grown up in the real world. He thought goodness would prevail. What a joke. I've grown ever more cynical.

I still read diligently. Books are my silent refuge, my temporary oases. Ironically, the silence is also a prison; all the thoughts that the stories create rush around in my head with no escape.

I wonder who he discusses books with now. Probably Jocelyn, fellow doctor, his partner, his collaborator. My opponent.

The pewter light shining down on the single brocade chair kindles a ridiculous hope that he's kept to himself in his small cocoon — he and my son — but I've envisioned a tryst between Sinclair and Jocelyn for so long, the hope lingers only fleetingly.

Sinclair's wearing plaid pajama boxers and his old Duke T-shirt, long faded from the deep Blue Devils color it was when we were dating. So much has happened since then.

Seeing him alone in this setting deflates me of any remaining bravado. I hang my head, purse dangling at my side, and cry.

He pushes the door closed and takes me in his arms. For a moment I freeze, but strength ebbs until I drop the bag to the floor and collapse against his shoulder, against the soft worn cotton of his shirt and the firmness of his chest. I am broken. The distress of Steven's death is overload. The anger I've built toward Sinclair over the months evaporates momentarily under the need to alleviate the suffering of mind and body. My head still screams at Sinclair, but my heart is too heavy to listen to it. The fresh wound of Steven's death slices the cankerous boil. Love and hate so entwined. I lift my face up, my lips toward his, and feel the warmth of him breathing. His lips brush mine, tantalizing, passing in the night, teasing for more before he sets me an arm's length away.

CHAPTER FOUR

I force my eyes open to the morning sun streaming in an unfamiliar window, and then I remember where I am — in the guestroom of Sinclair's new house. The sheets are knotted around my feet. I came with nothing, and so I am clad in one of Sinclair's cast-off dress shirts that I took from where it lay on the bathroom floor, presumably peeled off during Seth's bath. Sinclair wore the starch out of the bleached white cotton during the course of the previous day so that it falls softly over my curves. I let the smell of him wrap around me.

I pull on my jeans and pad barefoot down the hall in search of the coffee wafting in my direction. Seth is seated on the family-room floor, lining Hot Wheels up in a straight line. He's always been like that, all orderly, no matter what he played. His hair is rumpled from sleep. His face is etched with concentration. It always is, unless he's asleep.

He's beautiful when he's sleeping. His skin takes on an ivory pallor, and his lashes look thick and black enough to be false, to be an adornment added to a china doll. He sleeps on his side, curled up with one hand tucked under his pillow and the other grasping Binks, this huge stuffed rabbit he got in his first Easter basket, a monstrous basket I bought at Claire's Flower Shop.

Miss Claire specializes in baskets for every occasion. She has some generic baskets on display, but most she makes up special at the request of her customers with all kinds of trinkets in them, good stuff you'd never think of yourself. Sandra Bollen, this real snooty lady who hangs out with Sinclair's mom, gave me one as a baby present in the hospital when she came to see Seth. It had a silver pocket watch in it with Seth's birth date etched inside the cover *to mark the times of his life*, she said. I love that. Her daughter-in-law Amy was pregnant at the time. I think she was giving out really good presents that year so Amy would recoup the same, but I didn't care. It still meant the world to me. Now I buy baskets from Miss Claire all the time. I sent one to Amy when her son was born. And I sent one to my mom once.

I told Miss Claire that Mama didn't have many interests. Mostly she drank and smoked, and when she was sober, she liked to smoke, watch television, and cross-stitch. Miss Claire is about a hundred years old; she's seen a lot in her life, I think, because she didn't bat an eye at my description. She makes baskets for lots of snooty people, but she's pretty down-to-earth herself. I wouldn't be surprised if she has a mother like mine, or maybe an aunt or a sister. Anyhow, she knew exactly the kind of basket to make for my mom. She put in a cross-stitch pillow kit surrounded by sampler liquor bottles and two highball glasses hand painted with the same design as the cross-stitch pillow. I think it's the only present my mom ever got excited over. She really liked it. After that, I decided I'd never buy a basket of any type from anyone other than Miss Claire. So I bought Seth's first Easter basket from her. Not one of the ones in her window display, but one she made up special for me with his favorite candies, some little cars, and Binks, this huge orange and yellow rabbit with floppy ears that are about a foot long.

Back when Seth first got Binks, he and the rabbit were about the same size. I could measure his growth spurts when he was sleeping at night by how much longer he was than Binks. That's how I picture him when I'm alone at night. Not at school or playing or anything, but in bed asleep with Binks, with his face relaxed and smiling, because then I can imagine him still loving me, not thinking of me as the mommy who abandoned him.

Sleep is magic. Maybe God takes children in his arms and holds them while they sleep so they resemble angels, making parents fall back in love with them every night, no matter how rotten they may have behaved throughout the day.

When Seth is sleeping, I can't remember a single bad thing he did.

I know better in the daylight. He's tense even when he's playing, prickly and on guard, but as I watch him on the floor, I don't want to remember anything awful about him, not even the things he did this past weekend, like dumping his cereal on the floor because it wasn't Cap'n Crunch. I had only Special K because I didn't know Sinclair had let him start eating kiddie cereals. Usually when he has one of his screaming spells, it's because I didn't know something new about him. It's my fault for being such a failure as a mother, leaving him and all, so I try not to dwell on what he's done wrong.

I like to think of him as the perfect child, never growing up, never being anything but the innocent child he is when he's asleep; and when he's good, like now, playing by himself on the floor, concentrating on his toy cars.

He's wearing a pair of red pajamas I've never seen. I didn't buy them, and suddenly I wonder if Sinclair is shopping for his clothes or if his mother has taken over that privilege. Or someone else?

I want so badly to be a part of that perfect life we had before that I ignore my instincts. I tempt fate. I step closer. "Hi, darling. Mommy's here."

Seth's eyes flare wildly as he falls backward. "Why are you here?"

"I just came to visit."

"It's not your day."

"I know, darling."

"I have to go to school. Mrs. Beazly is bringing a guitar today."

"What fun!"

His face isn't registering fun. It's wide-eyed with defiance saying, *Don't touch me.*

I remember him as a baby wrapping his little fist around my fingers, and holding on as he learned to walk. I never thought he'd lose that grip on me. I never thought he'd quit reaching for me. Despite everything, I still yearn to be held just once by my mother the way I want to embrace Seth this minute.

He's a different child here in front of me than he was *before.* Before the break-up. Before Caroline's death. Before real life ended. Or maybe it was the fairytale that ended and real life that recently kicked in.

In our perfect life, Seth laughed with me.

I remember his second Christmas. He was too young on his first Christmas to understand much about it, but his second Christmas was different. I woke at five in the morning and lay in bed waiting for the sun to peek over the horizon. As soon as the first rays hit the bedroom window, I pushed at Sinclair until he opened his sleepy eyes and yawned at me. "What's wrong?"

"It's Christmas."

"Merry Christmas," he said and rolled over, pulling the covers with him.

"Get up! Go get Seth. We have to open the presents."

"Some wise person somewhere said, *Let sleeping babes lie.*"

"That's sleeping *dogs,* and Seth isn't a dog. I'm going down to turn on the Christmas lights. You carry him down."

"In an hour."

"No, I can't wait that long."

Sinclair didn't understand. I'd never had a real Christmas with a fancy tree and decorations and presents to give out to people I loved. Oh, I'd bought things for my mother — soaps, perfume, a nightgown, and such — but she'd yawn and fall back asleep on the sofa, complaining of a migraine that was more likely a hangover. My own little son to open presents was the best gift I could ever have for Christmas, and I couldn't wait another minute.

"I'll make some coffee," I whispered as I rubbed his shoulders.

"Ummm. That feels good."

I kissed his neck, and he moaned as I nibbled his flesh and moved my hands over his sleep-flushed body. He turned to me with searching lips.

An hour later, he carried Seth down on his shoulders, the two of them singing "Jingle Bells" to Batman lyrics and giggling at their own intelligence until they reached the midway landing that looked into the living room. There, Seth gasped at the stack of presents. Santa Claus had been generous.

He opened exactly three presents before stopping. The third one was a little thing I'd found in an old-fashioned toyshop I'd happened across during a road trip.

I can't remember where the toyshop was, but I remember taking an exit off a highway, looking for a cold drink when I found the place — an old log cabin with small square windows under a wide front porch that had a swinging sign: *Novelties*. A bell strung to the door jingled as I stepped inside. The interior smelled of raw cedar and lemon wood polish. Twelve-inch floorboards gleamed in the dull light, and a woman as old and wrinkled as time sat in the back corner reading a Nora Roberts romance novel.

I almost turned around and walked out, but colors on the shelves stopped me. Not bright, glistening colors of today's plastic toys, but muted, antiqued hues with the finest of details etched carefully into wooden surfaces. I trailed around the shelves, the woman's attention flickering between me and the entrancing words of the novel in her lap. There were dozens of old-fashioned amusements — things that flipped and rolled with bells that jingled and heads that turned, pull-along animals with slinky-like springs wiggling their hindquarters, and board games actually painted onto hinged wooden boards with carved playing pieces. I admired them all, but there was only one that I couldn't leave without.

The box, small but not cheap, was handcrafted from mahogany. The toymaker had carved funny faces on every side and etched the end of the wooden turning spindle.

Seth wasn't sure what to do with it. Sinclair didn't even know what it was. I joined Seth on the floor, sitting behind him with my arms and legs enfolding him, and placed the box in our laps. As I turned the handle, carnival music tinkled from inside, and still Seth didn't know what to expect. He'd never seen such a contraption. I turned the handle and turned it some more until he'd almost given up on seeing anything happen, when suddenly a colorful clown with a funny wooden head and a huge red nose popped out. Seth was shocked for a second, then threw his head back, laughing. His entire body shook with glee. I wrapped my arms around him, and we laughed together as we rolled on the floor. Sinclair grabbed up the jack-in-the-box and wound him up again and again, laughing with us as it popped out. It tickled Seth just as much the tenth time as it did the first.

If I had that toymaker's address, I'd send him a thousand dollars for that memory.

That same excitement flows in Seth's words as I watch him stand so adroitly in front of his lineup of little cars, but his body isn't smiling. His face isn't even smiling. "I get to do the weather chart. Daddy says it's going to rain, but it's sunny right now, so I get to put up the sun, the clouds, and raindrops. Nobody hardly ever gets to do that." He's not exactly happy. He's measuring himself against the promises of his day, trying to gain self-worth from other people and activities. I know the feeling. I used to do the same during those years I climbed the social ladder to reach Sinclair.

I move closer and crouch beside him, but he edges backward. "Sounds like you're the luckiest kid in class."

"You can't make me miss school today. I don't want to go to that stinking pool house to stay with you."

I will myself not to stiffen. "No, darling, you don't have to go to my stinking pool house. I can't even go there. That's why I'm here."

"Why can't you go there?"

I imagine a spot taped out on the floor where Steven's body was found and the bloodstains left behind. To ever sleep again in the midst of that remembered violence seems impossible. "There are workmen cleaning it up right now."

I see him relax somewhat, his body standing less rigid. "Maybe they'll get the stink out of it."

"Maybe." Will they be able to get the blood out of it, or Steven's spirit? The murder will hang in it forever. "So is it okay if I stay here for a bit?"

His eyes narrow at me. "How long?"

How long? I wonder. I reach out to touch his shoulder, but he sees my hand coming and backs up, leaving my hand reaching into emptiness and dropping limply to my side. "I don't know how long." Time has become meaningless. Days run together. I don't know anything. I don't know who he is or who I am, anymore. I don't even know how long Caroline's been gone.

Sinclair has been watching us from the kitchen. He walks over and takes my arm and escorts me toward the coffee. "Breakfast in a bit, Number Three," he hollers back at Seth.

He likes reminding Seth that they share a history of family and names. Seth was named Joseph Sinclair Winters III, after Sinclair and his father. We tried to call him Joseph, but it was too much for him as a toddler and he continually shortened it to *'seph,* which people misinterpreted as *Seth.* Eventually we found ourselves calling him that, too, and quit fighting it. Seth suits him more than Joseph anyway.

In the privacy of the kitchen, Sinclair runs his hand across my neck and kisses my cheek before he hands me a cup of coffee. "You can't stay, Rachel. It's too confusing for him."

"Confusing?"

"Yes. He doesn't know if you're going to be a part of his life or not. He accepts that we're on our own, and then here you are back again. He needs solidarity in his life. His psychological welfare is at stake. You can't just pop in, stay a while, then leave again."

Then let me stay, I think, but I don't say it. We'd end up screaming at each other, again. We'd end up casting those mile-deep looks that accuse each other of bearing fault. We'd hate each other inside a week. Or at least that's what we both fear would happen. I wish it could all end differently. I wish we could all walk away hand-in-hand into a perfect sunset where nothing bad would ever happen again. I thought that's what I'd done when I married Sinclair, but I was wrong. Life doesn't work that way. Cinderella and the Prince probably had warts, bad morning breath, and love affairs.

CHAPTER FIVE

Yesterday I said I wouldn't visit my mother. That was yesterday. Now Steven is dead, my apartment is a crime scene, and my husband has once again expelled me from his house, wearing yesterday's jeans and one of three blouses from the shopping bags I had with me.

It's a five-hour drive to my mother's house, but I don't have anywhere else to go. I don't have a friend to call. I'm not the typical mom of toddlers. The group of women that passed as friends six months ago won't call anymore. Why should they? My baby is gone. My son is living with his father. The last thing they want around is a depressed single woman with mental hang-ups.

The high-society ladies I served on behalf of the Winters' heritage allow me into their houses only as a topic of conversation over Monday-afternoon bridge. By now, even that interest has probably waned.

In my early days of motherhood, I disregarded my mother's indifference and took to visiting her with the baby in tow. I felt renewed warmth for the woman who must have loved me in infancy as I loved my children, but she didn't latch on to being a grandma. I doubt she ever thinks of Seth. I don't know if she remembers baby Caroline or not. She probably only remembers what the television showed, not the real thing, not how my baby cooed and drooled and fell asleep in my arms.

I don't know what has possessed me to take such a ridiculous trip, but I follow the blacktop ribbon across the state until I find myself driving through the familiar grimy neighborhoods that lead to my childhood home.

The faces are different. The children racing across the parking lot and screaming at the windows aren't the same ones who lived there in my day, but the same noises persist: the motion of city-bound children, of basketball at the netless hoop, of lounging on car hoods, of music blaring out of colorless apartments.

I realize with sudden clarity how long my mother has remained in the same beige box. She could have bought a house in the time she has devoted to her bland apartment, but she has always lived ready for flight. She has never hung pictures or lined the kitchen cabinets with shelf paper. The windows still bear the commercial draperies provided by the apartment complex; the floors are still carpeted with brown shag.

From the car I can see into the kitchen and the family room beyond. She's not home, or she's in bed. The fleeting disappointment gives way to relief and then anxiety. I have nowhere else to go.

As I contemplate a plan, a GMC truck pulls in several spots over. My mother emerges from the passenger seat, joined by the driver: a tall fellow with a long beard and long hair, a navy ball cap on his head, and jeans that sag around his flat butt. He's at least ten years her junior. I watch them laugh heartily over some shared joke, and I see his eyes, laughing eyes. She's dressed, as usual, in painted-on jeans and a deep green shirt that hugs her figure and cuts a deep V over her cleavage. The chuckles die out as she sashays down the sidewalk at his side, and I see she's aged. The corners of her eyes and mouth are accentuated with lines. I wonder what her escort sees in her. Usually her makeup is too thick, clumped on her eyelashes and standing out as pink circles on her sagging cheeks, but today she wears almost none. Her hair is curling loosely around her head, not fixed and sprayed into place. Hints of laughter remain around her mouth and twinkle in her eyes. He's brought a laughing woman to the surface; it's unlike her to be jovial.

How long have they been dating? And where did they meet? He isn't her typical fare. Why hadn't she gravitated toward his sort while I was under her roof? My mother dated some bad ones in her day, but I paid the price for her choices. Like Kyle.

Kyle was the wealthiest of Mama's boyfriends. He constantly bought her things, which made up for his ugly face. He had some big job downtown. I wish I knew now what it was, but back then I didn't care. Every time I looked at him, all I saw was his wide nose and pockmarked skin.

He started out buying Mama dresses and shoes and pocketbooks, then hooked her with a diamond pendant necklace. Mama didn't know what to do with herself. He had more class than any guy she'd ever been out with. He drove a new Cadillac and often arrived in a suit coat. Normally such attire wasn't a turn-on to my mother, but he wore it so casually, like somebody off Miami Vice, that she began to fancy him as an exception to the suit-and tie league.

He was okay with me. He didn't bend over backward to have me around, or anything, but he was polite enough to ask me how my classes were going and if I needed a dress for the prom. That wasn't a problem; I was only fourteen and had no intention of going to the prom. I'd been put off boyfriends for a while after Susie Millis went around writing obscene notes about Kevin Smith and me on every blackboard in school.

Kyle and Mama got pretty tight, but he never moved into our house. He had a much classier place out toward Wake Forest Road, so he'd only come pick Mama up and off they'd go, sometimes for days at a time. I thought he was feeling bad about me being alone all the time when he started bringing me gifts. At first they were small things, like hair bows and a hairbrush, perfume, and a couple of T-shirts. Mama kept telling him not to, that I didn't expect such treatment — in fact, I think it made Mama jealous that he'd buy me something because it took away from her getting gifts, somehow — but she let things slide for a while. After a month or so, the presents got a bit more extravagant: a necklace and a dress. He made me try those on to be sure the dress fit properly. Mama stood there tapping her shoe, telling me to hurry it up because they had plans for the night. I came out of the room feeling like a model, swishing my hips and twirling on the runway. He smiled real big. He had that little gleam in his eye that told me the dress flattered my figure. My breasts had fully developed by then and stood up with the pertness teens have without even trying, and my slim waist, usually hidden beneath baggy T-shirts when lounging around the house, was accentuated by the dress's trim fit.

Mama flashed her eyes from him to me. "Great, it fits. That was mighty generous of you, Kyle, but you've got to quit spoiling her. You can see it's going to her head. Now go on, Rachel, get changed. And don't stay up late. You got school tomorrow."

I didn't see Mama or Kyle for a couple days after that. Jennifer Mayer came to spend the night with me one night so we could study biology together, which, if her mother had known we were alone, she never would have been allowed to do. The next afternoon I was slumped in front of the television when Kyle walked right into the apartment without Mama.

"Is Tammy still at work?" he asked.

"I reckon."

"I brought you another present," he said as he turned and shut the door behind himself.

I perked up a bit and turned to look at him. "Another dress?"

"Something better. Come see."

He handed me a bag with a bikini inside. "Go try it on," he said.

"Summer is months away."

"I know, but you know how they start putting out the swimsuits way ahead of time. I thought you'd want the newest thing out."

I skipped off to the bedroom, totally oblivious to his intent. In hindsight, most of Mama's boyfriends were what I would now classify as creeps, but none of them had ever made a pass at me. Rodney, the guy she was dating when I was ten, had slapped me around a few times, but I never told Mama about it because I figured she would get mad and tell me I deserved it. I thought she'd yell more, and I'd end up with a real beating for causing problems with her boyfriend. One day she saw it happen, though. He'd pushed her around a bunch of times and she'd pretty much tolerated it, but that day he raised his hand to strike me for not taking the garbage out to the dumpster right when he told me to. Mama stepped between us and told him nobody was going to lay a hand on her kid except her, and if he didn't like it, he had better get out. When he left, she told me to get the trash out to the dumpster or *she* would slap me.

But none of them ever came on to me, until Kyle.

I stepped out of the bedroom and strutted across the kitchen in the new blue bikini, thinking about getting Jennifer to invite me over when the pool opened at her apartment complex.

Kyle stood there leaning against the kitchen counter nodding. "Fine. Just fine. Twirl around. Slowly now. Turn around, let me see the back. Now walk this way. Swing your hips. That's right. Oh, is that prime. Yes, sirree. Now back across the room."

He followed in my footsteps, shadowing me with his tall, heavy frame, and placed his hands on my shoulders and coiled his fingers into my waist-length blond hair. I stopped dead in my tracks, unsure what to do. His hands slid around my body. I wanted to scream. This was my mother's boyfriend. This was an old man. What did he want with me? He scooped me up in his arms and carried me through the bedroom door. I beat against his chest with my fists. "Leave me alone. Put me down. Let me down."

"I'm not going to let you down," he hissed. "And you're not going to let me down either. You're going to be a good little girl. Think of all the lovely things I've bought you. You owe me, little girl." He bent his face toward me. I yanked his hair. He responded with a whopping slap to my face. I screamed. He slapped me again and pinned my arms beneath his.

Tears streamed down my face. "Stop. Please stop."

"Relax, little girl. Enjoy it. I've got things to teach you."

"Mama," I murmured. "Where are you, Mama?"

I tried to pull my mind into a shell, away from what was happening, but my ears felt electrified, sounds intensified. I heard Mama's car. I held my breath and counted. Ten footsteps from the car to the door. *Ten steps, Mama. Hurry.* Finally, the door opened. Kyle didn't hear it.

She must have realized he was there. His car was outside. But she didn't call out his name. I was waiting for her to come, waiting. Then it occurred to me that maybe his car wasn't outside. I hadn't heard him pull up. Where had he parked?

Mama's keys landed on the kitchen counter, like usual, tinkling together. Kyle raised his head and glared at me. "You better shut up, or I'll tell Tammy what a slut you've been, prancing around half-naked."

I had more guts than he knew, though. I kicked at him as hard as I could and opened my mouth to scream. "Mama, Mama! Help me!"

Mama came running in, beat on his back and yanked him off the bed. She screamed at him. "Get out of my house, you pervert!"

He acted all casual about it, fixing his clothes back in place like he hadn't done a thing. "Oh, Tammy, you know how she is, strutting around all the time. I was just teaching her a lesson before she learned it the hard way from a real pervert."

Mama's face was stone. "Out, now." Her left hand reached up to her neck, feeling for the serpentine chain with the diamond pendant, and yanked it free of her neck. "And take this with you, you jerk. My daughter can't be bought." She flung it at his chest.

He let it drop to the floor and sneered at her. "You don't know how lucky you've been to have me this long."

"Right. Lucky me. Now get out."

She stood there like that, stone-faced, unmoving, while he sidled past her and strode out the door, slamming it so hard it bounced back open again and stood that way in the afternoon sunshine as he pulled away from the far end of the parking lot some minutes later.

Mama waited until she saw his car pass by the open door before she turned to me. I'd ridded myself of the bathing suit and pulled on jeans and a sweatshirt. I didn't want any of my body showing.

She stepped from the doorway to the bed and settled beside me with a hand on each shoulder. "Are you okay?"

I nodded. "I am now."

She pulled me closer and caressed my head.

"I love you, Mama."

I wanted so much for her to say the same thing. She did, but in her own way. She said, "You're my flesh and blood. I'm meant to take care of you."

She didn't date anyone for a while after that. We spent a lot of nights watching old movies and putting together puzzles on a huge piece of cardboard she brought home from the plant where she was working. Eventually she got bored. When the flowers started blooming and we shed our winter coats, she had a new guy on the line, but that was okay. I knew to keep to myself more, and I convinced myself that deep inside she loved me more than she did him, no matter who the "him" was, even if she hadn't really said it.

That was the only time she made the choice between me and one of her boyfriends. There were too many nights of being set aside, of being chastised, struck, and condemned to consider myself secure. I was afraid to ever test the theory again.

Cast from Sinclair's house, I sit in my car and watch my mother enter the apartment with this new man and think of calling out to her, but I don't. I imagine wistfully of belonging to a normal mother and being enveloped in a welcoming embrace. Sinclair never hesitates to greet his mother. And she would move the world to take him in her arms. But moments of serenity with my mother were few. I am afraid that if I call out to her right now, she's likely to stop in her tracks, stunned for a moment, and then ask what I want.

I start the car and drive away without a word, this time heading to Durham, where Jennifer, my old school friend, still lives. I picture us having coffee and a long talk about everything in our lives. Nothing of importance, nothing below the surface, nothing like our deep conversations in high school. Nothing that matters. But that's what I need. Something easy. Something normal.

I cruise into her neighborhood and stop at her driveway, and as I stare at her quiet yard, the wide front porch topped with three dormers, her empty house silently simmering in the heat of the afternoon, I realize I haven't talked to her in ages. Maybe our friendship has evaporated like everything else in my life.

I keep going.

As the afternoon wanes and the sun sets, I drive all the way back to Asheville and decide to spend the night at the Grove Park Inn. I always wanted an excuse to stay there. All the clothes and accessories I could possibly want lie within the vast scope of the world-famous resort. I stop at a grocery store and buy a gallon of Moose Tracks. I plan to check in for the weekend to get lost in ice cream, movies, the spa, and sleep — nothing different from any other day of my currently miserable life, in which time only ticks away an eternity of uselessness.

I sit in my idling car in front of the mammoth stone façade of the Grove Park Inn with the resort sprawling around me on the rolling, mist-covered hills, and I feel as wretched now as I did groveling at the feet of pimply-faced teenage boys. This time I don't see a way to escape. The brightest thing in my future is another funeral.

Another funeral. It reminds me I have the picture of the nun in my pocketbook. I pull it out and stare at the nun's face, young and serene. I see peace in her face. I turn the card over. *How sweet is the way of love,* it says. *Society of the Little Flower.*

I haven't been to church since the funeral. There are too many people in churches. Too many people to stare and whisper at me.

Steven's funeral will be the same way. I shake just thinking about it.

I turn the card back over and stare at the nun's face once more before I shove the card into the clip on the sun visor to ponder later, and surrender my car keys to the hotel valet.

CHAPTER SIX

Colette holds the service at the funeral home instead of a church. It's the same funeral home we used. The same room, even. I remember sitting in a sedated stupor as I endured the lines of people paying their respects. The room should have been a soft, mournful blue. But it's not blue. It's red and gold. Red carpet, red walls, with gold cushions on the stackable chairs carried in for the service. I feel bathed in blood.

I sit in the third row from the back on the far end, away from the entrance, and close my eyes to shut out the blood. I don't want to remember where I am. Caroline's spirit sweeps over me. I feel her baby breath upon my cheek. My breasts stir with the familiar ache of needing to nurse her. *She's gone.* I see her in my mind's eye in the coffin, her dress pink, her ruined face too pale, too still. I swallow and grip my abdomen. *I miss you, Caroline.* My gut retches and catches in my throat.

She fades away, slips into a mist of white, and then I see Steven step forward. He's not dressed formally, like his body stretched out in the casket at the front of the room. Instead, he appears to me wearing blue jeans and the green polo shirt I bought him at the mall last month. His black hair is mussed, as usual, and his brown eyes radiate a calmness I've never seen in them — serene, in fact. *She'll tell you.* He doesn't say the words, exactly. They just echo in my head as he smiles at me and then follows Caroline. They dissipate into the mist in my mind.

I open my eyes and stare at the casket. *Oh, Steven. I miss you already.*

He was a neat kid, on the brink of manhood, but still a boy at heart. He used to come visit me in the pool house. The first time I laid eyes on him, I was unpacking a few belongings. It was mid-afternoon. I'd left the huge patio doors open to let the breeze blow the mustiness from the place, the cloying smell of pool water and mildew. My rooms were to the back of the building, a kitchen with a counter area open to the large party room, and a bedroom off to the left of the kitchen, which was meant to be a change room for guests. I installed a bed, dresser, television, and overstuffed chair, and called it home.

I was sliding clothing into the drawers when Steven wandered in.

"Oh, hi. You must be Mrs. Winters. Mama mentioned you'd be moving in here. I forgot."

I turned and smiled at him. Sweat adhered my T-shirt to my breasts. At first, I thought he hadn't noticed, but as I worked, I caught him watching me. He quickly averted his eyes and moved across the room. Embarrassed, I figured at first, but as I got to know him better, I learned it was a sense of propriety, something I play-acted without fully comprehending until I got to know Steven.

Steven nodded toward the bed. "I like the furniture. Classic."

I played along with his diversion. "Thanks. The bed's one of my favorite pieces." One of my only pieces since the split. Sinclair had everything else. But this bed was special. It had previously furnished our guest room, chosen because the curly-cued black wrought iron reminded me of a childhood I'd never had. Caroline was meant to grow into it someday. I thought sleeping in her bed would somehow keep her within my grasp.

Steven wandered around the room, touching my books, my clock, my radio, while I moved around the bed, stretching the sheets into place. When I unfolded the bedspread, he took one side and helped me. I figured it was probably the first time he'd ever made up a bed. Colette's maid, Betts, all but lived with them. She did everything for them on a daily basis. I'd had a weekly cleaning woman when married to Sinclair, but in my real life, no one washed my sheets or clothes except me — certainly not hired help, and never my mother. Growing up, I generally took care of my mother's mess, too, just to avoid the backlash of her temper when the apartment wasn't kept in order.

As I watched Steven smooth the bedspread, though, I imagined him as a skinny little kid following the maid of the moment around just for attention. He was like that, always hanging around with people you didn't expect. He was proper in every sense of the word, adhering to everything his mother ever taught him, but he didn't have her sense of class consciousness. He was nice to everybody, and his manners weren't put on like Colette's and mine. He was exactly who he portrayed himself to be. He probably would have followed the maid around and asked her conversational stuff, like how her kids were doing in school and what she planned to give her mother for Mother's Day and what her favorite kind of cookies were. He'd been taught to open doors for women and to carry their packages, so he applied it to the help, too, carrying the vacuum down the stairs for Betts and helping her with her coat in the winter. It didn't stop him from dropping his clothes on the floor and leaving his bed unmade. Cleaning up after him was a job that belonged to Betts as sure as being a gentleman belonged to him. I wish I could see things as clearly as Steven had.

Red and white carnations arranged on metal tripods stand around Steven's casket like castle guards. I have vowed never to have carnations in a bouquet. They are equated with funerals and other uselessly formal affairs. I squirm in my seat. I want to run through a field of wild daisies, set free like a butterfly to skim across the petals of flowers and never be grounded in reality again.

I feel the weight of a man settle into the pew beside me, and I know it is Sinclair before I even turn to look. I can't live with him, but he'll sit with me at the funeral. He takes my hand and I lean on his shoulder. Another funeral, too soon.

The man hosting the service is a stranger. I don't listen to a word he has to say. It irritates me to hear someone try to preach about love and heaven and the goodness of the dead soul when they know nothing about the person. It's pathetic. Colette should have called the pastor who knew Steven, the one from the church where he attended youth group with kids from school. Or maybe Colette didn't know that Steven went to church. Maybe he only confided in me about his outside activities.

I turn my gaze from the podium to look out the window and think about Caroline. I probably would have listened to every word at her service except I was too drugged up even to stand on my own.

I'm not drugged into numbness this time. I wish I were.

Caroline. My baby.

I want to sink into her, fill my brain cells with memories of her, and pull her back into conscious being. If only I could have that day back again, to live over, to change the course of our lives. I could fix it. I could fix everything. I would hold her in my arms all day long.

But if I could, I would go back even farther. I would tell them to get rid of the new partner, Jocelyn, too. I'd tell them to never hire her.

I don't want to think about Jocelyn now. Sinclair is here beside me, not with her, not today, so I won't dwell on her. I want to think about the day I found out I was pregnant with Caroline, seeing that little stick turn blue and Sinclair kissing me, twirling me around and then taking me back to bed to show me how much he loved me for being the mother of his children. I squeeze his hand thinking about it, and he squeezes mine back with no idea what's going through my mind.

I was so excited about the pregnancy, I couldn't wait to share the news with his mother. I told her that afternoon while Sinclair and his daddy were at the office. As usual, she was in the kitchen. She spent a lot of time in the kitchen, but she wasn't much of a cook. That day, she was dicing vegetables and dropping them into a pot.

"Another grandchild. How wonderful!" she exclaimed, waving the knife in the air. "We were afraid there would only be Seth. Sinclair was so lonely as a child; we didn't want that for Seth. Do you think it will be another boy? A boy needs a brother."

I didn't think Seth needed anybody. He was a loner from day one. He sat by himself in preschool, absorbed in his own games. He was never aggressive toward anyone else; he just didn't need anyone.

"It's a blessing to be so independent," Dr. Winters often said of him. "That boy will go far. He's got more sense of self than most adults."

Seth's self-absorption certainly made him an easy child. He didn't need to be entertained. He wasn't noisy. He wasn't boisterous or hyper. He had his moments of whining and complaining, and when he set his mind on something, he was more determined than a politician at the polls, but no one could say he upset a household.

"Was Sinclair like Seth when he was a boy?" I asked Mrs. Winters.

"Heavens, no. Sinclair ran me ragged. He always had a ball in his hand. Sometimes I thought I'd given birth to a golden retriever."

"What?"

"Oh, I forget you didn't grow up with a dog, dear." She went back to chopping carrots. "My family always had goldens. Ah, Goldie, I remember her best. She had an insatiable penchant for fetch. I couldn't walk through the yard without her on my heels with a slobbery ball in her mouth. She must have had dozens treasured away."

I pictured Mrs. Winters — Elaine, or "Lainey" to Sinclair's daddy — as a young girl, a miniature of her adult self in tailored clothing with a golden retriever at her heels. It didn't fit.

She must have read my look. "I loved animals as a child. We lived out in the country, near New Bern. I had three dogs, four cats, and a wild sparrow I'd saved when it fell from a nest." Her eyes went off to some other place. "I loved peeling out of my oxfords and walking down the road in summer with the hot gravel pressing into my bare feet." She grinned. "Funny thing is, we were wearing pedal pushers back then, just like girls now."

"Pedal pushers?"

"Oh, you know, capris they call them now. We wore them so our pant legs wouldn't get caught in our bicycle chains."

I did a reconfiguration of "Lainey" in my mind: curly bobbed hair, pedal pushers, white bobby socks and oxfords, frolicking with dogs and saving birds. I fast-forwarded the image to her as a mother chasing a rambunctious little boy in a ball cap and jeans, the two of them riding bikes through the park. It was a new vision of my mother-in-law.

"Of course, some people called them clam diggers instead of pedal pushers, especially there on the coast. I'm so glad they've come back in style." She turned to the stove and added canned chicken broth to the pot. It would lack spices, I knew, and become watery, tasteless slop, which is why she hired caterers for her social gatherings. Nevertheless, she devoted herself to the task and stirred the mixture a few times, which set her to thinking. I could see the gears turning in her head as she watched Seth playing with his action figures on the floor. "I don't really know who Seth takes after. I can't imagine Sinclair's daddy being that quiet as a child. He's certainly not a quiet adult."

Dr. Winters was a male social butterfly. He talked to every living soul he met. "No, he doesn't take after him, that's for sure," I said. I couldn't help thinking about my faceless father, the man I never saw, never heard about. Perhaps he took after *that* grandfather. I would never know.

I could tell Mrs. Winters was thinking the same thing. And probably thinking about blue-blooded Susan Chance, whose parentage was documented back to the Mayflower.

At least I was producing babies. Mrs. Winters was getting what she wanted. I had to keep her focused on that. I rubbed my still-flat tummy. "Well, I'm hoping it's a girl. We can shop and paint our nails together."

Mrs. Winters smiled. "A girl. That would be different."

When Caroline arrived seven months later, she was definitely different. She started out with a piercing scream followed immediately with a dreamy look that was far too satisfied for a newborn. She smiled early, she sat up early, and crawled at eight months. Where Seth was quiet, she was loud. Where Seth deliberated over choices, she demanded without hesitation. She was a Winters child through and through. Everyone doted on her. She couldn't be in a room without drawing attention to herself. She was too vivacious to be ignored.

Attention didn't linger long on the newest member of the Winters family. When she was six months old, Sinclair's father invited us over to Sunday dinner and made an announcement over fried chicken, baked beans, and slaw. "You're settled, son. You have your family established. It's time we look for a partner. I want to cut back to three days a week. Your mother and I intend to travel, and I'm going to get my pilot's license."

I think the pilot's license shocked Sinclair more than the semi-retirement. "Really, Dad? Wow. I didn't know you wanted to learn to fly."

"Sure you do. Remember all those model airplanes? The RC club we were in when you were in elementary school?"

Sinclair nodded. "Cool, Dad."

I was still thinking about the semi-retirement. It seemed like an office discussion, not a casual lunch statement. Sinclair wasn't even reacting. Maybe he'd seen signs of it already. He'd mentioned how his dad was slowing down, forgetting things, losing his temper over small stuff, but I figured it was just the two of them spending too much time together and being more open with feelings than non-related doctors. My concerns were purely selfish. "What will you do without your father there? The workload . . ."

Three pairs of eyes turned my way. Maybe it had been quietly discussed off and on throughout Sinclair's college years, and I was the only one outside The Know of the long-range plans. "We'll take on a new partner," Sinclair said with that tone that wondered how I didn't see it plainly already.

"Oh."

It sounded simple, but in my gut I knew it wouldn't be.

I was right.

After a month of sorting through letters and resumes, telephone interviews began. They narrowed it down to five to meet in person. The first three were disappointments. They didn't click. The fourth was a maybe. Then she came. Jocelyn.

Seeing her bio on paper and meeting her in person were equally impressive, but in totally different ways. I heard enough of the talk between Sinclair and his daddy. Their first question to every applicant was why they were interested in joining a small private practice in Asheville, North Carolina. Her answer had been perfect. She was tired of the Atlanta rat race, and she'd been raised in the hills of Tennessee. The lure of the mountains was calling to her. I wish she'd gone back to those same hills. She could have moved to Chattanooga. You can't get prettier than Chattanooga. Why'd she have to come over the border to North Carolina?

But she had an answer for that, too. Her brother had settled in Asheville, and he was all the family she had. Sinclair liked the idea of family calling to her, and her comfort with mountain life. He wouldn't lose her because of the steep, icy winter roads or the curse of winter dragging on for months while people were boating and fishing along the coastal lowlands. Her record was impeccable. Her big-city experience was diverse. She had civic-duty titles hanging like Boy Scout badges under her name, along with the list of awards she'd earned in college and in the medical profession. Sinclair was totally impressed.

When Sinclair and his daddy finally interviewed her in person, he came home lighthearted; full of talk about how lucky they were to find her, and what a boon she'd be to the practice. Whatever she'd put on paper had faded to nothing compared with whatever she'd said in person.

One look at her and I knew why.

For some reason, I had figured girls with enough brains and concentration to actually make it through med school wouldn't be much to look at, but when I walked into the country club on Sinclair's arm for dinner to officially celebrate her acceptance into the practice, I realized how wrong I was. Jocelyn could have been straight from a television medical soap opera. Her body was better than slender; it was athletically toned. She ran triathlons. She skied in Aspen the week before officially starting at the office and arrived tanned and relaxed. Her long brunette tresses were knotted on her head and cascaded to her shoulders. She was too physically fit and sharp of feature to be beautiful; rather, she was handsome, with dark eyes and olive skin, the flipside of my fair delicateness. She wasn't cocky or highbrow; she was very confident and self-assured, which is ten times more potent. If she'd been sitting at the table in blue jeans, she would still have been in total command of her situation because she knew who she was. Everything that I winged by impersonation, Jocelyn was to the core. Manners and carriage were inbred, as natural to her as breathing, but she didn't put on airs or place herself above anyone; my poor ego did that for her. Her superiority was earned with easy conversation and obvious, although not affected, intelligence. She had that rare quality of poise, a definite aura of intelligence, and spoke with the graciousness of a queen without my insecurities. I felt diminished next to her. She was the real thing. She was a diamond. I was a crude zirconium on display in a fourteen-carat-gold setting.

Very little of the dinner conversation had to do with medicine, but had much to do with the medical field, which left me out. I became the corsage, the decoration on Sinclair's arm, the obedient show wife. I shouldn't have resented it, and never had when the doctors were all male, but Jocelyn's inclusion in their conversation made my exclusion all the more obvious. After all, even with a ring on my finger, I valued the ego stroking of other men's appreciative appraisals.

I'd met my match, and I knew it.

Life went downhill from there.

CHAPTER SEVEN

Sinclair jostles me off his shoulder as Steven's funeral service ends. "I'm not going to the gravesite," Sinclair says.

"I can't go alone."

He sighs. "Okay." He takes my arm and guides me out with the throng of people. His mother is waiting outside the door. I suppose she sat with some of her cronies. My head is so confused with past and present, I haven't the strength to speak, so I nod to her and remain affixed to Sinclair's arm. He leads us to her car and eases me into the back seat.

"We'll come back for your car later," he says as he helps his mother in and takes the driver's seat.

Half the town has turned out for the burial. Teenagers mill around between gravestones, some crying, most somber and silent, wondering who would have killed their friend and classmate. I can't imagine Steven having any enemies. I can't imagine anyone having such anger toward such a sweet kid that they would stab him repeatedly until his life ebbed away.

Eyes follow us, women turn away, as Sinclair guides me toward the crowd and stands dutifully at his mother's side while a camera snaps pictures of us.

"Rachel," she says, and reaches a hand toward me, a show of affection for the public. She's trying to make us look like a family. Appearances. Everything is for appearances.

I pull from Sinclair's grasp. I give him over to his mother and step away. I'm overcome with shakes. Graveyards aren't the spooky stuff of horror movies or pretty parks for Sunday strolls. They are pits of despair made up of lost dreams, a dead end of life.

The wasteland of souls cries out to me from beneath the pathetic markings of granite, scrawled names, and dates that do nothing to justify the lives lived and lost.

Tears fall uselessly for Steven all around me, but his loss isn't real to me, yet. I know it will come. It will come with sudden alacrity when I see a young boy toss a football, and realize it isn't him; when I open my mouth to ask Colette about his plans for college and realize there are no longer any plans; when I hear a noise in the pool house and turn, expecting it to be him coming to visit.

I stumble down the hillside to Caroline, the small mound that was her. I fall to my knees and press my hands to the grass. *Feel me, Caroline. I am here. I love you. I love you.*

I feel eyes turn on me, feel them thinking judgmental thoughts about me and my baby, and I don't care. I am not of these people. Where I come from, I have no fear about following my own rules and desires. I'll grovel on my child's grave and not be ashamed.

The graveside portion of the service is short. People begin to disperse.

Sinclair arrives at my side. I see his black Rockports in the grass and make myself stand.

He inclines his head toward his father's grave, a mound almost as fresh as Caroline's. Sinclair's eyes are closed. I wonder if he's praying, or conjuring images of his father to grasp at like minute wormholes into a dimension of past reality. His cheeks are moist with tears he's wiped away.

After a quiet moment, he holds out his hand to me. "Come on. Time to go."

I take his hand and placidly follow him back to life, to our separate lives. He'll deposit me at my car, and I won't see him until it's my turn with Seth again.

At the top of the road, blocked by the departing crowd, I see a flash of brown gown and white cape. I stare at the spot waiting to catch a glimpse again, a face framed in white cloth and black veil. The nun. People shuffle and move, and there she is for a fraction of a second, her face there and gone again, the nun I saw at Caroline's funeral. I had hoped she would be here. I pull the picture from my pocketbook and stare at the face. Both young, but I'm not sure they are the same. I wish I'd seen her up close.

I pause at the top of the hill and glance back and forth between Steven's grave and Caroline's, recalling the words whispered in my head by Steven. *She will tell you.*

Who will tell me what, Steven?

CHAPTER EIGHT

☙❧

Thursday's forecast calls for freezing temperatures. I sit inside the pool house, listening to the steady drizzle of rain on the roof. The police have vacated the scene. Sinclair has returned to work. Seth has gone back to school.

I watch rivulets of rain slide down the sliding glass doors until dark settles over the city, until Colette's lights go out and the world falls silent. Finally it is time. The red arrow on the outdoor thermometer has tilted downward. I slide the door open and stand in the dark, slashing rain beside the pool, just outside the circle of light cast by the spotlight. The end is there in front of me, crystal clear by day, and yet black as pitch, churning with minuscule whitecaps as the rain and wind stir the surface.

I take one step. My body is enveloped in severe cold. I bob to the surface, unwillingly suck in air, and let the water rush over me again, but I don't sink. I don't die. I can't even make myself sink. My body panics and flails at the water despite my brain screaming for all systems to stop, to shut down, to let me drown.

And then there's a voice, bitter, crackling at me like shifting ice. "You're pathetic," it says.

A pale, thin arm reaches out and pulls at my clothes, heaves me to the side.

"Leave me alone!" I scream.

The delicate hand slaps me across the face and pulls again at my clothes. "I'm not strong enough to pull you out. Climb out."

My teeth chatter as I shake my head.

"Fine. Drown."

She stands.

I cry. "Help me!"

She turns and reaches for me, even though her face radiates disdain, maybe even hatred. When I'm out of the water, she pulls me to my feet and guides me back inside.

She is as wet as I am, her black raincoat shedding water like a duck, spilling from her hood, down her shoulders to the floor. She hauls the door shut and forces me to the bedroom, strips me, pushes me onto the bed, and covers me up.

"Next time, try a razor blade. That might actually work."

"Why didn't you leave me there?"

"If that was the answer, I would have joined you."

She flips off the lights and slips from the room like an imagined spirit as I lay shivering under the blankets, wondering what she was doing standing outside the pool house. Was she watching me?

Days pass. I don't know how long. Time is unreal to me. One day is the same as the next.

I sit on the sofa and stare at the wall.

Lilly appears at the door, a moonbeam body clothed in black jeans, black sweater, the sun braising her back as she peers in between cupped hands. She steps inside.

I stare past her at the door. I thought I had locked it. I locked everything. Every window. Every door.

"You haven't left this place in over a week. I thought maybe you'd found some razors after all."

My mind is blank. I don't know what she's talking about. Razors?

She circles the room, touching my things like Steven. Nervous energy. I'm not sure why she's come to see me.

"Where's Steven?" I ask her.

"You really are nuts." She says it with her whole face. "Steven was murdered. How could you forget that? You were at his funeral."

The shock falls over me like cold water. My brain is full of holes. I think it's the medicine, the anti-depressants and sleeping pills, but the doctor disagrees. He says everything will come back over time, that my mind is trying its best to deal with what happened to Caroline. That's where he's wrong. I don't think I can deal with it at all, ever. I see the days stretching ahead of me in a stupor of nothingness. Death would be better than my life.

Death. I shiver as I remember my midnight dip in the pool. I already failed at suicide.

Death. I remember Caroline. I remember Steven.

I remember his casket. I remember his gravesite.

I look around me, noticing my surroundings for the first time since then. New blue carpet covers the floor, soft beneath my feet as I move across the room. I wonder where on the unmarked floor Steven was found. How often have I stepped on the spot where he drew his final breath?

The smell of fresh cream paint hangs in the air, replacing the old smell of pool chlorine, at such cost. I rest my hand against the wall and guess at how many coats of paint it took to cover the splatters of Steven's blood.

"You never used to visit me," I say to Lilly.

"Steven used to visit you."

She says it with an attitude, her pale eyes darkening from watery blue to cold steel like Henry's, but I excuse her emotions and smile at the memory of Steven's visits. "Yes, he did."

As she pulls a barrette from her hair, runs her fingers through the strands and refastens it, a necklace slips from beneath her shirt, the gems glinting in the light. "Nice," I say.

She frowns, scorning my envy. "Henry."

I try to remember where I saw one like it. "Cache?"

She rolls her eyes. "Tiffany's."

Real diamonds. I should have known. Her father showers her with everything she could possibly want.

She slips the necklace back under her shirt and tosses her hair over her shoulder. "You never go out." She says it as an insult, or maybe as an explanation for why she's come to stare at me, which is funny, since I've never seen her have friends over. No teenage pool parties or cook-outs or even a gaggle of girls giggling in the backyard.

She obviously doesn't see her solitary life as being anything similar. "You'll grow old here," she continues, "and kids will make up stories about you being a hermit, an old witch with evil powers."

Maybe she means it as a joke, but it rings too true to be funny. I don't want people stopping me in the street, looking into my eyes and probing my mind. I don't want to see the thoughts forming in their heads behind their eyes, judging me, guessing at what happened or what I am thinking.

Before Sinclair kicked me out, I knew they wondered what Sinclair and I said to each other in the black of night when we couldn't sleep and there was nothing between us but thoughts of Caroline dead in the car. I hated venturing out even to the post office or the grocery store. I made Helen, our maid, run all the errands. I made her buy everything, even my tampons and my liquor. She didn't mind buying the tampons, but she refused to buy my liquor at first. She said it was against her religion. I handed her an extra twenty for her church collection plate and told her to consider it medicine. She pursed her lips like an old schoolmarm, but she bought my vodka without another word.

Sometimes I had to go out, like when I had to take Seth to the doctor in June. His allergies were kicking in with all the pollen in the air. Sinclair said to take him to Mac, an allergist in town. Sinclair was adamant about sticking to his patients and letting other specialists diagnose us. So, I took him.

Our reception was worse than I expected. They all stared at me. They would talk sweetly to Seth, then look up at me and ask how I was doing, as if I could answer such a thing. What was I supposed to say? "I feel like my guts have been ripped out, thank you. How are you today?" So I didn't say anything. I just stared at them blankly and thought about when I lived back in the dump of an apartment with my mother, where no one expected anything of me. I didn't have to please anyone or be anyone. I could have stayed high throughout high school and no one would have cared.

Here, I couldn't have a normal conversation. I didn't want to. I saved up all my words and shot them at Sinclair in the evenings. I put so many holes in him, he couldn't bleed anymore. That's why he kicked me out. He said Seth couldn't take the arguments and anger. But it was more than that. Sinclair couldn't feel anything anymore. It was my fault. I killed his heart with my verbal abuse.

It's all left me feeling so wretched that I can't even meet my own eyes in the mirror. I brush my hair blindly, facing the wall, not caring how I look.

I am safer in this cave. No one takes my picture and writes nasty things about me on the Internet for the world to read, but if Lilly is right, they may start showing up at the door to get a picture of me as a witch. I turn to the mirror and make a grizzly face. "Hmm. I'll have to keep practicing."

I should be unsettled, remembering I'm standing where a murder took place, but Lilly spooks me more than thoughts of Steven's ghost. Dark circles rim her pale eyes. She moves like a cat, silent, slipping from place to place, keeping to the edge of furniture as if she has a need to stay half-hidden, ready to dart to safety in an instant.

Reality is coming back to me. "Have the police said anything yet?"

"Lots. But they're way off track."

"What do you mean?"

"They're questioning his chemistry teacher. Lovers' quarrel, they think."

"A woman strong enough to hold him down and stab him six times?"

"Steven wasn't any taller than you and was thin. Lots of women could hold him down. But the chem teacher is a guy. Perry Willis."

"Why does society suggest everyone is gay nowadays? It makes me crazy. Steven wasn't gay."

"No, but Mr. Willis tried to convince him he was."

I harrumph. "Because he didn't have a girlfriend."

Obviously my comment doesn't merit a reply; Lilly moves to the kitchen counter, where she helps herself to a drink of water.

"Did they fingerprint the knife?" I ask.

She drinks the entire glass of water, staring past me out the glass doors between gulps, and sets the glass in the sink before answering. "Who would stab somebody and then leave a knife with fingerprints? What they didn't find was the flashlight."

"What flashlight?"

"The one the killer cracked him over the head with to knock him out." Every syllable she spits out comes with a *you're stupid* attitude attached to it. I suspect it comes from having pulled me from my death. Nothing like a little superiority to give a teenager an attitude. I can't say she's wrong.

I try to mollify her a bit. "Your parents sure are forthcoming with info. I'm surprised they've told you so much."

"You're so lame. My parents tell me nothing." Her sneer says more than her words.

"You don't like your parents much, do you?"

"How'd you guess?"

"I can see it in your eyes," I say, then I realize she was being sarcastic again. "You're pretty easy to read."

There's a chip on her shoulder about the size of my dresser. "Who are you to know anything about me?"

I flop onto the sofa. "You don't know much about me, either, do you?"

"Sure. You were a pampered wife until your baby died and you went nuts."

I laugh. "That's who I've become, but it's not who I am."

"What's that supposed to mean?"

It's too much to explain, so I take us back down the other path of parental relationships. "My mother didn't like me. Still doesn't."

Now she laughs, but it's not a funny laugh. It's like something out of a horror movie. "You have no idea about mothers who don't love you."

"Colette adores you."

"Colette does not even *like* me. And she isn't my mother."

"Do you remember your real mother? She died when you were a baby, didn't she?"

"No. My mother is off in the Bahamas, or Thailand, or the Galapagos Islands, for all I know," Lilly says. "She took off with some soccer player when I was five days old. All she left behind was a stupid doll. My father says she couldn't handle having a kid. I don't think that's it at all."

I knew all about making up excuses for a mother. "So, what's your theory?"

"She couldn't stand my dad."

"Why do you say that?"

"Because he's a pervert."

I'm not sure if she means it as a teenage insult or what. I sit a moment waiting for her to expound, but she doesn't. I push her forward with my own story. "My mother had a string of boyfriends, but never any that lasted more than a year. A couple of them were okay, but most of them were jerks. They treated me like dirt."

I wait to see if she takes the bait. She doesn't.

"One of them really was a pervert, though."

Her eyes light up for a second. "What happened?"

I don't want to put images in her head in case she's using the word without really understanding it. She's probably just mad at her dad for being overprotective. Henry rarely lets Lilly out of his sight. I think of some way around the delicate words. "My mom caught him."

She frowns. "Oh."

"She kicked him out."

"Like I said, you don't know anything about bad mothers." She picks up an apple from a dish of fruit on the counter and tosses it from one hand to the other. "So where was your father?"

Her question makes my gut clench. I asked my mother about him once. She looked at me hard, not wanting to reply. "Don't matter who he was," she said. I held back the pain. I refused to let my mother's words hurt me. Still, Mama saw it all clearly on my face because she conceded just a tad. "I never told him about you, so don't think he abandoned you or nothing. I kept hoping he'd come back of his own accord." I nodded, not understanding her reasoning, but understanding what she was trying to say: *I didn't want him to come back on account of a baby; I wanted him to come back on account of me.* I give Lilly the short version. "I've never met my father."

My admission must put us on more equal ground. She moves directly in front of me and stares me down. "That's not as bad."

"Not as bad? I don't even know who my father is," I say.

"Lucky you."

"What?"

"Your father might not even know you exist. My mother knows I exist. She gave birth to me. That's not something you forget. And then she left me. With him, living in a hellhole."

The kid lives in a mansion with everything she could possibly want, and yet she says she lives in a hellhole. I think of Henry, so upstanding, so successful in business. He was often outside tossing a football with Steven, or swimming laps in the pool alongside Lilly, or taking them to the movies. He is a wonderful father.

She would never have survived in my place.

She glances down at the coffee table and sees the picture of the nun on top of a stack of books. I must have set it there after the funeral. "What are you doing with that?" she asks.

"Found it."

She picks it up and straightens a bent corner. "Found it?"

"In a parking lot."

"*Life . . . a thing of suffering and continual partings . . . I knew nothing then of the joy of sacrifice,*" Lilly says.

The joy of sacrifice? "Huh?"

"It's something she wrote. I have it on my Facebook page."

Lilly quoting a nun. Wow. "Do you know her? She came to Caroline's funeral and Steven's."

"That couldn't have been her. This is a picture of Saint Thérèse. The Little Flower. She's been dead for ages."

Lilly knows something about a saint? "Well, maybe it wasn't her," I say, "but it was a nun. Didn't you see her?"

Lilly ignores my question. "She sends roses when she hears pleas for help."

Now who sounds nuts? "Roses? A dead nun sends people roses?"

She places the card to one side without responding, selects a book, and sprawls on the floor. I can't understand why she's made herself at home, but it's nice to have some company, to have someone to talk to. I never see anyone anymore.

I glance at what she's chosen. A classic. Salinger's *The Catcher in the Rye*. How apropos. She ought to appreciate the narrative voice.

When she leaves, I go to the kitchen and pull out my pills. I want to forget life again. *Give me my haze of delirium, O false happiness, O pill of subdued emotions.* I stare at the pills in my hand and am struck suddenly with my most lucid moment of the day: if the police hadn't *found* the flashlight, how did Lilly *know* it was a flashlight?

CHAPTER NINE

✥

I am seated in Dr. Arick's office, receiving my required weekly dose of psychobabble.

"I'm worried about all the time you spend inside. You need to get outside more," Dr. Arick tells me. "Sunlight helps relieve depression. So does exercise. We need to put you on an exercise regime."

"I like being depressed."

"Explain."

"No one expects anything of me, and I can spend all day sleeping."

"Do you want to spend your entire life sleeping?"

"If it will make it go by faster."

He writes that down. "What about your son?"

"What about him?"

"Would you feel better if you got to spend more time with your son?"

"He doesn't like me. He has no desire to spend more time with me."

"How does that make you feel?"

Being pushed away by a four-year-old boy has lasting effects. I can't foresee a time when Seth will run eagerly into my arms. But I don't want to explain all that to the doc. It takes too much effort. I revert to his statement about exercise. "You're right. I need to get better. Got any ideas?"

"Well, what do you think of bicycling? There are trails all along the Blue Ridge you could explore. Fresh air and exercise."

I nod. "Good idea. I think I'll do that."

Dr. Arick shifts in his seat, flips a page in his notes. "I also think we need to move you out of the Gordins' apartment. The scene of their son's murder is not a healthy place for you in your mental state."

"It's okay. They painted it. New carpet, too. I like living there."

"Really? Tell me about it."

"There's this really sweet little girl, their daughter, Lilly. We're best friends now."

He nods and scrawls something in his notebook. I figure he likes the idea of me bonding with a little girl. I'm his prize patient. I'm fairly certain that he's writing a journal article about me, about how crazy I am and how he's curing me. Let's hope he doesn't interview Lilly. I stand up. "I have to go now. I have a hair appointment. If you could just renew my prescriptions . . ."

When I get home, I sink to the sofa and stare at the wall for a while before I decide to seek diversion in a fictional world. I reach toward my stack of books but pause halfway. There's a book sitting in the middle of the coffee table with a picture of the nun on it. *The Story of a Soul: The Autobiography of Saint Thérèse of Lisieux.*

The sentence Lilly quoted has been reverberating through my head — *suffering and continual partings* — but I know I didn't buy that book. At least I don't remember buying it.

I pick it up and leaf through it. It falls open at a page marked with a ribbon where text has been highlighted: *Even the brightest day finishes with the dark: only one day will be without end — that of our first and everlasting Communion in heaven.*

I read it five times. All I have in me is bitterness and sadness, and even though I think of heaven in some abstract way, I have never really considered heaven as a reality that had anything to do with me.

I turn to the first page and begin to read.

Bitter cold descends over the mountain. The wind rattles the windows at night, and the pool house feels ever damp and cold. I remain in bed, cocooned against the world for days until the sky clears, a beautiful blue so crisp and bright that it draws me from beneath the covers to peek out at the world.

I see Colette sitting by the pool under a thick blanket, reading a book in a spot of sunshine, sheltered from the brisk wind by the pool house and main house. It's the first time I've seen her since . . . since the night of Steven's murder. She's been in hiding. I've been too lost to seek her out.

I reach for *The Story of a Soul*, then change my mind. I'm reading it slowly, seeking out bits of wisdom as I go. Even if I were clear-minded rather than doped up, I know I can't do that with Colette staring at me. Instead, I grab my latest novel purchase and head outside. I figure Doc may be right; sunshine and fresh air can't hurt.

Maybe Colette and I will talk.

The book in Colette's lap is from the library. No surprise there. Colette is such a tightwad, she squeaks. That's why she's willing to rent me her pool house. You'd think she was poor or something.

She sees me without even looking up. "Well, look what the cat dragged in."

"Hi."

Bruce the yardman is crouched by the pool, checking chemicals, but Colette ignores him. He's a non-entity. "You're despicable," she says, still staring at the words on the page.

"I know," I say, although I'm clueless as to what specific thing in my life she's commenting on.

"My son dies, and you go check yourself into the Grove Park Inn and relax in the spa for a week."

I'm on my full dose of medicine this week. I have no emotions. Nothing will upset me today. I shrug. "You were having the place recarpeted and painted. And there wasn't anywhere else to go."

"I ought to kick you out."

"I wouldn't blame you a bit." I take a seat beside her. "Why's he checking the pool? It's freezing out here."

"Winterizing it."

He moves to the end of the pool and lifts the cover from the pump housing as if it's made of Styrofoam. He's Superman. Wide shoulders.

Fit from yard work, but a gnarled face, as if he spends his days thinking ugly thoughts. I avoid the yard when he's around. He must feel me
watching him because he looks up, his eyes narrowed at me. I turn to
Colette. "What have you heard from the police?"

"Nothing."

"Nothing?"

"They think it was a drug deal."

"A drug deal gone awry?" I am stunned in a satiated, drugged up,
can't-really-focus-on-it way. Steven never did drugs. If anyone had a
drug deal going on, it would have been Colette, because she's been a
user as long as I've known her.

I met Colette at the first wedding Sinclair and I attended together
in Asheville. Colette was standing by the buffet, eating cake, when she
saw me looking at her. "I couldn't resist," she said, nodding at the cake.
She snickered when I cut myself a small slice. "Better watch out eating
that much. You'll get fat."

She was making fun of me. She's a large woman — heavy-boned.

"I'll have to work it off later," I said.

She eyed me as I eyed her. "You're not from around here, are
you?"

"No. Raleigh."

"Oh, that's you. Well, I see why, now."

"See what?"

"Why he was willing to ditch his inheritance."

"Sinclair?"

She glanced around her back, then began licking the icing from her
fingers. "Didn't tell you, eh? Elaine, his mama, was fit to be tied, but
she had to give in. He wouldn't budge."

My face must have frozen at the thought of Sinclair risking his inheritance for me.

"You didn't know, huh?"

"No, I didn't." It was the first secret shared between us.

Mrs. Bollen walked up. A physical change swept over Colette as if a
fairy godmother had passed a wand over her and raised her up on glass

slippers. "Sandra, darling, how are you?" Colette said. "I heard that sweet daughter of yours is off to Princeton in the fall. What will you do with her so far away?"

I stood my ground. I knew how to do the princess act, too. "Oh, so you're Mrs. Bollen. It's a pleasure to meet you. My mother-in-law, Mrs. Winters, has such nice things to say about you."

Colette raised one eyebrow and quirked one corner of her mouth, trying to keep from laughing at our mutual change of tone. Before we left the celebration, she slipped her calling card into my hand and told me to drop by for a visit.

I went to see her the next week. She offered me a snort about ten minutes after getting there and was slightly peeved when I declined. "You're gonna act like you didn't use crack where you came from, Miss Hoity-Toity?"

She didn't exactly know where I came from, other than the city of Raleigh. I guess she considered all of Raleigh to be a cesspool or something.

I never did take her up on the drugs; I have all the medication I need without taking stuff I would have to buy in alleys. But she liked the idea of being able to offer them to me. She can let her guard down around me, and I won't get whacked out over it like the rest of the upper echelon.

She was a good mother, though. I doubted Steven and Lilly had any idea she did drugs. I'd never seen any sign of it around Steven. I didn't know Lilly well enough yet.

Bottom line, though: if the murder had anything to do with drugs, I was sure they were Colette's drugs, not Steven's.

"Yup," she said, as if reading my mind, "they think Steven was a drug dealer. They found my stash and jumped to the wrong conclusion. Now I can't get a buzz in case the cops come back around." She snaps her book shut. "Let's go see a movie."

So much for fresh air. "Sure."

"Great," she says as she stands and gathers her blanket, "*Law Abiding Citizen* is showing at the dollar theater."

She actually says it with a straight face. I snicker, wondering if it's the title that's attracting her or if it's just typical Colette unwilling to waste any of her wads of money going to a new release. Probably both.

Colette goes after her keys while I grab my purse from my bedroom and make a quick attempt at brushing my hair and putting on lipstick.

Bruce the yardman watches as I pull the door closed and check the lock twice.

CHAPTER TEN

I t's my weekend to have Seth. Sinclair called to say he would drop him off after preschool. I offered to pick him up, but Sinclair said no, it would be better if he brought him to the pool house. Now that I think about it, I haven't ever picked him up. Not since the accident. Part of the *agreement*. My son isn't allowed to leave the school premises with me.

It's probably just as well. If I picked up Seth, he'd probably start screaming in the middle of the parking lot, refusing to get in the car.

They arrive at five, which is an hour earlier than usual. I rush out to the driveway to meet them. Orange and red leaves swirl around us in currents of air and flutter to the ground.

He assesses me as he hands me Seth's bag. "Are you okay this week?"

What he's asking is whether or not I can handle Seth for the next forty-eight hours. I lift my chin and meet his eyes with a look I hope exudes more confidence than I feel. "We'll be fine."

Bruce the yardman, working up a leaf pile in the middle of the backyard, stops raking to stare at us. Henry sticks his head out the back door and yells at him. "Bruce, get the blower and clear the leaves off the driveway before you leave. Lilly, come get changed. I'm taking you out to the mall and then to dinner."

Father-daughter date; Colette has gone to a jewelry party given by the daughter of one of the country-club cronies — one of those horrible events you can't get out of without looking like a cad. Colette will buy more than anyone else just to maintain her status.

I follow Henry's gaze and spot Lilly sitting at the base of the big oak tree in the back corner of the yard. Two guys in hoodies are standing over her, one leaning against the tree trunk, the other standing to the side, arms crossed, talking to her. They see Henry eyeing them and creep away through the trees and undergrowth that block the house from the back neighbors, down a path I've never noticed. Lilly drags her feet as she heads to the house, her shoulders hunched as she stares at the ground. Her hair hangs limp around her pale face. She's wearing a long, black sweater thing that hangs to her knees. She looks like something from a gothic music video. I wonder what the boys think of her. Are they attracted to her? Or selling her something?

Sinclair raises a hand to Henry. Henry waves back, his smile brightening his striking face, tanned from a recent business trip to Florida. He disappears back inside, and I turn my back on the yardman and Lilly to face Sinclair. "This is a surprise. No patients this afternoon?" I ask.

"I have a convention to attend this weekend."

His words speak volumes.

"I'll have my cell phone if you need to reach me, of course. And Mama will be home." He hands me a paper with a Florida address. "Here's where I'll be staying."

I wonder if all men take their girlfriends to Florida this time of year. "Jocelyn is holding down the fort alone, is she?"

"No. Patrick Bollen said he would as a favor."

Patrick Bollen is the husband of my friend Amy — at least, she was my friend in my old, normal married life. I don't like Patrick. He's too arrogant, always making Amy feel subordinate, criticizing her Midwestern accent, her cooking, her lack of domestic skills.

I don't want to know the details of Sinclair's trip beyond that. I don't want him to confirm that Jocelyn will be at his side, accompanying him out of town, probably sharing a hotel room with him. It has all come to pass as I expected.

I think back to my recent stay at his house and realize her belongings weren't scattered around his house with sloppy abandon like some women might have done. But I expect caution from Jocelyn. She is independent. She won't move in until Sinclair and I are officially divorced and she has his last name tacked in between hers and the long list of academic letters trailing behind.

I knew from the beginning she was trouble. Sinclair was too pleased with her, too satisfied with her work. He extolled her virtues to anyone at the club willing to listen. Jocelyn sailed into his life with all the grace and professionalism a woman can possess, while I was at home, saddled with a stubborn four-year-old and a baby who rarely slept. I was a wreck. I hadn't lost the weight of the pregnancy, yet. I have now. It's surprising what a mere death and depression can do for one's appetite. But it wasn't just my weight. I was constantly tired, overburdened, and emotional. I felt as bad as I looked.

I remember trying to see things objectively. I tried to decipher what was going on at the office and to convince myself all was okay, but every time I looked in the mirror, doubts restored themselves. I continually pressed Sinclair. I sought affirmation that all was fine with us, that my fears of Jocelyn displacing me were unfounded.

"How's the new girl working out?" I asked about two weeks into her tenure.

"What new girl?"

"Jocelyn."

He frowned at me. "She's not a hired hand, Rachel. She's a medical doctor."

"I know that. Haven't we been discussing her position for months? How's she working out?"

He turned back to his papers. "Fine."

"Does the staff like her?"

"Yes."

"Does she get along with everyone?"

"Yes."

"Does she consult with you on patients?"

"Sometimes. I'm more likely to seek her opinion. She's been practicing longer."

"So you get along well with her, then?"

He looked up. "What's with the twenty questions?"

Men are so dense. Obviously I wanted to know how close they'd become, if he was physically attracted to her. "You spent so long looking for the right partner, I just wondered how things were working out."

"Great. Things are great."

Seth chose that moment to shuffle in and lay his lollipop on Sinclair's papers. "Mommy, I need to go potty."

"Oh geesh, look at that! I'm trying to work here, Rachel. Quit with the questions. Get the sticky candy out of here and leave me alone."

I left, taking the lollipop in one hand and Seth in the other. I felt forty years old, worlds away from where I'd been such a few years earlier.

I washed Seth's hands and stared into the mirror. My belly was still flabby. My butt was huge. My face was bloated and pale with lack of sleep. My eyes were bloodshot. I looked a mess. I'd lost my figure and my glow. I was a college drop-out; a dumb blond; an aging mother with two anchors tied around my neck, never free to do anything, never full of fun as I'd been such a short time earlier.

I'd thought a second baby was the perfect thing to round out our family, but that was before Jocelyn arrived. With her around, the two kids only made me feel matronly.

Now Caroline is gone, and I would give anything to feel matronly again, to have her back and wrap my whole life around her.

My figure has returned, but Jocelyn is still there, evident in the piece of paper dangling in Sinclair's hands, the convention address, a tangible line drawn between us. We are separate. He makes plans that don't include me, and if Jocelyn is joining him, he has no need, no obligation, to tell me so.

Seth glances from Sinclair to me. He is too young to catch the innuendos, but he feels the strain between us. "Daddy . . ."

"No, Seth. We talked about this. I'll be back."

I reach out to take the address and let my fingers linger against his hand. He must remember the magic we were together.

His eyes close for a fraction of a second, and I know I've connected with him. It's enough to make him pause, to turn his hand to grasp my fingers, but not enough to make him stay. He lets go and turns away to take long strides back to his car.

Not even a kiss for Seth.

I hope it's enough to change the course of his weekend.

Seth stands beside me, watching Sinclair's car disappear down the road and states his case with quiet defiance. "I want to go with Daddy."

"I know you do." My emotions over Sinclair, the love and hate, the jealousy and the repulsion, grapple within me, but the truth, however contrary, stands clear. "I want to go with him too."

But we can't, so I take Seth's bag and retreat to my rented fortress.

I need a battle plan.

CHAPTER ELEVEN

S eth is as rattled by Sinclair's departing as I am, so I make him a sandwich and settle him in front of a *Bob the Builder* video; then I pick up the Saint Thérèse book and read back over a page I marked the previous night:

> *The sun shines equally both on cedars and on every tiny flower. In just the same way God looks after every soul as if it had no equal. All is planned for the good of every soul, exactly as the seasons are so arranged that the humblest daisy blossoms at the appointed time.*

I conclude it means that in God's eyes, I am as important as Jocelyn. I don't think society agrees, but I've decided it's pretty obvious God's opinion ought to matter more.

When I turn back to the kitchen for a drink, Lilly is there, leaning on the counter. I jump. "Cripes! How'd you get in here?"

"I'm a ghost. I came in through the walls."

"Funny."

"The back door, genius."

"I had it locked."

"The key is under the broken brick."

She comes and goes. I realize Lilly must have left the book for me, but I don't mention it. I have to ponder the significance of its being from her, of her having read the words I'm struggling to absorb as reality. I thrust the thoughts away and concentrate on the moment at hand.

"There's a key right there, outside the door? Oh, that makes me feel secure with some murderer running around. Why didn't the police find the key? They must be totally lame investigators."

She shrugs with that lazy, disgusted look she gets. "It went missing for a few days."

Her abrasiveness irritates me. I don't understand why she bothers to visit me, why she teases me with clues that are meaningless. "Is there something you aren't telling me?"

She laughs; actually, she cackles. "There's a lot I'm not telling you."

About the murder or about herself? I'm curious, but at the same time I don't really want to be privy to either one. I have enough to sort out in my head already. "Don't you want Steven's murderer to be caught?"

"The cops know there's a back door. They know the killer didn't force a way in." She spits the words at me as if it's my fault they haven't solved the case. "Obviously the door takes a key." She walks around me. "Anyway, I didn't come to talk about that. I came to make sure you're still alive. And to see Seth."

She sits beside him and stares at the television as if she actually wants to see the show.

He looks up at her. "Hi, Lilly."

He's been around Lilly only a few times. She used to come with Steven to take him trekking around the backyard in search of grasshoppers and such, but he seems to accept her as a fixture without hesitation.

I wish the same could be said of me.

I go through the kitchen to the back door and look around. I'm not sure what I expect to see. Maybe huge footprints or a bloody handprint. But there is nothing more than grass and a stone walkway edged with pansies recently planted to flourish in the increasingly cool weather and shortening days. I sit in the sun and close my eyes, wishing the answers to life could be found written on the insides of my eyelids. The sun warms my skin, but not my soul. Darkness grows from the inside, a fear, a sickness holding me captive.

When I open my eyes, Bruce the yardman is standing outside the pool fence staring at me. I try to smile at him, but the smile doesn't quite reach my face.

I pick a handful of pansies and carry them inside. I have a glass jelly jar under the sink to stick them in.

Lilly says, "There were footprints. Men's size-ten Nike tennis shoes . . . Steven's."

How does she know these things?

As I bend down to retrieve the jelly jar from under the sink, a voice blares out behind me, "Lilly!"

I whack my head pulling it out of the cabinet and turning around. Lilly springs to her feet. "Got to go."

"Who was that?"

"Henry." She always calls him Henry, never Daddy. She points to a tiny speaker embedded in the wall by the back door. "On the intercom."

"The intercom? I didn't know it worked."

Lilly shakes her head at me. "Obviously Steven didn't know either."

"But I've never heard it before."

"I turned it on when I came in so I would know when Henry got home."

With that, she slips out the door and disappears around the corner.

I had seen the speaker before but assumed it didn't work. Looking at it gives me the creeps. I look closely and see a tiny switch in the corner, which I flick to *off*, and stare out the glass doors to the big house beyond the pool, wondering if Lilly was in trouble for something. She looked scared.

Then I think about the murder. Could the intercom have had anything to do with it? What if it was turned on? Could that have spurred a murder? Unless . . . I look at the intercom. The switch could be pushed in the opposite direction so that someone in the house could hear what was going on in the pool house. Had they been listening to my conversations? But still, would that have anything to do with Steven? If the killer was in the house, did he come here seeking Steven because he heard him over the intercom?

Then a new thought dawns on me. Maybe Lilly heard everything that happened in here that evening. If so, why didn't she stop it? Why didn't she call the police?

Maybe she had.

When Sinclair calls that evening, I can tell from the dishes clanking in the background and the hum of voices that he's on his cell phone in a restaurant. "How's it going?"

"Fine," I reply. What does he expect? That I've let Seth drown in the pool or something?

"Good. I forgot to tell you that Seth has a birthday party tomorrow at the Bollens'. Two o'clock."

"Oh." The thought of having to talk with a group of mothers I've avoided for months knots up my stomach.

"You can take him, can't you? I already RSVP'd to Amy and Patrick saying he would be there."

"Thanks for checking with me."

"It's not like you have anything else planned, do you?"

"No."

"Great. Well, let me say goodnight to Seth."

So much for conversation between us. I hear a woman's laughter close to the phone and know he's conversing with *her*. He always had time to talk to *her*. He'd do anything for *her*. "I'd drown in work if it weren't for her," he'd say. "I can't afford to lose her."

He took Saturdays and on-call Sundays to give her freedom. He replaced their consultant on her advice, and the office manager. White-haired Iris had run the office throughout senior Dr. Winters' reign, but Jocelyn convinced Sinclair to replace her, too.

I stopped by to give Iris a retirement gift on her last day. She held her chin up bravely. "It's long past time for me to retire. Even my grandbabies have grown up while I've been chained to this place," she said without emotion, but regret shone in her eyes.

I kept my tears at bay. "You've meant the world to Dr. Winters and his patients, Iris. Don't let anyone make you feel that your dedication hasn't been appreciated. Dr. Winters couldn't have done better than you."

She nodded, unable to speak, while I tried to convince myself to take my own words to heart. Sinclair could have married someone better than me, but the point was he'd married me, not Jocelyn. I wasn't about to be cast aside like an inept receptionist.

After Jocelyn's arrival, Sinclair's daddy continued to practice for a while. That was the plan. He'd stay until Jocelyn built up a large enough clientele to support her position. It didn't take as long as expected. The patients loved Jocelyn and had no qualms about being rescheduled from senior Dr. Winters to young Dr. Jocelyn Harper.

At the inception of the search for a new partner, his father was only looking forward to retirement. Six months later, he was seeking respite from raging headaches and bouts of nausea. Being a doctor made him that much more stubborn about acknowledging he had a significant ailment. "It's stress," he argued for weeks before giving in and undergoing tests. The tests confirmed the worst; he had a brain tumor.

Sinclair was exhausted every night. Despite intensive care, his daddy continued to worsen. When Sinclair was home, he pored over medical journals and read studies online. He knew intellectually there was nothing further to be done for his daddy, but his heart ached too badly to give up. He was a doctor; he had to seek a cure. "What more can you do?" I asked. His father had already undergone surgery. Most of the tumor had been removed, with chemotherapy following to battle a recurring portion.

"Something. I'm looking into . . . well, it's experimental, but it may work. I want to understand it completely before we take that step, though."

What he really wanted was a miracle.

I would have left him alone if he'd been working with a man. I'm sure of it. But Jocelyn hung over us, over our relationship, like a storm cloud threatening disaster. I understood his concern for his father, but I suspected he was finding more than medical answers at Jocelyn's side. He'd stop by the house long enough to eat half his supper, change into jeans, then head off to the hospital and medical library. Maybe he went alone. He never said. But I always pictured Jocelyn meeting him there, poring over the books with him.

"Maybe you ought to let it go, Sinclair. He has good doctors. They know what they're doing."

He turned on me like a snake ready to strike. "Do you understand? He's dying! And you want me to just trust someone else to do everything possible for him? I'm a doctor, Rachel, and his son. No one is in a better position to help him than I am. If I can't save him, he'll die. He'll die! Do you understand?"

I felt a shadow pass over me. I really had no idea what he was going through, except philosophically. I'd never known my father, so I didn't know what it would be to lose one. I barely had a mother. I'd never had anyone to whom I meant the world other than Sinclair. Our fears were dominoes. He was afraid of losing his father, and I was afraid of losing him. But it wouldn't be to the clutches of death.

His voice dropped to an agonized whisper. "It's not a game. It's life or death."

Back then, I couldn't fathom death. It wasn't real to me. I'd never known anyone who died.

Caroline chose that moment to wail from her crib. The irony of the moment was clear all too soon.

When Caroline died shortly after that, it should have brought us together in our misery, but Jocelyn was there for him twenty-four/seven. I wasn't even there for myself.

Even now I struggle to stay cognizant for Seth. I could fade into nothingness in the confines of this pool house, but I must keep myself focused during his visits for his sake. "Talk to Daddy," I say. I hand Seth the telephone and walk away to microwave our frozen dinners.

Sunday afternoon we arrive late to the birthday party. I allowed thirty minutes to shop for a present, but Seth couldn't make up his mind between a Transformer and Legos. Had it been a girl's party, I could have picked out a Barbie doll and left in five minutes.

If I study the cars lining the street, I can guess who is attending, but I'm hyperventilating as it is. Seth walks up the steps in front of me, a little man in his navy slacks and his red sweater. His hair is neatly combed, and he's wearing his loafers, not his tennis shoes. Sinclair would be proud of me for getting it right, but it wasn't my doing. Seth knows the drill. He's four now. He laid out the clothes his father packed and changed without my having to tell him to do so.

As Amy answers the door, I realize with a flash how much I've missed her. She's a bouncy brunette with over-tweezed eyebrows. Both our children were born within months of each other. We took our kids to the park together, and out to lunch. We left our babies in the club nursery and sat around the pool, watching the boys splash in the water, and slept in the sun while the boys had swimming lessons. She was a Midwest farm girl with an enchanting smile and spontaneous laughter that bubbled into the sunshine with irrepressible glee.

Today her easy smile fades as she holds the etched glass door open; the shock of seeing me waves across her features. "Rachel. Hello. I expected Sinclair to drop off Seth."

"He's in Florida. At a medical conference."

She's unsure what to do. Her eyes shift from me to the women in the room. Amy has always struggled to fit into the circle of society. She doesn't know how to fake it like I do; she's too honest for that. She's afraid of making a wrong move. She wants to do everything by their rules so they'll keep her in their throng. "Won't you come in?"

I knew better. She meant: *You don't want to come in, do you?* I'm not a safe bet anymore. I had a breakdown. My family is broken. My husband is having an affair. I'm not a neat little package that fits into their ideal lives.

Beyond her I see the other mothers sitting in the living room, nibbling on appetizers and sipping punch. I know with a glance that the buffet was brought in by caterers. Amy did better with my help last year; I taught her to make clam dip and canapés. We laid out fresh vegetables and homemade dressings. The children had chicken strips so zesty and flavorful that the women ate them as well, with pasta salad on the side.

I look into the face of each woman: Maureen, queen bee, sips from her crystal punch glass with her pinky just so, alongside Andrea, her best friend and neighbor, both of them Old Money, born into their rank by daddies who did the same. Next is Penny, an overweight red-head who lives on the fringe and is oblivious to the fact that they talk about her every time she leaves the room. Zoe, the dark beauty who constantly strives to outmaneuver Maureen, eyes me with interest. And in the corner, Cora and Darla, two plain round-faced women pregnant with their second and third babies respectively, hang out to have a good time and don't care a whit about who thinks what.

The chatter and clatter of dishes in the room falls silent. All eyes are on me. I repeat my new mantra: *The sun shines equally both on cedars and on every tiny flower.* Darla speaks up. "Hello, Rachel. How are you doing?"

I hate that question. They want me to say I'm fine. They want me to go back to being a happy mom with nothing else on my mind but the next party or mommy meeting. I can't do it. I can't. I steady the pounding of my heart and breathe deeply so my voice will sound normal. "I'm coping. Thanks for asking." I hand Amy the present. "I'll be back to pick him up at five."

The sun is setting by the time we get home. Seth is full from all the party treats, so I nuke myself a frozen dinner and watch him watching television, then we play Chutes & Ladders. He wins three times.

I fold up the board and set it in the box. He stays beside me.

"I miss Daddy."

"I do, too," I reply, and he lets me put my arm around him. "Do you do fun things with Daddy?" I ask.

"I played golf with him."

"You did?"

"He said I got the highest score."

"I bet you did." I imagine Sinclair's golf game with Seth in tow. "Did Jocelyn play, too?"

"I don't know. I can't remember the names."

I sigh. At least she hasn't become a household fixture in his life.

We are still sitting together when I hear Sinclair's car arrive. Seth hears it, too. He jumps to his feet, heaves open the sliding glass door, and runs across the patio. "Daddy! Daddy!"

I watch him fly into Sinclair's arms. He must not remember what his daddy did to his little sister. How could he, and still be so anxious to be with him?

I carry Seth's small suitcase to the car and retrace my steps without a word. Sinclair is wrapped in Seth and doesn't even notice.

Inside, I pull the book from the table and seek the confines of my bed and the comfort of some secret that will wash the pain away. As I settle onto the pillows, I close my eyes for a moment and listen to the stillness, the aloneness of my space. The emptiness, the nothingness of what has become of my life.

Eventually, I open the book and again read the passage about the wildflower:

He has created the poor savage with no guide but natural law, and it is to their hearts that He deigns to stoop. They are His wildflowers whose home-liness delights Him. By stooping down to them, He manifests His infinite grandeur. The sun shines equally both on cedars and on every tiny flower. In just the same way God looks after every soul as if it has no equal. All is planned for the good of every soul, exactly as the seasons are so arranged that the humblest daisy blossoms at the appointed time.

Planned for the good? Where is the good, God? How can any of this be good?

I keep reading.

CHAPTER TWELVE

✶

Lilly visits on Wednesday. She doesn't have much to say. She glances around the apartment and gazes into my eyes and down at my wrists before sitting on the sofa and picking up a book. I'm guessing she's judged me mentally sound for the time being.

"Don't you ever have any homework?" I ask.

"No."

"Why not? I always had tons."

"Teachers don't like to grade it."

"What? You mean they don't give you any because they don't want to grade it?"

She doesn't answer, her usual tactic when she thinks a question is too dumb for a response.

"Got a new boyfriend?"

She doesn't respond.

"The guys out by the oak tree — who were they?"

She speaks without looking away from the book. "I told them to get lost."

"Why?"

She turns the page of *Emma* without answering.

I reach for my pocketbook. "I've got to go. I have an appointment."

"With who?"

I consider not answering her, but I'm trying to be nice. That's what the Saint Thérèse book is teaching me.

I'm not like Saint Thérèse, not in any way imaginable. Both her parents adored her. And although she admonished herself for being sinful, she never did anything bad, not really, not like I did. I think she must have been a saint from the day she was born. She thought about God all the time, about how much she loved him and wanted to be with him. And the Virgin Mary appeared to her while she was sick as a child. I am nothing like her. I'm not sure I love God. In fact, some days I don't even believe in God.

Maybe that's why I keep reading the book. She makes me want to be a better person because I feel wretched about how bad and self-centered I've been my whole life. So I smile real friendly and answer, "It's my weekly visit to Donald Arick."

"Who's that? Your hair stylist or something gaggy?"

"I wish." I conclude Lilly doesn't believe in going to salons. Her hair hangs halfway down her back, jagged on the ends as if last cut with kitchen scissors. I'd done that out of necessity as a teen. I don't understand why she would do that, considering all the money at her disposal. She wears Tiffany jewelry dangling from her wrists, and she plucks holes in her Abercrombie sweatpants like they're cheap and disposable, but she chops off her hair with kitchen scissors. She is spoiled, but plays the deprived teen.

I pick up my keys. "Donald is my shrink."

"Oh. Maybe I ought to come along."

"Naw. He's a quack. I only go because I have to."

She smirks. "Donald's a quack."

"Yeah."

"You don't get it?"

"What?"

"Donald Duck. Donald Doc. He's a quack."

"Ha ha. You quack me up."

"You're more quacked than me, that's for sure."

I start giggling. "Lilly's quacked. She needs a quacker."

The humor smolders in the depths of her eyes as she jumps and flaps her arms like wings. "Lilly wants a quacker. Lilly wants a quacker."

"Lilly needs a quack 'cause she's quacked."

She stops flapping her arms and collapses on the couch. Her face falls into her hands, and she weeps. What am I to do?

I look at the clock. "I have to go, Lilly, or I'll be late. You can come with me if you really want to. At least ride in the car with me?"

She shakes her head without looking up.

"Lilly ..."

"Go."

I feel torn. "I can't skip, or he'll call Sinclair, then I won't get to see Seth."

"Can I stay here while you're gone?"

I reach for the door. "Yes, stay here. Don't leave. I'll be back as soon as I can."

"Good, because Keith is coming to fix the cable again."

I don't bother trying to figure out who or what she means by that.

I can't help smiling throughout my appointment. *Donald Doc's a quack.*

Donald Doc just thinks I'm happy for a change. "How was your relationship with Sinclair just prior to Caroline's death?"

"I was fat."

"Explain how that affected your relationship. Did you feel unattractive or worry Sinclair found you unattractive?"

I'm still laughing. "Both. I had a harder time losing weight after Caroline's birth. And he started spending time with Jocelyn. Put two and two together."

"Tell me what you think they were doing."

"Having an affair."

He stares at me, trying to figure out why this is making me laugh. The answer is easy: *I'm quacked.*

The cable guy's truck is blocking my parking place when I get back, so I have to park in the street and walk all the way down the hill to the pool house. My feet are frozen by the time I get inside, and Lilly is using the last of my bread to make toast.

"Feel free to make yourself at home," I say.

She scowls at me, the humor we shared dispelled to a distant memory. "Were you saving it for something?" she asks.

I wonder if she is mean to me out of spite or if she treats everyone this way. Maybe she didn't understand the *being nice* part of the book. Or maybe she is being nice and it's me misinterpreting her intentions because of the sour looks she gives me. I turn from her to deposit my pocketbook and shoes in the bedroom. "Talking with Donald Doc puts me off food for the rest of the day." I change subjects to something we have in common — Steven. "Have the police found anything else?"

"Yes. The dirt on Steven's shoes didn't come from our backyard."

I roll my eyes. "Now that is truly useful information. Did they suppose he never left home?"

She shrugs.

"They really referred to the dirt on his shoes?"

She shrugs again.

I go along with her suggestion just to humor her. "So, what now? They're going to test the dirt all over Asheville, and what will that tell them?"

She gives me one of her *You're an idiot* looks. She thinks I'm making fun of her. I don't want her to think that. I got enough of that in my youth, being treated like a jerk by my mother's low-class boyfriends, so I offer a more serious train of thought. "What about carpet fibers and hair, and all that stuff they show in movies?"

"The only fibers they found in here were from you and me and Colette and Betts and Henry."

She can't possibly know that, but I go along with it. "That figures."

"And a strand of someone else's hair they can't identify."

That makes me pause. Maybe she has some inside scoop. Maybe she's listening in on police talks or has access to their records or something. Or maybe she's making it up to make herself feel in control of the situation. "Well, there you go," I say. "Maybe that will lead to something."

"You're so stupid."

I don't understand. She says it like I'm her enemy. She gives me a book about a saint, but then she's hateful toward me. Maybe we ought to discuss it. "I've been reading that book."

She cocks one eyebrow at me.

I fetch the book from my bedroom and flip open to a page I marked: "*Suppose the son of a clever doctor falls over a stone in the road and breaks his leg. His father rushes to the spot and, with loving care, uses every ounce of his skill to heal him. His son is soon healed and is grateful. There's no doubt the boy is quite right to love such a father. But now let us suppose that the father learns that a dangerous stone lies in the road, goes there before his son, and unseen by anyone, takes away the stone. Now the boy, who knows nothing of the mishap he has been spared by his father's loving foresight, will show him no particular gratitude and will love him less than if he had been healed by him.*"

She bites her lip.

I ask, "Do you think she is saying that God let Caroline and Steven die because without their deaths he wouldn't have had the opportunity to heal us? To make us grateful for his love?"

She closes her eyes and sighs. "You don't get it." She snatches the book from me, runs her finger down the page and reads, "*Yet if the boy knew the danger he had escaped, would he not love his father more?* That's what she's trying to say. Think of what you still have. Think of all that could be wrong but isn't. We constantly blame him for the bad things. She's saying God loves us even though there are a zillion things he does for us that we never thank him for."

What do I have to thank Him for? I can't think of anything but my loss: Caroline, my marriage, the love of my son. I am bereft. So I say nothing in response.

Lilly turns away, her thin, white body a mere wisp of a living being. I don't think she is any happier than I am, and I doubt God could possibly bring joy to either of us.

CHAPTER THIRTEEN

The phone rings. Panic engulfs me. My stomach leaps to my mouth. I don't want to answer it. Lilly's string of clues has me thinking about the killer. I keep thinking he's watching me through the windows.

The phone keeps ringing. I let it ring five times before I snatch the receiver. "Hello."

It's Colette. "Come join us for supper. Henry's gone on a business trip. It's just me and Lilly."

I imagine Lilly glaring at me through dinner for fraternizing with *the enemy*. But Colette probably needs me. She needs someone to talk to, and I've been ignoring her, lost in my own world. "Give me ten minutes."

I hang up the phone and glance around, the creepy feeling persisting. If this were a TV movie, I'd notice something significant at this point, something that would lead me to the killer. But I feel clueless, wrapped in drug cotton. I make an effort to get clarity, to notice little things. The intercom is turned off. The windows are all locked. No one will sneak in while I'm gone. I grab my tiny pocketbook, slip on the clogs by the door, and twist the lock into place. I tug on the door. I check it twice. It's locked.

Dusk is hanging over the yard, but a few birds are still twittering in the trees. I look for the extra key hidden in the yard by the back door. It's gone. My nerves tingle from my toes to the roots of my hair. Who took it? Lilly? Colette? Henry? Bruce the yardman?

Lilly. It must have been Lilly. I will ask her.

I circle around the pool, out the gate and down the walkway to the back deck.

Colette is leaning on the railing, staring at something in the woods. Those boys again? I don't see them or Lilly.

Through the tall glass windows, I watch Betts the maid set the dining-room table, and suddenly I am filled with angst. She turns her head and peers at me from afar. I think of the missing key, the clues, unseen eyes watching me, and I shiver. Where does Betts fit into it all?

Colette sips at a gin and tonic. "Hungry?"

"What'd she make?"

"I haven't the foggiest. I don't ask for anything anymore."

Lasagna. We sit in the formal dining room. Betts serves it on the fine china with sprigs of parsley on top and salads on the side. She doesn't realize I eat out of frozen-food containers. Or maybe she does. I see her look at me sideways as she sets a plate in front of me. Maybe she knows I'm nothing more than her and never have been. I was a maid all along. A maid with a ring on my finger, doing what I was told to do. I don't need any more enemies in my life, so I smile at her. "Thanks, Betts. It looks delish."

Colette raises her eyebrows. "Yes, it looks great, Betts." She downs the rest of her gin. "It's getting late. Why don't you go? We'll stack our things in the kitchen."

Betts nods and leaves without a word, but her eyes linger on me a moment too long. It gives me the creeps.

"Where's Lilly?" I ask.

"She decided to eat in her room."

I nod and take a bite of garlic bread. It melts in my mouth. "So what's up with her?"

"She's just in a mood. I'd rather she eat by herself anyway. She sulks all the time, and it ruins my supper."

"I'm sure she misses Steven."

She picks up the fine-stemmed crystal goblet of wine with no more care than a plastic tumbler. Her eyes glisten, maybe from liquor, maybe from tears. "It's her fault he died."

"Her fault?" I say. "Certainly you don't suspect Lilly killed him? She's so tiny."

"I didn't say she murdered him."

I think about Lilly's attitude and spooky ways. Is her attitude a result of Steven's death, or is there something else going on? I choose my words carefully. "She seems *troubled.*"

Colette concentrates on her food.

"Like she's hurt," I add.

Colette raises one eyebrow.

I stumble over what to say. I want to help Lilly, but I really don't know what I'm talking about. Not yet. I detour. "Maybe she needs to get out more, to take her mind off things. She's stuck at home all the time."

"I really don't care," she says with a shrug.

"Why won't Henry let her go out with friends?"

She pounds the table. "Do we have to discuss this over my supper?"

I jerk backward. "It's just a question."

I see her thinking it over. She picks up a forkful of lasagna and stares at it. "I wouldn't say this to anyone other than you, but you're not likely . . . Shoot, you don't talk to anybody anymore. She's a slut." With that, she pops the lasagna in her mouth and chews.

"How do you know?"

"A mother knows, trust me."

My mother certainly didn't. Or maybe she did. She probably didn't care. She probably didn't consider me a slut; she was worse. "Maybe she could go out with groups of kids. Safety in numbers and all that."

"Orgies in numbers are more like it."

Somehow, Lilly just doesn't seem like the type. She reminds me of myself in a lot of ways, but not as a girl who's been around. I can spot that. I'm not *that* far beyond those years. "Maybe she could go shopping with me, or something."

"Why would you want her to do that?"

"Like you said, nobody talks to me anymore. Company might be nice."

Colette shrugs. "Whatever. You'd have to ask Henry."

I dive into my lasagna with gusto. Colette has no motherly ties to Lilly. I'll figure out what's wrong with Lilly one way or another by myself.

CHAPTER FOURTEEN

A nother sleepless night. I'm walking across my bedroom to get the novel from beside my bed when I hear a noise. I stop. Every nerve is tingling.

My life may be in danger. It may have been *me* the murderer was after, not Steven. There are people who think I'm an unfit mother, like the crazy lady who tried to convince Social Services that Seth ought to be put into foster care, no doubt with designs on getting custody of him for herself; the people who wrote letters to the editor about what horrible parents we must be; friends who turned their backs on me. I shouldn't have asked Sinclair to take Caroline to his mother's house that day. I shouldn't have relinquished my responsibilities!

The murderer has realized they offed the wrong person. He's come back to rectify the error.

I close my eyes, waiting for the blow to my head.

Nothing happens.

I hear the noise again and whirl around.

Through the bedroom door, I see a thin figure, like the wisp of a ghost, a shadow in the dark, faintly backlit by the spotlight that shines continuously on the pool. My first thought is that it's one of the boys Lilly was talking to by the back fence. I saw one of them creeping around the back patio the previous night, almost hidden in the dark, leaving something on the deck. I looked for it the next morning after Colette and Henry had left, but it was gone.

I press myself flat against the wall and watch the figure move closer.

I gasp and collapse on my bed. "It's you," I say with a sigh. "I should have guessed."

"Don't get so excited. You're no big thrill either," Lilly replies as she slinks from the shadows into the light. Her long, wispy hair hangs limply over her shoulders, framing the paleness of her face so that the dark circles of black eyeliner look like stage make-up for a horror film

It dawns on me how hard she works at making herself repulsive. She hasn't realized yet the power she holds in being female. In fact, she seems to do everything possible to disguise all traces of beauty, wearing her expensive clothes and exquisite jewelry in such an odd, mismatched way that she appears wretched. No wonder she has no friends. I feel for her. She is pathetic in her abrasiveness. Donald Doc would say she's reacting to Steven's death with anger and frustration. Who am I to ridicule her for that? And yet I still feel I can help her in some way.

She climbs onto the bed beside me and lies on her back.

"Thinking of him tonight?" I ask.

"Every day. Especially today. We had plans. It's my birthday. We . . ." her voice trails off. "He always got me the best presents."

I am sure Henry and Colette gave her a stack of presents.

The thought must register on my face. She replies, "Not things that cost a lot, but things that mean a lot." She looks out at the window. "But not this year."

A picture flashes in my mind — a red glossy bag. "He did buy you something." I say it and then wonder how I know. Did he tell me? Another picture flashes of me paying for something, something black that the clerk carefully folds into a red bag. I falter. *I* purchased something, not Steven. But my gut tells me differently. I search my mind, trying to bring Steven back into the picture.

Lilly folds her arms defiantly across her chest, across the black Carowinds' logo on her T-shirt. "Like he'd tell you."

She always wears black, he'd said. Where were we when he said it? I see the bag in my mind's eye again and feel that odd dizziness pass over me, a piece falling into a puzzle. I held the red bag in the mall on the night Steven was murdered. And I'd seen him there, in the mall, from my table in the food court.

As I bit into my egg roll, I saw him across the way in a clothing store — a women's clothing store. I took another bite and watched as he flipped through the rack. A salesgirl approached with a red silk gown held up for him to see. Steven shook his head and moved to another rack. He moved around the racks pausing, touching, rejecting, until he pulled out a black knee-length dress, fitted at the top and flaring into layers of lace at the hips. He held it tentatively at arm's length. I knew then whom he was shopping for. I snatched up my purchases and abandoned my lunch.

"It's perfect," I said breaking my silent approach between the maze of racks.

He turned and smiled. "You're right. I look good in black."

I laughed.

"She'll never wear it," he said. "She only wears jeans and baggy shirts."

"She'll wear it for you." As I said it, I wondered if I was the only one who had seen their relationship for what it was. If they had met in high school, they would have dated openly, but because Lilly's father happened to marry Steven's mother, they hid their feelings from the world, afraid of appearing incestuous. At least, that's what I surmised. But I'd seen them together and knew from the glow in their eyes what they held in their hearts.

Steven stared at the dress as though he couldn't imagine Lilly's thin body inside it. "She might hate it."

I pulled him toward the corner. "Come on, I'll try it on. You'll see."

As we approached the dressing room, I saw first the camera and then the man holding it, walking toward the checkout counter. A reporter, skulking in the mall, looking for something for his yellow journalism to sell. I could see the headline featuring Colette's teenage son at my side. I grabbed Steven's arm. "Quickly, in here." I pulled him into the dressing room, clasping the black dress in my hands. In my haste, I tripped on an outfit someone had left on the floor. Steven yanked the door closed and caught me in one fluid motion that toppled us both forward, crushing me between the wall and him, with his right hand accidentally cradling my left breast, the other wrapped around my waist.

As my pounding heart slowed, I met his eyes and saw the hungry look born there as he became aware of my body next to his, the curve of my hips beneath his hands, the softness of me pressed against his chest, the proximity of my mouth to his.

I'd forgotten his innocence. I, barely twenty-five, and he, seventeen, gazed at one another. Eight years and a lifetime stretched between us. His chivalry hadn't been an act. He was as virginal as a newborn babe. His eyes told a dozen stories of dreams unfulfilled, dreams that hadn't been of me, but from one touch and the look smoldering in his eyes, somehow entangled me.

"Go," I said, "get out of here."

His dazed expression briefly searched my face as he reached for the door. I had to do something. I had to ease the hunger in his soul. "Meet me at the grove in an hour."

He left without a backward glance. I wasn't sure he even heard me.

I bought the dress and headed for the grove. Every teenager in the area knew the grove, but no one would be there on a Sunday evening. We could talk in peace. At least I had planned for us to talk.

I shake the memory away. Lilly is staring at me.

"It's a dress. He bought you a dress." I unfurl my body from the chair, stride across the room to the kitchen and pull the red bag from a bottom cabinet. I thrust it at her and grab my pocketbook and keys. I don't want to watch her unfold it. She needs to cry. I need to cry, too.

I step outside and pause in the crisp air, wishing I had thought to grab a jacket. I intended to get in my car and drive somewhere, but something turns me away from the road toward the land sprawling out behind the house. Beyond the luminous, still blue water of the pool, I pass across the cement patio and out the wrought-iron gate to the soft green manicured grass sloping upward to the base of a huge oak tree that stands like an extravagant shadow in the yard. I trudge up the incline.

Then I remember the two teenagers. Are they there somewhere lurking in the dark? I stare into the woods, but it's fruitless trying to see anything in the shadows. The woods are silent. The moon is full, lighting the yard. So I relent and flop against the tree trunk. The bark presses into my back, but I seek its abrasions. I want to be uncomfortable. I want to cry, to wash the pain from my heart with a flood of tears, but as I lean my head back against the tree and stare up at the stars flickering with eternal wishes, the mourning catches in my chest like a tear-soaked sponge, and my mind whirs away on its own path to that night in the park.

I remember it well. The grove is a small plot of grass amid a thick clump of trees off a footpath on the outskirts of town. I followed the narrow trail through the twilight, hoping I wouldn't be emerging from the forest of trees alone in the dark.

I needn't have worried. Steven was waiting when I got there. He was lying on the grass staring up at the sky with a long, man-sized black flashlight at his side. I smiled; he was an Eagle Scout, always organized, always prepared.

I craned my neck to see what he was looking at. "What is it?"

"First star. I'm making a wish."

I sat down beside him and laid the bag to one side. "Wishing for what?"

"Can't tell."

"Come on."

He looked at me, then turned skyward again. "For Lilly, that things . . . will work out for her."

I brushed his comment off as meaning something at school, or life in general. I had no idea what he meant. "Sorry I rushed you out of the store. I panic every time I see a photographer anymore, but I got the dress. She's going to love it."

"Think so?"

"Yes. Want to see it?" I reached for the bag.

"Try it on, please."

I hesitated. "Will you close your eyes?"

He clenched his eyes shut, and I turned my back to him while I stripped and pulled on the lacy black dress. The sun had transformed to a red globe in the tops of the trees, and sucked the daylight warmth from the land in its parting. The chill raised goosebumps across my shoulders. I rubbed my arms and spun around. "Okay. Open your eyes."

The bodice was too tight, and it was too short, too youthful for me, but none of that registered in Steven's eyes. The layers of lace wafted around me as I playfully danced around him.

I push the memory aside and turn from the twinkling night sky to peer toward the small building I call home. The lit interior blazes through the night with the clarity of a drive-in theater. Lilly is still standing mid-room, clutching the dress. I watch her as if with his eyes, and I see her as if for the first time.

She is hurting. Despite her posh surroundings, she is a mirror of my youth, but scarred and hollowed out. I know so little about her, yet I sense she lacks the driving courage to escape whatever demons are haunting her. Contempt for something — or someone — smolders in her eyes and pulls the color from her face. She is a shell of a child with an untold story.

I am drawn back down the hill, watching her through the window as she slips the dress over her head. Had others watched me this way from the main house? Had Steven?

Lilly's eyes are bloodshot. Her mouth is a thin line. The dress hangs from her thin shoulders. Then she arches her arms over her head and rises on her toes. Her body bends and sways and she steps out nimbly into a pirouette, spinning gracefully and coming to a stop with her heels together and her fingers striking a graceful pose in front of her. I never figured her for a ballerina.

I wasn't as graceful dancing in circles around Steven. He sat up and turned back and forth following my path around him. "Stand still. I can't see it."

I laughed and spun faster. He stood and reached for my hand. I twirled within the clasp of his palm and came to a standstill flushed and breathing heavily. His eyes met mine, laughing with me, then traveled down the dress while one hand involuntarily traveled from my bare shoulder and skimmed along my arm to my hand. I shivered in the cold, but flushed under the power of his attention.

He held my hand in his and examined it as if it were some rare jewel.

"You're delicate, but you're not as frail as Lilly. Her hands are so fine. She . . . She's like shattered glass carefully held together by some invisible glue. I'm always afraid of breaking her." He touched the fabric by my waist. "She'll never wear it. She'll hide it away like a dream to hold onto of who she could be if she were free."

"Free?"

His gaze moved from my waist and hands, to my cleavage, then to my face, to my eyes, as if I could understand what he meant without words.

"I can never touch her. I am her sanctuary." He caressed my cheek.

I could give him what he wanted. I'd answered that look for so many men, one more wouldn't matter. But this was Steven. Just looking at me had torn away a resolve I'd seen in him before to be different, to be stronger than his desires. To give in would destroy all I admired in him.

"I'm not her, Steven."

He raised my hand to his lips and kissed it like a gentleman, so completely the Steven I knew, but with a new hunger behind his actions, an insatiable carnal knowledge transferred from adolescent dreams to me. "Dance with me."

Lilly leaps across the room like a gazelle, lands on her toes and spins. When she stops, her head drops to her chest. I can't see the tears on her face, but her tiny frame shakes with crying as she collapses to the floor in a crumpled heap.

I step forward, ready to go to her aid, to comfort her, but I stop. I think of putting my arms around her and running my hands across her shoulders, and I am filled with images of Steven there doing the same — touching her meekly as a consoler — and I am filled with remembrance of his hands upon me. It's more than I can bear. I can't help Lilly. I can't even help myself.

I turn to the driveway and seek out the solitude of a long car ride to nowhere. I end up at the grove. Steven's spirit beckons to me. I follow the trail through the woods, stumbling in the dark, and lie on the grass, staring up at the star-studded sky with secrets as deep as forever. I close my eyes, thinking he'll step from the trees to join me, but I remain alone with my thoughts, with my memories.

His hands were different from most. For some, who I was as a person was unimportant. I was an image to them, a conquest to be hung on their resume of life as an achievement. In their anxiousness to meet victory, my needs became unimportant. The first few times, when I was so insecure that I couldn't bear the thought of being alone, I wanted them so desperately to need me that I led them to bed offering my body as a sacrifice for reparation of my wounded mind. I lay like a doll beneath them, knowing they were mentally and emotionally detached from me.

In those early years, I sought only to provide what was necessary to keep from being alone, to escape my mother's house. It took me years to realize that being desired lay nowhere close to being loved or even valued. Nevertheless, there were a few boys who actually fell in love with me. Ironically, they worried so much about pleasing me that they lost the edge of being attractive. I'd never had a role model of affection. I didn't know how to react to it. I didn't know a man could coddle a woman and still elicit respect. I didn't know a man could be both macho and sensitive. The men in my mother's life were domineering and brash. I looked for the same qualities, the egotistical jerks who normally had no interest in me beyond passing time in high school. So, when boys plied me with sweet words and endearing caresses, I found them weak and lacking. It wasn't until much later that I began to discern a difference between pathetic and sympathetic. It's the difference between a man who lets a woman rule him, and a man who manages to place a woman on a pedestal without placing her above himself.

Neither love nor sexual attraction motivated my pursuit of Sinclair — initially I was driven by financial security, appearance, and suaveness. Nevertheless, Sinclair had the perfect balance of tenderness and dominance, which is why my plans for marital security were thwarted by love. I let my heart interfere with my head. I could have saved my marriage if I'd remained detached.

Nevertheless, as I stood in the grove that night, as I stood wrapped in Steven's arms, I found myself in a totally new predicament. Here I was facing the eager teenager of my youth while I was armed with a lifetime of experience. I knew what he wanted, and I knew I could give it to him. But this time it was Steven, a mere boy in my eyes, one I respected and cared for. If I succumbed to his desires, our relationship would never be the same. The thought of sleeping with Colette's son was despicable, and it tumbled backward through my mind, redefining what I'd been: a groveling whore.

I touched his face, wondering what thoughts were racing through his mind. What did he expect of me? Was he one of the naïve young who, as I had, equated sex with love? Or did he merely want release from his dreams?

His cheek felt warm beneath the palm of my hand. His chest rose and fell gently at my chin. I felt the strength of his need.

I'd been an island for months, set apart, emotionally stranded as an outcast. A part of me needed him as much as he wanted me. I didn't need him as a lover; I needed him as consolation and assurance that all was right with me, that I was still who I'd always been, that I wasn't contemptible, that I wasn't a freak who had failed at marriage and motherhood with nothing but isolation stretching into the future.

I wouldn't lead him on. I only conceded with one small action. I lifted my face to his.

He accepted the invitation. He brushed his lips against mine.

I began to wonder if I had misjudged his innocence.

"I used to think you were old." He had misjudged me too.

I stroked his face. "I used to think so, too." I felt like I'd lived an entire lifetime already. I started down this road too young, at twelve, when other girls had barely abandoned dolls and dress-ups.

His touch, so tentative, struck me as what my first experience should have been like. I imagined a virgin couple exploring each other and discovering their passion with similar awe and ceremony. I was filled with longing to have that lost moment back. I wanted to redo the moment, to replace it with so wondrous and sacred a moment as this moment seemed to Steven.

My first time hadn't been a moment of discovery or passion. My encounter at twelve had been a rough groping. Jimmy knew nothing and cared nothing about love or tenderness. He only sought to relieve his pubescent urges.

I've often thought back on that night with Jimmy and wondered whether, if I'd taken a different route in life, if I hadn't run into Jimmy while meandering the streets en route to see Jennifer, I would have turned out differently, whether I would have remained miraculously virginal and pure throughout high school. Would a night at Jennifer's house instead of wrapped in Jimmy's embrace have changed my entire future? My answer is always no. Life with my mother and her many partners had erased all sense of propriety from my soul. I attached no value to my virginity at that point. Why would I? What role model did I have? Television sold sex like lollipops to children. High school did the same. And obviously my mother approved. There wasn't a thing in my life telling me it was wrong. I needed love, and in the equations presented to me at that point, love came in some skewed fashion from sex. It wasn't until I saw my life through Jennifer's eyes that I realized my folly.

Some of my subsequent partners had more talent than Jimmy, but by then, my virginity was long lost and I lacked the tremulous anticipation of The First Time.

Standing in the grove that night, I knew Steven wasn't in love with me. I was the body of convenience, the available fuel for a passion held in check for a long time. He was in love with Lilly. Nevertheless, his tenderness moved me as I was moved by only one man — Sinclair.

Sinclair knew more or less where I had come from, but I'd gradually built myself into a new person, a woman with charm and finesse, a woman with scruples. I had to live up to being that person. It wasn't easy.

Sinclair wooed me with expertise. It wasn't all fancy restaurants and gala affairs, although there were enough of those types of dates that I was thankful I belonged to a sorority where I could easily scrounge up an array of evening gowns from others' closets.

Formal dinners weren't a problem for me. I could maintain my new identity in satin and lace with crowds watching my every move; I merely played the part. I was an actress on stage in my finest attire. It was the less formal dates that tested my will.

Mid-May he arranged a trip to the beach, a reprieve after graduation before real life set in. Emerald Isle was still deserted, an oasis of sea spray and sunshine waiting for Memorial Day weekend to officially call guests to its haven. For us, it was time in a bottle.

We walked along the edge of the ocean, the surf's white bubbles numbing our feet while the sun dripped down our backs like butter slowly melting. Seagulls took flight with loud complaints. A trio of pelicans skimmed along the peaks of waves.

Sinclair held my hand.

With all my experience, I had determined there's nothing more intimate than holding hands, feeling the solid flesh and steady heartbeat of another person enfolded in the comfort of your palm, a simple contract given and received, saying, "I'm here with you of my own free will. Be with me. Join me." It has nothing to do with lust and everything to do with accepting one another. His hand in mine summed up my image of him, of how a relationship with him made me feel: warm, coddled, secure.

We came to a rivulet of water charting a course from a shallow tidal pool back to the ocean, a miniature reproduction of lakes and rivers flowing seaward. Like a little boy, Sinclair pulled his hand free to stoop and dam it up just for the fun of watching the water spill over the chamber walls to continue its journey homeward, then he fell to his knees to bank the sloppy sand into a curved wall and rushed to dig out a tiny reservoir with his bare hands. I squatted on the other side to re-inforce the crumbling walls with scoops of wet sand mortar, but the water continued to outpace us. He laughed as he gave up, rinsed off the gritty sand in his moat of seawater, then clasped my hand again to drag me to the warm tidal pool. As we talked of common friends, trips, and supper plans, his grip directed our path. A squeeze of his hand, and I knew to stand still and follow his gaze toward a small sand shark trapped in the vanishing pool, its smooth black skin glistening like a living opal. We sloshed around up to our knees like children, my hand safely enclosed in his as we followed the tidal pool until it pe-tered out, then back along the breaking waves, his hand signaling mine with a nudge around a jellyfish stranded inches from retreating waves.

Sinclair had eyes open to life. Everything was a new discovery, even if he'd seen it a thousand times. At his side, I felt the wonder of the beach as if for the first time. He made me savor the sand between my toes and the sun on my face. The salt clung to my skin and stiffened my hair, and I reveled in the sensation of it coating me with a new di-mension of life.

He held my hand in his all the way to the distant fishing pier — the only one on the strand not swept away by hurricanes — and led me down the wooden planks. He paused to ask the fishermen about their catches: two old ladies with gummy smiles, a skinny man, black as pitch, with one foot propped up on a five-gallon bucket while he stared seriously into the depths of the ocean as if he were watching a fish circle his bait, and farther down, three men resting their beer guts on their laps as they chatted and laughed at themselves with little at-tention paid to their fishing rods. All the while, he held my hand ten-derly in his, a connection to him, a promise of what we were becoming to one another. I wondered if the act of belonging to someone filled him with gulps of headiness, facing the enormity of what a future with one person could mean, but it wasn't something I would ask. I knew my singularity in the world wasn't normal. Other people had bonds with family and friends. My yearning to belong was too frightening to admit to anyone. The desire to remain with him beat in my chest until my heart felt it had swollen beyond the capacity of my ribcage. Tears of need escaped, tiny droplets at the corners of my eyes. I blamed it on the sun blinding me. It wasn't the sun; it was him. He was brighter than any future I had ever hoped for. He was an open book: sincere, smart, and full of goodness. I wanted so much for the whole image to be true, to really be the girl I pretended to be.

We spent hours on the beach before returning to the beach house, where we'd only paused upon arrival to deposit our bags inside the door.

I'd been prepared to purposely withhold exclamations over what I anticipated his family's beach house to be like — it was one thing to compliment a home, but quite another to appear envious or stupefied by possessions, a mistake I no longer made among my new class of peers — but in the case of the beach house, there was no need. It was a simple cottage with three bedrooms upstairs, and an open kitchen and family room downstairs. The view was spectacular, but the windows were ordinary six-over-six panes that left me feeling cheated indoors. The exterior paint peeled and curled in the afternoon sun, and the veranda railings proclaimed their age with gray, weathered wood. I felt totally comfortable. It was my kind of house, free of the arrogance in which I'd bathed my new identity. If I hadn't been playing the part of the perfect girlfriend, I could have been myself, a person I worked hard not to reveal. The real me didn't have airs or poise. She couldn't make conversation. But in the cottage, the lines between the girl I had been and the part I played became blurred. I ached to snooze in the ragged hammock hung in the shade of the screened porch, settled in a place I could call home.

The feeling was mutual. Sinclair relaxed. He sank into the yellow sofa and kicked his feet up onto the knotty-pine coffee table while I busied myself at the kitchen counter a few feet away. I'd planned a scrumptious meal for us. If there was one thing I'd learned as a latch-key kid, it was how to cook. I'd watched more afternoon cooking shows than soap operas; who needed soap operas with my mother around?

Before returning to the beach house, we'd walked down the road a piece to a small brick ranch bearing a wooden sign that simply stated *Fresh Shrimp*. The briny smell of fish seeped through the walls to the stagnant air of the side stoop where we rang a bell for service.

"My family has bought shrimp here forever," Sinclair said. "There's nothing like shrimp fresh from the ocean. Even a hundred miles in-land, they're likely to sell you frozen stuff from who knows where."

A woman shuffled to the door and smiled with recognition. "Come in, come in. How's your mama? I haven't seen her yet this year. Y'all down for a spell?"

"Yes Ma'am," he replied, his voice becoming tinged with her lazy drawl. "This is my friend Rachel. We're celebrating. I finally finished up at Duke, and I'm taking a breather before I join Daddy's practice."

She appraised me with a Southern smile that hid whatever she was thinking beyond the slight widening of her dark brown eyes, and I wondered if I was the first to be paraded into her home, or one in a long lineup. She revealed nothing in her reply. She turned back to Sinclair. "Well, don't that beat all. I guess I got to call you Doc, now, eh?"

"Not you, Miss Hattie. I need a pound of shrimp if you have it."

"Certainly, Doc. Coming right up."

Sinclair peeled money from his wallet.

"Not on your life, young'un. You celebrate your graduation."

"Why, thank you, Miss Hattie. I couldn't ask for a better send-off than some of your shrimp."

"Say hello to yer Mama for me."

"She'll be along by the end of the month."

He held the door open for me, the treatment of a lady, but I felt Miss Hattie's eyes burning into my back, lighting a scarlet *A* where for once it hadn't been earned.

As we followed a worn footpath along the edge of the island road back to the cottage, I fought off the urge to examine "us" too closely. Maybe it was a fairytale weekend. Maybe I was another notch on his days of freedom before his doctor life kicked in, but I was going to immerse myself in the role. I was going to be the girl I wanted to be: Sinclair's girl. I'd learned my part so well, it wasn't such a great leap to believe it. And so, as the heat of the day eased away under the fingers of a rising breeze, I stepped into my new persona. I quit acting. I became Rachel, the upstanding girlfriend, the one who met Sinclair at the end of his long trek through school and studies and preparation, the one ready to step out with him into life as an adult.

Being in the cottage made it easier than any other place I could have chosen. The kitchen counter had worn spots. The pans had seen better days. The plates were mismatched. In that kitchen, I could cook. I felt at home.

Sinclair sat watching me with a soft smile playing across his face. "The walk was good for you. You seem at ease."

His words could have pulled the mask back over my face, but I was enjoying myself too much. I didn't want to hide from him. I side-stepped the truth: I was more at home in this worn cottage than I could ever be in his family's spotless mansion. Instead I said, "I had a wonderful time today. I felt like I was seeing the beach for the first time."

"I've spent a portion of every summer here for as long as I can remember. This house was here long before most."

"Lucky you."

There was an edge of curiosity to the tilt of his head. "You don't mind it being old and worn, do you?"

I paused. Was this a test? We were at a great divide and I had to have the magic answer to make the leap. I felt slapped by reality and did something I would never have done if I'd been given time to think it out. I told him the truth. My eyes spoke more than my words. "Sinclair, you know ... I've hinted at my past enough ..."

He saved me, catching me halfway. "But some girls expect everything to be upper crust. I'm not like that. I want you to understand."

It was the most honest thing we'd said to each other at that point. I nodded. I didn't need to add anything. I didn't want to expound on where I'd come from, and I wasn't ready to push his explanation to the point that it might broach whether or not there may be an "us" in his vision of who he was. We knew where one another stood for the moment, and I kept it at that. I went back to rinsing shrimp. "It's lovely that this beach is still mostly cottages, not hotel after hotel."

"True. It's small and private. Even the condos haven't impacted it with great crowds except during the height of the season, and I rarely visit then. I like it abandoned, like it is today."

I glanced up from rinsing shrimp. "Me, too. It's like a private world."

That night, I left him on the sofa with a glass of wine in his hand.

"Not yet," I whispered into his ear as I stroked his face and pulled away. I trailed up the staircase with my sun-kissed shoulders held proudly back when all they wanted to do was droop under the weightless white cotton of my sundress, under the duress of false pretenses.

He stayed there, staring out the window, sipping his wine long after I climbed into bed. I recited besotted lines of Elizabeth Barrett Browning until I finally fell asleep, waiting for footfalls on the stairs that never came.

He was in my room when I woke the next morning, slowly rocking in an old wooden rocker that had probably rocked him to sleep in his infancy. Early rays of daylight cast their urging caresses across the worn, white coverlet of the bed, into my eyes, making Sinclair a dark blur, but I could tell he was looking at me.

I gazed at him with foggy eyes. "I'm sorry. I've slept late. You should have woken me."

"It's the sign of a Southern lady to keep a man waiting."

I had the decency to blush at his innuendo. I was no lady, and few men had waited. I sat up, letting the covers fall. The sheer blue of my nightgown left little to the imagination. "Sinclair . . ."

He came to my side and touched my face. "I thought a lot last night."

I held myself perfectly still, waiting for the gentle letdown. I knew the dream was too good to last.

"I've dated a lot of girls."

I laughed. I couldn't help it. It was not at all what I expected him to say.

He shook his head and joined my laughter. "That's not what I meant. I mean, I don't want you to think this is a freaky thing, saying this, that I haven't had time to get to know you, because I have. I have instincts about people."

I could have laughed again, but I didn't. I stared at a worn spot on the coverlet. "When I said we needed to wait, I didn't mean ..."

"I know you didn't. But when you left, went up to bed, I realized that I wasn't disappointed."

That time, I couldn't keep from laughing. "Great. Now I feel better."

"This isn't coming out right. I did want you, more than anybody ever, but as I sat there by myself, I thought about what it was like having you here with me, upstairs, as if you're already part of my family, about all the places we've been together and how easy it is to have you at my side. You're not a strain on me. You're not full of expectations and demands. You take everything in stride. You delight in everything we do and everywhere we go. You make me feel good about myself. I knew you were upstairs, and I knew I didn't have to have you last night because I could have you forever, and that would be so much more than once or twice or a dozen times, or even a year of nights that would end in gossip and stares, and more searching. I want you forever. I want what my parents have had all these years, an easy relationship, relaxed and content. You don't make me try to be more than I'm content to be."

I felt numb, trying to absorb it. I couldn't even unravel how his position was so opposite to mine — that he was being totally himself and I was trying so hard to be what I had no right to be. But I thought of the walk the day before, the making of our dinner, and how it all felt more real than anything had in years. I needed someone to pinch me, to wake me up. I held my breath, waiting for the punch line.

"What I'm trying to say is let's get married."

I looked at him as if I'd been slapped. "Married?"

"Yes. Married. I'm ready. I'm joining Daddy's practice. I'm ready to put down roots and start my own family, and you ... You're every-thing I want. You're warm and caring; you're easy to be with. You're real."

His words worked magic on me. I believed him. I dared to believe I was who he thought I was. After all, I'd had that revelation, too. I'd felt it the day before, and there he was saying the very thing I'd been feeling.

I pulled him close and kissed him, and showed him how real I could be.

When we consummated our marriage, what I shared with Sinclair was far beyond anything I'd ever experienced before, not because he was more skilled, but because it was sacred. It rose as a bond made be-tween us, a physical representation of our words, a blending of our souls. We gave and took of each other freely with no secrets or shad-ows between us. We became one. It made me regret every man who had ever come before him. It made me realize what a grave mistake my youth had been. I realized the meaning of making love, of commit-ment, of the joining of souls.

The night I stood in the grove with Steven, clad in a black dress meant for Lilly, I recalled that turning point in my life, and I realized I was doing both of us a great disservice. He didn't love me; he loved Lilly. I could never give him what he wanted. And though I was sepa-rated from Sinclair, I was still committed to him; I still loved him. I couldn't go back to being what I was in my youth. Despite the pain and rejection enveloping my mind and body, Sinclair had changed me for life. I couldn't use Steven to mend my wounds, knowing in the long run I would wound him as I had been wounded throughout my youth. There would be a chasm of dishonesty between us. I loved Steven too much to mistreat him so profoundly.

I stepped away from him. "We can't, Steven. It's not really me you want."

His eyes glowed. "Yes, it is."

He reached for me, but I turned away. "Everything you're feeling, you're feeling toward Lilly, not me. It's Lilly you must share it with."

"I can't. Can't you see that? I can only dream of Lilly. But you . . . I can love you."

"No, Steven. You're a . . ." I wanted to say he was a boy, but I knew he'd take it as an insult, and I didn't want to hurt him in any way. "You're confused. Let's think about it first. Let's take it slow." I turned back to him. He had tears in his eyes. "Kiss me, then. Kiss me and think of what you want."

"I know what I want."

I kissed him deeply, more thoroughly than he'd ever been kissed, I knew. When I pulled away, he was electrified. "Now, go home and see Lilly and look in her eyes, and think how you'd feel if we'd made love."

The image was beginning to dawn on him, the message I was trying to convey about what guilt could do to a relationship. I could give volumes of lessons on guilt.

"Go on, Steven. Go home."

He grabbed his flashlight, stumbled to his feet and hurried away through the woods. I sat in the moonlight until I heard his car pull away, and ages beyond. I listened to the birds' chatter peter out as they drifted to sleep. I listened to tree frogs begin their nighttime serenades, and the rustle of nocturnal animals scampering in the leaves.

I thought of Steven back home, searching out Lilly, and where it might lead, and it led me back to Sinclair, to that first morning, again, and to the weeks beyond.

When Sinclair and I returned to town after the beach trip, me to the sorority house and he to his parents, I began to put life into perspective. The dream of the beach seemed impossible. He showed up a few days later, a grin on his face, a bouquet of flowers in his arms, and a ring in his pocket to make it all official.

I'd had time to think. I looked at the flowers in his arms and remembered the look on his mother's face when we first met. She was in the living room, cleaning up the last of a bridge club luncheon. She was stooped over the coffee table collecting teacups — fine bone china with fluted edges that were etched in gold. Each cup had a single, delicate rose painted in goldenrod yellow. The bouquet of roses on the side table were so exact a match, I imagined her carrying a cup into the florist and asking her to dye a dozen to match the cups.

The furniture wasn't anything to rave about. I'd seen finer in my climb up the social ladder. There were houses in Chapel Hill, Durham, and Charlotte that would take a person's breath away — brocades, velvets, and suede on curved sofas, wing-back chairs, and day chairs. I'd seen rooms that represented more money than people in my old neighborhood spent on their lifetime mortgage. In comparison, the Winters' furniture was dated, square solid pieces with some light-colored etched wood. Not pine, but hickory or pecan. It didn't bother me one bit. I'd lived with chairs that were duct-taped together. But I could read a house well at that point. Mrs. Winters went for quality and durability. She didn't waste money, and she expected things to last.

She raised her eyes toward the door and straightened when she saw me. "Well, you've brought company."

"Mama, this is Rachel. Rachel, this is my mama."

"Pleased to meet you, Mrs. Winters."

A polite demeanor settled over her. "You must be the one from Raleigh. I hear Sinclair met you at a sorority party."

"A luncheon, yes, Ma'am."

"He was dating Susan Chance, then."

"Yes, Ma'am."

"I like Susan. She is from a very upstanding family."

Her words fell with the all the weight she intended.

"Well, come along to the kitchen. We have lots of goodies left from the luncheon and I'm betting you're hungry, aren't you, Sinclair? I've never known you to come through the door without looking for a meal."

She was cordial enough after that, to my face at least. I heard words between her and Sinclair while I was in the bathroom later that evening, but she was the epitome of a hostess in front of me. Gradually, as the weeks passed, she warmed to me, even laughing with me from time to time. She has a deep love for her only son that takes precedence over anything else in her life, and she accepted me for his sake because it was what he wanted. I knew it was a façade, but it smoothed things over.

Facing a lifetime of her looking down on me, though, was another thing. Between the morning of his proposal and his showing up with the flowers and a ring, I spent nights dreaming of her staring at me. When Sinclair pulled out the ring, the diamond dazzled me with the light playing on its many facets, reflecting promises of happy tomorrows. I wanted to keep my mouth closed. I wanted to grab the golden ring and run with it. But I couldn't. Not when it came right down to it. I didn't think I could fake it for the rest of my life. I shook my head. "I'm not right for you, Sinclair. You know that. I'm from a different world. You said everything seems new to me, but that's because it is. I'm from downtown Raleigh. I went to college on scholarships and grants. My gowns are borrowed. I had to teach myself how to speak correctly so I wouldn't sound like a bumpkin. I don't even know who my daddy is. I'm Cinderella! This is all just a fairytale ready to go poof."

He smiled. "You may be Cinderella, but that entitles you to a happy ending. You've swept the chimney. You've toted the wood. It's time to slip on the glass slipper."

"Your mother doesn't like me."

"Look, I'm a big boy. I've lived most of my life being what they want me to be. You said you were Cinderella? Well, remember Prince Charming agreed to marry as the king requested, but only if he got to choose the bride. Same deal. They want grandchildren. I want you. They'll be happy as long as we give them kids."

"They want grandchildren from Susan. Babies with blue blood."

"I don't love Susan. She's not happy unless every hair is in place and there's a mirror readily available to check her makeup. I have no intention of marrying her. I want you. I want to have babies with you, and a house, and spend Saturdays puttering around. I want us to take long holidays together for the rest of our lives."

I was melting. He could tell. He moved closer and whispered in my ear. "I want to marry you and carry you up a long flight of stairs to a room flickering with candlelight where we will share champagne, and I will slowly pull the pins from your hair and undo the long row of buttons running down the back of your wedding gown, and I will show you a million times over how much I love you." He nibbled on my ear and ran kisses down my neck. I felt weak in my knees. His kisses trailed down my shoulder, down my arm to my hand. He kissed my finger and slipped on the ring.

Resistance was futile. I'd been assimilated.

While Lilly dances in the pool house in a dress bought by Steven, I sit quietly in the grove, staring up at the star-filled sky and recall every nuance of that evening with Sinclair like it was only yesterday.

An owl hoots somewhere nearby as clouds pass over the moon. As the moon reappears, I brush the leaves from my clothes and make my way slowly out to my car, back to the wreck that has become my life.

CHAPTER FIFTEEN

L illy seems a bit softer the next time I see her. Her nails are clean and pink instead of black, and her face is devoid of black eyeliner. Maybe the gift from Steven has brought her some comfort, or maybe she's let her guard down a bit, not putting on her masquerade for me like she does for the rest of world. She's probably realized I'm not worth the effort.

She seems to be dealing with Steven's death better than I am with Caroline's.

I venture out for supplies and spend the rest of the day drowned in my own tears because I saw a polkadot hair bow in a store and remembered that's what Caroline had in her hair the day she died. It brought her face back to me, tear-stained, crying.

I bite back a new flow of tears. I can tell by the way Lilly is fiddling with things in the room that she has something to tell me. I sit quietly on the sofa and wait. She moves around the room for five minutes before she speaks.

"They found a pair of shoes with blood on them."

"The shoes, again. You told me they'd tested the soil on his shoes."

"Another pair. Unfortunately Betts washed them."

"With blood on them?"

"She said she's just a maid, not paid to think about crime investigations. Of course they're useless as evidence, now."

"Do you think it was Steven's blood?"

She rolls her eyes and picks up a magazine from the coffee table.

"But Steven was wearing the shoes with the mud from somewhere else, right?"

"Yes."

I'm a bit slow. I can't figure out why he would have a second pair of shoes. She flips through the magazine while I think.

He couldn't have changed his shoes; he was dead. Then I realize someone in the house may have changed them. Or worn them. "But if one was to make an assumption that the killer wore them to prevent another pair of footprints, wouldn't it have to be someone from inside the house?"

Of course Lilly is way ahead of me. She settles on the sofa to read something that's caught her eye. "Your intelligence astounds me."

If it was someone in the house, that narrowed the field. One of the people I converse with daily killed Steven. Henry, Colette, Lilly . . . or Betts. There has to be another explanation. "How did the investigators not find the shoes beforehand?"

Her quirky smile lights up her face. "I'd say they went missing until wash day."

"Why didn't Betts call the police instead of washing them?"

"Good question."

She reaches toward the books, but I beat her to it. I sift through the stack and pull out *A Tree Grows in Brooklyn* from the pile. "I got this one for you."

As she flips through it, my thoughts flicker to the money-saving tin can I kept in my closet after reading that book, something Lilly definitely won't do. She's wearing more money on a chain around her neck than I saved in six months' time.

My childhood seems like a distant memory.

When she leaves, I stare at the wall and think of possible killers. I can't believe it's someone in the big house. I refuse to accept that as a possibility. I decide to find the real murderer. I start looking into men's faces. I look for Steven's murderer everywhere. I'm sure I will recognize him when I see him. He'll have beady eyes full of anger and evil.

I watch Bruce the yardman all morning. He's not a homeless wanderer with some secret cult life. I'm fairly sure by looking at him that he is the grandfather of twin redheaded boys with freckles and toothy smiles like he says he is. He's definitely got the red hair going. But his eyes are a hard blue, not soft and smiling. He looks like he'd have a go at an Irish temper and the bottle, but that's me stereotyping him from television movies. What I need is a motive.

Betts is beady-eyed if ever anyone was, but I can't think of a motive for her, either. What did she have against Steven?

Then there's still the drug theory, but not the way the police are considering it. I think it has something to do with Colette's drugs and Steven caught in the middle. Someone planted the extra shoes as a diversion.

So, I keep looking in the faces of everyone who crosses the yard. I believe mean people have mean eyes. Ricky taught me that.

Ricky was one of my mother's beaus. I knew straight off he was different from my mother's previous boyfriends. He arrived on a Harley, which wasn't really notable except to state he had more money than the previous slug Mama had living with us. Ricky had tattoos down both arms, which was also nothing new. What made him different from the others was the way he talked to me. The first thing he did was sit beside me on the sofa. Mama had walked in before him and strode to the bedroom. "Make yourself comfortable," she hollered without a backward glance at him. It hadn't been twenty-four hours since Bubba had left, and she still had pieces of him lying around on the floor to dispose of — his dirty socks, nasty underwear, and his stinking cigars. He came back later for those. I could hear Mama hustling around her bedroom cleaning it up. Ricky probably thought she was getting dressed or something normal. I almost told him to watch out about sleeping in that bed. I sure hadn't changed the sheets anytime lately, and I knew Mama wouldn't have. I shuddered at the thought of anyone having to sleep on top of Bubba's germs. But as far

as I knew, this new guy Ricky was as creepy as the rest, and I didn't care
what he slept on.

Ricky just sat there, pretty as you please, looking at me. "You must
be Tammy's daughter."

"Yeah, so what?" I replied. I wasn't much into manners at that point.

"She didn't mention she had a daughter."

"Surprise, surprise."

"So what's your name?"

I didn't take my eyes off the Dating Game playing on the television. I thought about saying Tammy Two just out of meanness, but
then I'd have to explain my real name and I didn't feel like talking that
much. "Rachel."

"How old are you?"

I threw him a look of disgust. "Not legal."

"What?"

"I'm fifteen."

"Oh."

If I'd looked at his face, I knew from his voice it would be crest-
fallen. It had that turn to it.

"I had something I wanted to show you, but you probably wouldn't
be interested at fifteen."

I hadn't forgotten Kyle. I would never forget Kyle. "Pervert," I
hissed under my breath. I wondered how long I'd have to live with
this one.

He looked at the television for a few minutes, but the show didn't
interest him. I could tell because he picked up one of Bubba's cycling
magazines and started flipping through it. He leaned back on the sofa
and crossed one leg over the other like a lady would and bounced his
foot impatiently. I figured he had ADHD or something.

Apparently he wasn't really reading the magazine. He'd probably
already read his own copy since he had a Harley. "Do you like animals?" he asked.

The question caught me off guard. The television was blaring an ad
for face cleaner to protect teenagers from zits. I remember it distinctly

because those kinds of commercials always made me self-conscious around other people, especially when I had a zit coming up on my chin, so I was relieved he wasn't paying attention to it. I would rather carry on some inane conversation than have a man staring at my zit during a zit commercial. "What kind of question is that? Do I like animals? What kind of animals? Rats and snakes, or something decent like tigers and horses?"

"Well, rabbits."

I studied his face to see if he was being serious or making fun of me. He had a round face with large brown eyes and a fat brown mustache. His hair was thinning, but he didn't look old, really, because he didn't have any wrinkles and his arms were muscular. He wasn't a hunk, he wasn't that good-looking, but there was something about him that made me like him. There was a gentleness about him, a kindness to his eyes I'd never noticed or even looked for before. I almost trusted him, which I never said about any of my mother's partners before or after him. But I'd learned to be suspicious. I wondered why he was throwing me a line about rabbits. Maybe this innocent look of his was his angle.

"Rabbits? I don't know. I ain't ever seen one." My grammar wasn't very good back then.

"You've never seen a rabbit before?"

"Well, in books and on TV and stuff, but not in real life."

"Haven't you ever been in a pet store?"

I shrugged. "I guess not. I had a cat once." I wasn't sure why I admitted that to him. I rarely told anyone anything about myself.

"I don't like cats. They're too sneaky," he said. "I like wiener dogs, though. They're about as open an animal as a body can tame. But rabbits, they're the best. They don't bark like dogs, they don't eat much, and they're soft to cuddle."

I stared at him good and hard. Here was this Harley-riding guy in his forties with tattoos all over his arms, and who knew where else, telling me he thought rabbits were cuddly. "I guess I'll have to take your word for it."

"I'll have to get you over to see my rabbits."

The show came back on then. I looked at him a long minute, wondering if he really had rabbits or if this was a ruse to get me somewhere alone.

Mama came out then, all changed into a short red dress that usually meant she was expecting dinner and a good time. "Bye, Rae," she said. "Don't wait up." It was her standard line when reeling in her newest catch.

After they left, I turned off the television and stared into the tight, now clean space of my mother's gaudy green and yellow bedroom. I was admittedly bored just sitting there, so after a while I got up and washed her sheets, just in case Ricky really was a nice guy, and in case he really did have pet rabbits and a wiener dog.

Turned out I had days and days before clean sheets were needed. He dropped Mama off that evening at eleven o'clock, walked her to the door, then zoomed off on his Harley, loud enough to wake Mr. Humphrey upstairs in 3B, and he was as deaf as they come. I was still up watching television. Mama stripped off her high heels on the way across the room and tossed them into her bedroom before sinking into the new recliner she'd wheedled out of ol' Bubba.

Mama was smiling. "He's got to get himself off to work early tomorrow," she said in response to my unasked question.

I nodded. That meant he had a real job. Mark up another difference between him and most of Mama's usual fare.

It was two weeks before the subject of rabbits came up again.

I still didn't completely trust him, but I was curious enough that I was willing to climb on the back of his bike and wrap my arms around his waist. He patted my hands, which made my stomach flip over, but I didn't move. We roared off on his bike, the wind whipping through my hair and tugging at my clothes, making the flare of my jeans flap wildly. Mama had many a boyfriend with motorcycles, but this was the first time I'd ridden with one of them. He slipped through traffic, the Harley whining and blaring as he accelerated, and rumbling when we got stuck at traffic lights. Then he turned off to a more rural road, and he swept the bike sideways as we whirled around a corner and flew up a hill. About two miles later, he slowed and pulled into a neighborhood of little brick houses with black shutters and cement patios. I figured we were cutting through the neighborhood to a trailer park or something, but he turned down the next road and pulled into driveway. The grass was cut, even trimmed around the driveway, and there were flowers in the garden around the edge of the house. A little sedan of some sort was parked in the carport beside a fishing boat. *Mama's struck it rich*, I thought.

He held out one arm to help me slide off the bike before he got off. "Come on," he said, leading the way to a side door in the carport. I was disappointed. I wanted to go in the front door like a real guest, but then I figured taking me in the back way made me almost like family or a close friend, which was better. The kitchen was brown and yellow, scattered with a few dirty dishes, but mostly clean. A fish aquarium glowed in one corner. The family room beyond was dark; the shades were all drawn.

He set his helmet on the washing machine by the back door. "Want something to drink?" he asked.

I said yes just because I was curious to see what he'd have in his refrigerator. He had beer, but he also had a little jug of milk and a carton of orange juice. I almost asked for orange juice, but I was afraid maybe he drank it straight from the carton, so I opted for some water instead. Then we went outside, back through the carport to his backyard, which had a short chain-link fence running around the perimeter to keep in his Dachshund, a little bowlegged brown fella that came yapping up from the far end of the house where an elderly woman stood by an open door.

"Hi, Mama," Ricky hollered. "I brought a little friend by to see my rabbits."

"Well, hello, child," she hollered back in a husky voice that suited her bobbed hair and handsome face. "You come on in here and get some cookies when you've had enough of them rabbits." The screen door slammed behind her.

"You live with your mama?" I asked. That accounted for the house and pretty yard, anyhow, but it still didn't seem to add up to a guy on a Harley with tattoos who raised rabbits and was interested in dating my mother.

"No, it's a duplex. I divided the house up after Daddy died and told her to come live here so as she wouldn't be so lonely, but we both have our own space. She don't hardly ever come to my side, but I eat supper with her a lot. She's a better cook than me."

He loved his mama enough to give her half his house. This guy was somebody special, which was plain even for me to see at fifteen. I knew if I had a pretty little brick house in a neighborhood, I wouldn't have split half of it off for my mother, and when I married and was rich, I didn't even offer her a pool house in my backyard, which makes me feel rather wretched, now that I think about it.

The dog kept yapping at my feet, so I bent down and scratched his head. His fur was smooth, but nothing compared to the rabbits'.

The rabbits were housed in cages in the back corner of the yard, which was only about twenty steps from the back door, but bigger than any yard I hoped to have at that point in my life. There was a little utility building with a long roof leaning off the back side. The bunny cages hung under the roof from long cables. There wasn't just one bunny, but bunches of them lined up in cage after cage. I counted fifteen altogether.

"Wow. All these are yours?" I asked.

"Yup. I raise and sell them."

"Sell them to who?"

"Friends, people at work, sometimes to pet stores."

"Do you make a lot of money?"

He laughed. "Anybody looking to get rich don't need to raise rabbits, not by the time they pay to feed 'em all year. And they die pretty easily, especially the babies. Mostly I do it 'cause I like 'em."

I looked at him sideways. "Really?"

"Really. What's not to like? Like I told ya, they're quiet and they're soft to cuddle." He opened a cage and pulled out a long-eared white one with black spots down its back. "This is Jack. He's a broken Holland Lop."

"He's broken?"

Ricky ran his hand down the bunny's sleek spotted fur as it leaned against his chest. "The spots down his back classify him as what's called a broken. He's been daddy to lots of babies. Here, hold him."

He carefully laid him in my arms. After I got comfortable with him, I nuzzled my face in his fur. I'd never felt anything so soft in my life. It was different even from rabbit-fur coats in the mall — softer somehow.

Ricky pointed one by one to each of the cages. "This is Snowball. She's a rare blue-eyed white, but a Netherlands Dwarf, not a Lop. See how short her ears are and how they're standing up instead of flopping down the side of her face? And her body is a lot smaller. Lops get big. Now, Rudy here is a Tort. See, the brown fur is etched in black. I love Torts. Then there's Taffy, Giggles, Evie, Taz, Pearl, Turner and Hooch, Kanga and Cocoa Puff. These three are babies. I'll be selling them in another week or two. Want to hold one of them?"

"Sure."

He put Jack back in his cage and laid a palm-size baby in my hands. It was the most precious thing I'd ever held in my life. I was speechless.

"Are you gonna name this one?"

"No. But this one here needs a name." He pointed to the cage on the end where a white rabbit with beige spots sat looking at me.

"A broken Holland Lop, right?"

"Very good. Why don't you name her?"

"Can I hold her?"

He took the baby in one hand and scooped the bigger rabbit out of her cage and into my arms. "I just got her last week. She's a show rabbit, perfect conformation."

The rabbit relaxed against me as I stroked her back. "Peachy."

"Peachy?"

"Her fur looks like peaches and cream."

"Okay, Peachy it is."

"I wish I could buy one of the babies, but Mama would never let me have a pet."

"I'll tell you what, Peachy here will be yours and you can come see her whenever you want."

"Really?" A red flag rose in my head and made my back tingle with suspicion. Why would he do such a thing for me?

"Really. In fact, whenever she has babies, you can sell them to friends at school and keep the money, you know, for movies and stuff."

I didn't believe him. He didn't have any reason to be so nice to me, but he was good to his word. Peachy kept me in spending money throughout high school in bursts of litters of five babies at a time every few months. Sometimes she lost babies, and Ricky would be as upset as me, but I learned a lot through the experience. I learned that not all men were domineering, and that kindness and compassion weren't the signs of being a wimp. Ricky taught me there was a whole world of men out there that could make me feel special in a way that had nothing to do with sex or what I had to offer them. Ricky taught me how to love. He forever changed the type of boys I dated; I learned to look carefully at their faces, not to see if they were handsome, but to see if they had that soft openness to their expression and compassionate eyes that spoke of sincere kindness.

He asked my mother to marry him after six months, but my mother said no and dumped him. She apparently didn't learn the same lesson as me. She said he was too soft, but I never trusted that to be the real reason, and she refused to say more.

She never knew I continued visiting him long after their break-up. He was more family to me than she was. In my best dreams, he was my daddy and I'd at last found a real home.

So, I know I can find Steven's murderer by looking into visitors' eyes. Whoever it was, their eyes will give them away.

Rain pours from the sky and washes down the glass doors as I tell Lilly about Ricky and what he taught me. Every once in a while, she turns a page of the *Better Homes and Gardens* magazine she has lying on the floor in front of her as I talk. When I'm done, she tilts her head to one side and narrows her eyes at me. "How about my eyes? Am I evil? Could I be the killer?"

Lilly is a lot of things — spooky, mysterious, unpredictable, shy — but I don't say that to her. "Steven loved you deeply, and I know that feeling was reciprocated. If your eyes show anything, it's love for him."

She closes her eyes, to stave off tears, I think, and nods.

"So tell me about the intercom. Can they hear what I'm saying?"

"Only if it's turned on."

"That's a relief. I've never turned it on."

"And for sure you're the only one who ever comes in here." Sarcasm has returned to her voice. She wears it like a shield.

"You're implying Colette or somebody turns it on to eavesdrop."

"I didn't say that."

"So what does the intercom have to do with the murder?"

She got huffy. "Who said it had anything to do with the murder? I thought you'd want to know you're being listened to all the time."

That gave me the creeps. I couldn't imagine why Colette would want to listen to an almost entirely silent apartment. Were she and Henry so protective over Lilly that they listened in on her conversations? Did Colette expect to overhear me talking bad about her? Maybe she expected to catch me doing something with someone? But who? I never had anyone over.

Except Steven.

"Steven is the only one who has ever visited me here," I say. Then I think of the grove, of what almost happened between Steven and me. "She wouldn't have figured on me and Steven, you know . . . He was a kid."

"No. But Steven could have called down here to see if I was here."

"You mean you and Steven met here when I was gone?"

She rolls her eyes. "It was our place before it was yours."

"Does Colette know?"

"I made sure the intercom was always off, if that's what you mean. But I wasn't here when he got here that night. I was supposed to be, but Colette wasn't around, and Henry, well, I had to take care of him first, for the second time that day. Then he sent me on my bike down to the grocery store to get him some Advil."

"And it happened while you were gone?"

She looks away from me. "Not exactly."

"Who found Steven?"

"The police."

"The police? But what made them start looking for him?"

"Someone called from a pay phone."

"You?"

She doesn't answer.

"If you know who did it, Lilly, you have to tell. We need to tell the police so they can arrest the murderer and end all this."

Finally her eyes break the deadlock glare she's had on me. "You are crazy and naïve."

"Me? Naïve?" I feel like I've stepped back to my childhood. My mother used to call me naïve. I haven't been considered naïve since I was twelve. Her insinuation makes me feel stripped naked of every-thing in my past.

She looks at the magazine and turns another page.

Conversation over.

I stare at my spot on the wall as I figure things out.

The rain seemed to last forever. Night and day kept passing away under the steady pounding of it on the roof and windows. But it ended late last night. Today I sit on the sofa looking at the bare branches reaching up through the gray sky with little hope of finding a single ray of sunshine. The room is silent except for Caroline's baby talk echoing around me. I'm afraid if I move, I will silence her voice. She will drift away into the grayness outside.

I watch from the corner of my eye, hoping to see her move through the room.

There is nothing but shadows.
Caroline, come to me!

I wake on the sofa, cramped and hungry. I have no idea what day it is or how long I've slept. I click on the television. The cable is out again.

I have to get out of the apartment to see if the world is still revolving around the sun.

I shower, dress, even put on makeup, then trudge up to the main house. The sun sparkles across the pool and yard. The air hangs warmly around me, the cold washed away. The cable man is kneeling in front of the cable box, fiddling with wires. I wave. He nods. I try to analyze his eyes, his demeanor and personality, but he's too far away.

It's not hard to analyze Betts. She's staring out the window, first at the cable guy and then at me, as if my friendly wave indicates I'm in cahoots with him over something.

She almost growls at me when she answers the door. "She's gone. Come back later."

I trudge back across the yard, but instead of going inside, I stretch out in a lawn chair and gaze toward the back of the yard at the old oak tree to think about friends. I'm not sure Colette is really a friend anymore. We don't really talk about anything that matters. I'm beginning to think I don't have any friends at all. I haven't talked to Jennifer since Caroline's funeral. And I haven't seen Ricky in years. It's sad because they are the two people in the world who helped me escape reliving my mother's life.

Somehow I have let them both fade away.

I feel desperately alone.

The next Saturday, I decide to take Seth to Raleigh so I can see Ricky. I'm hoping he'll offer some words of wisdom to fix my life.

Sinclair wouldn't have let me have Seth if I'd told him I was going to Raleigh. I'm not supposed to leave town with him. Part of the *agreement*.

"I'm taking you somewhere special today," I tell Seth.

I haven't seen Ricky since my wedding. The wedding was huge, but mostly friends, relatives, and associates of Sinclair's family. I didn't invite many people to the wedding: my sorority sisters, Jennifer, my mother, and Ricky. Ricky gave me away. We both seemed to take the gesture literally. He handed me over to Sinclair, and we both knew I would lean on Sinclair in the future instead of him. He evaporated from my life. He liked Sinclair and probably understood I had finally found my place in the world, so he felt like an unnecessary third wheel. We quit conversing by phone and mail, but he was always in the back of my mind as my childhood lifeline.

When he said goodbye at the wedding, he chucked me under the chin and kissed my cheek. "I knew you'd turn out in the end." If only he'd known. If only I'd known.

It's a long drive to Raleigh, but we leave early in the morning and Seth endures it well.

Ricky's yard looks different, which isn't surprising after five years. The Harley and boat are both gone. A pickup truck stands in their stead.

Given the length of my absence, I decide it would be more fitting to go to the front door. A short, square woman in her mid-fifties answers. The smell of something Italian wafts from the dim interior. "May I help you?"

"Is Ricky home?"

"Ricky Bathay? 'Fraid not, sweets. He got married a few years back, and I've been renting this place ever since. His mama still lives next door, though."

"How about his rabbits? Are they still in the backyard?"

"Oh, he gave those up. His wife didn't want them cluttering up the backyard and all. They live in one of those uppity neighborhoods with all them ordinances and such."

Heavy-hearted, I lead Seth next door. I'm ready to greet his mother with a warm hug. We'd been close during those rabbit years. "Hi, Ruth."

"Rachel. What brings you here?" She seems cold compared with the grandma figure who used to welcome me.

"I'm looking for Ricky."

She nods toward Seth. "This your surviving child?"

I understand. Caroline's death and all the press. My body suddenly feels hollow. I turn to go, but pause. Maybe Ricky feels differently. Maybe he still cares. I can't find a scrap of paper in my pocketbook, so I pull a blank check from my checkbook and hand it to Ruth. "Here. It has my address and phone number. Please give it to Ricky."

She fingers it as I stride away. Her voice rises behind me. "He got married. Lives in Knightdale, now."

I raise my hand in a wave and toss her a slight smile, but I don't stop my trek to the car.

I take Seth to Pet Lovers and scoop up a black Holland Lop from a cage of various rabbits. "Run your finger down his fur, Seth," I say, holding out the tiny fur ball.

Seth shakes his head and takes a step backward.

"He's soft, Seth. He's a baby. He won't hurt you."

"I don't wanna."

I take Seth's hand and place it on the bunny's back. "See how soft?"

"Lemme go. I want Daddy. I wanna go home."

I flip the rabbit over and look at its genitals. It took me a long while to discern the difference between males and females, but after years of selling baby rabbits to friends, I eventually learned. "Aw, it's a boy just like you, Seth. How about we take him home for a pet. We'll call him Ace of Spades, Ace for short."

Seth wrinkles his nose at me.

"I had one named Queen of Hearts, once. And one named Peachy. She was my first rabbit. Boy, did I love that rabbit."

"It stinks in here. I wanna go home."

I sigh. As young as Caroline was, she had already displayed a love for every animal she saw.

"I hate you," Seth says. "I wanna go home to Daddy."

As Seth backs away from me, I try to keep the horrible thought from surfacing, but it is there: *Why did it have to be Caroline who died?*

The thought rocks my world, tilting me. *I am a horrible mother.* I hold myself together long enough to get us back home, but feel my self losing reality; I want to forget everything.

CHAPTER SIXTEEN

I rise from a deep sleep to rapping on the front door. I stumble out of bed and down the hall. Something about the house seems odd, but I can't put my finger on it. I feel like I'm walking in a fog and my surroundings aren't clear, aren't in focus. Everything seems to have been rearranged.

The world is at a tilt as I tiptoe down the hallway, doing my best not to make a noise. I see Seth as I pass his doorway. He's slumbering, curled around his stuffed rabbit, Binks.

A young girl is at the door. I recognize her thin frame and long hair; I know her, but I can't place her. I'm stuck in a void in my mind, lost, unable to connect the flashes of perception.

She reminds me of myself as a girl, and I feel like I'm talking to myself as I speak to her. "Don't you know you shouldn't come calling mid-afternoon? You'll wake the baby with all that knocking. She'll wake up screaming and then the entire afternoon will be ruined. She's cranky when she doesn't get enough sleep."

The girl gives me a strange look. "The baby is sleeping? What baby?"

"Caroline, of course. She sleeps until three-thirty every day. If she doesn't sleep, she'll scream all bloody afternoon. Have you ever had to listen to a baby scream all day and all night?"

"No."

"Who are you, anyway?"

"Lilly . . ."

"Lilly? Lilly? I don't think I know you. What do you want?"

The girl bites her bottom lip. "Nothing. I . . . Never mind. Sorry I disturbed you."

She sprints away like a frightened deer.

I wake mid-afternoon in Sinclair's new house, feeling disoriented until I remember I am minding Seth. He wanted to go home to his own bed rather than the pool house. I can't blame him. The pool house is depressing.

The remnants of a strange dream sift around the edge of my mind, of slamming the door in Lilly's face. I can't think why I would do such a thing.

Being in Sinclair's house, though, surrounded by the things we shared when Caroline was a part of our world raises her lifeless shadow around me. I feel the absence of her. Her voice is missing from the family room. The sound of paper tearing and toys being flung to the ground, the sound of her garbled baby talk as she plays with a spoon and dish beside me in the kitchen, the wail of her waking in the morning. Her missing sounds are like holes in the fabric of daily life.

That's what came between Sinclair and me. I lived with her lifeless shadow every waking moment. Sinclair was at work. He didn't feel the black hole of her absence sucking at his memories, keeping life from moving forward.

He would walk in the door to catch me crumpled in tears over a toy or a picture book. At first, he coddled me, but the emotions wore him down. He wanted to shut the whole thing out. He expected me to be stronger than I was.

"Pull yourself together, Rachel," he said one day toward the end.

"Don't look at me like that. You look at me like I did something wrong. It's not my fault. Why won't you talk about it? You act like she was never here."

"I've had a long day, Rachel. Let it rest."

"You never want to talk about her."

"There's nothing to talk about. Talking doesn't change anything."

"I miss the noises she made."

"She's gone, Rachel."

The finality of his words was punctuated by the ringing of the phone. Sinclair picked it up, anxious for the world to build a wall between us so we wouldn't have to talk, so he wouldn't have to talk to me. He murmured into the receiver, so I knew who it was. *Her.* Jocelyn. She was the only wall I couldn't scale to reach him. Sinclair's face lit up in her presence. She could talk on his level. She was a part of his hour-to-hour existence all day. She never faltered — not in action or responses, as if she had some all-seeing eye preparing her for every encounter.

I often found them with their heads bent over a case file, talking in earnest hushed tones. Sometimes at home he'd exhibit an anxiousness to be shed of me and the children, to get out the door to a meeting with Jocelyn, to give her a present, a "bonus" orchestrated to reward her for being such a godsend to his practice.

There was nothing I could do to combat her pervasion into our lives then.

There is nothing I can do to stop it now.

I wander down the hall and crawl back into bed with Seth. I feel his heart beating through his backbone, and sleep envelops me again.

CHAPTER SEVENTEEN

L illy stands at the glass doors, making a strange face until I walk over and let her in. "Are you okay today?"

"As opposed to when?"

She looks around shifty-eyed and then back at me. "Are you alone?"

"Who else would be here?"

"Um, no telling." She relaxes and shuts the door behind me. As she turns back around, I see her again at the door of the house in my dream, a flash of recognition and gone again. *A dream?* My brain is the moon, full of craters and dark shadows.

Concentrating on her, I almost forget the bunny in my hands until she notices it.

"What's that?"

"My new pet."

"You can't have pets in here."

"Why not?"

She shrugs and sits beside me. "Can I hold it?"

"Sure." I show her how to wrap her hands around him.

She, like everyone, holds the bunny to her face and lets the soft black down waft against her cheek. A look of contentment momentarily eases the lines of her face.

"His name is Ace."

"That's good," she says. "I was afraid you named it Caroline or Steven."

"That would be pretty creepy."

"Were you singing to him last night?"

"Huh?"

"Last night. Were you singing lullabies to the rabbit?"

"To a rabbit?"

"I heard you —"

She whips around at the sound of a car in the driveway. "Oh, no. Henry's home."

"So? Aren't you allowed to be down here with me?"

Her breathing becomes labored, and her face becomes strained. "He was supposed to have meetings today. He left a message saying so on the intercom tape at the front door." She shoves the bunny into my hands and runs out the back door.

I run to the door. "Wait! I wanted to ask you . . ."

Bruce the yardman looks at me from a hole he's digging in the back corner. Lilly is gone.

Donald Doc watches me over his spectacles. "You bought a rabbit?"

"Yes. I had a rabbit when I was a teenager. They're good pets, you know. They don't make any noise. Well, some noise if they get angry, especially when they're pregnant and don't want to be touched. They growl, but not like a dog."

"I see."

"And they're nice to cuddle."

"I can understand how it would feel good to hold and cuddle something again. I know you miss doing that with Caroline." He tapped his pen against his chin. "Do you ever imagine it's Caroline?"

What a dorky question. I want to tell him I feel like strangling him till his eyes pop out just to see the reaction on his face. Instead, I tell him the truth. "I close my eyes and imagine I've been transported back to those years when the future offered release in a new independent life, not a dead-end trail of useless days."

I've said too much. He scribbles away on his pad before he speaks. "What makes you feel like your days are useless?"

I shrug. "I don't know. I have no purpose. I feel empty."

He nods.

I stop myself. What is it Saint Thérèse said in her book? I wrote it on a card to think about: *Though I have never heard him speak, I know he is within me, guiding me.* Can I believe that? Can I release myself to believe that there is more than darkness and pain filling my soul?

CHAPTER EIGHTEEN

S eth comes for the afternoon the next day because Sinclair has a
meeting and his mother has gone to visit her sister. I'm tempted
to ask Sinclair why this won't confuse Seth, but inside I've convinced
myself that Seth asked to be with me for the afternoon. I don't want to
be told differently.

With little else to do in the pool house, he wants to hold Ace. I
smile, seeing the little black bunny nestled to his chest. Seth talks intently to him in quiet tones I can't hear. I turn to pour us drinks and get
Seth a snack. It's going to be a good day together. I'm going to read
him a story and then take him shopping and out to McDonald's so he
can play in the play space and pig out on french fries. Then I'm taking
him to the toy store. I feel good just thinking of the smiles I'll wheedle
from him today.

As I turn back to him, drinks in hand, Ace scrabbles in his arms.
Seth drops him. I rush to pick him up, my soft baby bunny. He con-
vulses in my hands a few times and dies.

My small bit of contrived cheerfulness evaporates, and I plummet
back into the abyss.

I am staring at the lifeless bit of fluff when Lilly saunters in. She
speaks but I don't answer. She scoops him from my hands. "He's dead."

I nod and walk away. I pick up my drink, go to the kitchen and take
my pills from the cabinet. There are ten left. I wonder if that's enough.
I dump them into my palm.

Lilly steps up, snatches them away, and throws them in the sink. "It's a rabbit. It's not worth killing yourself over."

"That would be impossible since I'm not alive. I'm just a body walking around with lungs inhaling and exhaling and a heart that keeps beating. I need to donate this robotic flesh to a hospital and let them put some poor dying soul in here that still has feelings, that still has a reason to live."

"You have a reason to live. Look at Seth. He needs you."

Seth squats eye level in front of the dead rabbit where Lilly laid it on the coffee table. After a minute, he finds a pen on the table and pokes at it a few times, first at the still sides of the ribs and then at the open mouth, until he feels me watching him. He meets my gaze for a split second, drops the pen and plops in front of the television to stare at it like a zombie.

"Seth doesn't even like me," I say. "Tell her, Seth. Tell her how you hate me."

"It's those stupid pills. They numb you, Rachel. You can't even think straight anymore. You talk to Caroline, and she's not here. You sit on the couch and stare into space for hours at a time and never even see me come and go. You forget to eat. You don't leave this stupid apartment."

I can't keep up with what she's saying. Her words are running too fast.

"You need healing. You've got to start looking outside yourself, Rachel. Wash those pills down the sink. Come back to life."

I hear her, but I don't move. Wash the pills away?

She turns on the water, and I watch the pills dissolve and slide down the drain.

I am stretched out on the couch staring at the ceiling when Sinclair comes to get Seth. Lilly is still here, playing Chutes and Ladders with him. We didn't go to McDonald's or the toy store.

"How'd it go?" Sinclair asks.

"Fine," I reply without moving.

"Are you okay?"

"Just tired." Tired of life. Tired of trying to go on.

"I'm glad you got to spend time together today because he won't be able to visit with you this weekend. I'm taking him on a little trip Saturday."

That explains the change in schedule. "Where are you going?"

"The beach house. It's supposed to be unseasonably warm on the coast this weekend — in the eighties."

The beach house. Our beach house. I picture Jocelyn pulling up with him, walking into the cottage, my haven. I turn tear-filled eyes on Sinclair and wish he could read my thoughts, feel my breaking heart.

He gathers Seth in his strong arms and leaves.

Lilly stands at the glass doors and watches his car pull away. "You still love him, don't you?"

"What would make you say that?"

"You ought to put up more of a fight. If you don't let him know, he'll end up marrying that lady doctor . . . what's her name?"

"Jocelyn. Doctor *Jocelyn* Harper."

"Yeah, her. He'll marry her and go on without you. You have to get back with him. Get well and get out of this pool house, Rachel, before there's more trouble." She crosses the room and sits on the coffee table in front of me. "You have to get better. You have to get out of here. Come with me."

"Come with you where?"

"The healing place."

"Where's that?"

"If I tell you, you won't go. You have to trust me."

Trust her. I unconsciously shiver from head to toe. She slips in and out of my house like some sort of spirit and speaks in riddles and makes proclamations like some pretend adult from the Twilight Zone, but I'm supposed to trust her. "Gee, let me check my schedule. Oops. Sorry. No can do. I'm all booked up." I kick my feet up onto the coffee table and lean back with my eyes closed.

"I didn't mean we were going right now. Tomorrow at three. I'll meet you by the oak tree."

I search inside my blank head to try to think up an excuse. When I look up to answer her, she's gone.

"He has already gone on without me," I say to the empty room.

I am alone.

CHAPTER NINETEEN

❧

I perch on the edge of the sofa and watch the minutes tick by. Three o'clock. I'm still not sure I want to go, but my body stands and my feet propel me forward.

Lilly is waiting at the oak tree. I stop beside her.

"Let's go," she says as she steps forward.

I don't follow. I don't want to go. She steps back to my side and slips her hand into mine. "Come on. Hurry or we'll be late."

I let her lead me. We follow the path through the woods. At first, I think the teenagers will be waiting to pounce on us, but I dismiss that idea and dream up a black-cloaked witch, hideous and old, waiting in a mystical cabin. I imagine the smell of potions drifting through the woods and the cackle of incantations echoing around us.

I'm wrong. The path weaves through the woods, around the back neighbors' houses and comes out on a road. For a moment, I'm disoriented, but Lilly isn't. She knows where she's going. She doesn't pause. She pulls me up the sidewalk and stops at the bus stop.

"The bus? I could have driven."

"You wouldn't have. You would have said no."

The bus arrives before she finishes her sentence. She must have known the schedule.

We sit on the vinyl seats side by side as passengers alight and depart. No one sees me. No one recognizes me. I stare out the window at the slope of the mountain falling away beneath us and at the array of colorful leaves painting the landscape orange, yellow, and red. The bus travels downtown. I wonder if we're going to the Sensibilities Spa. Perhaps Lilly is into aromatherapy. There's been a sense of calm about her lately.

She stands and pulls me with her, and we plod down the steps of the bus to the sidewalks busy with tourists spending their money on T-shirts and art and pastries. Lilly doesn't follow pedestrian rules or normal manners. She moves against the flow, dodges between people, her thin body slipping between bodies like a ghost through walls, pulling me behind, bumping me into people and packages until we pass the library and reach the civic center. With a quick glance at traffic, she dashes across the road to the basilica.

"What are we doing here?"

"It's the healing place."

"A church?" Now it makes sense. This is how she knows about Saint Thérèse. I may be reading the book, but I'm not ready for church. I'm still listening in my head, trying to hear God in the silence of myself. "I'm not going in there."

"Come on," she says and tugs again.

People are looking at us. I give in and follow her up the wide steps and through the doors.

It's dim inside. Candles flicker on the altar. Lilly doesn't walk down the aisle to a seat. She moves along the back wall and joins a line. People are taking turns going into a closet.

My heart pounds in my head. "You want me to go in there? No way."

"You talk. The priest listens. It will heal you."

"I don't need healing."

"Yes you do. You have to get well and move on."

Some old bag of a lady hisses at us. "Quiet!"

I snatch my hand from Lilly's grasp. As I turn, I glimpse a nun kneeling in the front pew. I hesitate. Is it her? I can't stay to find out. Fear pounds in my heart — fear of what, I'm not sure — but it presses upon me so that I can barely breathe.

I run out the door.

CHAPTER TWENTY

❧

I stumble into the apartment, my vision blurred by tears.

My son hates me. My husband has abandoned me. I don't even have a memento of my daughter except the bed she never grew into.

I move to the bed and lay my head on the pillow and think of her. She was so different from me, full of life and laughter. I would have tucked her into this bed with stories and kisses. At twelve, when I was crawling into bed with boys, she would have been telling me secrets and giggling over school escapades before crawling under the covers. As a teenager, her bed would have been a sanctuary in our happy home for peaceful rest.

But she never got the chance. Instead she sleeps eternally in a box in the ground, a bed she will never outgrow.

I feel like my skin's been peeled off and my skeleton, my muscles, and all my nerves are exposed to the atmosphere. My emotions are as raw as my open flesh. I need more than anything else at that moment to be surrounded by Caroline, to touch and feel everything that was hers. I have nothing of Caroline's in the pool house except this bed. Sinclair has everything else. At least, I hope he still has everything. He wouldn't have thrown it away, would he? I've been gone so long, I don't know. I've been disconnected from everything. I don't know what happened to her things. I pull my car keys from my pocket and take off in my car.

As I pull into Sinclair's driveway, I realize how early in the day it is. Sinclair is still at the office, no doubt treating strep throat and flu

cases. I remember him saying one day he got to feeling he could diagnose most patients without even stepping into the exam rooms.
Sometimes something new would come along and he'd have to jerk
himself out of complacency to even think about the possibility of di-
agnosing something less than run-of-the-mill viruses. He didn't say
that anymore, though. His dad had been something different, something unsolvable. He never wished for anything other than the usual
anymore.

I sit in the backyard on a wooden porch swing hanging in the shade
of an old oak tree that overlooks a breathtaking view of the valley. The
view reminds me of the room they stuck me in after Caroline's death,
where I sat staring out a small square window most of the day, so the
view is wasted on me. I've lost heart for the mountains. I never think
of them as serene anymore. A part of me yearns for flat, open land
where no memories can invade my senses.

Hours later, I hear Sinclair's car pull in the driveway, but I don't
move. I know the routine. Seth will gather up his school things,
Sinclair will walk down the driveway to collect the mail, and Seth will
get the newspaper. I have five more minutes to waste at least. Sinclair
will see my car. He will know I am there. I want him to wonder where
I am.

When I think they're settled inside, I walk around to the front and
ring the doorbell. Sinclair comes to the door alone. "Where were
you?"

"Out back on the swing. Can I come in?"

"I don't want to confuse Seth, again. He didn't understand coming
home from school with you the other day."

There it is, again — confusing Seth. I am more confused than Seth,
I think. "You asked me to pick him up. It was your idea."

"What do you need, Rachel?"

"I want the pictures of Caroline. I want to look through them. You
have them still, don't you? And her clothes? Please, Sinclair, I need to
touch her."

The spirit in his face flees to some other distant place for a moment. "Maybe another day, Rachel. This isn't a good time."

I return home, rejected and alone, and crumple weeping onto my bed, and fall sleep. Days? Hours? I don't know.

I am at the bottom of a sandpit. The sun shines down on me, but cannot penetrate the blackness of this pit. I look up and see the blue sky, but it's foreign, a world apart from me. I hear voices laughing and talking; they are like claws scrabbling sand upon my face.

Do-gooders call into my cavernous prison, but I know behind their masks, they are faces of scorn, fleas rising from the sand to feed upon me, making raw, oozing wounds upon my flesh.

I try to escape from this pit, but the walls crumble when I try to climb out. There is no fleeing this torment.

My other self, the one not attached to heart, the one that watches from the outside, she tells me I can control this despair. I can smile. I can make myself behave nicely. I can raise my face to the sky and let its energy suffuse me with vigor and renew my well-being, but I don't.

I don't want to bear a false façade. I want to cry the tears. I want to scream the screams. I want to be angry.

I hope it will help, that it will wash the leaden gloom from my soul, the entombing despair from my heart, the screaming madness from my head. I hope.

But it never does.

I cannot eat. I cannot sleep. Madness lives in my brain like an alien worm taken hold that I cannot dispel, a ghoul I try to hide from, but he knows all my secrets. He knows all the places I go to be by myself, and he waits there with haunting eyes.

I will never be whole.

I cannot live with myself. I cannot live with the memories of what we were and what I've become. I cannot live without her.

The people have gone away. They have abandoned me for newer causes. They think I should have healed by now. They say I should have unplugged myself from her death. I should have stepped forward into the light.

Maybe they are right, because the light is fading. I plead with the sky not to give up, too, but it turns gray. Rain pours down, splattering me. The drops enlarge, and quicken, soaking the sand, puddling beneath me. The pit is a quagmire, sucking at my feet. Perhaps they are tears.

Are they my tears, God, or yours?

My soul concedes to the enemy.

Let it end.

Let me die.

CHAPTER TWENTY-ONE

I wake in blackness with Caroline alive in my mind. As the last of the medicine dissipates from my body, emotions reach up through me like spring blossoms striving for sunshine and make their seeds more recognizable: they are hands reaching up from the grave.

I know what I have to do.

I slip on a clean shirt and grab my keys.

Riverside Cemetery's wrought-iron gates are closed and locked, but that doesn't stop me. I haven't climbed a fence in years, but adrenaline courses through me and I scale the wall like I'm twelve again and land on the other side with a soft thud, like a cat. I hesitate, listening. The air is heavy with the slumber of the dead. The hounds aren't after me yet.

The sun peeks through the trees to caress the grass with its fingertips, wiping away dew as I weave between the gravestones. The cold moistness chills my bare feet and soaks the hem of my jeans until they feel stiff and weighted around my ankles. I am cold, shivering, and I know she is, too. It urges me forward.

I see the Winters' huge gravestone across the way, down one hill and a few steps up the side of the next, nestled in the shadow of an elm tree. Caroline's small brass plaque is there. They made me come to watch her burial through the blur of drugs they pumped into my veins and forced down my throat. They said I needed closure. They said I wouldn't be able to face the truth unless I saw her being put into the ground. Dust to dust. Gone forever. I stood with Sinclair holding me up and a male nurse from St. Joseph's on the other side. I tried to turn away, but I became transfixed like a moviegoer unable to shut my eyes against the unfolding horror.

They sat me in a chair with a throng of people standing around. Everyone we knew had gathered to gawk at my baby being put in that nasty hole in the ground. I crawled inside my mind to shut them out, but I kept looking out, seeing them. I couldn't make them go away.

They all had to say something. Dumb things. They told me everything would get better. They said God was holding her now. They offered to bring me food and help take care of Seth. I didn't want to talk to them. I didn't like the feel of their eyes on me, thinking about what had happened.

I don't know how long ago that was, but they're all gone now. The graveyard is empty.

I pass a tent with a hole dug and overlaid with a slab of carpet, ready to swallow another person. I stumble past it and hurry to the Winters family plot. Urgency rips through me. I've waited too long. I've waited too long! Despite the cold, distress born in my gut emanates outward to my skin as perspiration, and makes me shiver uncontrollably.

The mound of her grave is so tiny, I wonder how I ever left her here. I drop to my knees on top of her and pat the ground. "I'm here, baby. I haven't forgotten you. I'm here." I see her in that satin-lined box, cold, crying. I have to reach her. I have to save her.

The corner of the sod planted on top of her is still loose, not yet grown uniformly with the surrounding plots. I grasp the edge and tug, but the roots have burrowed deep into the ground. I tug and tear at it, pulling it out piece-by-piece, hunks of grass and roots dripping with dirt I fling away. I scrape at the earth with my fingers, digging into it with my nails, scrabbling like a dog.

The ground is hard, but I persist. She's crying. I hear her wailing. My breasts fill at the sound and ache with the need to nurse her. I want to rock her to sleep. I want to caress her face and look into her eyes, touch her lips.

Her crying has escalated. Nothing will soothe her now but breast-feeding. Sinclair says she is too big to nurse. She isn't. She still needs me.

She's stuck inside that box. She can't get out.

"I'm coming, sweetie. Those bad people did this to you. I told them not to. I told them Mommy's baby doesn't like the dark."

I hit a rock. I scrape the dirt from around the edge of it and try to pry it up.

She's reaching for me, her tiny arms raised up to me. She loves me. She wants me.

I push and pull at the rock, and dig at the soil.

"What are you doing?"

The voice catches me unaware. I twist around to see Lilly staring down at me.

What is she doing here? Is she following me? *She is spying on me.* Her fine blond hair has been pulled away from her face, caught loosely in a ponytail so that her wide blue eyes command attention, red-rimmed and damp from tears, tears of her own lost cause.

She squats beside me and grabs my wrist. "Look at your hands. What have you done?"

Dirt clings to the flesh on the tips of my fingers where they are shredded and bleeding. I stare at my hands, knowing the pain is searing up through my arms and burning at the base of my brain, but I am numb to it.

"We have to get you to the hospital. What were you thinking?"

"Caroline . . ." Her name escapes my lips as a cry. I can only think of her alive, screaming for release, scratching at the inside of the cas-ket, trying to reach me as I try to reach her. I scrape at the dirt again. The pain in my hands begins to register, but I keep on. Tears splash on my hands. I cannot see, but I can feel the dirt. I absorb the pain. I need the pain. I want all the pain I've been holding in my head to explode through the tips of my fingers and empty out my heart. I dig at the earth with renewed intensity.

Lilly clutches my arm and pulls me backward. "You can't dig her up. She's dead. She's been dead ages, months now."

I shake her off. She doesn't know what she's talking about. She's in cahoots with the rest of them. She was there when they stuck Caroline in the box in the ground.

She grasps my shoulders and shakes me. "What's wrong with you? Don't you know what you're doing?"

Saint Thérèse whispers to me, *There are trials and crosses for you, and they will make you worthy of God's kingdom.*

I push the words away.

I knock Lilly sideways with the sweep of my arm.

She crouches in front of me, places her hands on my face and forces me to look her in the eye. "She's dead. She's cold and hard and rotting in there. You can't dig her up."

I pull away from her. My eyes focus, and I see the dirt as dirt, a pathetically shallow hole. The pain in my hands is suddenly unbearable. My fingers curl uselessly toward my palms, trying to escape themselves. I stare at my fingers, torn and bleeding and crusted with dirt, and I begin to realize what I've done. "She's calling me."

"No, she's not. You've flipped. She's dead. She died in the car, remember? You found her dead."

I see her through the car window, limp and lifeless. It's Sinclair's car. I know because the paint is black. It's the Expedition. Sinclair left her in the car. I see her, and I scream now as I did then. "She can't be dead. She can't be dead!"

Lilly stands and pulls a cell phone from her pocket. I stare at the dirt-sodden knees of her jeans as she talks to someone, "Hurry! Hurry, Dr. Winters. She's gone nuts."

Have I gone nuts? *You've gone nuts. Now they'll call Donald Doc. Now we'll go back to our safe white room.*

I don't care. I am filled with pain, filled with grief. I fold into a ball, rocking back and forth on my feet with my fingers tucked protectively against my stomach. Tears flow from some sick deep place in my soul. "My baby."

Lilly sinks to the ground in front of me and starts smoothing the dirt back over Caroline. "She's not there, you know. Not really. Her body is, but her spirit is gone, flown off to heaven like Steven." Lilly stares off toward the mound where Steven lies. "I came to say good-bye to him in the quiet, but then I realized he's not here in the ground. He was too full of spirit to be stuck in that old body. We're so bound up on earth, we forget that when we die we get to fly free and soar. Look up." I follow her gaze upward. The sun has edged upward, backlighting the trees, giving a gray haze to the horizon. "Listen to the birds in the trees. They're just waking up, singing to each other. Look at the sun, like light from heaven shining on the trees, and at the clouds skirting across the sky. Steven and Caroline aren't here. They are God's creations, and their souls have been freed from their bodies, made as beautiful and weightless as the air and the birds' music. They're with God now in heaven, not in the ground."

Lilly's face glows before me, her skin luminous. Her watery blue eyes glisten.

I wipe my eyes with my wrist. My fingers are screaming with pain as she eases to my side and puts an arm around my shoulders. I tremble in her arms and weep. The hole in my soul will never be filled.

Sinclair arrives some time later. His words are soft, like when he rocked Caroline, and when he spoke to Seth at bedtime or caught him doing something naughty. "Rachel . . . my poor Rachel. Look at you. Those hands will take some fixing. First things first. Then Donald is going to see you. I've already called him. He'll meet us at the hospital."

He supports me with one arm and pulls me to a stand.

I'm spent, but still cognizant. *Not Copeland.* I remember the last trip to the hospital, being confined on the fifth floor, the psych ward. "Not to Copeland again. I'm all right. I just went off for a bit."

"We'll see what Donald says."

"I just miss her so much. Don't you miss her?"

"I miss her, but I don't want to dig her up. She's passed, darling." He sweeps hair from my forehead. "Do you know she's dead? Really? Do you?"

I see her still body in the casket. She's not moving. She's not crying. She's stiff and coated with makeup to make her look normal. I wanted her to be scratching trying to get to me, but I know she's not. "Yes, I know she's . . . gone. But I don't want her to be. If only we could do the whole day over again. I wouldn't send her to your mother's for the day. I wouldn't ever send her anywhere. I'd hold her all day long and never let go of her, not for anything."

Lilly turns away from me, not wanting me to see the tears flowing down her cheeks. She sprints between the gravestones and is gone.

Sinclair places one arm around my waist and helps me up the hill. "You did always take care of Caroline, Rachel. You held her all the time. She knows how much you loved her."

It's my turn to look at him crazily. He was the one who was supposed to take her to his mother's house for the day. He's the one who forgot. "Your mother said she'd watch her. You were supposed to take her."

Tears are streaming down his face, too. He nods his head and frowns but says nothing in his defense.

"I was so tired, remember? She wasn't sleeping at night. I needed a break. Your mother offered to help for the day."

"Everyone knows how tired you were, baby. I told them you weren't sleeping at night. Here we are at the gate. I'll have to lift you. You can't use those hands."

He scoops me into his arms. I smell the muskiness of his skin, that morning smell in bed before he's taken a shower. The stubble of his unshaven face brushes my shoulder. *I wish you had told me you didn't have time to take her that day.* The words batter around in my head and mouth, but I bite them back. He's trying so hard to make it up to me and I'm so tired of carrying the weight of it alone. I relax into him and let him take charge. I love him at that moment as I haven't in a long time. I love him the way I did when he planned surprise trips and elegant dinners, when he wooed me in candlelight and made love to me on a sand dune. I love him for taking care of me as no one else has ever taken care of me. I love him for letting me be the child, the needy, the dependent. I let him carry me on the tide of time, through the pain of the moment like a silver-clad prince come to my rescue.

I can't open the car door with my hands. Sinclair sets me on the ground and steps around to open the door for me, and I look through the hazy glass to the back seat, willing myself to get in. I know my baby is dead, buried under that little pile of dirt in the graveyard. I know she isn't in the car anymore, strapped in her car seat and staring lifelessly at the floor, but I'm still afraid of seeing her there. I make myself look. I make myself see the seat empty. My vision connects with my brain, and I see something. It takes a moment for the fuzzy form to take shape on the seat, lying spread eagle. Panic rises with alacrity, screaming out of me faster than the form fully taking shape in my brain. I want my hands to work, to snatch the door open, but I don't want to see, either. I back up. I can't look. "Not again. Not again. How could you? Not again."

Sinclair grabs me. "What is it? What's wrong?"

"Seth! First the baby, now Seth. You left him in the car. How could you do it again?"

Sinclair holds my shoulders. "What? Seth isn't in there."

I scrabble at the door with my useless hands, but I can't open the door. "Get him out. Get him out!" I pound on the door with my elbows. I hate him. All the love of a moment ago has been wiped away. I hate him. "How could you risk it? How could you do it again?"

He yanks the door open. "See? It's not Seth. It's Binks."

It is Binks, his long, fluffy ears stretched out over his head like a child's arms, his floppy legs spread across the seat. Anxiety and relief collide in me, and I collapse to my knees, swallowing vomit. "Sixty-nine degrees. It can happen at sixty-nine degrees with the windows cracked. Didn't they tell you? They explained it to me. It doesn't have to be hot."

"It's Binks, Rachel. Seth is fine. He left Binks in the car when I dropped him off at Mama's house."

He bends down and smoothes my hair. "You're a mess, aren't you, sweetheart?" He shakes his head. "Come on. Let's get to the hospital."

My chin quivers as I look at him. Where does he get his strength? How can he keep going on like nothing happened? How can he put one foot in front of the other?

It's as if he can read my mind. "You won't have to do anything. I'll take care of it all. Just get in the car and close your eyes. That's a good girl. Sing me that little song you used to sing about the sunshine on your shoulders. The one you sang for me at the beach when we were dating."

I know he's distracting me. He's the doctor, I'm the patient. Maybe he's the husband and I'm the wife, still. I want to be distracted. I want to go back to being a couple on the beach with life spreading out before us as long and unending as the ocean. I need him to carry me for a while, farther than across the graveyard to his car. I want him to carry me home, to make everything go back to normal.

I lay my head back against the headrest, and I sing.

CHAPTER TWENTY-TWO

From deep inside my shell, I sense the room is dark. Someone's pulled the shades. Somewhere at the tips of my arms, my fingers burn with distant pain; I can't move my arms. The dark is a mist circling my soul. My screams echo in my head and never make it into the silent room. I can't get far enough inside to hide from myself. There must be a hiding place somewhere in the dark of my subconscious. But I can't find one. The mist whispers to me. I can't escape myself. I can't escape the words of my subconscious: *You know she's dead.*

Yes, I know. Why do you have to keep telling me?

Because you don't listen. You don't face it.

Yes, I do. Leave me alone!

Then tell me what she looked like.

I don't want to.

See?

See what?

You won't face it.

You sound like Donald Doc. Leave me alone.

He said you have to face this.

I don't care what he says. He's an idiot.

Tell me what she looked like.

Okay, she was blue.

Was not.

Was too.

No, she wasn't. She was red. She was burnt.

Her lips were red.

Yes, her lips were red. How'd it happen?

Don't you ever let up?

No. How'd it happen?

He left her in the car.

There you go again.

What do you mean?

Tell me what happened.

If only I hadn't been so tired.

Quit the if-only route. It won't work.

I was tired.

You're still tired. Making excuses won't make it go away. Tell me . . .

It was Sinclair's car. The Expedition. Seth was in the house.

Keep going.

I couldn't find her. She wasn't in her crib. She wasn't in the house. There she was in the car. She was in the car.

Yes . . .

She was in the car!

Was she sleeping?

No, she wasn't sleeping.

Was she breathing?

Leave me alone.

Was she breathing?

NO!

She wasn't breathing?

No, she wasn't breathing. She wasn't breathing.

She'll never breathe again.

No, she'll never breathe again.

Where is she now?

In a box, in the ground.

Yes. See, you can say it. She's in a box, in the ground.

Lilly says that's only her body. She says her spirit is free now.

Do you think she is?

I want to think so. Is she?

Go to the healing place. Ask that priest.

I thought you knew everything.

I know something you don't. You're so dumb.

What?

You keep trying to forget everything so you won't feel bad anymore.

You have a better idea?

If you forget her, she won't exist anymore.

Huh?

As long as we keep thinking about her, she's alive through us. We can keep her forever, right here inside this cavern you call our brain.

CHAPTER TWENTY-THREE

✾

Through narrow slits of half-sleep I see Sinclair lean forward in the chair by my hospital bed, his head in his hands.

"I wish . . . it's so useless to wish. I can't change the past. Oh, how I wish I could! But I can't undo it! What's done is done."

He sobs into his hands until his nose runs, and he snatches a paper towel from the dispenser by the sink to swab his face clean.

His voice whispers out, more resolute than before, "I can't undo it. If only you could see that, Rachel. If you could see we only have the here and now, that with today we can shape our future, then we might have a chance. Why can't you step out of the past?"

He finally looks at me. "Oh, I didn't know you were awake."

In my mind I am smiling, but I don't think the expression reaches my face.

He runs his hand down my arm. His voice sighs, "Rachel."

I don't know what to say to him, or even if I can speak. I feel like I'm locked deep inside my body, unable to react.

"I got the best surgeon possible to work on your fingers. They'll be sore for a while, but they'll heal."

My hands are nubs of bandages at the ends of my arms. The pain is a dull throb from somewhere distant; I am well sedated.

"Donald says you're going to be fine, too. He says you went off your meds, cold turkey. Why'd you do that?"

"L-l-l-l." *Lilly.* I can't get it out. "L . . . L . . . Lilly." My voice sounds raspy.

"Lilly? You mean Colette's daughter? What does she have to do with your medicines?"

I'm too exhausted to talk. I just want his voice to wash over me and soothe me back to sleep.

"You have to stick to your dosage and ease off them. You know that."

I nod.

"But it's a good sign that you want to get off them. It tells me you want to get beyond all this and get on with life."

Get beyond all this? Is that possible? Ever? His face swims before me, slightly out of focus, but clear enough to show the earnestness of his words. Is he trying to say he wants things back on track? *Meet me halfway, Sinclair. Tell me you think about her every day. Tell me you miss her as much as I do. Tell me you often cry when no one's around, and that your arms ache to hold her.*

Tell me you're not starting over with Jocelyn. Tell me that someday Seth will look at me again with love in his eyes and we'll sit together in the spring sunshine and talk about what Caroline would be doing if she were there, and that there will be smiles in our voices even if there are still tears in our eyes. Then I'll have something to live for, to strive for in the tomorrows stretching out before me.

I want to say it aloud, but I can't get the words to rise from my heart to my throat. I close my eyes and relax as his voice caresses my sleepy mind.

". . . then there might be a chance for us."

I wonder if I heard the words or if they're part of a dream. *There might be a chance for us.*

He is gone when I wake again.

As much as I've cried, the tears should all be gone, but they come again, flowing from the emptiness of my soul. Can I love again? Can I *be* loved? Am I worthy of it?

I cry until I can cry no more, until my breaths become gasps, and then, shallow, and finally steady and slow again. I wipe my eyes, my nose, my wet cheeks. When the blurring of my teary vision clears, I see a package on the side table: my Saint Thérèse card and the book.

Lilly.

Lilly isn't allowed in the psych ward, but it's as if she knew my mind was searching for the words.

I reach out and clasp the card with my fingertips, desperate for guidance. I stare at the youthful face shrouded in the black headdress. I have read much of her autobiography, listened as she told me her secrets, and I don't hesitate to share mine with her. I have no doubt she can hear me. "I want to believe, Saint Thérèse, but I'm struggling to survive. How can I ever hope for love? How can I find forgiveness when I can't find my way through an ordinary day?"

I hear her whisper, *I am a wildflower beneath the towering cedars.*

I sniffle, stymieing the tears before they flow again. *Yes, a daisy. He loves me, he loves me not.*

I reach for the book, wanting to finish it, to discover the golden nugget she must be saving for the end.

Inside, Lilly has placed a note handwritten in her thin script on a pale pink and lime-green striped slip of paper: *She was a saint, and she felt the same darkness!*

I hadn't reached the page she has marked. I sigh, expecting a lecture, a pleading for me to go to that church, but I'm trapped in my cell and I need nourishment in whatever form I can get it, so I set Lilly's note to the side and read:

Instead of letting me see any ray of hope, God afflicted me with a most grievous martyrdom . . . I was alone in a desert waste — or rather, my soul was like a fragile skiff tossing without a pilot in a stormy sea. I knew that Jesus was there, asleep in my craft, but the night was too black for me to see Him. All was darkness. Not even a flash of lightning pierced the clouds. There's nothing reassuring about lightning, but, at least if the storm had burst, I should have been able to glimpse Jesus. But it was night, the dark night of the soul. Like Jesus during His Agony in the Garden, I felt myself abandoned and there was no help for me on earth or in heaven. God had abandoned me . . . I wish I could express what I feel, but it is beyond me. One must have passed through this dark tunnel to understand its blackness . . .

I close my eyes and let tears seep down my cheeks as I let my pain and fears mesh with hers. I am not alone. This saint, this innocent who had never done anything that compared to the vile sins I trailed behind me, had felt as bereft as I!

How did she believe? How did she not give it up for lost?

I read on:

Sometimes, I confess, a little ray of sunshine illumines my dark night, and I enjoy peace for an instant, but later, the remembrance of this ray of light, instead of consoling me, makes the blackness thicker still.

And yet never have I felt so deeply how sweet and merciful is the Lord.

I close the book and hold it to my chest. I whisper into the dimness of the room, "Show me mercy . . ."

Another day, I hear Sinclair's voice. I don't know if it's real or a dream. I can't get my eyes to open, but his voice washes over me, warming me like a soothing shower.

". . . I know you think I've forgotten about her, but I haven't. I think about her every day. I loved her as much as you did. How could you ever doubt that? I just don't want to talk about it. If I speak her name aloud, it destroys me, it shatters my reserve. I like to hold her memory quietly inside of me, where no one can change it or tarnish it. She was so special, so much like you, like everything I love about you: vivacious and smart and beautiful."

I think I've wished the words into being, but it's a nice dream, so I let it continue to wind along.

"I know you still love me. There's just so much between us. Why can't you go back to the way you were? Why do you keep doing these crazy things?"

His pitch changes. "Like the rabbit. How could you do that? How could you mail that dead rabbit to Jocelyn? I didn't tell her it was you. You're lucky the police don't know it was you, but I know. Who else would do such a thing? I thought you were getting better."

Dead rabbit? I didn't mail a dead rabbit to Jocelyn. What is he talking about?

"Oh, dear God, there is so much to overcome. How can we ever fix all this? Heal her, God, and heal *us*."

I've never before heard Sinclair pray aloud except the blessing over dinner at his parents' house.

We attended his parents' church on special occasions — Christmas and Easter and the odd time in between — a nice church with a pleasant pastor, but I had no interest in God back then. The sermons reminded me of all the sins of my life, but I already knew them all so well that his words fell like rain on a full bucket; they spilled over the edges and slipped away.

Sinclair went because he was supposed to. Sinclair did everything because he was supposed to. "It's the downfall of being an only child," he told me once. "Everything my parents ever wanted in a child falls on me. Sometimes I wish I'd had a dozen siblings so I could have blended into the background and all the responsibility of turning out right could have fallen on someone else."

The thought of just doing what he wanted and ignoring his parents' expectations never occurred to him. He was the stitching that held them together; it was his place in the family to become what they molded him to be, as if his parents were God and he was Adam. I said so to him, but he got mad. "It's a matter of wisdom. Why would I disregard what experience taught them?"

He makes it all sound so practical, but inside him it's not that sensible. His quiet acceptance of his planned life is full of holes. He couldn't play football because his father had ended up with a bum knee. "It's hell standing on my feet seeing patients all day, son. Makes my knee throb. You don't want to do that to yourself." Because, of course, he had to follow in Daddy's footsteps and be a doctor too.

"Being a doctor is what kids dream of, though. Didn't you want to be one?" I had asked him.

"Maybe I would have if it hadn't been expected of me. It's all right, though. Once I was in med school, I was glad I'd followed Dad's example."

What he wanted to be was an astronaut. I tried rewriting our life, picturing him in that role, him in the space shuttle looking out the

window while orbiting Earth, and me seeing him far above, a bright
light moving across the sky, mistaken by children as a star in the night
to cast wishes upon before falling asleep.

What happened to my dreams and wishes?

Sinclair's voice peters out to tears. "God, I love her, but I don't
know how to make it work . . ."

Inside my cocoon, I, too, start to cry. And to pray.

A couple of weeks later, I sense him in my room, sitting, watching
me, saying nothing. After a while, he kisses my forehead. "Merry Christmas, love," he whispers and leaves me to the silence of my room.

I am a daisy swaying in the breeze, my petals being plucked off one
at a time. *He loves me, he loves me not.*

Days pass. I have no idea how many. I don't remember when I went
in. But I finally become cognizant. I sit. I read. I work on a crossword
puzzle.

Talks with Donald Doc have become routine, although I don't
really remember anything we discuss. Nothing important. Nothing
significant that has made me feel I've been restored to normal. My
heart is still in my throat, but my painkillers and anti-depressants have
gradually been reduced, and I feel more in control.

Sinclair helps me into the car. I have been released to his care, but I
must visit Donald Doc twice a week, and I promise to stick to the pre-
scription schedule he gives me.

I know I will be staying in the pool house again, but Sinclair takes
me to his house first. He doesn't say why until I follow him back to the
bedroom. He pulls a box from his closet to the side of the bed and sits
down. "Mama packed up most of Caroline's things and gave them
away, but she saved a few things. Just mementos. I'm sorry I didn't
share them with you before. I should have."

I stare at it. It is just a box, an ordinary plastic storage container
from Wal-Mart. On the side, a sticker shows a child hiding in it, with a
huge X across it to show the danger of suffocation. I imagine Caroline

as the child. It could easily have held her body if she had scrunched down in it to hide, like she did at the end of the couch. She thought it made her invisible if she closed her eyes.

Why didn't someone take off the sticker?

I glance sideways at Sinclair. Maybe Mrs. Winters left the sticker there on purpose to keep driving home the point. Babies die from ignorance. Our ignorance.

I stare back at the box. Suddenly I'm afraid it's too early. They should not have released me. I am coming apart, shattering into a thousand pieces, blasting to all points of the room from an internal sonic boom. I want to crawl into that box and pull the lid down and never look anyone in the face again. I don't want to wonder what they are thinking about my baby. I don't want to keep remembering everything over and over again.

But life just keeps flowing forward. It is my punishment to be kept alive, to endure the torment of facing it all again every day. I lash myself with memories. I make myself think of her, red and blistered with dead eyes beneath long lashes that used to bat at me when she giggled and hang damp with tears when she got upset. She'd been upset; there was a trail of salt left running down her cheeks.

My hand shakes as I reach to open the lid. Waves of grief churn at the base of my spine, contort in my stomach, and spread through my limbs, making me weak all over.

Sinclair reaches over and pulls the lid off for me and sets it to one side, then lays one hand on my back as if to nudge me forward.

On the top lies a tiny white sweater from her layette, knitted of the finest angora. I remember slipping her tiny arms into it before bringing her home from the hospital, such delicate fingers and toes. I lift the garment and bury my face in it. It smells of Downy, but not of her.

Beneath that lies a floppy rag doll with frizzy brown hair and an old-fashioned pink dress, a Christmas gift from Sinclair's parents that sat pristinely on Caroline's dresser.

Two dresses lie wrapped in tissue paper, fancy things with lace and smocking worn for Christmas and Easter. Her christening gown is

wrapped in broadcloth. It was handmade for her at Mrs. Winters' request. Caroline was baptized at Sinclair's family church when she was
three months old, with a reception afterward that I thought might rival
her wedding. Not so. She will never have a wedding.

I run my fingers down the pleats of the christening gown. I remember how it draped off her body and cascaded down, so much silk and
lace for such a tiny little princess. It seemed ridiculous at the time, but
now it is comforting, in case all the fuss about baptism is true.

I think about the prayer I heard Sinclair utter in the hospital. Was it
real or a figment of a dream? I wonder as I did many nights in the echoing confines of the hospital ward what Sinclair thinks of God now. I
wonder if he asks God if our baby is in heaven. I wonder if he asks
God if our crime is so horrible that we'll never join her there.

It makes me want to believe in God. I am filled with new convic-
tion that I can't die until I've come to terms with God, because I have
to get to heaven to be with Caroline. I have to hold her in my arms
again to tell her how much I love her.

We used to be so philosophical about God. We both believed that
God and salvation boiled down to being a good person and loving one
another, doing unto others, and had nothing to do with attending
church. I had no church history. The times I attended with Sinclair, I
did so only because I relished doing everything ordinary families did.
I became my mother-in-law; I did it for appearance's sake.

Now I know otherwise. Saint Thérèse has opened my eyes, and I
have opened my heart. I have heard Sinclair pray with sincerity, and I
have followed suit. I realize I must learn more about God, but the idea
is a vague, meandering notion and I must find the gumption to follow
through. I'm not there yet.

It's as if Sinclair reads my thoughts. He follows my fingers as I trace
the stitches around the lace. "I go to church now to talk to God. And to
Caroline. I like to think she can hear me when I whisper to her at church."

He speaks to Caroline in church? His admission stuns me. I know
he loved her as much as I did, but he's been so stoic about it all that I
imagined he'd shut her away, out of his consciousness.

I will tell him about my prayers, about my conversations with Caroline and with Steven and Saint Thérèse, but not yet. For the moment, I want to bask in Caroline, in all that was her.

I set the christening gown aside and pull her baby book from the bottom of the box. All the loose clippings I saved are floating in the pages: her birth announcement, the pink sheet from her hospital bassinet, photos of sitting, crawling, and lying naked in her baby bathtub. There's the society news clipping about her baby shower, and her first invitation to a birthday party. I scrawled notes on every page, filling out the date she smiled, the day she cut a tooth, the day she ate real food. Only one page at the front of the book is blank: the family tree. I couldn't fill it out, knowing my half would be blank. I stared at the page, thinking of the day I almost filled it in with fictitious names, but I didn't. I didn't want to pass my legacy of falsehood on to my daughter. Let her present family suffice.

Now it would remain blank. There would be no next generation from Caroline.

I flip to the middle, to where the book ends, and stare at the photo of her seated in her highchair smeared with chocolate cake. It isn't a unique picture. There are millions like it across America. The first birthday. But this one is of my baby, my Caroline. I touch the picture, wishing I could have the moment back, the prayer of many a mother, of many a lover of the dead.

Tears trickle down my cheeks. My baby is not in the plastic box of keepsakes. "If I could only touch her once more."

Sinclair walks to his dresser and pulls out a Ziploc bag holding the precious remains of her first haircut, a few curls of her fine blond hair. "Here."

I take it from him with more care than a diamond-studded necklace. Here is part of her to touch. I want to take it home and hold it under my pillow.

He pulls an envelope off the top of his dresser and empties its contents, then plucks a curl from the Ziploc bag and deposits it safely inside. "Now we can say we've split hairs," he says.

Despite the gravity of the moment, I smile. It's been a long road, but I'm beginning to realize men deal with issues differently. "That's totally unlike us, you know," I say, "to worry about splitting hairs. We never got to the nitty-gritty. We got on famously on every issue."

"Yes, we did."

He turns and takes my hands in his. "Let me see how your fingers are healing." He peels away the bandages and examines the puckered looking skin. "They seem to be healing. Are they still painful?"

My fingers throb steadily, as much a part of me as my heartbeat, but numbed by medicine, a thing to be ignored. What I feel more than the pain is the energy of his touch on my skin. "It's not bad. The medicine helps."

He caresses my palm, avoiding the tender tips. "Let's leave the bandages off for a bit, let the skin breathe. I'll bandage them again before you leave."

I hold my breath. Does he mean I'm to stick around for a while?

His fingers travel up the smooth skin of my inner arm, and then to my shoulder, to my neck. He pulls me toward him, and we kiss, his lips soft and welcoming, tender.

He leans back and looks at me, looking for permission without asking for it aloud. I smile just slightly, and I nod.

His lips are tender trying to express the multitude of emotions our box of memories has opened between us.

CHAPTER TWENTY-FOUR

L illy sits on the counter and stares at the floor. She is in the dumps.
"Lilly, what happened to Ace?"

"He died."

"I know. What happened to him?"

She wrinkled her nose. "He was stinking up the place."

I don't have to ask if she sent him parcel post to heaven. I know it was her. It had to be her. I wouldn't have done that. *I didn't, did I?* I let it go. Let them blame it on me. They already know I'm crazy. But it makes me wonder how many cracks she has that haven't been discovered yet, chinks in the armor she's built around herself that go soul-deep.

I pick up the cross-stitch pillow and run my fingers over it. *Live in harmony, rest in peace.* I used to wonder what my grandmother meant by it, but it makes more sense nowadays. If I could live in harmony with what life has dealt me, I could sleep better at night. I'm thinking my grandmother was speaking of eternal life, though. She was on her deathbed. Mama said it was the last thing she cross-stitched. Mama had to help her with some of it because her eyes were failing and she was coughing so much, she couldn't aim the needle through the right hole.

Mama was nineteen when her mother died. She got pregnant with me the night after the funeral while finding consolation in some guy's arms. Not that my grandmother's death was a surprise. She'd been sick for ages, and bedridden the last full year of her life. Mama had to do everything for her, so when she found out she was pregnant with me, it didn't upset her. She thought taking care of a baby had to be easier than taking care of an old dying lady, she told me once, but found out too late that was wrong. Old ladies stay in bed and become more gravitated to one spot until they don't move at all. Babies do just the opposite.

Mama's always kept a picture of Granny sitting on her nightstand. Granny was a beautiful woman, despite her blond, bouffant hairdo. I can't picture her old. She is cast forever at midlife. Even as I imagine her on her deathbed, I see her with that beehive of blond hair stacked on her head.

I like to think of her and Mama sitting on the couch together in their little white house in the country, with their heads bent over a piece of embroidery, my grandmother guiding my mother's hands in making the fine stitches. The image makes Mama seem more American, more ordinary. It makes me imagine her drinking Kool-Aid and eating Oreos, and watching *Father Knows Best,* even though her daddy had died of old age when she was a kid. In the winter evenings when Mama and I cooked together in our ratty apartment kitchen, Mama would tell me tales of her childhood, of how Granny had been my grandfather's third wife; the first two had died. My grandfather had a thing for young women. With him being seventy on their wedding day, I guess my grandmother, being thirty-eight, seemed like a spring chicken to him. Mama said when she thinks of him, she's enveloped by the smell of tractor oil and moist dirt, sandy southern soil enriched with a load of manure. Her daddy spent a lot of time gardening, raising up corn and okra and rows upon rows of pole beans and peas. Sometimes she'd tend the garden with him, helping him plant the seeds or harvesting the vege-tables in warm sunshine after a day at school, but mostly her daddy kept to himself and she'd be stuck helping Granny in the kitchen, can-ning or cooking supper. She remembers the sense of him, how the skin hung off his thin arms, the boniness of his lap when he held her, and the deep, deep brown of his eyes embedded in a face of wrinkles.

Mama taught me to cross-stitch when I was ten. She said her mama had taught her because that was one of the things a girl needed to know to land a good husband; it was how Granny hooked up with my grandfather. She met him at a church fundraiser. He admired her cross-stitch work and asked her right then to marry him. I'm thinking it wasn't her cross-stitch he admired at all, especially if Mama and I inherited our figures from her. I never said so to Mama. She said the cross-stitch hadn't done her a lick of good, but maybe it would help me.

It did. I cross-stitched a graduation gift for Sinclair — a formal declaration of his graduation from Duke in the school colors of blue and gold. On the night of his graduation, we went out with his whole family to celebrate. Everyone had given him presents. Mine was third in the stack. He tore the sparkling blue paper off and then stalled out. He rubbed his fingers over the glass, not just reading the words, but almost feeling the stitches through the slick surface. "You made this?" he asked. I nodded. His face lit up as if shocked that I had created such a thing and then held it up to show his mother. "Look, Mama. Look what Rachel made," more aptly interpreted as, *See, Mama, she can do real wife-like things; here's proof.*

My grandmother may have missed the mark on my mama, but it was definitely a point-maker for me. If I hadn't inherited her figure, though, I don't think all the cross-stitching in the world would have helped.

I run my hands over the pillow again. *Live in harmony.* Maybe my grandmother knew something way back then. Maybe she could foresee the turmoil that would land in her yet-to-be-conceived granddaughter. Or maybe my mother lived in turmoil, too, and it's just been passed down the line, right along with the pillow.

I look at Lilly's downcast figure and picture her boxing up the rabbit and mailing it off. She's as messed up as me. My mother isn't perfect, but at least she didn't outright reject me like Lilly's had her. I wonder for a moment if she ever thinks of Lilly, if she regrets her decision, and how she would feel if she knew what abandonment did to Lilly. In her own silent way, Lilly is crying out for help as loudly as me. We both need to learn to *Live in Harmony* and *Rest in Peace*. She needs me. In fact, we need each other. "Tell me what's up."

"Forget it. Nothing's going to change. I've got two years, two months, and five days, then I'm out of here. I'll be legal. I can leave, and they can't stop me. They can drop dead for all I care."

"This is coming from the girl who tells me to read a book about God and love? I guess it didn't work for you."

"That was for dealing with death, for figuring out about Steven."

I haven't heard any updates on Steven since I went into the hospital. "Have the police discovered anything new?"

"No, and they aren't likely to, either. Last I heard, they were checking phone records, as if that's going to connect them to anything."

"Steven didn't do drugs, did he?"

"Ha! We left that to Colette."

I think of the two teenage boys lingering by the woods and visiting the deck in the dark of night, but I do my best not to react. Were they there to talk to Lilly? Or were they asking her to get Colette to come outside? Sometimes I think Lilly says more than she really knows, and this may be one of those times. She may be fishing for someone to confirm Colette's addiction. I'm not about to play the fool.

"So why could that church fix one problem and not the other?"

"With Steven, it was a healing of my heart. No one at a church can do anything about my parents. I have to bide my time till I can get away."

I laugh. "You could do like Saint Thérèse and become a nun. They could shut you away in a convent or something."

"You are so *not* funny." She heads to the door.

"I'm sorry, Lilly. That was mean. Don't go. I rented a movie. Stay and watch it with me. We'll order pizza with lots of mushrooms."

"Extra cheese?"

"Definitely."

I'm relieved as she settles beside me on the sofa while I pick up the phone to order pizza. I don't want to be alone. I'm afraid to be alone. The pills restocked in the cabinet are calling to me, and I need Lilly as a barrier.

Besides, I've got to find a way to keep communication open with her. I know the signs. I've been there. She has something to tell, and if I can't do anything else right in my life at this point, I'm going to offer Lilly a lifeline like Ricky gave me.

It's a matter of how . . . and what.

CHAPTER TWENTY-FIVE

H ow long have I hidden from the public eye?
I know it's time to face the world. My brain is waking. I can't sit
here, entombed with my thoughts. They pound in my head like resur-
rected ghosts. I have to fix my life, and I can't do it shut away. Today I
bypass the bookstore to go to the library. It's more public, and yet I
won't have to worry about talking to anyone. It's a practically voiceless
world. And the library has a lot more books.

I stand in the middle of the library and think about all the writers
out in the world making up stories. There are so many of them even in
this small library, no one will read them all. I wonder why writers do it.
I wonder if they live such quiet lives, they have to make up adventures
to keep themselves sane, or if their lives are so exciting, they have to
write them down.

I keep hoping some book will open some secret door that will suck
me in, make me forget myself, and offer some new alternative to my
life, or the answer to my crazed mind.

Donald Doc says just admitting I'm crazy means that I'm making
progress.

"May I help you find something?"

I turn to see a delicate woman, probably in her thirties, smiling at
me as if she's selling evening gowns in a fine boutique — until she
sees my face, and recognition dawns on her. She doesn't lose the smile,
but she pales slightly and stiffens just enough that I know she knows

who I am. I've become an expert at reading expressions. She knows about Caroline. The moment passes in a flash, though, and her smile returns with sincerity. She knows and doesn't hold it against me? I warm to her immediately. "I'm looking for something to take my mind off things, but I don't really know what. I'm a cover-and-blurb shopper."

"I'll leave you to look in peace, then. My name is Donna-Lynn. Just ask if I can be of any help. Keep in mind the newest releases are on a separate shelf up front."

I thank her and go back to perusing the shelves. It takes fifteen minutes, but I finally find one that intrigues me. I sit at a table by the window to read a chapter, to see if it's worth carrying home, but my eyes won't stay on the book. I feel like someone is watching me. Through the window, I don't see anyone I know. I turn again to the book and read a few sentences, but the feeling won't dissipate. My head is tingling with apprehension. I glance around again, but see nothing. The traffic lights on the corner change. Traffic moves forward. A mother and child hurry up the road, hand in hand. A teenage couple reclines against the brick wall of the sandwich shop across the road. Two men head up the hill, up Haywood Street, talking animatedly about something. The clouds break, and sun shines through almost blinding in its intensity.

I blink and squint and refocus. My eyes settle on the basilica, and I think of Lilly leading me there. I wonder who took her there. A school friend? I need to talk to Lilly again. I wonder what she says when she goes into the closet.

Something catches my eye, a person, I think, coming around the corner, but then it's gone. I blink. There's no one there. I shiver.

I glance again at the book on the table and decide to read it at home in the bit of sunshine we're having today. Colette doesn't even notice my lounging around anymore. She sleeps most afternoons away under the fog of sedation, taking up where I left off such a short time ago.

I check out the book. On the sidewalk, I look once more toward the basilica, then turn away and head uptown toward the bistro at the top of the hill. Lunch is bearable with a book in my hand. Lunch and then home.

I finish reading the book in two hours flat. It doesn't help me drift off to sleep that night the way I hoped it would. I lie staring at the ceiling of my bedroom, thinking I ought to take a pill to knock myself out, but I don't want one. I keep counting sheep, and ceiling tiles, and all the boys I've been with in my life, which makes me feel more wretched and used up. The only time I felt like I was anything was when I lived my fairytale life with Sinclair, being a mother to Seth and Caroline.

Mrs. Winters expected Caroline to grow up in frilly dresses with patent-leather shoes. She liked Caroline's baby hair fixed in ribbons when we visited her house. She began talking about giving Caroline a tea party for her fifth birthday before Caroline could even stand up. I had no expectations of Caroline. I only wanted her to be herself. Caroline liked to laugh and squeal. She pulled her toys off the shelves and tossed them on the floor. She had no idea what Mrs. Winters had in store for her, of how she'd have to hold her pinky out when she drank her tea, and how she'd have to address the Garden Club members as Miss Ada, and Miss Olivia, and Miss Glenda. She didn't know her piano teacher had already been decided and a trust fund had already been established to send her to Mary Baldwin College in Virginia, to Mrs. Winters' alma mater.

I let Mrs. Winters make all the plans. I felt ignorant raising my children. The only thing I knew was that I had to tell them I loved them every day. Even days when I was tired and I wanted to be alone and I didn't want to hold them and fix their cuts and wipe their runny noses, I took them in my arms and kissed their heads and told them that I loved them so they wouldn't go looking for it from somebody else.

In my mind, I am standing with them back in time, waiting for Sinclair to come in the door, and I realize they don't love me as much as they love Sinclair. They rush to the door when he gets home. Caroline cruises and crawls to reach him, then latches on to his leg and squeals "Da! Da!" until he sweeps her up in his arms and spins her in circles. He kisses her soft round cheeks and tucks her under his arm, carrying her like a football off to the kitchen, where he mixes himself a drink and gives them both a glass of apple juice over ice with a cherry dropped in so it looks like his.

I concentrate on those happy times. I reincarnate a day when Seth stood by my chair explaining why Tyrannosaurus Rex had short little arms. Caroline lay in my arms nursing, stopping every once in a while to look up at me and grin in her impish way, her face lit up from the inside. Sometimes she would examine my nipples with her fingers, rubbing them as if considering how they worked, and then she'd snatch at whatever necklace I wore and pull at it until I loosened her grip and reestablished it around my index finger.

I close my eyes and let the image flow through me. I let it carry my thoughts into drowsiness, but as I drift off to sleep, they take their own direction.

In my dream, I see her in the car. We have been to the ice-cream parlor downtown and she's eating rainbow sherbet, stripes of different colors running through it: pink, yellow, orange, purple, and blue. It's dripping down her face, and she's laughing as she's licking the sticky mess. Seth is eating vanilla ice cream. He has a dish and a spoon, and he eats carefully so it won't drip on the shirt Mrs. Winters bought him last week. He has his new Nikes on, too, and sports socks with red stripes around the ankles that match the red of his shirt. He likes clothes more than most little boys. I expected him to have ragged T-shirts and dirty knees, but Seth doesn't play ball or tag, or anything else that causes boys to slide their bodies across the ground. He likes to build things indoors and to play games that require total concentration. Mrs. Winters doesn't think it's strange. She's says it's a blessing he's so orderly.

I see Caroline's shining face in front of me. The sherbet is red on her cheeks and blue on her tongue. Her eyes are squeezed shut in glee. Ice cream drips down her chin and leaves splotches of brown on her dress. The car comes to a stop and Seth steps out, pristine, dish and spoon in hand. Caroline sees him stepping out. She puffs out her lower lip. Her chin begins to quiver. My view changes. I am no longer in front of her. Glass has risen between us. I am outside the window. Tears seep silently from her eyes. The ice cream on her face fades away, except for the red ice cream around her mouth; it deepens and becomes her lips. Her eyes fly open and stare at me wide-eyed, and then she becomes still.

That's not how it happened. If only I could take her for ice cream once more. I would wipe her face and kiss her cheeks and love her.

I wake in a sweat. I am alone in my bed in the pool house. I stare at the ceiling, at the little squares of white fiberglass tiles, and I try to conjure her face again, the smiling one, the one coated with ice cream, but she won't come back to me. I reach beneath my pillow and clasp the silk-wrapped clump of baby curls and cry into my pillow.

The next night, I dream of her again. We are on the back porch. Seth and Caroline are in the blue plastic baby pool. Seth is floating his boats around in circles. Caroline splashes him and sends a tidal wave over his orange boat with a kick of her chubby legs. Seth splashes her back, but she isn't upset. She squeals in delight.

"You sank my battleship," he says, and sets his boats to rights again, one following the other.

Caroline pulls herself out of the pool and half-crawls, half-toddles across the yard toward the sandbox. I cringe at the thought of sand sticking to her bathing suit, her arms and legs, but she keeps going past the sandbox, past the swing set, and around the corner. She reaches the car, and somehow the door opens. I yell at her to stop, but she doesn't hear me. She climbs in, and the door shuts behind her. I run to the car, but the faster I run the farther away the car seems to be. I can't reach it. I can't get to her. I'm so tired, I begin to crawl and half-toddle like she did, and it takes me down her path to the car door. I reach for the handle. It won't open. I close my eyes. I don't want to look in. I don't want to see the scene unfold again, but the dream keeps going, and there she is. The window has turned to water, and she is at the bottom of the blue pool, in the blue water, strapped in her car seat, limp and still.

The third night, she is in her christening gown. Baptismal water is being poured over her head, but I am not the one holding her. I am in the crowd watching. A movement pulls my attention to the left, and I see a nun sitting in the audience. Saint Thérèse? I call out to her, asking what is happening. She remains focused on the baptism. I try to move forward, to reach the woman holding my baby, but I can't move. She's a tiny woman dressed in a long gown of royal blue. Her hair is as pale as moonbeams and longer than mine ever was, hanging down about her shoulders to her waist, shielding most of her face. I don't recognize her. Her attention is on Caroline, watching the water drip over her head. In the woman's eyes I see aged wisdom. Her features change from young, to old and wizened, then young again. *Give me my baby back*, I scream from my seat, but she only smiles at me, and looks adoringly down at my little girl. *My* little girl.

I wake with arms that ache as if they've been carrying loads of firewood up a mountainside, and a heart that feels like it's trying to pump molasses through my veins. I feel weighted down and lifeless, but calm, as if I'm being carried along in the eye of the worst storm imaginable.

I fall into a sound, exhausted sleep and don't wake until noon. I feel coated in the ugliness of my dreams. I need to get out, away from the pool house. I need to let the air blow over my face and sweep away the clouds in my mind.

I am ravenously hungry and can think of nothing I want except a crepe from Café Soleil. I riffle through my drawers for jeans and a passable shirt, and head to the shower to wash away the remnants of the dream. The water pours down on me, enveloping me in a rush of steam, and beats me with a stream of water upon my flesh, but it only revives the dreams, the pool, the water, my baby.

I pull on my clothes and head downtown, hoping lunch and air will ease my burden.

When I reach Patton Avenue, I keep going down the block. I feel beckoned. Perhaps another book from the library. Maybe a pastry from the bakery. But that's not it. I keep going and come to a standstill at the corner, the basilica towering over me.

I stare up at it stupidly. Lilly has bewitched me or something. A church doesn't call someone, least of all me. From the outside it doesn't even appeal to me, despite its fame. It's old architecture, stone with twin bell towers, built up next to the road. There's no sweeping lawn and walkway welcoming wanderers. Of course, a person can't live here without knowing something about it. I've walked by it a million times and seen it from distant hills. I am familiar with its massive stone structure and legendary dome roof. It's as much a landmark to western North Carolina as Mr. Vanderbilt's house, a statement of continuity through a hundred years, designed by Rafael Guastavino, the Biltmore architect. As he had for the mansion, Guastavino gathered bits of artwork from around the globe to edify the structure — statues, mosaics and whatnot. I've heard tales of a painting of Mary damaged in a war that tears itself anew every time it's repaired, and of miracles granted to those who enter the church. Despite the changes in people, in lifestyle, in the failure of the Vanderbilt family to dwell even the span of a single generation in the spectacular house on the hill, the church remains as the architect intended — not a moneychanger's attraction, but a house of worship.

From God's sky view, it must be an icon, but from the street, it's just an old stone building sitting on the edge of the sidewalk with a white stone carving over giant wooden doors. The bell towers are too high to appreciate, and the roof is hidden from view. I've never really looked at it as more than a piece of history.

A heavily bearded homeless man with a tent pitched on the grassy border of the ill-kept parking lot stares at me as if I'm the odd one in the scene. Cars whiz by, their tires whirling on the pavement with exclamations of places to go and people to see. I have no more direction in my life than the homeless man. Perhaps less. That's what I've come looking for.

I turn away to head back to the library when I see a figure out of the corner of my eye, like last time. It's a woman with a bundle held to her chest. Blankets. A baby. I look at her face and gasp. It's the woman from my dream, young and serene, fine boned. I realize it's not hair I saw in my dream; it's a cloth draped over her head and shoulders, flowing out like a cape behind her. I'm sure the bundle of baby is Caroline, right there in her arms. She races into the church in a fluid movement, a blur.

I stand shocked a moment. *My baby.*

I run across the road, seize the heavy latch and step inside.

I remember little of my previous rushed entry and exit with Lilly. Today I pause. The reception area is dim and castle-like, empty except for a small table of prayer books, cards, and brochures set out to answer visitors' questions. To the left is a vestibule hidden by a wrought-iron fence. I step inside. Candles surround an image of a little boy wearing a crown, his arms stretched skyward. *Infant of Prague*, it says, and I suspect it is Jesus as a child, but I'm not sure.

The woman is nowhere in sight.

Another person, a middle-aged businessman, enters the main doors and passes through swinging doors adorned with leather and stained glass that lead to the sanctuary. I follow, easing the door open with trepidation. The man walks forward a few steps, then falls to his knees in the aisle, his gaze trained first upon the crucifix on the altar, and then toward an alcove off to the right. "Praise be to you, Lord Jesus Christ," he whispers to the air. He makes the sign of the cross and eases into a pew, then lays his head in his hands in prayer.

As I take in my surroundings, my senses are overwhelmed. This isn't an open space with pews and an open pulpit with a microphone. It's dark and silent, full of ancient mystery foreign to me. Stone walls and domed ceiling cast me into another time, with carvings and artwork at every turn. I can scarcely take it all in. Along each wall are alcoves housing statues. Saints, I presume, as gray and timeless as the walls so that my eyes flicker over them for mere seconds before being drawn to the altar, to the blood-red backdrop and the crucifix it frames. Jesus hangs there on the cross, a nearly life-size replica of the man, his head drooping to his chest, his skin sunken around his ribcage. I am struck by the scene as if I've never known about the crucifixion because it glares at me from the altar and forces me to face the truth of what was done to this man, this son of God, in the name of faith. His suffering hangs there daring me to look away, to ignore his sacrifice.

But I do look away. I ignore the mosaics on the wall, carvings calling my name from their century-old faces of stone. I have to find my baby.

There are a couple of people near the front of the church — an old man and his wife, and a group sitting in an alcove to the right. I don't see the lady from the street.

Where is she?

I know in my heart it can't really be my baby. I've faced the fact that she's gone. She's dead. And yet, I still want to linger, to see if the woman returns. And to see what these people do.

I watch the man praying. I want to ask him where she may have gone. He's obviously comfortable in this place. He's deep in prayer, worshiping God. I imagine that's how Saint Thérèse prayed. I take a deep breath, wanting that feeling to take over me so that I can feel the light, the hope, the love. I want to be overwhelmed with emotion. I want to be carried away to somewhere full of such deep compassion and faith like him, but I feel like a jack-o-lantern, carved out, bearing an immovable expression. I know only fear and sorrow and regret. I know love and hate live entwined within me, but they are uncontrollable reactions to life. Did this man learn to love God, or did it just happen, like the burst of love I felt at the birth of my children? I can't *make* myself love someone. I don't think I can make myself not hate someone, either. As much as I love Sinclair, I can't help but hate him, too, for the loss of Caroline. That is my problem, the hole I've dug myself into.

I feel wooden standing by the door. Embarrassment makes me want to leave, but I feel incapable of leaving. I slip into a seat and watch.

The interior is dim but fragrant with candle wax, and vibrating with the quiet murmur of prayers from the alcove at the front of the church, where a small group kneels, heads bowed. I wonder why they are grouped there.

I look more closely at the statues. To my right, high up on the wall in a tall brick archway, a cement woman stares soulfully across the room. Further along, a statue of a man dressed in long robes and crowned like an early Saint Nicholas stands with a staff in his hand. Two other statues perch on the opposite wall, figures from history I can't identify. But none of them captures my attention like the altar. There, flanking Jesus are tile mosaics of six saints. Or are they angels?

As I sit there, staring at the grandeur, I find myself becoming more grounded. I'm discovering a new quiet place within myself, and yet it's coming from somewhere outside of me. My attention rests again on the crucifix. I think about this man, Jesus, whom so much of the world worships, and I wonder at his suffering. I have suffered all my life and yet not suffered at all, not like him, not physically upon a cross. Is that what draws people to him?

I turn away from the cross. It hurts too much to look at it, and that's not where the lifeline is. It is a statue like all the others. It's not real. It can't talk to me or sweep away the agony in my soul.

There are areas off to either side of the altar — bays, rooms, chapels — I don't know what they might call them, but they have pews and candles and statues. I look to the one on the right, where the people are kneeling and praying, and my heart pounds with expectation. I slip from the pew and move forward, but I feel so ignorant that I stop midway to slide into another pew to watch them. A man lights a candle and makes a sign of the cross, touching his forehead, his chest, his shoulders. I don't understand why. Two women kneel, one praying, one weeping. Another holds a rosary, the beads slipping rhythmically through her fingers as her lips move silently over words I don't recognize. Their actions are so foreign, I feel like I'm visiting an alien planet. I don't speak their body language. Their rituals are mystical to me.

I close my eyes and concentrate, at first too much. I concentrate on trying to find myself, but I'm so tangled in my own life, I am enveloped in darkness and despair, caught in a web of knots and lies. The blackness of my life rises in my veins like boiling pitch to fill my organs.

I feel like an outsider here, unable to reach in and grasp the sweet honey from the hive that the others seem to be drinking so freely.

No one is sitting in the chapel to my left, but I see candles flickering beneath a picture, and I wonder if it's the damaged one. I move toward it, keeping my footfalls as noiseless as possible.

It's a Spanish print titled *Virgin Mary of Guadalupe.* To my right is a painting: *The Visitation of Mary to Elizabeth,* ancient, but in good repair. I turn to the front of this small chapel area and see above me in an arched alcove trimmed with sculpted doves, a statue of the Virgin Mary, her eyes turned skyward while angels, bent in prayer, kneel at her feet. As I look up at her, I find my eyes drawn upward, as hers are, and gradually I quit thinking of myself and think only of my nightmares, of Seth and Caroline, of life. I slide into a seat and stare at her. As I study her, recognition dawns on me. She is the lady in my dream, and the very same woman I saw running into the church. She is the one who was holding my baby.

My baby. How could you take my baby? The pitch in my veins rises to my head and pours out in tears. *I may be a horrible person, but I was her mother. She's my baby. How could you take her away from me?*

A door in the side of the chapel opens and a middle-aged man, lean and tall, steps out. He is dressed in black with a white clerical collar, and looks straight at me. I bite back my tears. I've been caught by the priest. He's going to know I'm not Catholic. Someone told him I'm here, and he's going to kick me out.

I'm too insecure to stand and face him. I turn my head stiffly toward the statue and stare at Mary as I defiantly wipe away my tears.

The priest pauses a moment, glances to the church entrance, then at his watch, and then at me as he weighs something in his mind. His ruddy complexion speaks of an active man who loves the outdoors, and yet as he eases between the seats and sits beside me, he doesn't move like an athlete. He moves like a lion, I assume from years of making his way quietly around all the sacredness of this church. He has good eyes — green and gold with a sad kind of love shining out. Boyhood freckles blend with age spots, and his hair is white. "Mary will listen to your problems if you need her to, you know," he says.

"I'm not Catholic. I'm not praying to some dumb statue." I feel like Lilly, pushing away the hands that want to help me.

He looks at the floor, his green eyes lighting up as he tries to hide a smile, and I like him, despite my snide reply.

"We don't pray to statues," he says. "We surround ourselves with statues to remind us of how Mary and Jesus and the saints lived their lives."

Anger wells in me, and I feel the need to shove his religion in his face. "Idolatry." I say it defensively even as I silently admit I've been talking to Saint Thérèse.

Even that doesn't anger him. He chuckles. "They're like family photos. We don't worship them or the Virgin Mother. But we do ask the saints to pray for us."

I think of my Saint Thérèse holy card and realize I understand in a way that I never would have a few months ago.

He sees me mulling over his words, and continues. "We often ask friends to pray for us. Why do we bother doing that?"

"I don't."

"But you know you should." He sits back in his seat, settling in for more than the one short statement he'd intended. "Did you know Jesus performed his first miracle because his mother asked him? He said it wasn't his time, but she sent the waiters over to him anyway. He told the waiters to fill barrels with water, and Jesus turned it into wine, all because his mother asked him to. That was the wedding in Cana."

I try to imagine being the mother of God's son and asking him to perform a little miracle for me. Wine at a wedding almost seems an unchristian miracle to have asked for, similar to saying, *I sure would like a steak dinner, son, instead of this meatloaf.* It sounds like something I'd do.

The priest looks at me. "Because Jesus made it obvious that he honors his mother, we ask her to intercede on our behalf, to ask her Son to do favors for us. Men in general tend to have soft spots for their mothers."

He hasn't met Seth.

But then I remember how Seth used to make me cards and pictures in preschool, and how he brought me drinks when I nursed Caroline, and found me things to watch on television when I rocked her to sleep in the afternoons. Maybe Seth doesn't see me enough anymore to remember I'm his mother.

I stare at Mary. She had to have been perfect. God picked her out. She raised his son. She has nothing in common with me. "How can she relate to me? I bet she never yelled at Jesus or made stupid mistakes. She wasn't filled with all this . . . this bad stuff, this failure."

"Certainly she was. She was human." He looks up at her stone image. "Did you know she lost Jesus for three days? She and Joseph were on a trip with a whole caravan of family and friends. They were out on the road a full day before they realized Jesus wasn't with them."

I look up at the perfect mother. "You're kidding."

"Nope. Seriously." He must love to tell stories. He leans toward me, his eyes lit up as he continues, earnest and yet sad. "They were frantic. They thought he was hanging out with cousins or something, but he wasn't. Eventually they found him in a temple talking to the rabbi."

"I bet they didn't yell at him, did they? How could you yell at God's son?"

"I don't know if they yelled, but they did reprimand him. Jesus just looked at them and said, 'Why did you not look for me in my Father's house?'"

I hear a whisper through my mind — Caroline's voice. *You've found me in my Father's house.*

Could Caroline truly be here?

Then reality screams at me. I wonder what I'm doing in God's house, talking to a priest. If he knew how horrible I was, he'd kick me out. If he knew how our baby died, he would be disgusted. He would step around me like scum, like everybody else who knows. I want him to know. I want to shock him. I want him to know I'm nothing like Mary. "The point is they *found* him. He wasn't dead."

"No." He holds his breath for a mere second, his back stiffening just slightly, his eyes clouding over. "She let him die on a cross."

"She didn't have any control over that. Soldiers dragged him away, didn't they?"

"Yes," he says, looking me in the eye, his voice begging me to understand, "but she knew it was coming. She knew he would be beaten and crucified, and she stood aside and let him do what he'd explained he would have to do to redeem the world."

"But it wasn't her fault. She didn't have to feel guilty about it."

Dismay crosses his brow as he leans forward. "Do you think that made her feel any better about it? Do you think she went to sleep that night, snuggled into bed without a care?"

His words slap me across the face.

He sits back again, his hands folded in his lap, watching me digest Mary's emotions. Her anguish is mingling with mine. Or maybe mine is mingling with hers. A bond forms between us in the sharing of our loss.

It settles in me, and I sigh. "I guess it doesn't matter how children die; part of the parent dies with them."

The priest isn't done. He takes my hand. "Now you have to hear the hard part."

I look up at him. The Irish laugh lines around his eyes belie the solemnity he now bears.

"His crucifixion was everyone's fault, just as surely as if we hammered the nails in ourselves. He died for us. We killed him. We crucified him with our sins."

Great. I need a bit more guilt on my shoulders. I wonder where Lilly is now. Where's the healer she was talking about? He must only hang out in the closet.

"He died so that our sins would be forgiven. All we have to do is ask forgiveness."

I want like anything to pull my hand out of his clasp and run like the wind, but I imagine the Bridge Club wagging a finger at my lack of manners, so I stay put, hoping he's almost done. I look him straight in the face, hoping that will make him stall out, but what I see is that he doesn't really seem to be talking to me. His eyes have gone glassy, as if he's not seeing further than something inside himself.

I sit quietly and watch him covertly, wondering what secret he's aching over. After a minute or two, he comes back to himself, glances at his watch, and turns to me. "Don't try to understand it all at once. Just open your heart and pray, and the rest will come with time."

I nod. "Thank you."

He eases himself to a stand. "Maybe we can talk again. You're welcome here any time. " He strides away, turns, and genuflects toward the altar, then jogs down the aisle to the front entrance.

I think of all he's said, and all Saint Thérèse teaches about love and faith even in the bleakest darkness, and I want to believe. I really want to. I want to sit here and have God open a window to heaven so I can see Caroline and know I will be with her someday. But I am filled with doubt. How can asking God for forgiveness take away the ulcer in my soul?

CHAPTER TWENTY-SIX

❧

Lilly doesn't know I've been to the basilica. I'm not going to tell her yet. I want to dwell on all these new thoughts privately before I share them with her. I pretend to be absorbed in my latest library book.

She searches through the stack of books until she finds one of interest, and reaches up to turn on the standing lamp. Her peasant-blouse sleeve slips down, revealing a bruise encircling her arm.

"Lilly, what happened?"

She pulls her sleeve back down. "Nothing."

"Who did it?"

"It's nothing. I tried to get away."

"From who? Who did it?"

"Doesn't matter."

Her attention remains fixed on the book.

I string together past events. "Was it those boys who were hanging around out by the oak tree?"

"Give it up, Rachel."

"Who are they? Drug dealers?"

She puts on her teenage *you're retarded* look. "Duh! Am I buying drugs from them? No. Have you ever seen me high? No. If anyone around here has a drug problem, it's you and Colette. So leave me alone."

I feel sure those boys have something to do with Steven's death and Lilly's abuse. "Are you sleeping with one of them?"

She slams the book closed. "Do I act like I'm hooked on some stupid guy? Do you see me hanging out somewhere waiting to run into them? Do you see me moping around, writing out some idiot's name on notebooks or staring at my cell phone, waiting for a text to roll in? No. I don't talk to anyone. I don't go anywhere. Give me a break. I thought we understood each other better than that."

I am taken back as the reality of her existence rises before me. Steven wasn't just her true love; he was her only friend. Now, by choice and circumstance, we are each other's only friends. We are both social outcasts. I wonder if hers is by choice, or maybe because Henry won't let her go out. I gaze at the floor and whisper, "Why don't you have friends, Lilly?"

She shrugs. "It's too much trouble."

"Too much trouble?"

She picks at the carpet. "I can't call. I can't text. I'm not allowed to go out. If he catches me online . . ." she looks up at me with fire in her eyes, "it doesn't matter because I don't like people anyway."

Her admission says more than she knows. I see her, the girl in class who can't participate in anything, who has an attitude because she's built a wall of self-defense. She's convinced herself that she doesn't like her classmates so that she doesn't have to face the fact that they don't like her. She's made it *her* decision instead of *their* decision.

I push her a tad more. "Then why do you come see me so often?"

She stiffens. "Because Steven liked you, and you need help."

"Because Steven liked me?"

I see the shell breaking as her shoulders shake and her voice quivers. "I feel like I can hold onto a piece of him when I'm with you. You let me remember. You let me miss him."

I pull her into my arms, her taut, thin body, and hold her there until she softens and leans into me to cry, but she allows herself to give way for only a minute before she pulls away and wipes her nose on her sleeve. "I'm fine."

"You're not fine. Someone is abusing you. If it's not those boys, who is it? That moose of a yardman?"

She smirks. "Bruce? Wow. No." She shakes her head.

"Have you told your parents? Does your dad know?"

She snorts. "Just leave it alone, okay? Stay out of it. You'll only make things worse."

Her face remains stoic.

"Look, if you won't tell me who he is, at least tell me what happened."

"He was ticked that I said no to him."

"He must have squeezed the tar out of you."

"It's nothing new. Leave it alone."

"It's wrong, Lilly."

"Could have been worse. He could have slammed me against the wall."

"I'll put a stop to it."

She shakes her head.

"I'll call the authorities."

"Please don't."

"Is it a teacher?"

She looks at me with such pleading eyes, I drop the subject. But I *will* keep an eye on her.

Me. A crazy, doped-up woman with a failed life track.

CHAPTER TWENTY-SEVEN

❧

I see through the back door that Colette is arranging a bouquet of flowers on her dining-room table, so I enter without knocking. "Did Henry send the flowers?"

"Yes."

"What's the occasion?"

She glares at me. "No reason. Because he loves me. Some women don't have any problems holding onto their husbands, thank you. I couldn't ask for a better husband." The statement sits there between us like a challenge. "I've had more than I can stand of people pointing fingers at us for everything under the sun. I'd expect better from you. Henry has done everything he can to take proper care of us, to keep the media away, and help with the investigation, and he's never stopped being the best lover I've ever had. You of all people ought to understand what we've had to put up with. That's what the roses are for, because everything is so right between us despite everything. Wonderful. Perfect. In fact, never better."

The lady doth protest too much, methinks.

"My apologies. Good to know you two are solid." I say it, but I wonder. She's right, though, about being in the public eye; I've been under the microscope and know what a strain it is on a marriage.

Betts brings us both cups of coffee, mocha roast to celebrate the icy breeze swirling around outside. The aroma wafts around me and wraps me in memories of happy Christmas breakfasts with the Winters family. My heart slows. My body relaxes. I see us by a roaring fire, laughing, talking, hugging. I want to stay in the memory, but then I remember the reason for my visit.

"Do you think somebody at school is picking on Lilly?"

Colette is preoccupied with a rose that won't settle into the arrangement quite the way she wants. "I wouldn't be surprised. She's not the easiest person to get along with. Too willful. What makes you ask?"

"I noticed a bad bruise on her arm, like someone snatched her roughly."

Colette laughs. "Oh, that. I did that. She was in my medicine cabinet, trying to get into my prescriptions."

"Oh." I picture it in my mind: Lilly sitting on the edge of the sink, reaching up to the top shelf to pull down a bottle of Valium, and Colette walking in behind her, yanking her from the counter and cussing her out. I've been subjected to worse. In fact, I'd subject her to worse myself if she was really after drugs.

I remind myself that Lilly is a teenager; she is me in an earlier life. She can't be taken at her word. And if she won't tell me what's going on, what can I do?

Moonlight suffuses the dark with its clandestine glow as I try to shake the remnants of a bad dream about the horrors of my life, about guys in high school and Kyle-the-pervert.

I force them away. I think of Sinclair, only Sinclair. I am a new person with him. I mentally wrap myself in his body. I feel his lips upon mine. I am safe in his arms.

I drift back to sleep, watching myself with him as if I am floating above the bed, reveling in our two bodies entwined. He is my protector, shielding me. I am safe. I let myself be there with him, feeling his warm breath fill my ears with soft whispers, his hands claiming me as his own.

I sink into my body to feel his love. There is an aura around us. I feel like my body is glowing in his embrace. We are solitary in an eternal night, sheltered in peace, two lone figures made into one, secluded in the dark.

In my sleep, I turn my head and open my eyes, expecting nothingness. Instead I see Colette.

Is she really there?

Her face comes closer, more menacing, her hand raised with a dagger. "Stay away from him. He's mine, you hear me? He's mine."

Him? My head has been so full of Sinclair, he is all I can think of. Why would Colette warn me away from Sinclair? "Sinclair is my husband," I say.

"Henry! Get away from Henry! I knew I would catch you together."

Henry?

My eyes pop open.

I am alone. I'm not with Sinclair or Henry.

Colette's voice is still ringing in my head, her words running through again and again until I remember an argument I had with her. She was at my house, standing in the foyer, red-faced and flustered. She was screaming at me, accusing me of sleeping with Henry. "He's having an affair; I've seen the signs. And I know it's with you."

She wouldn't be consoled. I couldn't stop her tirade and threats.

I sit up in bed as I try to remember how it ended. *When did we have that argument?* And how did we get beyond it, to the point that she would allow me to live in her pool house within easy grasp of her wayward husband? Is her demeanor now just an act?

Maybe the fight never really happened. Maybe the memory is just another bad nightmare I can't shake off. *What really happened?*

The answer won't come. I wonder if I made myself forget for some reason. But why?

I bury my head under my pillow and try to recreate the scene in my mind. What happened? Why does it feel like a black hole in my head?

Please, God, make me whole again. Let me remember. If you can really hear me, Saint Thérèse, help me!

Nothing comes.

But it will. I trust it will.

CHAPTER TWENTY-EIGHT

I wake to a new day and need something to occupy my mind to chase away the horrible remnants of the dream, of the forgotten argument. I plan to cook something scrumptious to take up to Colette, something to warm her heart. Maybe I can lead the conversation to find out more about the forgotten argument.

Cooking has always been my secret weapon. When I gave up the bad-girl image in my teens to hang out with Jennifer, I was inspired by a cooking show to start trying gourmet recipes. I made up grocery lists with all kinds of ingredients we'd never kept in our two kitchen cabinets. Mama gave up shopping for me after two weeks. "I can't find this stuff you have listed. What's wrong with fish sticks?" she asked, plopping three boxes on the counter. That was easy for her to say. She went out to eat with her bozos at least three nights a week. I was the one stuck with fish sticks. So, I convinced her to give me the grocery money. I had to shop frugally. Spices were priced like gold, but lasted a long time, so I ate fish sticks and rice three weeks running until I'd accumulated what I needed. Then, I started to cook.

My first few attempts were runny when they were supposed to be thick sauces. The meat was overly spiced and undercooked, but I didn't give up. Before long, I was preparing better meals than they served downtown at The House of Fine Cuisine. Mama started staying home for meals. Then her boyfriends started eating with us, too. But when winter came along and night descended early, Mama dashed through the house long enough to change clothes and stayed gone.

I started going home with Jennifer after school and taught her how to cook. Her mother was a fairly formidable cook, given her grand size and need to keep up with a very large appetite, but more in the fish-stick range of expertise than chicken à la king.

In tenth grade, we signed up for home economics. We didn't learn much. In fact, we ended up teaching Ms. Smith a few things. But nothing keeps boys away from girls faster than knowing they're taking Home Ec. It reeks of *I'm looking for a husband*. That was fine with both of us.

In the long run, the cooking lessons were a good thing for Jennifer. She studied business at Meredith College, then started a catering company. She lives high off the hog in Durham, serving pâté to professors and their wives at their cocktail parties and collegiate functions.

But the cooking lessons also served me well. Sinclair's mother had accepted me only to keep from alienating her son, and I was determined to prove my worth. I figured I had two options: One was to really suck up to her, something I'd had my fill of over the years. The other was to get in her face and just boldly state she could quit looking down her nose at me. With Sinclair at my side, I finally felt a strength and confidence that didn't exist before. I became a person, not a puppet. I had married her son, married into position and wealth every bit as she had. Why should I be scared of her or anyone else in her pissy society?

So I decided to show her how many ways I could outdo her. First, I sewed her a quilt as a gift, a marriage-ring pattern as old as time, in her favorite colors — baby blue and yellow, a washed-out version of Duke's school colors that Joe kept their house drenched in. In the bottom corner, I cross-stitched a square that said, *A lifelong union*.

Then I invited her and Joe over to supper. Normally, they had us over to their house. She loved playing hostess and catering to her son's whims, so it was unusual for them to have supper with us. It was her purpose in life to entertain, and entertain often.

I set the table with our fine china. Our crystal glinted under the chandelier. Wine stood ready on the buffet.

It wasn't the table or wine Sinclair's mother commented on when she entered the house, though. It was the menu. "It smells divine," she said. "What is it?"

"*Poitrine de Veau Farcie*," I replied. I didn't grant her the English version. I knew she hadn't a clue what it was.

"I had no idea you spoke Italian," she said.

"It's French."

"Oh."

She visibly shrank just a tad. For a moment, I felt like a louse. She may have talked bad about me when we first met, and she probably gossiped madly about me to all her cronies, but she did let me marry her son. Then I remembered that the outcome would serve a greater purpose. We would come out of this as equals.

As the veal came out of the oven, I went into action, straining the pan juices and vegetables, pushing them through a sieve with a wooden spoon, and scraping them into a pan to reheat with olives, pine nuts and parsley until the sauce came to a boil. Leaving that for a few minutes, I strained the tiny new potatoes and quickly heated a puree of green beans.

She stood in a corner, looking baffled and helpless. "You've worked so hard on all this. Really, it wasn't necessary. I'd have been just as happy with fried chicken and mashed potatoes."

"It's nothing," I said with a smile. "We eat like this all the time."

"You do?"

Sinclair arrived with his father, his entrance timed perfectly as if we'd conspired beforehand. "Oh, shoot. Not *Poitrine de Veau Farcie* again? We just had that last week. I was hoping it was *Poulet Vallee d'Auge*."

"*Demain, mon cherie*," I replied with a twinkling thank-you in my eye.

"Sure, tomorrow," he muttered. He turned his back to his mother as he poured himself a glass of wine and grinned at me with pride sparkling in his eyes.

"I had no idea," his mother mumbled again.

Exactly. I smiled. "You're right. We hardly know a thing about each other, do we?"

Point made. She began to see me in a new light. Until the accident, that is. Then she remembered where I came from, and made sure everyone else did as well. Not that I ever heard it from her myself. I just felt it. I felt it in people's stares, in whispered words, in closed doors. I'd lived up to my past, is what she probably told them. A good-for-nothing destined to fail.

That's why Sinclair ended up with Seth. I'm sure of it.

So, I'm back to being the girl from the wrong side of the tracks, but Colette has never cared where I came from. Or maybe she does. Maybe that's why she suspected an affair between Henry and me.

I will ply her with food to find out exactly what happened, to find out how much of my shattered memory holds truth.

Today's menu will be something special, something I haven't attempted in a while, something to loosen Colette's tongue.

I reach into the back of the bottom cabinet for my double boiler and my pasta pot. The pasta pot feels unusually heavy. As I set it on the counter, something clanks inside. A smaller pot? No. It's a heavy black metal cylinder. A flashlight. *The* flashlight? It must be! It's Steven's; I recognize it from the night in the grove.

I'm not sure what to do. Should I call the police? If so, they'll want to know why. I'm not supposed to know there was a flashlight involved in the murder.

I pull it out with a paper towel wrapped around it. It looks clean. No blood or hair. Nothing that I can see.

I set it on the end of the counter and stare at it as I scrub out the pot and rinse it with boiling water.

Lilly shows up as I stir the crème sauce in the double boiler. I glance at the intercom. It appears to be turned off, but creepy thoughts have eaten at me for the past hour, and I don't want to speak aloud for fear of being heard by some unseen person, so I nod toward the flashlight.

"Took you long enough."

"You knew it was there?"

"No. But I knew it was somewhere. It was missing from his closet."

"I better call the police."

"To tell them you found his flashlight? They searched the premises and didn't find it, right? So it's not like you were hiding evidence."

"That's true."

"Did they ever find the knife?"

She shakes her head, not really listening. She's staring at the flashlight. She walks forward and takes it in both hands and clasps it to her chest, then settles on the couch with it nestled in her arms like a baby. Her body shakes with sobs.

Cooking for Colette is no longer important. Digging for answers can wait. What Lilly needs right now is compassion. I sit beside her and take her into my arms.

CHAPTER TWENTY-NINE

✽

Donald Doc is distracted today. Or maybe he's bored. He's not twisting his pen around in thought. He's not firing questions at me. Even if I did trust him, which I don't, I've realized he is never going to be my doorway into self-revelation. I decide to turn the tables for a change.

"Dr. Arick tell me: What do you think of God?"

His face flashes a *what* for a second before he regains his composure. "That's a rather open-ended question."

"Do you think he's for real?"

He looks uncertain, as if he's afraid of being sued if he answers. "It's *your* thoughts and feelings that are important here."

I decide to help him out. "I'm thinking of going to church. I used to go, but I was just attending, not really talking to God. And I'm wondering if it will help."

He actually smiles, so I ask him again, a different way. "Do you believe in God — that he can wipe our slates clean so we can start over?"

"A belief in a higher power can be very reassuring to people. A higher power has been utilized for decades to help alcoholics through recovery. There are also support groups and prayer meetings available at churches. You might feel safer sharing painful emotions and personal problems at a support group rather than with family or friends who often don't know what to say."

Painful memories and personal problems. That is how he classifies my life. Everything I was and am reduced to a definition.

He clicks his pen open and begins to write. "Have you chosen a church to attend?"

I won't give him the satisfaction. "It was only a philosophical question."

The gleam in his eyes melts away with disappointment.

I wake to a quiet rustling outside. I peek out the back door, expecting it to be Bruce the yardman trimming bushes or something, but it's a detective brushing against the foliage as he paces off the length of the yard. I consider opening the door to tell him about the flashlight, to ask what evidence they've found. I go so far as putting my hand on the doorknob, but I change my mind. I'm afraid. I'm afraid they'll implicate me somehow, and I have enough to deal with.

I crawl back into bed to read and doze the day away.

Lilly perches on the edge of my bed after school and pulls the Saint Thérèse book off my nightstand. "Did you finish reading it?"

"Almost." I think about my pleas for the restoration of my memory and the healing of my life and marriage, and even for the flame of faith to burn within me. I haven't seen answers to any of them. "I've tried praying. It doesn't help."

"She said she prays even when she feels horrible, even when she feels like her faith has dried up." She picks up the book and flips through it to a place she had underlined. "*For me, prayer is an upward leap of the heart, an untroubled glance toward heaven, a cry of gratitude and love which I utter from the depths of sorrow as well as from the heights of joy. It has a supernatural grandeur which expands the soul and unites it with God. I say an Our Father or a Hail Mary when I feel so spiritually barren that I cannot summon up a single worthwhile thought. Those two prayers fill me with rapture, and feed and satisfy my soul.*"

As I listen to Lilly read, her attitude is hard to mesh with Saint Thérèse's words. She's so abrasive, so prickly and rude, so opposite to everything Saint Thérèse teaches that it's hard for me to believe that she truly takes to heart what she's quoting.

I don't say that to her, though. I remember how I was in my youth when my life was so confused. If having an attitude preserves her well-being, perhaps God and Saint Thérèse understand that.

I wish I could believe as strongly as her present voice suggests she does.

"At least Saint Thérèse felt him in the beginning," I say. "I've never felt him."

"Because you're still too caught up in yourself."

That's more of an insult than I'll take even from Lilly. "Try looking in a mirror, kid." I walk out of the bedroom to the kitchen nook.

She follows me. "You would have loved Caroline no matter what she did, right? And you love Seth even when he doesn't love you. God's the same way. Doesn't matter if you love him or recognize he's there. He loves you anyway."

I have to admit that she's right. That is what Saint Thérèse said. Maybe it's working for Lilly even if she doesn't show it. "So praying and going to that church, they've helped you come to terms with Steven's murder?"

"Yup."

I see a huge ravine yawn between us. "How can you say that so flippantly? Doesn't it eat at you every day? He's dead and there's nothing you can do about it. You can't bring him back. You'll never see him again."

"I'll see him in heaven. I know that. He's the one who took me to church."

She sounds like a textbook. "I thought Steven belonged to that little white church in town where he went to youth group."

"He went to youth group there, but we attended the service at the basilica. They have a lot of different Mass times, so it was easy to go and not rile Colette or Henry."

A household where kids had to sneak off to church — that was a new dimension to add to my image of Henry and Colette.

"But how has it helped? How did it make the pain go away?"

"Acceptance of God and living for love didn't make it go away. It helps me deal with it. Jesus helps me carry the burden."

"You could help your burden by telling the police everything you know, by helping to solve his murder."

She places her hands on the counter and leans forward, her eyes as serious as I've ever seen them. "They aren't ever going to solve his murder. They botched the investigation step after step."

"Purposely?"

"Who knows? They let friends and family into the area before they finished gathering evidence. The fibers they collected turned out to be useless. Most were from us, you included."

"He died in my apartment."

"Exactly. There were a few others from strangers, but they haven't connected them to anyone. They've been through everybody at school, teachers and so forth."

"But they haven't closed the case."

She shrugs.

"There was somebody nosing around the yard just this morning."

"Bet he didn't find anything."

"You think somebody paid them to quit?"

"You said it, not me."

"So we are back at square one. How can you set that aside?"

"Because in the long run, it doesn't matter. Steven is at peace. *Grant me the serenity to accept the things I cannot change, the courage to change the things I can, and the wisdom to know the difference.*"

"Sure. That's why you're Miss Bright-and-Cheery."

She turns away and sinks into the couch. "Some things are harder to accept than death. I offer them up, but I still have to endure them."

Hard to accept — her bruise. "Let me see that bruise again." She lifts her sleeve. The patches of black and blue are fading to brown and yellow.

"Colette says you were getting something out of the medicine cabinet. Drugs, she says."

"Ah, that would be this bruise." She lifts her other sleeve where a new bruise is still rather black.

"So, you were in the medicine cabinet."

"Yes."

"Getting what? Please tell me it was Tylenol."

"Birth-control pills. She confiscated mine, so I went to get hers."

Colette's proclamation comes rushing back to me. *She's a slut.*

I think back to my teenage years. I sure wasn't perfect. My mama wouldn't let her boyfriends smack me around, but she smacked me when I deserved it, and it's easy to see Lilly isn't the easiest person to live with. Still, I wonder what's really going on in that house.

The meds are wearing off. The thoughts pounding in my brain are too loud. I need a distraction. I need company.

I walk across the pool patio, through the wrought-iron gate, and down the path that leads to the back deck. Bruce the yardman is nipping brown leaves from the resplendent rhododendrons. I sidestep him without a glance. I see Colette through the wide glass windows seated on the sofa, staring at the television. Colette rarely watches television, especially during the day, so I wonder if something else has been exposed on the news that has her transfixed.

I slip in without her noticing and settle into the distant armchair to catch what's on the screen without disturbing her concentration.

Betts comes to stand in the corner of the room and watches me with scornful eyes.

It's not news. It's a home video of Steven as a child, running down the beach with a kite trailing behind him. He's wearing blue bathing trunks that have slid to his hips, and his hair is stiff with sand and salt. The kite keeps bobbing from sand to sky, bumping along in rhythm to his faltering steps as he runs while glancing back to see if it's taken flight. His figure gets smaller and smaller until he trips over a shell seeker and tumbles to the sand. The kite wafts along and lands on top of him.

The camera tilts sideways as the cameraman sprints across the distance to help him up. Colette is there brushing him off, wiping the sand from his lips and hugging his face to her breasts. A hand, thick and muscular, definitely not Henry's, comes around the camera and tousles Steven's towhead. I've never seen a picture of Steven's father, but from this glimpse of his hand, I build a picture of him, heavyset and well built, and I wonder where Steven got his lanky, long bones.

"He was such a sweet thing back then," Colette muses aloud. "He loved me so much. I wish he could have stayed that way. So good. Such a good son. If only he hadn't grown up and changed."

I've invaded her private space. I stand to go and make it halfway to the door, my path blurred with tears floating unwillingly in my eyes.

"You don't have to go."

I don't answer. I feel like I've caught her naked in the middle of the day. I feel worse than naked.

I drive around a while. I go to the park. I sit in the grove. I think about how far I've come, and I realize that maybe Colette is falling into that same abyss. Maybe she needs me, and I have abandoned her.

I go back to her house, thinking we'll talk about Steven and Caroline, and cry on each other's shoulders.

The house is darker than usual. I drop my keys and pocketbook in the pool house and follow the walkway up to the back door. The television is flashing a myriad of colors on the dark wall. A light shines from the kitchen doorway, probably left on by Betts.

I step inside, my footfalls whispering in the silence. The television is muted. I stride across the room to the lone figure hunched on the sofa. I stop halfway there when I realize it's not Colette. "Oh, Henry. I'm sorry. I thought . . ."

"Colette's not here," he says, sitting up straighter. "Come join me."

I glance at the video. It's still Steven's childhood on replay.

"It was in the machine."

"I know. Colette was watching it earlier."

He nods. "She's never gotten over him."

Never gotten over him? Are men all the same? "I hope she still thinks about him every minute of the day! He was her son."

He frowns and points to the screen. "Not Steven. Her ex. She's always comparing us."

Men are so dense.

I debate the situation a moment, a part of me wanting to flee the house to return to my small prison of solitude, but a flash of memory assaults me — Henry bringing me a bottle of wine my first night in the pool house, setting it on the counter, telling me it might take the edge off the place, and patting my back as he left. He offered me comfort, such as it was, when I was at my lowest.

I sit beside him and place one hand on his shoulder. "I don't think that's why she was watching the video, Henry. She was thinking about how sweet Steven was when he was a little kid. Apparently men don't need those moments, but women do."

He evaluates me a moment before his arm slips up around my shoulders. "Some men do. We can comfort each other."

"Sure, Henry," I say in camaraderie. "I need a friend tonight."

"Me, too." He moves to the bar. "Let me fix you a drink."

"No thanks," I say.

"I hear you're getting off your meds. You need something to take the edge off."

I stare at the television. The sound is off. A five-year-old Steven moves to the staccato clinking of Henry's spoon against glass.

He passes one of the drinks to me and settles on the sofa at my side.

We sip at the drinks as we stare at the screen, at Steven playing with a young boy's abandon. I fight the emotions it creates. It's making me weepy. My head throbs with the effort of keeping my brain in check.

Henry leans toward me. He means to kiss me.

I push him away. "No, Henry."

He sits back. "Come on, now, darling. Who do you think you're fooling?"

"Huh?"

"You and I both went fishing for gold. We understand each other, don't we? We married for money. We scout for good loving."

Fishing for gold. Colette said that to me the day of that argument! *Henry went fishing for gold, and I was the lucky fish snagged on his hook.* She was yelling and crying. *He's having an affair.* The memory is there and gone again, whisked away into the mist of lost moments. "I don't know what you're talking about."

"Everyone knows about you, Rachel. Your mother-in-law has been clucking for months about her son's mistake in marrying you, bringing him down. And then you move in here and dance around in that pool house like a fish in a bowl, dancing and twirling. If that's not an open invitation . . . I knew you would come calling one of these nights. I've just been biding my time."

I pull away to stand. "Well, you can bide it from now till hell freezes over." Dancing around? I haven't! *When will this nightmare end? What's happened to my life?*

Henry's professional demeanor falls back into place. "I guess I misunderstood."

I smooth my shirt. "I guess so."

I pause at the door, feeling his gray eyes upon me, and notice just how hard they are. Business eyes, I'd always thought, but now I reconsider. Business? Or bitterness? I feel dizzy and sick to my stomach. I run all the way back to the pool house. I lock the doors and collapse on the sofa. I close my eyes, but the world keeps spinning around me.

CHAPTER THIRTY

※

He comes to me in the night, invading my sleep, intruding into my dream world, his hands grazing my skin, his lips seeking mine. I push him away, but he's too heavy, too strong. I'm a little girl again, a frail teenager. His face lingers over me. "Mama, Mama," I cry. And he is there, still pushing at me, his hands groping. His face. I see his face through my tears, at first as it was a decade ago, so pompous, his wide nose flaring with the effort, his pockmarked skin so oily, it gleams in the moonlight. I push at his oily face, his nose pressed to my flesh, his eyes soft in their sockets beneath my fingers, the wet of his mouth against my palms, trying to stop him, to shove him away.

I want to wake up, but I can't. I am chained to the nightmare.

He slaps me, his hand meeting the flesh of my face with all the power of his age and weight behind it, a hard blow that lights every nerve in my cheeks and knocks my jaw sideways.

For a moment I can't see. My eyes sting. My brain careens around in my skull. When my vision clears, it's not Kyle I'm grappling with; it's Henry.

I find my voice. "I said no. I said no!"

I beat at him. Laughter spills out of his mouth in breaths of damp vapor that swirl around the bed until we're hidden in a cocoon of murky fog, until his mirth becomes maniacal and his face spins in circles above me, faster and faster, creating a vortex my eyes can't follow. My brain begins to spin with it, purple, orange, red, and blue sweeping around me, a rainbow swirling rapidly, the colors mixing, melding, becoming black as the night.

And I awake.

Cold air sweeps through the room.

The glass doors are open.

When morning dawns, I am lying in a ball on the floor by the sofa with the blanket from my bed carefully tucked around me.

Lilly? Were you here?

Nothing moves but my eyelids flickering over my sleep-soaked eyes as I think back over the vaporous images of my restless night. How much was real? Or was it all a dream?

He is a pervert, Lilly said. Oh, Lilly! How did I not believe you? How did I not see it? The gifts, the control, the hardness in his eyes.

He's having an affair, Colette said.

Another memory comes to me. I had been to the mall that day. Seth ran up the steps ahead of me while I hauled the bags into the house.

The phone rang. Who called? I can't remember. Someone I had to talk to. Someone I couldn't put off. Snooty Maureen's mother, Mrs. Chilston. I had to be nice to her. Propriety. She was planning a luncheon. So many useless details to decide. She had to tell me everything. *Just be nice to her,* Sinclair had instructed when I complained about listening to her tedious plans and her strings of gossip. It was important to talk to her. She ran the women's auxiliary. She made me nervous. She could see through my thin disguise. I had to play the game. She represented all the old ladies of the town. If she rejected me, everyone would.

I walked through the house with the phone plastered to my ear and popped a video in for Seth in his bedroom. It was time for his nap. He crawled into bed with Binks, and I covered him up, so sweet against his pillow, Little Boy Blue asleep in the hay. He was engrossed in the video, his eyes drooping, before I closed his bedroom door.

I finally managed to get off the phone, but when I reached the foyer, Colette strode in, her face contorted with anger.

"I know you're sleeping with him," she said.

"With who?"

"Henry. He's having an affair. I see the signs. And I know it's you."

The whole argument comes flooding back, just like in my nightmare.

I was flabbergasted. I couldn't fathom ever having an affair with Henry. I didn't want anyone but Sinclair. "It's not me."

Her face was flushed with anger. Sweat beaded on her forehead. Her eyes were two dark slits spitting bullets at me. "Who else has reason? You're looking for another sugar daddy to jump into bed with. Well, let me tell you, if Henry leaves me, he won't get a dime. I'll leave him broke. He went fishing for gold, and I was the lucky fish snagged on his hook. He was in ruin from bad deals, and I saved him. It's my money, and I won't let him get his grubby hands on it. He ruined Marge, but he won't ruin me. I'm no fool."

I looked at her, and I knew what it was to be filled with that fear. For months, I had been living with the fear of Sinclair leaving me. An ulcer in the heart. But her theory was wrong. "I have no interest in Henry. Why would I want Henry?"

"Why would you want Henry? Because Sinclair is on his way out. You've told me yourself what's going on between him and Jocelyn. Everyone in town knows about it. You're a joke. Everyone laughs at the show you put on. You're old news."

I couldn't listen to her. I couldn't think about Jocelyn being with Sinclair. I moved toward the living room to the wet bar and poured myself a whiskey straight up. I swallowed one and then another. I wanted to drown the pain. "I love Sinclair. He wouldn't do this to me."

"You don't fool me." Spittle gathered at the corners of her mouth. Her hair was disheveled. Her skin progressed from flushed to splotchy. She was ugly. "You're only after money. But Henry doesn't have any, do you hear me? It's my money. Mine! And Henry is mine, too. I've paid for him, lock, stock, and barrel, and no one's going to take him away."

I cowered under her anger. "I have no interest in Henry."

"He's dialed your number five times this week on his cell phone."

"He and Sinclair are working on his investments."

She rolled her eyes. "Like I haven't heard that one before. Would you like to know what happened to the last tramp he had a fling with?"

"Colette, I'm your friend. I would never have an affair with your husband."

She listed the fates of girls she destroyed financially and socially. "You're an easy target. The easiest I've had to deal with yet," she said. "So get out of Henry's life, or you'll regret it." She strode out the front door, slamming it behind herself.

I was totally shaken. My thoughts spiraled in circles around her and Henry, and then around Sinclair and Jocelyn. I stood trembling, trying to collect myself.

I ease my body onto the pool-house sofa with the blanket pulled around me. How could I have lived with her all these months and not remembered that fight?

Then I realize, *No one else knew about the fight except the two of us. No one else would think it odd that she let me live in the pool house. In fact, it would make sense; it would make her appear generous, considering we used to be best friends.*

I'm not so befuddled that I miss the writing on the wall. She did it to watch me.

But why watch me? I'm innocent. I did not have an affair with Henry. This is not my life, not anymore. How have I come full circle? How have I been carried back to where I started?

I have to wake up.

I must find Colette and tell her. It isn't me that Henry was sleeping with. It's Lilly. She's being molested. *Raped.* How stupid of me not to realize it earlier. She'd called him a pervert, and she meant it. I, of all people, should have known. So blind. So self-absorbed, self-pitying. I have been a fool.

My stomach wretches.

I have to save her.

I rush outside and stand in the driveway. The cars are all gone. Lilly has left for school. Henry is off to work. Colette must have met friends for breakfast.

Colette's mansion stands in front of me, pale gray bricks, palladium windows, a gabled roof, and an entryway of heavy mahogany doors flanked by glazed windows. I pause. *The intercom tape at the front door,* Lilly said. I trek up to the door. I never noticed it before, but visitors can leave messages on the intercom system. I press the button. "Colette, come down to the pool house this afternoon. We need to talk."

My voice echoes in the foyer, and I wonder how Betts reacts. Does she turn to the pool house and think of me with spite?

Perhaps she thinks nothing; I am not worth her time.

Lilly slips in the back door that night, smells coffee brewing, and helps herself to a cup.

I want to admit to her that she was right about Henry, but I have to have a plan. "Where's Colette? I left her a message at the front door, but she hasn't come to see me."

She takes a seat on a barstool and stirs in a spoonful of sugar. "Probably no tape in it."

I think of the day — how long ago was it? before I went into the hospital — when she went tearing out the door because Henry got home early. "But you told me once that you left Henry a message."

"It's probably gone missing since then."

"Who would have taken it?"

She shrugs.

Her evasion irritates me, so I give her the same treatment and turn back to my magazine.

She assesses me from across the room as I turn the pages and sip my coffee. Her eyes on my face should be unsettling, but I've become used to her strange ways. Still, I know what she's thinking. It was her who was here in the middle of the night.

I hide behind a blank mask and stare at the fashions in the magazine until I can't stand it anymore. "You were here, weren't you? You put the blanket over me," I say.

She remains poker-faced.

"You're right." I begin to cry. "He is a pervert."

Tears trickle down her cheeks, and the floodwall breaks loose.

I take her in my arms and console her. She is me, and I am her. I am consoling my own teenage self, thin arms wrapped around thin, quaking bodies, pale faces grown paler with heartache. All the pain and confusion pours out of both of us in streams of tears until she falls asleep in my arms and I lie back with her heavy breaths wooing me into deep thoughts. I have to do something to help her escape. But what?

I won't call the authorities. I've known girls in bad foster homes. Sometimes living with the enemy is better. And now, after thinking about it all day, after holding Lilly in my arms, my gut tells me that Colette isn't the solution. She is too devoted to Henry to hear anything against him.

Maybe I can get custody of Lily, and we'll find somewhere else to live.

But in order to help her, to protect her, I have to be seen as being sane and fit myself. I need to rebuild myself inside and out. I need to flush the blackness from my heart and soul. I need to feed my body and my spirit, gain strength, and stand up again.

I keep thinking about what Lilly said about being healed in the closet. I am ready to be healed. The drugs aren't working. Life isn't working. Donald Doc isn't working.

I think about Saint Thérèse. She never gave up on God.

Maybe Lilly is right. Maybe I should give the closet-thing a try. After all, no one kicked me out during my last visit. The priest said to visit again if I wanted to.

I tiptoe into the church and glance around. There isn't a line at the closet. There are a few people kneeling up front again, but other than that, the place is empty.

I step over to the closet and peek in. It is empty, just a square closet with a kneeler against one wall and a little window.

A voice suddenly speaks behind me. "Can I help you?"

I spin around to see it's the same priest. "Hello, again," I say.

"Well, hello. Glad to have you back. You've been on my mind. I don't think I introduced myself last time. I'm Father Jacobsen, but most people call me Father Jay."

I have no intention of telling him my name. "A friend of mine told me I could be healed if I go in this little thing. Does it work?"

His expression flattens. "Does for some. Others aren't sincere, so for them it doesn't."

"Sincere about what?"

"Being sorry. Seeking forgiveness."

"Oh." I stare at the box, and wonder.

He sits down in a pew. "Why don't we just talk out here like last time? Come sit in a pew with me."

"I've already done a lot of talking with the doctor. It never helps."

"Something happened to your child."

I sit down. "She died."

He doesn't say anything. I guess I was expecting *The Lord giveth and the Lord taketh away* kinda crap that everyone's always quoting to me, but he doesn't say anything. He just nods, waiting.

"I keep seeing her face."

He nods again.

"In my dreams, I mean." I'm afraid he thinks I'm crazy.

He nods again. "It happens."

I wonder if all priests are so vague. Maybe he doesn't realize I want him to help me. "Lilly told me you could make the pain go away."

"Why do you think you see the baby?"

He sounds like Donald Doc. It's a stupid question. "Because I miss her."

"I think there's more to it than that."

"Like what?"

"Are you afraid to let go of her?"

"I don't know what you mean."

"Are you afraid to face the fact that she's not coming back?"

"I've faced that fact a hundred times every day."

"But are you comfortable with it?"

I know my face shows the dismay and disgust that shoots through me. "Am I comfortable with it? What kind of an idiotic question is that?" My voice rings out in the silence of the church, and I blush, realizing I've called a priest an idiot. He doesn't look flustered, though. His expression is as calm as it's been all along, and I think maybe he has three older brothers who took turns calling him an idiot when he was a kid.

"I mean, have you made peace with her being gone? Or are you filled with guilt over what happened?" His focus moves from me to the crucifix on the altar. "Have you made yourself picture her in God's care and thought to yourself, *Okay, God, she's yours to take care of now. I can go on with my life knowing you're holding her in your arms. She's safe in your kingdom.*"

He trains his eyes on me again. My face is probably as blank-looking as my brain feels. Can I bring myself to say those words and mean them? "I don't think I'm ready to say that."

His face becomes strained. "She's not coming back. No amount of arguing the point with yourself is going to change what happened. You have to start picturing her with God, and accept that she's there waiting for you."

I look up at the crucifix and try to picture Jesus holding her. I can't.

Instead I say something I don't mean to admit. "I had a dream once. Not about Jesus or God or whatever." I pause, not wanting to go back to the memory. He waits silently. He's good at that. "I saw Mary holding her. It was Caroline's baptism, and Mary was holding her instead of me. I thought it was a lady with long white hair, but then I saw that statue over there, and I realized it was her."

He nods. "Baptism washes us clean and makes us open to salvation. I think it's very fitting you saw her that way. That's a good image to start with. Now think of Mary rocking your baby in heaven and Jesus looking over her shoulder, touching her cheek, delighting in her beautiful smile."

I try, but I'm not ready for that yet. I picture Mary holding her, and I still want to pry her out of Mary's hands. I want to hit Mary with a stick and tell her Caroline is *my* baby. I don't tell Father Jacobsen that.

In some deep part of me, I understand where Father Jacobsen is going. If I can get to the point of picturing Caroline with Mary and Jesus, I will be able to release her to death, to accept that she's in heaven and not coming back. I can say it to myself a million times, but I have to make myself believe it. And he's right, I have to become comfortable with it or I won't ever really lay her to rest.

"But I don't understand why God would do this to me. Why would he take my little girl away?"

"God didn't do it. He allowed it, but he didn't will it. Nevertheless, sometimes it's the trials that bring us closer to God more than the happy times."

I remember that from the book. I paraphrase it. "If a father fixes a loose stone in the road and his son doesn't trip, the son remains safe but never realizes what his father did for him. But if the boy trips over the stone and the father catches him, he does."

His eyes widen with surprise. "Ah, you've read *The Story of a Soul*. Exactly. God often protects us and saves us without us knowing. It's when we've fallen that we call out to him."

"So, I'm on my knees. Now what?"

"Look up."

When I enter through Colette's back door the next day, Betts is leaning against the wall, saying something to the cable guy, who appears to be installing a new cable by the desk in the corner. She twists around when she hears me, her face a wall of stone. She hates me, or she hates wasting her day standing guard over the cable guy. I think she ought to smile because she's not having to do laundry or clean toilets.

"What do you want?" she asks.

"Hello to you, too, Betts. Where's Colette?"

She sneers at me, and points me up the stairs to a spare bedroom Colette has deemed her craft room. Colette fancies herself an artist of sorts. She makes mosaic frames from broken tiles and sells them to gift shops. *Everyone needs to do something, and no one can ever have enough money,* she said when I asked her why she puts so much time into them.

She is bent intently over a tiny frame she's filling with ivory chips. She speaks without looking up. "That detective was back here today. He's been here every day this week."

"What is he looking for? Do they have a lead?"

"He's trying to implicate Henry. That is so ridiculous. Henry is a good man, an upstanding citizen. Everyone knows him. The idea is so preposterous; I can't believe he can get away with even insinuating him as a suspect."

Sure, he's so upstanding that he molests his daughter. But is he capable of murder? "Are things okay between the two of you now?" I ask.

"You keep asking that. Why wouldn't they be?"

I wonder again if she's faking it, and if so, why? I'm sure my memory about the affair accusation was real. *Connect, brain, connect.*

Colette is totally engrossed in her project. I admire her calm. She keeps her emotions so contained.

I try to think of other suspects. "I wish you would get rid of Betts and that yardman. They give me the creeps."

"Good help is difficult to find. Betts works hard."

"Her eyes are shifty."

"Oh, that's a good reason to fire someone."

"How about that cable guy downstairs? He was here that day. Have they checked him out?"

"Cable guy?"

"Yes. Remember? He was fixing a cable that got sliced."

She nods and stares vacantly out the window, fitting it into the events of that day, I surmise.

I turn to what's really on my mind. "Colette, do you picture Steven in heaven?"

She drops the piece of tile from her tweezers and frowns. "Ashes to ashes, dust to dust."

"You don't believe in heaven?"

She chooses another piece without even glancing at me. "No. It's like the tooth fairy and Santa Claus."

Even I know the legend of Santa Claus is based on the life of Saint Nicholas. "Saint Nicholas was a real person."

"Was. Then he died."

"So how do you deal with it? Knowing Steven is just gone."

"I mourned him, Rachel, but he's gone, and going crazy won't bring him back. We all die. It's a fact of life."

I don't know if she really feels that way about Steven, but it is abundantly clear what she thinks of me and my inability to deal with Caroline's death.

I turn and leave.

CHAPTER THIRTY-ONE

The whir of a car in the driveway doesn't draw my attention keenly enough to pull me away from the book I'm reading, or make me rise from beneath the warmth of the blankets stacked upon me to ward off the dampness of the pool house. Colette often has company. But after a couple of minutes, a voice crackles through the intercom, hesitant and unsure. "Uh, I'm looking for Rachel Winters." My first thought is Detective Brown, but it's not his voice.

I throw back the covers and rush to the glass doors. I wait a moment, hoping that whoever it is will step away from the door so I can see his face.

"Uh, if this is her house, please tell her Ricky Bathay stopped by." Ricky!

I dash out the door and up the driveway, no coat or shoes, as he heads toward his car. "Ricky! Ricky! I'm here."

He turns to me, his pleasant face stretched with a mile-wide smile. "Rachel." He opens his arms, and I'm in his grasp in a moment. "You've done well for yourself by the looks of this place."

I take his arm in mine, ballroom style, and lead him down the driveway. The cold of the cement driveway bleeds through my thin socks, but I don't mind. I am flushed with warmth at having Ricky at my side. I am a schoolgirl, again, giving him my report card. "I used to have a house every bit as grand, but this isn't it. Sinclair and I separated. This is a friend's home. I live in her pool-house apartment."

"Separated? Oh, Rachel."

There's so much to tell him. "We want to work things out. It's just so hard."

"It usually is. If life was easy, everyone would be happy."

We reach the pool house, and I offer him a cup of coffee. He props himself on a barstool and lets me fix it the way I did so often at his duplex, a spoonful of sugar, a drop of milk. "You say not everyone's happy, but you're always happy, Ricky. I've never known you to be miserable."

"A matter of outlook. I try to concentrate on what's good in my life."

"Like your rabbits. You used to cherish your rabbits, but I hear your wife made you give them all away."

"Oh, you would love Maria. She's very beautiful, like you, Rachel, and such a good person."

"You didn't invite me to your wedding."

"We eloped. I met her one week and we got married the next. Isn't that wild? Anyway, why would you want to be bothered with some old man from so long ago? You would have felt like you were obliged to come if I'd sent an invitation. I didn't want that."

"Ricky, you are one of the most important people in my life. I would have loved to have come to your wedding."

"Then I wish I had invited you. I'm so lucky to have Maria. And as for my rabbits, she is worth far more to me than they ever were. She prefers cats, so now we have cats."

"And you're happy with that?"

He grins. "Like I said, concentrate on the good and let go of the negative. It's wasted energy. You've got to look for the positive."

"There isn't anything positive in my life anymore," I say as I take the stool next to him. "I've lost it all."

"Well, there's your avenue, then. The only place you have to go is up!"

I laugh. "Only you could see it that way." My spirit is buoyed by his presence. He is the hope I need in my life. I want him to save me, like he used to. "I've needed you, Ricky. Why haven't you called? I gave your mother my number."

He clucks his tongue and pulls a folded paper from his wallet. "Girl, didn't I teach you better than to hand out blank checks to people?"

"It wasn't just anyone; it was your mother, and I only gave it to her so you'd have my number. I didn't have anything else to write on."

"Don't you know not to trust people?"

"Not even your mother? She's so sweet. And she makes great cookies."

He unfolds the check, written out to Charles Smithe for the sum of a thousand dollars. "She left it by her phone and this kid came by . . . well you just better be glad I was around that day with my eagle eyes watching everything."

"He forged my name on the check?"

"Land sakes, yes. Girl, trust in God, and no one else."

"I can trust you, Ricky. Out of everybody in the world, I've always been able to trust you."

He looks at me more deeply. He sees the puffy dark pouches beneath my eyes and the scars in my soul. "You're hurting pretty bad, I can tell. But it's up to you this time. You can do it. You can get your life back together. You're stronger than this. I've seen you overcome so much in your life, you're not about to roll over and give up."

He pulls me close and hugs me, and I feel loved, as I haven't in months. We sit like that, wrapped in each other's arms as I sob out my sorrow of how empty and broken I've become. I can bare my soul to him, and he won't laugh or turn away. He's seen me at my worst in life. He loved me even when he was pulling me out of the gutter. I can ask him. "You say *trust in God*, but do you really believe that? Do you really trust in him?"

"Of course I do. I couldn't tell you a thing when you were a teenager. You knew everything there was to know in the world. But now that you're a dumb grownup like the rest of us, I'm going to set you straight." He holds my face in his hands, and I can tell from the look in his eyes, he's seeing me for all I've become. "You need Jesus in your life, girlfriend. That's where you'll find your revival. Not from me, or pills, or a bottle, or even from Sinclair. Once you've healed, then you'll be ready for life again, and maybe you'll work things out with Sinclair."

He wipes the tears from my cheeks. "That's enough of that. Last time you cried was when Becky Snyder made homecoming queen. Now, that was something worth crying over."

I can't help but smile.

"You come on with me. This place smells like chlorine, and I'm starving. Considering I just saved you a thousand grand, you can take me out to supper at some swanky place with lobster or something yummy before I head back home."

I hug him fiercely, then find my coat and shoes, and escort him out the door.

Later in the week, with the help of Donna-Lynn, the librarian, I carry a stack of books on death and angels, and a couple about Jesus to a table to look through. Since Ricky said this was the right track, I was willing to go to the next step.

After a few hours, it becomes apparent that Saint Thérèse is right. Jesus' mission was about love. But nothing can be resolved so simply in my mind.

I return to the shelf for something meatier, something that will delve into the history of Christianity. I find a huge volume with color prints of period paintings throughout that depict phases of the Church.

As I turn back toward my table, there is a man in the aisle. I don't recognize him at first, being outside the church, but as he nears, I know him in an instant. "Father Jacobsen. Hello." I whisper in the quiet tones of library conversation.

He smiles. "Good afternoon. Doing a bit of in-depth reading?"

I lay my hand upon the cover and nod. The silence of the library is as heavy as the silence of the church. It lacks the sanctity I feel within the walls of the basilica, but there is still a sense of security and of secrecy in the hushed atmosphere. I can confide my deepest mcandcrings. "I've been thinking about what you said, about picturing her in heaven," I whisper.

He nods.

"I know now why I'm afraid to let go of her."

"Why?"

"Because if I let go of her now, I'll feel like I'm letting her down, again."

He nods. I picture him in seminary school with an old monk standing at the front of the classroom teaching a room full of them how to nod.

"So, I can't let her go."

"Can't you see that this time it's for the better? She's in God's kingdom. The whole purpose of life is to gain entrance into his kingdom, and she's there. She's made it. You just have to be willing to *let* her be there."

My chin starts to shake. My mind and body are filled with the awful truth of all my doubts. The vile blackness I've kept at bay with pretty thoughts lately comes out of hiding and sweeps through me, consuming me, making me face the thought that's controlled me all along. "What if it's not real? What if there's no such thing as heaven? What if I let her go and she's not anywhere? Not here, not in heaven. Just rotting away in a hole in the ground?"

He sighs and points to the book in my hands. "I can show you the Bible. I can show you historical documents that proclaimed Christ's coming. I can tell you about all the miracles Jesus performed and all the prophets who told of his coming. I can show you documentaries that explain why we believe what we believe. But in the end, you have to take it on faith. It comes down to a relationship between you and God, accepting that he's there. You dedicate yourself to him, or not. Only you can take that step. I can't do it for you."

I want him to do it for me. I want him to set faith before me and force me to take it like my mother forced me to eat when I was five. Put on the timer and demand I accept it in the next ten minutes or I don't get any dessert.

He seems to know my mind. "God gave us all free will to make up our own mind. He won't force you."

Heaven. That was the dessert. "I can do without eternal life if it's as hard as this mortal one."

"You can't say that because you haven't experienced the love of God. They say being in his presence is so overwhelmingly fulfilling, our love on earth can't even compare."

"Love here hurts too much. I don't think I could take anything more powerful."

"That's where you're wrong. Heaven is love perfected, the most awesome love imaginable."

There is only one love I'm interested in, the answer I've been looking for in all the books. "Will I get to see Caroline again if I go to heaven? I just want to hold her again."

"*Caroline* is holding *you* right now, and caring about you, her mother, more than she could on earth. But Rachel, you won't find your healing anywhere else on earth except in the arms of our Lord. Follow him. Trust him. And know that Mary will cradle Caroline in her arms until you get there."

Mary is holding her. I want to believe. I really want to believe. But I don't really believe. I'm just repeating it like a mantra for my own ends.

He seems to know what I'm thinking. "Go across the road and sit in the church for a while. Christ is there, in the Eucharist, waiting for you. Clear your mind. Talk to God."

It's my turn to nod in silence as he walks away between the shelves of books.

I'm barely back to the pool house when tires squeal on the pavement up by the house; it's Henry's car, burning rubber as it streaks out the driveway. Something must be wrong. I jog up to the house. Betts runs from the kitchen to open the door, even though Colette is sitting on the sofa, staring into a gin and tonic.

"I thought I better check on you," I say as I rush to Colette's side.

"While you were gone, the cops came looking for Bruce — you know, the yardman. They finally have proof that he's a drug dealer. A couple of teens at the high school ratted him out."

"Wow," I say, wondering if it was the two boys I'd seen in the backyard with Lilly.

"Unfortunately, he's taken off. They can't find him."

I sink to the sofa beside her as the enormity of what she's saying explodes around me. "He might be the murderer." I reinvent every glance I ever exchanged with him.

Colette continues to stare at the ice cubes melting in the liquid gold in her glass. "So they say."

I place a hand on her shoulder. "You must be . . . what? Shocked? Relieved?"

She swirls the ice cubes and says nothing.

"So where did Henry go? Down to the station?"

"No. He's stressed out. He took off for a drive. He figures Bruce will tell them I was buying from him, but how stupid would that be? It would confirm that Bruce is a dealer."

"Henry knew about your drugs?"

She grunts a *your stupid* grunt and gulps down a huge swallow of liquor. "He's leaving for New York in the morning."

"Business trip?"

"That's what he says, anyway." She stands and crosses the room to the bar for a refill. "I'm glad of it. We need a break from each other. I'm sick of going in circles about all this stuff. I'm sick of him. And Lilly isn't helping matters. I don't know why I have to be saddled with her. I would ship her off to boarding school in an instant, but he'd have fits over it. He's so intent on having her in the house all the time. I personally wouldn't miss her one whit. I wish she'd left with her mother when she was born. But no, Henry had to have his revenge."

"Revenge?"

She lays her hand on her forehead, eyes closed. "I forget you haven't been around here as long as me. There's so much you don't know." She shifts her weight so that she can look at me while she talks. "Lilly isn't really Henry's daughter. Brenda, his first wife, was having an affair. When she ended up pregnant, he said the only way she was going to get a divorce settlement was if she left the baby behind. Not that he particularly wanted Lilly, you understand. He just wanted to make Brenda suffer."

I felt the blood drain from my face.

"Oh, don't look so stricken over it. Brenda got the better end of the deal. She took off without a care in the world. It's me that's suffered having to put up with raising Lilly, and look at how she's turned out." Colette lays her head back again. "Marge is to blame, though. You know, wife number two. She spoiled her rotten. Ruined her. Turned her into a whiney brat who sulks all the time. And a slut to boot, just like her mother."

"I think you have it wrong, Colette. She's not like that."

She turns and glares at me. "You dare suggest you know her better than me?"

I step back a step, and she drops her head back again, controlled. "Don't be fooled. She acts innocent, but she's not."

I need time to digest everything she's said, but the obvious question presses forth. "So who is it you think she's sleeping with?"

She cuts eyes at me that dare me to question her superiority. "As long as she does what Henry tells her to, I really don't care. If he's happy, I'm happy."

I try to read the truth behind her expression. What exactly does she know that she's not saying?

The topic obviously isn't open for more discussion, so I turn heel and leave, stopping on the deck to stare out at the huge naked oak tree to ponder it all.

Lilly isn't Henry's daughter. Revenge. What a different twist it put on the situation.

Was there some reason Henry had equal reason to take out revenge on Steven? Did he know that Lilly loved Steven? Would that have been reason enough for murder?

I couldn't go there. I couldn't even begin to believe that was possible.

I think again about the obvious step — calling the authorities — but I was taught from day one to be wary of police and social services. Maybe my attitude should have changed with age and social status, but given social services' part in limiting my rights to Seth, my old lessons have been reaffirmed rather than dispelled.

There has to be a better solution.

Oh, Lilly, if only we could find your mother. Like a bolt of lightning, I realize that is my new goal.

The timing is perfect: Henry will be away.

When Lilly curls up on my sofa to read that night, I see her with new eyes. She doesn't know her real mother or father, and Henry has been molesting her for years as revenge on his ex-wife. My childhood seems like a picnic.

Her eyes look hollow. Her skin is dull with winter pallor. Her hair hangs down her back, still jagged and in desperate need of cutting. She's wearing a navy sweatshirt that's huge on her. "Steven's?" I ask.

"Yes. Betts is clearing out his stuff, so I snatched this one up. It's soft."

And it feels like him, I add silently. I know that need to touch a piece of memory.

I imagine Betts going through Steven's things, and it turns my stomach. How can they not see the meanness in that woman's eyes?

I don't say so to Lilly. She's fighting off enough demons. I want to tell her about Henry not being her real father to release some of the torment, but it may raise hopes in her that I can't fulfill. I want to promise her I'll get her out of that house, but I don't. It's too big a promise to break. I have to work it out first. All I know about Lilly's mom is a first name — Brenda — and, according to Lilly, she's on a South Sea Island somewhere.

How can I find a faceless mother and father?

Pray, whispers Saint Thérèse. I close my eyes. *Forget what I've asked for myself, Lord. I've been so selfish. You gave me everything, and I lost it. Please, instead, help Lilly. Give her the chance you gave me. Help me help her. Lead me to her mother.*

I decide to go back to the basilica again the next day, not to talk to Father Jacobsen, but to listen to see if I can hear God, to see if I can hear an answer to my prayer. Lilly and I don't have much else going for us.

The church is empty except for a woman sitting in the alcove. There's always someone in that alcove.

I sit midway and close my eyes. Even with them closed, I see the crucifix before me, surrounded by the saints. I don't pray. I don't talk inside my head. I try to stay quiet in my mind to see if anything happens. I picture Jesus in my mind, and I wait.

I sit in silence for ages. The picture in my mind changes from Jesus to Caroline, to Seth and Sinclair, to my mother, to Ricky, to my old friend Jennifer, to Lilly. Faces flicker in my mind's eye, all feeding me kindness. And then Jesus' face comes back to me. I don't hear anything, but I feel something. I feel an urging and peace both. I feel the draw of something like light flickering in me. It is calming, like a warm bath, like a shot of whiskey as it flows out through my limbs. I like the feeling. It's like a drug against my pain, except it's not numbing me; it's washing the pain away. I relax.

Footsteps approach, and I open my eyes to Father Jacobsen on the altar. He takes care of something at the pulpit, then steps around to whisper something to the woman in the alcove. Turning back, he sees me, and strides down the aisle to speak.

"How are you today?"

"Better, I think. I'm listening . . . for God I mean."

He nods. "I saw your eyes closed. That's good. Listen. See what you hear. You know where I am if you need to talk."

He turns to go.

He knows me so intimately now, I am not embarrassed by my ignorance, so I finally get up the nerve to ask him the question that's been burning in me. "Father," the title sounds strange coming from me, "what is that alcove for? Why do people sit there?"

He sits in the pew in front of me, turned cockeyed to face me. "Someone is always present there, twenty-four hours a day, for adoration.

That's where the Holy Eucharist is held. Through the miracle of consecration, Jesus is present in the Eucharist. It is his most holy sacrifice, and parishioners take turns sitting in his presence, worshiping him."

"Huh?"

"That white wafer in the middle of the gold cross. That's the Eucharist, bread transformed into the body of Jesus. He told us so. *I am the living bread which came down from heaven. If any man eat of this bread, he shall live for ever; and the bread that I will give, is my flesh, for the life of the world . . . He that eats my flesh, and drinks my blood, has everlasting life: and I will raise him up on the last day.*"

"You mean to tell me you honestly think that piece of bread is actually Jesus?"

He goes into nodding mode again.

"And then you eat him?"

He nods again.

I can't keep the disgust from my face, but Father Jacobsen just smiles and pats my arm. "Keep talking to him. Keep listening. You'll see."

When he is safely back in his office, I creep forward and sit in the alcove. The smell of candle wax envelops me. I stare at the round wafer, wondering how such a thing could be true and why God would want it to be true. *It is his most holy sacrifice,* Father Jacobsen had said.

I close my eyes and sit as still as I can, letting the atmosphere or whatever it is — flow through me. I think of Christ's suffering on the cross and all that Saint Thérèse wrote. She offered up her pain and sorrow. She offered up the smallest things, like being accused of something she didn't do. Rather than getting angry when she was splashed by dirty water during chores, she rejoiced in it as another sacrifice to offer up to God. If someone spoke ill of her, she smiled. When the elderly nuns grumbled and complained, she served them all the more fervently, absorbing their complaints. Every offense she took with love as Jesus took the nails of his crucifixion. She made all her life into a walk with God, into a daily, minute-by-minute sacrifice. *Jesus has shown me the only path which leads to this divine furnace of love. It is the complete abandonment of a baby sleeping without a fear in its father's arms.*

I must try to do the same.

I hold my breath and picture all the pain in my body like red-hot lava flowing through me, and I offer it to God. I force it from my body, from the tips of my toes, up through my veins until it bursts from my head and flies to heaven.

It's as if my pain creates a chasm so that, for the merest moment, less than a breath or a heartbeat, I see inside. A ray of light pierces through, a light so illuminated, so perfect that even solid gold can't compare. It radiates purity and love, a bond I can scarcely describe. I gasp at the euphoria, pain and suffering transformed into tangible love and ecstasy. Rapture!

I am still filled with sorrow, but I have shared it with God, and I feel his arms close around me as I fall to my knees in the pew and weep.

Lilly is sprawled on my bed, reading a book, when I get home.

"Where have you been?" she asks.

It's time to tell her. "The basilica."

She nods, not as surprised as I expected. "I saw you there earlier this week."

I set my pocketbook in the corner and dig my slippers out from under the bed. "You did?"

"Yes. You looked like you were praying, so I didn't speak."

"I'm going for you, Lilly. I want to help you, but first I have to help myself."

"You can't help me. I just have to survive it. If you try to interfere, there will be trouble. And I have enough trouble in my life right now dealing with you." She manages a wan smile to let me know the last comment is a joke, then leans her head back on the sofa.

She seems so different from when we first met, and I realize we trust each other now.

CHAPTER THIRTY-TWO

S inclair steps from the car, his face drawn and tired, but his manners cordial. "You're looking more rested. Are you feeling better?"

"Much better. I'm getting out more. It's helping."

He sends Seth into the pool house, then turns to me with a sigh. "I know you want us to get back together, Rachel, but the phone calls aren't helping matters."

"Phone calls? What phone calls?"

"The prank calls to Jocelyn. The heavy breathing and hysterical laughter. You're really starting to piss her off, and I won't have my partner chased off because you've gone over the edge. I'll have you locked up first."

There are many dark spots in my memory, but I can't have called Jocelyn and not remembered. "I haven't made any phone calls."

"The police have traced them to the phone booth just down the road at the entrance to this subdivision. They've pretty much instigated you already, but now they've put a surveillance camera on it, so if you do it again, you're going to get caught."

The dark is creeping around me again, crawling across the ground and swirling around me like a tornado, sucking me in. "Why are you saying this to me? Why would I do such a thing?"

"To scare off Jocelyn? I don't know. You tell me. But it stops today. Understand?"

"I haven't called her." I'm not insane anymore. I would remember. Wouldn't I?

"Then who else could it be?"

"I don't know. Some pervert killed Steven; maybe he's looking for a new victim."

"Sure. That's a pretty big leap — from a teenage boy to a female doctor. Tell me how those two could possibly be related."

"I don't know! I'm trying to help people now, not hurt them!"

"Really? Who are you trying to help?"

"Lilly. She's being abused. Henry is molesting her."

His eyes bore through me. "Those are stiff charges."

"It's true."

He stares into the distance, and I know he's thinking of Henry, of everything he's ever heard or known about him. "Are you sure she's not inventing problems to get attention . . ."

He doesn't finish his sentence, but I know he thinks I'm incompetent, that I'm making the story into something it's not.

I give up. I snatch Seth's bag from him and leave him standing outside in the cold.

Lilly shows up that night after I've put Seth in bed. I'm in an ill mood. "Go back to your house."

"I came to see Seth."

"Why? Why would a teenage girl want to visit a four-year-old boy? Why don't you have friends, Lilly?"

She stiffens. "I thought we were friends."

I scream at her. "Why would you want to be friends with me? My husband doesn't even want to be friends with me. He thinks I'm a freak."

"You just have to get rid of that doctor lady. Then he'll want you back."

The phone calls — Lilly. "How would you propose I do that?"

Her lips are a flat line across her face, but I get the sense of a private smile. "I don't know. Maybe one of your friends can convince her to move somewhere else."

Why would Lilly take it upon herself to make prank calls to Jocelyn? "Funny you should say that. Someone has been trying to scare her off with prank phone calls, but the police are onto it. They have a camera stationed on the phone booth."

She smirks. "Too bad it didn't work. Maybe you can think of something better. After all, it's you who's her enemy, not me."

Anger broils in me as I realize it truly was Lilly, not me. I could smack her for the further harm she's done to my relationship with Sinclair.

But then I realize my true folly of the day. God has set trials before me all day long, and I have failed every time to follow what Saint Thérèse has taught me about reacting with love instead of anger, about offering up each incident as a way to show love in its most humble form. Like her, I feel unable to do anything huge, anything truly great, but I could do many tiny things all day long.

I am a very little soul who can only offer very little things to God.

Since I live in a cave, I don't have many opportunities to put *being nice* into practice, but like Saint Thérèse, I can offer what I have. I move to the kitchen as I gather my self-control, as I let peace battle down the anger, and find a glimmer of love deep in the dark of my ugly self. I open the refrigerator door and pull out milk and chocolate ice cream. "Would you like a milkshake?"

She glares at me and flops on the sofa.

I pull out two glasses and whip up two fantastic milkshakes, and add a dollop of Cool Whip on top for good measure. As I hand her one, I know I've chased the anger away.

Lilly slurps at it and halfway smiles.

We are both calm enough to discuss it now. "Lilly, you can't try to scare her off. Your little prank didn't help the situation; it made it worse. Sinclair got really mad at me. I can't make her go away. Instead, I have to make him want me more than her." The realization pours over me like warm water, as if I've been deaf to hearing it before now. I continue in a rush of words. "It's been easier for me to blame Jocelyn than to blame myself for our problems."

How sweet is the way of love . . .

Lilly looks up from her milkshake as if she has heard Saint Thérèse's whisper too.

I set my cup in the sink and turn away. I have a hard enough time loving the people who love me. How am I supposed to love an enemy like Jocelyn?

Hate and blame come so much easier than love.

Sinclair's birthday is coming up. I've got to make him see me in a better light again. I want to prove that I'm not nuts. And I'm definitely not bound for sainthood yet — I have purposely worked at coming up with a present Jocelyn can't match with a million dollars. I'm going to get him a remote-control airplane like he once flew with his daddy. He can take Seth to the park, and they can fly it together. It will unite them, three generations of flying high. Sinclair will like that, a tie between them like their names.

The problem is I can't find the store. It lies somewhere on the outskirts of town, a specialty shop with its own RC landing strip and field for enthusiasts. They have a club with meetings on Saturdays for competitions, something I'm sure Sinclair will end up joining.

I take the exit off the highway, and head down a side road through a small community I've never seen, past a grocery store and drug store, a strip mall of clothiers, shoe stores, and gift shops. The congestion falls away to woods and fields, past a strip of one-story houses lined up evenly on small lots and littered with toys, swing sets and old cars, but I see farther down the road it becomes more cosmopolitan. A subdivision, business center, and a mall I've never explored lie on the horizon. I'm through the next intersection before I register the words on a small wooden sign that points down the road to the right: *Ray's Airfield*.

"Shoot!" I pull into a gas station to turn around, but stop.

There, sitting on a bench, is Father Jacobsen, looking like a normal person in a leather jacket and blue jeans.

He's staring through the sparse woods separating the station from a trailer park beyond, where a lady is walking from her trailer to a row of mailboxes along the side road. He half-stands, his eyes intent on her, almost reaching out toward her, then slumps back onto the bench.

The lady is too far away to see clearly, but she's obviously not on her way out. She's wearing slippers with her sweatsuit. What interest could Father Jacobsen have in her? He's a priest. Dark thoughts rise up, but I force them away. I've been surrounded by liars and perverts my entire life. I know Father Jacobsen is not one of them.

I start to pull away, but change my mind and park. It's just too odd, him sitting on a bench in the middle of nowhere.

He jumps when I lay my hand on his shoulder. "Father Jacobsen, are you all right?"

He regains his composure quickly, but not before I see the strain on his face. I know that strain. It's not admiration of a woman. It's pain. It's heartbreak. Is he wishing he wasn't a priest? Or is it something else?

"Rachel. What brings you out here?"

"My car," I say, making a joke. "But I don't see yours."

He points toward the open bay, where a blue-uniformed mechanic is bent over an engine. "I'm having the oil changed."

I wonder if that's the truth. Why way out here? There are hundreds of garages closer to the basilica. But everyone has secrets; I'm not going to pry into his. What he needs is a way out of whatever is eating at him. Who knows that better than me? "I assume it's going to be a while."

"About an hour."

"Do you know anything about RC airplanes?"

His face lights up. "Are you kidding? My oldest brother used to compete. Why?"

"I'm on my way to pick one out for my husband. Care to join me?"

"Love to."

Father Jay is an expert on airplanes. He asks about motors, examines the wings, and checks out the controls. I'm looking at the pretty colors; he's asking about distance and ratios. We step out to the airstrip behind the store and watch the shopkeeper's orange plane make loops in the crisp blue sky. Father Jacobsen takes a turn, his eyes alight with merry memories. An hour later, I have a shiny red plane tucked in the trunk of my car and a grinning priest at my side.

"That was great fun," he says. "I'd forgotten how much I love planes. I'll have to call my brother Davey tonight and have a chat with him."

His happiness is contagious. My whole body is smiling as his memories fill the car with a happy glow, but reality is less than a mile away. "Now, tell me, Father Jay," I say, using his nickname, as I'm feeling rather chummy, "shall I drop you back off at that service station? I mean, is your car really being worked on?"

He looks at me with startled eyes. "Yes. Of course it is." He concentrates on the countryside passing outside the passenger window before whispering, "You saw her, didn't you?"

"Yes. Who is she?"

"My penance."

I know there's a story behind that, but despair has replaced his grin, and I know he's not ready to share it.

CHAPTER THIRTY-THREE

I like the church when it's empty. I don't want to sit in a crowd of people on Sunday. I don't want their noises and bodies interfering with my thoughts. I just want to absorb God on my own for a while.

"You told me it's all about forgiveness," I say to Father Jacobsen on Monday.

He nods. *"Forgive us our trespasses as we forgive those who trespass against us."*

I ponder the words a moment. "You mean he'll only forgive me if I forgive everybody else?"

"Hmm. Those were his words. You tell me."

It puts a new light on things. "Maybe that's where I'm going wrong here."

He sits, waiting.

"I can't forgive my husband. It was stupid. How could he do such a thing, forgetting our baby like that?"

He stares at the crucifix. "Are you sure it was all his fault?"

He wants me to take the blame. He wants me to say it was my fault for handing off responsibility of my child, even for a day. It's unfair. I can't be everything to everybody every day. No one can.

Silence stretches between us.

"Why should I take part of the blame? He did it. He left her there." I try to hold my tears back, but they pour down my face. "I told him I was too tired. She wasn't sleeping at night. I was exhausted. All I wanted was one day to sleep. Was it too much to ask for his mother to watch her for one day? Was it?"

Father Jacobsen says nothing. He rests his lips on the tips of his fingers and keeps his eyes on the crucifix.

"I asked him to take her to his mother for the day, but he forgot. He went on to work."

His eyes turn just slightly to look at me.

"He expects too much of me. I'm not perfect."

He lets my words hang there just long enough before he answers. "No one is. You're not perfect. Your husband isn't perfect. Even I'm not perfect."

His admission quirks one side of my mouth into a smile.

We sit. The eyes of the statues stare at me, waiting for my admission. The thought of trying to forgive Sinclair makes a ball knot up in my stomach. It makes my brain feel like it's on fire. It tugs at my soul.

"I have to forgive him, don't I?"

He nods.

"That'll be hard."

"Why?"

"You need to know the whole story."

"I don't need to know anything. But if you want to tell it, I will listen."

"I need to tell you the whole thing."

He nods.

"That day, when he was supposed to take Caroline to his mother's house, he didn't. He went on to work. When he got home, Seth and I had been napping. He woke me up. He said Seth was watching television but he couldn't find Caroline. I was still half-asleep. I'd taken a sedative. I needed a deep sleep to rejuvenate myself. So I wasn't quite with it when he woke me. I was groggy, like in a fog or something. So I wasn't thinking clearly. I didn't remember where she was right away. I went to her room, but of course she wasn't in her crib. She wasn't anywhere in the house. Then I remembered where she was. I started laughing, telling him he'd forgotten to pick her up. She must be at his mother's house. No, he said. He didn't take her there. I ran out to the car. I don't know why. I thought I'd find her baby bag. Maybe I pictured her sitting in her car seat, laughing, waiting for us to find her.

"That's where she was. She was still in her seat. He'd never dropped her off."

He nods.

"That's why I can't forgive him. He left her there to die in the heat of his car."

He nods.

I brush away tears. "So, it's his fault."

"He did it on purpose?"

"Of course not. He just put work above her. He was doing that more and more. Ever since his dad got sick. Nothing seemed to matter except his stupid medical practice."

Father Jay flattens his lips in thought a moment before he speaks. "I doubt Sinclair saw it that way. The practice is important to him. I'm sure he feels he has to do his best for his patients."

Everyone justifies Sinclair's actions. They don't understand my side of it. "Don't you see? He only cared about his patients. He avoided us. He'd come home a few hours and leave again." *To be with her. He was with Jocelyn every spare moment. Even right then at Caroline's death, he called her. Like it was any of her business.*

"So he was dedicated to saving lives, but he killed your baby on purpose."

"No, of course not. He's not a monster."

"It was an accident?"

"Yes, but he shouldn't have forgotten about her."

"You said you didn't remember her when you first woke up, but it's his fault because he put her in the car and then forgot about her."

I can't answer him. I don't want to answer him.

He waits.

I look at Mary and then at the crucifix. *Each of us drove in the nails. None of us is without guilt.*

I can't see the cross for the tears clouding my eyes. I turn to Father Jacobsen. He is so still, I wonder what he was like as a young boy. Did he fidget in church? Or was he always this good?

Quit avoiding the question. Is it all Sinclair's fault? I look back at the crucifix. I feel the nails piercing my skin. The pain is excruciating, but there's no way to stop it. The hammers keep pounding them in. I'm stretched out on the cross and the whole world is staring at me, pounding nails into my flesh, pounding the words in my head. "*I* buckled her into the seat!"

A million thoughts flare in my mind. A million pinpricks of guilt. Sinclair was not alone in the deed. I helped. I helped!

"You were doing it for her safety, not her death. You didn't want her to die."

"Of course not." The pounding stops.

Some inner knowledge dawns across his face as he stares at the crucifix. He digests it a moment, then turns to face me. "Neither did her daddy."

CHAPTER THIRTY-FOUR

The pool house is silent except for a drip that has started in the kitchen sink. Its steady *plunk, plunk* grates on my nerves. I can't read. I keep reliving my conversation with Father Jacobsen. *Neither did her daddy.*

I wait until evening, after supper, when I know he'll be home and Seth will be in bed, before I dial his number. Five rings. He's probably reading Seth a story. Or maybe he's washing the supper dishes. Or maybe he's staring at the caller ID and doesn't want to answer because it's me. Or maybe Jocelyn is there.

Eight rings. I hang up.

He calls back an hour later. "Sorry I didn't answer. I was online."

Online. He was online, not with her. "That's okay. It wasn't urgent."

"What's up?"

"I was just thinking about you. I wanted to hear your voice."

Silence.

He's thinking I'm like a stalker he can't get rid of. He hates me. Sobs catch in my throat. I try to swallow them, but they're stuck like huge gobs of goop and my voice has to stretch around them. "It gets lonely in this place."

"We ought to find you a better place to live."

He can't understand. It's not the place. It's lack of him and Seth. "No, it's not that. It's . . . never mind."

"What?"

I try to put into words everything flowing through my body. I know where it has to start. But I can't formulate the words yet. I can't tell him. I have to do more than admit my part in Caroline's death aloud. I have to live with it a while, first. I have to be comfortable taking part of the blame before I can lay it before him. It's too much anguish to put into a phone call.

"Nothing. It's late. We'll talk in a few days, okay?"

"Sure."

I haven't told Donald Doc about Father Jacobsen. I don't want my healing there to become some documented journal entry. His questions make me mad. But I have to give him enough meat to satisfy his little notebook, so I make an admission to him at our next meeting. "I remembered something this week."

He picks up his pen. "What was that?"

"I remember buckling Caroline into the car seat. I put her in the car, not Sinclair."

"So, you remember buckling Caroline into Sinclair's car."

"Yes."

"Tell me more about that."

"Sinclair was supposed to take her to his mother's house on his way to work."

"But it was so early in the morning."

I try to piece the day back together. He did leave early. I remember it was dark when he left. Why didn't I take Caroline later? I think about the week. We'd eaten supper at his mom's house the night before, and we'd taken his car. Why did we do that? We always took my car with the kids. The minivan had more room.

He took us home after, the kids and me. He dropped us off and left again. He had a meeting with Jocelyn, of course. But he could have changed cars when we got home.

I remember. The minivan was making a strange noise. We'd taken it into the shop to get fixed. We had to take the Expedition. Then, after supper that evening, he had a meeting with Jocelyn. I was left home alone without a car. I was mad, but I made a point of keeping my voice calm. "Cancel your meeting."

"I can't. I'll be home at ten."

"You promised you'd be home tonight. I'm going out."

"For what?"

"Mothers' night out. I'm meeting my friends at Outback."

"So get one of them to pick you up."

"You were supposed to watch the kids."

"I guess you'll have to get a sitter."

Frustration curdled in my stomach. I needed a break. But it wasn't just the need to go out; I could have hired a babysitter. It was the need to see him take part in parenting and being more than the money provider. I felt stranded at home with the kids. I felt abandoned by him. He was aching over his father; I knew that. But I wanted to be the center of his life again. I wanted him involved with the kids. I struggled that night to keep my temper under control because I knew it wasn't the outing that spurred my emotions, but rather, the knowledge that he was slipping away from me. Desperation was edging in.

The memory played across my features beneath Donald Doc's critical gaze. "Tell me what you remember," he said.

"My car was in the shop. He had the only car."

"Your car was in the shop, so you put the baby in his car that night to go to his mother's house."

"Yes, I put the baby in the Expedition."

"And again the next morning."

"Yes. I couldn't take her later. My car was in the shop."

That seemed to make him happy. He scribbled in his notebook for ten minutes.

He finally looked up and sat tapping his pen against his lips, staring into space. "Where do you think he was going that night?"

"Out with Jocelyn."

"You mean Dr. Harper?"

"Yes, his partner."

"For a business meeting."

"Sure, if you want to call it business."

"Ah, yes. Let's talk about this. What indications did you have that he was having an affair?"

I didn't want to go there. Talking about menial things didn't bother me, but I wasn't about to discuss my sex life with this jerk taking notes. "A woman just knows these things."

I knew because Sinclair became distracted around me. At first, before his father became ill, I attributed it to the pressure of getting Jocelyn to settle into the practice. Sinclair feared making a mistake. He sensed his father would be easing out of the practice and he had to be prepared to take the reins, which also meant being capable of dealing with his new partner. Then, when his father was diagnosed with a brain tumor, Sinclair became totally focused on saving him. I tried to comfort him and offer support, but his angst rose up in defiance, and he isolated himself with medical journals in an attempt to find an elusive miracle cure. He became distant, unreachable in his isolation. Jocelyn was the exception. She could join him in his research, aid him in ways I couldn't. He could prattle on in medical jargon, and she understood.

As I stare out the window at the bare tree branches, my vision blurs with tears. I have no intention of discussing the details of those painful nights. Why should Donald Doc know that Sinclair turned his back on me in bed? Why should I tell him how Sinclair looked at me? Six months after Caroline's birth, I still carried an extra forty pounds. I couldn't shed the weight. I couldn't quit bingeing, and the more distracted Sinclair became, the worse my weight problem became. I was ugly. I felt ugly. I felt his eyes look at me and label me ugly. I hated seeing his eyes rove over me because they no longer devoured me; they rejected me. I was a dumpy, married mother of two. I understood why he turned to Jocelyn. I didn't like myself; how could he? Jocelyn was beautiful and smart and fit. I'd degenerated into a sloth.

I won't discuss it with Donald Doc. Instead, I think back to the Expedition, to my hands buckling the car seat. "She was wearing her little red outfit. She cried when I put it on her. She didn't like the lace trim. But it looked so cute on her. She was such a pretty baby."

I am sitting in Sinclair's living room, on the sofa next to him. Seth is at a friend's house for the evening. I'm tingling all over, wondering why he's invited me over.

"I had a talk with Donald."

I stiffen. "What happened to patient confidentiality?"

"He says you're making great strides lately."

"He does, does he?"

Sinclair takes my hand into his and traces one finger down the length of each of mine. He can't bring himself to look in my eyes as he's speaking. "You know I love you, don't you? I want you to understand that."

He says it so calmly. If I had grown up in his shoes, I'd have been full of frustrations and rebelling at every turn. He accepts his life with total contentment and keeps plowing forward, even through the bad stuff, even through Caroline. His dedication to his parents' ideals had extended to marriage, too. I say what's on my mind. "Jocelyn is much more of what they want for you. Like Susan Chance was. Not a tramp like me."

"Are you a tramp?"

What he wants to know is if I've returned to that, if I've been sleeping around since we parted ways. I think of Henry and what may or may not have happened that night. Does that count? "No," I say. "I'm as virginal and cold as new-fallen snow nowadays."

He runs his hand down my arm. "You aren't cold. You're distant. There's a difference. You just have to scrape your way back to the surface."

He's trying to put the blame on me. He was the one having an affair. "All those meetings with Jocelyn . . ."

"What meetings with Jocelyn?"

"All those nights you dashed back out to the office."

"I was doing medical research and sitting with my father in the hospital. I told you that over and over again, Rachel."

"But afterward. After your father died, you still went out."

"Ah, those meetings. We had a lot of patient records to go over. Dad had a large circle of regular patients I'd been struggling to take care of, and I had to review their histories with Jocelyn so she could assume some of them. Things are much smoother now. In fact, we're adding a third partner. Patrick Bollen has decided to leave Family Med and join us. The practice seems to be growing in leaps and bounds with Jocelyn there, and we both want more time off. I want to work to live, not live to work."

I am incredulous that he's come to this new perspective on life; or should I say returned to his old perspective? He always focused more on family and living than work in our first years together.

I try to read the truth behind this revelation that's brought him back to me, and draw one conclusion: a problem must have risen between him and Jocelyn.

I say it straight out. "You pushed me away. Every time I turned to you, you pushed me away."

A queer look comes over him. "When my father was sick? I wasn't getting any sleep, Rachel. I barely had time to sleep, and I didn't have energy to spare, yet you kept putting demands on me."

"Not then. Later on."

He shakes his head. "Later it was you who turned away from me, Rachel. You didn't want to be touched."

The memory comes back to me as he says it, his hands reaching for me in bed. I didn't want him to touch me. I kept picturing him with Jocelyn. And I'd become so ugly, I couldn't bear his hands on my flesh. I decided he wanted only sex, not me. How could he want me when I'd become someone so unlike myself?

He places his hand over mine. "I know it was postpartum depression. It wasn't your fault. You needed space, so I gave it to you. I quit trying. I figured you would tell me when you were ready, and then Caroline . . . Everything seemed impossible after that."

Everything *was* impossible after that. We couldn't speak to each other, let alone make love. It wasn't just me who saw it. "Colette thought the same thing. She insisted you were having an affair with Jocelyn. Lilly thinks the same thing; that's why she did all those crazy things — the rabbit, the prank phone calls — that was Lilly trying to scare Jocelyn away."

"There is nothing between me and Jocelyn. There never has been." He kisses my scarred fingertips. "Whatever our problems, Rachel, I love you. I have always loved you."

His words are a salve to my lonely heart. I lean into him. His fingers caress my skin as he kisses me again.

I stand and take his hand. He understands the invitation. We may not be able to live with each other, but we need each other.

An hour later, he is slumbering at my side. I watch his chest rise and fall and lightly touch the roughness of his cheek.

I need you so much, Sinclair. I feel like a part of me is missing when you're not here. I can't go on alone.

I thought it was Caroline. I thought if I set her to rest, I could go on, but I can't. I've been without you throughout all this, when I should have been at your side, you holding me, and me holding you.

I cannot heal completely until I heal us. I become me when I'm in your arms. My wounds fade away. I feel like nothing without you. I need to be your wife. I need to be Seth's mother. I see you as a part of me. I can't be whole by myself.

If I close my eyes, I know my life only goes forward through you. You are my path back to sanity. Lift the lamp high, and guide me back to life. I can't find my way through this darkness alone.

Life is a trip through hell without you at my side. It has no purpose. It has no direction.

I am ready to reconcile.

I don't think I understood before. Everything was so ideal, I never fathomed how we were joined. I took it all for granted. I'd won the perfect life. I held the trophy I'd fought so hard to grasp. But I thought the trophy was something to set upon a shelf. I didn't know it was a melding of our hearts, a living thing, a union of our souls.

I want to lay spooned into your body forever, feeling your heartbeat next to mine, feeling you breathe in rhythm with me, the two of us a unit again.

How could I ever have thought I could go it alone? The worse parts of my life were alone. And so much of it has been alone. There are very few paths with footprints alongside mine, yet you were willing to join me, to take my hand and be with me.

Be with me again. Please.

I think all that, but all I do is caress his face and run my hands through the soft hair on his chest. His eyes flutter open, and I look into his soul. I say the words Father Jacobsen has been laying before me. "Please forgive me."

And I realize I've said it wrong. I wanted to tell him I've forgiven him. But what I've said is what I needed to say. He doesn't need to know the anger I had toward him. It is me who needs forgiveness for turning away from him when Caroline died. We both had our guilt to face, and we should have done it together. I should have stuck by him.

"Oh, Rachel. You don't know." His eyes close, and his chin quivers.

"Know what?"

"What you mean to me, what life has been like watching you from a distance."

I turn on my side and look at him earnestly. "I'm ready to come back."

"It's not that easy, Rachel. You can't just say that and move in, and then next week change your mind. We have to know this is for keeps. I have to know you're not going to walk out again, because even if I can handle it, Seth can't. He doesn't understand any of this, and if it's going to work, it's got to work first and foremost for him. I won't hurt him anymore. Let's take it slow. You show me that you're really ready."

I flop back on the pillows. "How am I supposed to prove something like that? You said Donald thought I'd improved. I have. I'm ready."

"You are improving, but you're not functioning normally yet. You're still a recluse. You don't talk to anyone except Colette, and she says you don't even talk to her as much as you do Lilly. And Lilly . . . well, you just told me the sort of things she does."

I sigh. I want to tell him about Lilly and how much that awkward girl means to me, but this isn't the time. "I am ready, Sinclair. I'll show you I'm ready." I lie there, conjuring up ways to prove myself to him, feeling more alive than I have in months.

And then it dawns on me. I know who can tell me what I have to do to make everything right again. I will put my life in order. And I will save Lilly, too.

CHAPTER THIRTY-FIVE

I sit in a pew for a few minutes, but more and more people keep getting in line. I'll never get to talk to him.

It's only a closet. It can't be that scary. It's not like he's a stranger anymore. I don't understand why all these people have to sit in the dark to talk to him. I talk to him more than any of them. I feel territorial.

I walk up and join the line and stand there, waiting, tapping my foot, edging slowly forward as people finish and leave. Finally it's my turn.

The closet smells of musty perspiration, like backstage nerves before a school presentation.

A tiny door slides open, just big enough to see Father Jacobsen through a screen.

"Hi, Father Jay. It's me."

"Rachel . . ." He's as stunned as I am at my being in the closet.

"I forgave him. I told Sinclair I was sorry. No, actually I was thinking about how much I wanted to forgive him, but what I said . . . what I asked was . . . would he forgive me."

Father Jacobsen leaned up close to the screen and whispered, "What'd he say?"

"He said he's never stopped loving me."

"That's wonderful, Rachel. Maybe we better talk later. This is a confessional . . ."

"No, I waited in line like everybody else. Now listen, here's the problem. He says I've got to prove I'm not just being flighty, that it's going to work. What should I do? How can I prove that I'm serious? That I'm back on my feet again?"

Father Jacobsen's face wrinkles up as he examines me through the screen. He looks off at the closet door, then leans toward me again. "Are you truly sorry, Rachel? Are you ready to ask for God's forgiveness?"

"Ask God?"

"Yes, ask him right now, aloud."

"You don't believe I said it to Sinclair, do you?"

"You need God to forgive you, too, Rachel. Forgiveness is but a breath away. Just ask for it."

I know he's right. I know the light I feel is not just rekindling my love for Sinclair. I'm seeing God. I'm finding a new center and a new purpose in life. It's not about obtaining things or pretending to be something I'm not. It's about love. God's love for us, and our love for each other. God is at the center of it all.

I can't just blurt out *I'm sorry*. I wouldn't mean it if I did it that way. I close my eyes and go to that quiet place I've come to know, that dim light deep inside me, hidden in the murky dark of my soul. "God, please forgive me for hurting Sinclair. I really didn't mean to. I was trying to protect myself, and I shoved him away."

Father Jacobsen nods. "Talk to him about the baby, Rachel."

This is hard. It is still a knot inside me that doesn't want to be untangled, but I've come this far. I wouldn't do this for anyone else, certainly not for Donald Doc, but this is Father Jacobsen. Right now, I feel closer to him than anybody on earth. He must think I'm ready.

Everything in me twists as I find the words. "God, I'm trying to get used to the idea of you reclaiming my baby, but it's hard." How can anyone, even God, understand? "I loved her so much!" They are nothing but words falling into the air. Nothing I say can embody what Caroline meant to me. "I'm so sorry I let her down that day. I would redo it all if I could. I was so tired. I'm sorry I was so tired."

I feel a rush of relief letting the words come. The blackness drains away, the dark mist falls away under the fingers of light penetrating my soul. "I know I have to quit making excuses, but I don't know how else to deal with it. I don't know how to get over it. I laid all the blame on Sinclair, but he didn't do it on purpose. Forgive me for hurting Sinclair when I know it was an accident. And Seth. And everybody else who's been trying to help me. Please God, forgive me. Help me get back on track. Help me put my life back together."

A sensation rushes over me like a bucket of cool water dumped over my head. I feel cleansed, emptied, squeezed dry of all the ghoulish impurities brewing within me. I am filled with light. I feel like I'm glowing.

I open my eyes to Father Jacobsen's nodding. He begins reciting some churchy words. When he's done, he looks directly at me. "Rachel," he says with a smile, "get a job."

"A job?"

"Yes. You have too much time on your hands. You think too much about yourself. Get busy doing something, anything."

He could have said, *Idleness is the devil's playground.* I'd heard Jennifer's mom say that lots of times, but I'd quit expecting Father Jacobsen to quote scripture and stuff. He never talked like a preacher, except for that bit of mumbo-jumbo.

"A job. Hmm. Okay. Thanks, Father Jay. Later."

"Wait, that's not all. You come back and let me know how it's going."

"I will."

"And keep talking to God."

"I will." I move to leave.

"Wait! I absolve you from your sins in the name of the Father and the Son and the Holy Spirit. Go in peace to love and serve the Lord."

"Thanks!"

As I step from the church, the glare of the sun stops me in my tracks as if I'm seeing it for the first time. I feel different. I sit on the curb a moment and think about Caroline to test myself, like poking at a bruise or a cut to see if it still hurts. It does. The wound is still there, and very deep, but maybe it's been doused in antibiotics. I'm not cured, but I'm refreshed, and it occurs to me that Lilly was right. Father Jacobsen is helping me heal.

I sit for a while in the sun, watching people go by, and I wonder where they are all rushing, and how they found their jobs. I travel up and down the street with my eyes. I pause on the library. I need a new book to read, but I resist. I must find a job. I can't sink into another fictional world. I stand and head down the street, feeling like a teenager out looking for a job. I'm not qualified to do anything. In college, I had intended to take pre-med courses, a B.S. in biology, but instead I gravitated to what I loved and ended up taking mostly art courses, and then quit to marry Sinclair. Worthless.

CHAPTER THIRTY-SIX

Three days of asking at every ice-cream store and temporary office in town has left me totally disillusioned. There are no jobs for me. I've decided Father Jacobsen may know of something, so I head downtown. After all, it was his idea.

I pop into the bookstore on the way, just on the off chance they need a cashier, but no, they've just hired someone. I trudge down the road to the church and take my seat, but Father Jacobsen doesn't show.

"God, I thought you were listening the other day. I said I was sorry and Father Jay said I need to get a job, but I could use a bit of help here." The more I talked, the more flippant I felt. Maybe it's all just talk. Maybe God and heaven don't exist and it's all crap, just like I thought. But as I think that, I feel the darkness curl around me. I don't want it back. "Come on, God. Help me. Can't you drop a job into my lap? Like a bulletin or something? A big headline in the paper?" The paper. That was pretty obvious and I hadn't even looked at one. "Thanks!"

I rush outside, heading back to the bookstore to buy one, but slow at the library. The library has dozens of papers from all over the state.

I settle at a table with the *Asheville Citizens-Times* spread out in front of me and start reading the ads. I'm halfway down the first column when a shadow falls over me. It's Donna-Lynn, the librarian. "This is a change," she says. "Not looking for a book today? I saved one off the New Arrivals for you."

"Thanks, Donna-Lynn, but I'm not here for entertainment today. I'm looking for a job."

"Really?" She turns a seat toward me and sits down. "Doing what?"

"That's the problem." I'm embarrassed to tell her it's because I have too much free time, but I've let so much out lately, I've decided honesty is the best path to feeling better. "I'm recovering, you know," this is so hard to say, "from the . . ."

She pats my arm. "I know about your daughter, Rachel. I'm so sorry."

I steel myself for more of the usual drivel, but it's not that after all.

Donna-Lynn continues, "I lost a baby seven years ago. Crib death. I still think about her. I still ache, wondering if things would have turned out differently if I'd only checked on her ten minutes sooner." She stops. "I'm sorry. You don't need to hear my sob story."

I take her hand. "I'm glad you told me. I feel so alone."

She pats the paper, and I see that she's as unable to go forward with her story as I am with mine. "So I understand. You need to keep yourself busy, keep your mind occupied."

How had two people in my life known this for months and not told me? Why does Donald Doc not know this if they do? "Yes, I need to be busy."

"I've got the perfect job for you."

"Here?"

"Yes. We want to start a story time three mornings a week for nursery schools. The children will come and hear a story, and then pick out books to take home. We hope it will encourage their parents to read to them, to build early reading skills."

I think about all those little faces turned to me, of little girls with curly hair. "I don't know . . ."

She knows my thoughts. "Seeing them won't make her haunt you. She will become solidified in your mind. Once you face them, after a while you won't be afraid to think of her."

I can only nod.

She looks like she's going to say more, then changes her mind. "You'll have to be creative, but I have a feeling that won't be hard for you. You know, puppets and felt people and things like that. You know what kids like."

I nod. "I've taken some art courses."

"Perfect. That's exactly the requirement I was thinking of posting. You're hired. Come tomorrow morning, and we'll get the paperwork done and start picking out which books to do first."

I'm beyond speaking. She knows. She leans forward, and we hug. I walk out the door, and she heads to the ladies' restroom, both of us with teary eyes.

On Wednesday, everything is ready. The first group of preschoolers comes in, shaking off raindrops. Twelve children. Raindrops hang on freckled cheeks, laughing eyes, and pouting lips. They're all wearing red T-shirts embroidered with *Miss Kay's Day Care*, but their uniformity stops there.

I expected to be nervous. I was nervous for a half-hour beforehand, but seeing the children opens me up to something I hadn't expected — joy. They clamor eagerly for seats close to me, ready to be part of the action. I settle in my chair with Pudgy Pig puppet on one hand and *Pigs in the House* in the other. Pudgy Pig turns the pages and makes wry comments throughout the story in my best piggy voice. I turn him into a great sidekick, letting him ask the kids questions throughout the story.

"Look at what that pig did. I wouldn't do that. Would you do that, little girl?" Pudgy asks a pigtailed girl in the front row.

"No way," she says, "but my brother would."

By the end of the hour, the kids all want a turn talking to Pudgy and Nettie-the-chicken, and I'm smiling, filled with a giddiness I haven't felt in a long time.

A second group comes in at ten-thirty. As they settle around me, I'm stunned. I hadn't thought to ask what groups would be coming to the library. Staring at me from the middle of the group is Seth.

I don't know what to do. Should I go hug him? Should I explain what I'm doing in the library? Should I invite him to sit on my lap?

His face is contorted with confusion.

I put Pudgy on my hand. "Hi, Seth. Surprise! Are you glad to be here?"

He frowns.

"Would you like to come sit up here?"

He shakes his head and hunkers down so he won't stand out. The other kids are looking at him. He doesn't like it.

"I want to sit with you," says a little redheaded girl.

I keep a smile plastered on my face as Pudgy turns to look at her. "Goody! Come sit right here, where I can see that pretty red hair. You're going to love this story."

I read the story with one eye on Seth. He's listening, but his head is down. He's casting sidelong glances at his classmates. The redhead is seated on the floor, clasping my leg by the end of the story. Two boys on the edge of the crowd have stood up to see more clearly. Another boy, wearing little black cowboy boots, creeps forward and pets Pudgy.

"Wasn't that great?" Pudgy asks the kids.

"Yes!" the kids answer.

"Will you come back next week and see me again?"

"Yea! Yes!" they shout.

Six children crowd around me to give me hugs and pet the puppets, but not Seth. He stands still in the middle of the movement and says nothing.

"Will you be here next time, Miss Rachel?" asks the redhead.

"Yes, sweetie." I touch her silky red locks, but I'm saying it to Seth, "Yes, I'll be here next week, too."

I didn't have Seth that weekend, so I didn't have a chance to talk to him. I go by Sinclair's twice, but they aren't home, and the phone is answered only by the machine. I ache inside with the need to talk to him, but I stay busy at the library with new groups each day, and spend afternoons at home going through picture books and planning my next week. Lilly joins me.

"You need another puppet," Lilly says.

"Why?"

"Some of these stories need a little girl or boy puppet, or maybe a puppy dog. Something besides Pudgy Pig."

"Hmm. You could be right. I wonder where they sell puppets?"

"Let's make some."

"Make them?"

"Sure."

I feel like I'm her big sister as we enter the store, the two of us working on a school project together. She becomes almost giddy as we pick out fabric, felt, lace, buttons and bows. She holds up jiggling plastic eyeballs. "Look at these. You have to get them," she says. I see the smile in her eyes, and I feel a glow of excitement stir within me. For the moment, we are both happy as we lay pieces beside one another and plan out how each can be used. Lilly has a creative bent she's never tapped into before — she is a natural puppeteer, and I am having fun.

The project is not a solution to her problem, but it's giving her some release, and Henry hasn't returned from his business trip yet. Colette says he had to extend it, but didn't say why, which makes me wonder what's up. Maybe they're still on the outs, unofficially separated. He often travels to New York, but not usually for as long as this. Colette hasn't been home much either, which is fine by me. Lilly is safe. For now. If she can just hold on a bit longer.

The next Wednesday starts the same. Seth spends the first story watching the other kids. During the second story, he scoots up on his knees and listens intently. When the kids hug me at the end, he stands by himself, watching me. I hold out my hand to him, but he won't come any closer. I decide not to push it. If he doesn't want to acknowledge me as his mother in public, I'm not going to force it.

"Isn't that your son?" One of the librarians asks.

"Yes."

"Why don't you talk to him?"

"He's an introvert. He would hate to have attention drawn to himself," I say, but I don't think they believe me. They think he's afraid of me. They probably think I abuse him or something. I want to slap their faces. I want to run and hide from their judgmental eyes. I feel tears coming, but I refuse to cry.

Donna-Lynn saves me. She steps up and puts her arm around me. "The kids are eating this up. You are doing a fantastic job. I never would have thought to interact with them with those puppets the way you have. You're a natural."

I know she's only saying it to change the course of conversation. I gladly accept the detour. "It's fun. I'm really enjoying it."

She smiles. "So am I. Come on, let's go to lunch."

She grabs her pocketbook from her desk and pulls me out the door, up the sidewalk to a café. We talk during lunch about the preschoolers and plans for spring and Easter themes. Then she takes an abrupt turn in thought. "I like to watch Marley."

"Marley? Who's that?"

"The little redhead. I like to imagine that's what Nicki would have looked like. My mom had red hair just like that."

Nicki was her baby, the one who died of SIDS.

I don't want to go there. Not today. Not when the story group has made me forget for a while.

"I like to think she follows me around at work, and that she was there, listening to the story today."

She is forcing me to blend the present with the past. She's forcing me to equate the preschoolers with Caroline. I think about my recent images of Caroline and the question that's been plaguing me rises to the surface. I can't help asking her. "Do you believe in heaven? I mean really, truly think there is such a place?"

"Oh, yes. I have to. If I didn't have heaven to look forward to, I wouldn't have made it through all these years. Someday, I'll see her there. She's waiting for me. I know it."

I sniff back tears. I know she's right. I now believe in God and heaven. But in my heart, I must totally abandon myself to God's mercy, as Saint Thérèse instructed. She suffered separation from her sisters, the death of her mother, and then illness, and rather than becoming bitter or lashing out, she turned to God and loved him with all her heart and soul. That's what I must do. I must let go of all the hate, anger, and blame that has kept me caged up and trust God to carry me with his love. *How sweet is the way of love . . . it leaves nothing but a humble and profound peace in the depths of the heart.*

If I can follow Saint Thérèse's example, if I can rebuild my life and outlook on Love, then, maybe, I'll have my life back again.

CHAPTER THIRTY-SEVEN

Sinclair arrives with Seth early Friday afternoon. "I thought you'd like some extra time with him this weekend."

"Yes, thanks." I hesitate, afraid of the answer. "I'd love it if it included time with you, too."

He nods. "Good idea. How about a movie and dinner out tomorrow, all three of us."

My heart flutters. "Perfect."

He touches my cheek and leaves.

Seth and I are alone two minutes before he gets to the point. "I thought you were living at the library now."

His confusion hits me. I remember the first time he saw his preschool teacher in the grocery store. He couldn't understand why she wasn't at the school. He hadn't understood that she only stayed there when the kids were there. My heart aches, thinking I should have talked to him the first day. "No, sweetie, I don't live there. I work there a few days a week, reading stories to kids like you."

"Why?"

"So I have something to do during the day, just like you go to preschool."

"I don't have to sleep at the library tonight?"

"No, dear. I come home, here, just like you go home. You know Daddy doesn't sleep at work, and your teacher doesn't sleep at school."

"Good. I brought Binks."

"Of course you brought Binks. Let's put him on my bed, then we'll have some ice cream."

We have a great time Saturday afternoon. Seth and I climb into Sinclair's car, and it feels like old times, except for the uncertainty scraping my nerves. We go to the matinee show and then head to Seth's favorite — Applebee's. I stop in my tracks halfway across the parking lot, thinking of the afternoon I was left outside watching Sinclair and Seth walk in without me.

Sinclair turns. He reaches his hand toward me. "Come on, beautiful." I join him. He clasps my hand in his, and I tingle from head to toe as I did on that day at the beach so long ago when I was another person, when I was walking placidly toward my future. Can happy endings possibly come around twice?

On Sunday, I'm washing breakfast dishes, smiling as I scour the sausage pan and think back on our family outing, when I hear something crash. Seth stands frozen, terrified, with the lamp from the table broken at his feet.

"I'm sorry, Mama. I'm sorry. I didn't mean to."

I shrug. "It's okay." I grab a garbage bag and pick up the pieces one by one.

"Don't be mad at me."

"I'm not mad. It's just an old lamp."

"Can I go home, now?"

"No. This is your weekend with me."

"I better call Daddy to come get me."

I pause to look at him. His eyes are as big as saucers. His face is flushed. He's terrified. "What's wrong?"

"Last time I broke a lamp . . ."

His words touch my mind and resurrect a memory. He and I were home alone. Sinclair was at work. I'd had a bad day.

Most mornings I woke with the sick feeling in my stomach of having to face another day without Caroline. Not that morning. I woke early. Maybe I'd forgotten to take my medication the night before. Maybe it was a peak in my hormones. Whatever the case, that morning I didn't remember I'd even been on any medications. It was an ordinary morning in paradise. I didn't even remember that Caroline was dead. I went to her crib to get her up, but the crib was empty. The bed was stripped bare. The curtains were drawn shut. Then I remembered.

I collapsed in the middle of the floor in tears, drowning in my grief.

Seth entered sleepy-eyed. His pajamas were buttoned crooked and there was drool on his chin. I should have wrapped my arms around him and loved him for being there, for being my surviving child, but my mind didn't perceive things that way. Anger and grief overpowered all else and became funneled into one emotion. I couldn't separate the two. I resented Seth's presence. I wanted Caroline so badly I became enraged at the sight of Seth. "Get out!" I yelled at him. "Leave me alone. I want to be alone with her."

His voice was so tiny, so quiet. "I'm hungry, Mama."

Always demanding, I thought. Always wanting something. "Go away!" I screamed. "I'll get your bloody breakfast when I'm ready. You won't starve for five blessed minutes. Now go away!"

He backed out the door and ran down the hall. I heard him thump down the stairs on his behind. He was going on with life, and I hated him for it. Life without his sister was no different for him than life with her. He still wanted his cereal and cartoons. He still wanted to go to the park and to get ice cream from Dairy Queen.

I focused back on the crib and thought of Caroline, picturing her in her crib reaching out for me. Her sweet, precious smile looked out at me with a promise of what life held before us — adventure. She was like me, ready to fight to hold the world in her palm. She would cut a swath through a jungle if that was what it took. She would go places, not plod down the path put before her. I was still smiling to myself, remembering her, when the crash came from downstairs.

When I reached the family room, Seth was perched on the edge of the sofa, staring down at the remains of a glass lamp. Not just any lamp, but a handmade lamp, an intricate design with gold trim, with an exorbitant price.

The anger I had tried to quell with memories flared again with added fuel. "You stupid oaf. Look what you did!"

"I was trying to turn on the light. It's dark in here."

"Of course it's dark. You shouldn't even be up yet. What are you doing out of bed?"

"I woke up."

"You should have gone back to sleep."

"I couldn't, Mommy. You were screaming."

"I was not screaming."

"Yes, you were. You were screaming for Caroline."

I stared hard at him. Had I been screaming? I didn't remember screaming. I just remembered being overwhelmed by her absence, by the sight of her empty crib.

His words didn't lessen the emotions exploding in me. "Of course I was screaming. I miss her. Don't you miss her? It's not fair that she died." I knew I was ranting and yelling in front of this helpless four-year-old, but I couldn't stop myself. I was caught in a torrent of misery. "You're just like your father. You act like nothing's happened. You don't even miss her. And now you've broken my lamp. What's wrong with you? You stupid little boy. Go to your room! Get out of my sight."

I shudder as I remember the rest of the scene: As he ran to his bedroom, I picked up pieces of the broken lamp and pitched them at him like rocks at a stoning.

Seth is in front of me, watching the memory wash over my face. Tears flood from me as I drop to my knees and hold out my arms. "I'm sorry, Seth. I'm so sorry. I'd forgotten about the other lamp. Mommy has been so sick. Sick in the head. I shouldn't have yelled at you. None of it is your fault, baby boy, none of it."

He doesn't come to my arms, but he doesn't run, either. He watches me warily.

I run my hand down his arm. "I'm trying so hard to put it all back together, Seth, and I need your help. I love you, Seth. You're all I have left."

I realize now what Saint Thérèse meant. She would have rejoiced in a broken lamp. She would have smiled and thanked God for another opportunity to express love instead of anger. *O glorious God, how I love thee! You love me as I love Seth, despite all my broken lamps! Despite all my failings and sinful ways.*

I crawl forward through the broken glass and Seth lets me fold him into my arms. He's stiff, unmoving, but he doesn't pull away, and I croon over him the way God embraced my own stiff, unresponsive soul. "My baby boy. How could I ever blame you?"

We stay like that for minutes on end until I reach to wipe the tears from my face and kiss his cheek.

"You're not mad about the lamp?"

"No, I'm not mad about this lamp, or the other one. I've just been very sad about Caroline, and sometimes it turns to anger, but I'm trying to stop it." I am going to rejoice in ways to offer love instead of falling prey to hate and anger! I understand Saint Thérèse! *My vocation is love! I will be love.* I will do all I can to offer up something every day during this *exile on earth.*

When it's time for him to go home to Sinclair, he packs his bag and sits on the sofa to wait for me. His face is serious and concentrated. I know he has a question weighing on him.

"So, what is it?" I ask.

"Huh?"

"Tell me what you're thinking about so hard."

"The library."

"The library. Yes, I'll be there again this week. I think it's helping me."

"Are you going to scream there?"

His question hits me like pieces of the lamp. I try to imagine being four years old in a group of my peers, wondering if my mother is going to go wacko at any moment, screaming in the cartoon dialect of Pudgy

Pig and Nettie-the-chicken while throwing books at kids. It would be like my mother showing up for my wedding on the back of a Harley, wearing skin-tight black leather pants. Only worse. I swore I'd never do that to my kids.

"No. I promise I won't go nuts at the library. I'm going to try my best not to go nuts at all anymore." I say it, and I hope I can make it true.

I curl into bed that night to finish Saint Thérèse's book.

I want to fly and imitate the eagles, but all I can do is flap my tiny wings. They are too weak to lift me. What shall I do? Die of grief at being so helpless. Oh no! I shan't even let it trouble me. With cheerful confidence I shall stay gazing at the Sun until I die. Nothing will frighten me, neither wind nor rain. If thick clouds hide the Sun and if it seems that nothing exists beyond the night of this life — well, then that will be a moment of perfect joy, a moment to feel complete trust and stay very still, secure in the knowledge that my adorable Sun still shines behind the clouds.

It is so much to absorb that I read no farther, even though there are only two pages left. I dwell on the eloquent statement as my heart sends up a silent prayer that doesn't even require words to make its meaning known to God.

CHAPTER THIRTY-EIGHT

I must force myself out the door to the library the next morning. I've had so many good days that I am rocked by the darkness that is suddenly enveloping me. The shadow of grief shrouds me. I'm in control, but sinking.

Sometimes, I confess, a little ray of sunshine illumines my dark night, and I enjoy peace for an instant, but later, the remembrance of this ray of light, instead of consoling me, makes the blackness thicker still.

Yes, Saint Thérèse, it does.

I force a smile, but Donna-Lynn can tell it's not sincere. She chatters on a while. I don't hear the words, only the noise of her voice scraping at the shell around me until the noise stops and she's waiting for an answer.

"What?" I say it gruffer than I intend.

She just smiles. She picks up Nettie-the-chicken. "Do you know any songs?"

"To sing?"

"Yes, to sing. What else would you do with a song? To sing to the children."

"You didn't say anything about singing for this job."

"I bet Pudgy Pig knows some songs."

"You really want me to sing?"

She's fidgeting with Nettie-the-chicken, but her expression is serious. "Singing is good for the spirit. It chases away those dark moments."

She slips Nettie on her hand and switches to a chicken voice. "Old McDonald had a farm . . ."

She goes through one entire verse before I join in. First I say the words, but after the E-I-E-I-Os, I add harmony. She's right. The blackness ebbs away. It's good medicine. "Thanks, Donna-Lynn."

Nettie-the-chicken cackles at me. "I don't get credit for nothing. I'm just the pretty face in front of the brains."

I take Nettie onto my hand. "Lots of thanks to you, too, Nettie. More than you know."

"I know," says Donna-Lynn. "I've seen the change. You can't be afraid of the darkness sneaking back up on you. You can't let it have its way with you. You have to fight it, because it's never gone for good. Seven years it's been, and it still creeps up on me. That's when I open my mouth and sing."

I gaze out the window at the sunshine and think of that first beach trip with Sinclair, walking hand-in-hand in the surf and singing whatever came into my head without feeling the least bit self-conscious, and often after that in the evenings, as I caressed him with my eyes. "I used to sing for Sinclair."

"It's time to start singing again. Sing for Seth, or sing for Caroline, or just sing for yourself. But you need to sing."

I add a song to that week's story time. The kids love it, singing along with their squeaky renditions. I can feel angels smiling around me.

One of the other librarians, the one who first asked if Seth is my son, approaches me afterward. "You have a beautiful voice."

"Do I? Thanks." No one's told me that before, except Sinclair. But he was supposed to say stuff like that when he was my husband.

The librarian waves in the direction of the basilica. "We could always use more good voices in our choir over at St. Lawrence if you're interested."

I should have known God didn't put her in my path by accident; of course, she attends church at the basilica. I laugh at the thought of me, the girl who so recently didn't even believe in God, being asked to sing in the choir. "That would be something," I say, but her words plant a seed that grows over the next few days.

I go to the basilica, but Father Jacobsen isn't there. I sit in the alcove by the Eucharist, the Adoration Chapel they call it, reading prayers from a book left in the pew. I look at the host and think about when Father Jacobsen first told me that Jesus meant us to eat his body and blood. First, it just seemed gross, but the more I sit in front of that little wafer, the more I understand it. To have Jesus there, present in the host, is such a miracle. I sit in front of him and feel his love, and feel myself falling in love with him. I remember the words from the Bible Father Jacobsen quoted, such a promise: *He that eats my flesh, and drinks my blood, has everlasting life: and I will raise him up on the last day.* A yearning is slowly building in me. I've got to ask Father Jacobsen what you have to do to be able to eat the host, to participate in Holy Communion.

Before leaving, I cross the church to the other alcove to look at the statue of Mary. I picture Caroline there in her arms, and I'm no longer angry. I'm sad, but I'm no longer hollow. "Kiss Caroline's sweet forehead for me please, Mary," I whisper before making my way out the side door to the parking lot.

Father Jacobsen is there, sitting in his small burgundy sedan, I assume setting off on church business. He rolls down his window to the biting breeze when he sees me. "How's the job at the library?"

"I love it."

A girl in a long brown coat rushes by us, and it spurs a question that's been nagging at me. "Father Jay, I've seen a nun . . . she came to my daughter's funeral and a friend's . . ."

He nods, anticipating my question. "It was probably Sister Mary Margaret." He stares beyond me a moment. A bittersweet smile settles over him as he collects his thoughts. "Her little sister died of some undiagnosed illness at two, while they were in foster care, and was cremated. No funeral service or anything." He turns back to me, his eyes glistening. "We couldn't go wrong in following her example; she probably attended as an act of love."

It sounded like something Saint Thérèse would have said.

Everything Father Jacobsen has said to me flickers through my mind, and I consider his contemplative words, his deep thoughts and faraway gazes. I've been so busy using him to help myself that I haven't considered what path he may be walking himself. Appreciation wells in me. "Thank you for helping me. You've made such a difference." The words are so inadequate.

"Not me. The Holy Spirit. Makes you want to sing for joy, doesn't it?"

Sing for joy, *yes*. "I think I need to sing . . ."

Lilly and I hang together all weekend. With Henry still gone, Colette has found something or someone far better than me to occupy her time; she rarely comes home. So on Monday after school, I take Lilly to the salon, and we both get our hair cut and our nails done. She sleeps on my sofa all night undisturbed until I wake her with the aroma of coffee brewing. She looks refreshed, still sallow, her eyes still rimmed with dark circles, her eyes still vacant, but improved.

"I'm going to be late for school," she says. "I don't even have time for a shower."

I pull my pastel pink angora sweater from the closet shelf and hand it to her. She peels off her black turtleneck and clunky jewelry, and slips it over her head. A transformation falls over her as if I'd waved a wand — her cheeks bloom.

She glances in the mirror as she runs her fingers through her freshly cut tresses, which fall perfectly into place in a silky mass that now ends at her shoulders. She tosses me a scornful frown, but as I hustle her out to the car, I see her smile to herself.

That night, I take her to dinner and announce that we're going to join the choir.

"I don't sing," Lilly says.

"You're the one who dragged me to the basilica in the first place. You're coming with me. You need to sing as badly as I do."

A dozen women are seated around the organ when we arrive. I take a deep breath and make introductions to no one in particular. "Hi. I'm Rachel, and this is Lilly. Father Jacobsen told me about the practice today. I've never sung anywhere really, except back in high school in music class, but I was hoping I could join you."

Two ladies on the front row turn and whisper to each other, while a woman seated on the stool beside the organist looks up from sheets of music, one eyebrow cocked. Lilly takes a step back. I don't know what is wrong. Either they know who I am, or I have broken some sort of protocol. I hope it's the latter. I can bear the latter.

Then the familiar voice of Donna-Lynn, the librarian, rings out from the back row as she maneuvers forward between the women to shake Lilly's hand. "Rachel, I'm so glad you came, and that you brought your friend."

The choir director looks up from the choir book in her hands and peers at me over her reading glasses. "I'm sure you meant Father Nolan sent you. Glad to have you join us, Rachel." She hands us a book each. "And Lilly, is it? We love to have the young people join us in song."

Lilly and I exchange glances. I suppose we both imagined the chagrin that my first words seemed to cause.

The next afternoon, I decide it's time to take action, to find a permanent solution to Lilly's situation, and there's only one person I trust to help me find it: Father Jacobsen.

I sit in the pew for a while, thinking he will come out as he always does. There are more people in the sanctuary than usual. More stream in the door. Altar boys light the candles as the organist plays a soft melody. It's a weekday, but a service must be getting ready to start. I've never paid attention to the service schedule, other than the Sunday Masses.

I slip from the pew and walk to the front, to the left alcove, where the statue of Virgin Mary stares down at me as she did on my first visit. I sit and look at her. "Are you holding her today, Mary? Are you rocking her?" My arms ache with emptiness. I still want so badly to kiss that sweet forehead myself, but at least now I can think about it without going crazy. I know she's not coming back.

As the church fills up, a different priest comes out with several altar boys, so I slip out down the side aisle and out the side door, thinking Father Jacobsen must be in the offices in the adjoining building.

In the main office, a jolly, plump woman sits at a desk, absorbed with something on her computer. I approach her quietly. She turns from her computer screen, startled to see me.

"Is Father Jay here?"

"Who?"

"Father Jacobsen. I need to speak to him, please."

She shakes her head. "You must have missed church the last few weeks."

I don't answer. There is a nameplate on her desk. Dottie Hamilton. She looks like a Dottie. Grandma Dot. Her silver hair is curled softly all over her head. Two smudges of blush run across her cheeks. She's wearing a light blue V-neck shirt with matching slacks, and I'm struck by the idea that's she's spent fifteen years or more behind that desk, filling her days since children grew up and moved out.

She's looking at me just as closely. She probably recognizes me from the paper. Or maybe not. My hope of hopes is that most people have forgotten about the tabloid stories now. Maybe she's just seeing who I really am. Even though I wear classy clothes, women seem to look through my learned mannerisms. I'm not offended. I've quit caring. It was probably stamped so firmly on my brow in my youth, I'll be wearing a scarlet *A* to my grave.

When she's done evaluating me, wondering what I'd have to say to a priest, she looks me in the eye. "Father Jay left two weeks ago."

"I just saw him in the parking lot on Monday."

She looks at me like I'm crazy. I'm not crazy. I've been crazy, I know, but I know I didn't imagine my last conversation with Father Jacobsen. I've heard a lot of voices, and I've imagined a lot of things, but not him. Not Father Jacobsen.

"He isn't the pastor here. He was only here on sabbatical," she says.

She expects me to leave, but I don't. I stand my ground. I want an explanation.

Grudgingly, she continues. "He was in a car accident in May. A little boy died in the other car."

My gaze doesn't leave her face.

Suddenly a dam breaks in her as if she's wanted to talk about it all summer and it's been forbidden. "He was in bad shape after the accident and stayed in the hospital for a long time. When they finally released him, he was so overwrought with guilt, he couldn't function. He came here for a while to pull himself together. He tried to speak to the boy's mother, but she wouldn't talk to him."

I don't move. "Was it his fault?"

She doesn't want to tell me. The struggle creases her face. "It was that weird time in the afternoon when the sun is so blinding it's hard to tell if a traffic light is green or not. It wasn't green. He ran a stop light."

Her admission rams me in the gut. I drop into the guest chair in front of the desk as I grasp the depth of what this means — Father Jacobsen killed someone's son.

She looks down at her hands on the keyboard. "He's such a good man, it's been hard watching him suffer through this. He's had a hard time letting go of what happened until just recently. Over the past month or so, he seems to have made great strides. I don't know what's finally helped him deal with the boy's death, but whatever is healing him is truly a blessing. He is such a dear soul. I'm afraid there's a part of him that may never recover."

Every conversation I had with him comes flooding back to me with new clarity. He was searching for forgiveness as much as I was. I refocus on Dottie. "He was afraid the boy's mother would never forgive him, wasn't he?"

She shakes her head. "She won't even speak to him, so I'm sure she hasn't forgiven him."

I turn and walk out.

I go to the grove, the last place I saw Steven. The sun is bright even filtered through the leafless trees, but does little to warm the cold mountain air. I don't mind, though. I feel like it's shining into the pit of despair that once held me prisoner and chased away the darkness. I feel lit up from the inside.

I think about Father Jacobsen. We helped each other, he and I. I wonder if he has healed thoroughly, or if he still suffers, knowing the boy's mother won't forgive him. And I think of the mother growing ever more bitter with hatred and blame aimed at Father Jacobsen.

Perhaps I can do something for both of them.

I call the church on my cell phone and talk to Dottie again. "What was the lady's name, the mother of the little boy who died in the car accident?

"I can't give you that information."

I could give up except that I feel like I know this faceless woman with the dead child. I can be her light. "Please, Dottie . . . I lost a child, too. I need to help her."

Dottie is silent a moment, deciding if she should tell me. Finally, I hear the rustle of papers over the cell phone. "It was in the newspaper, so I suppose it's not a secret. Her name is Brenda Leed. She lives on the far side of town." She gives me the address.

As I turn off the highway, I recognize the exit: the gas station on the corner where I ran into Father Jacobsen. Brenda Leed's home was in a trailer park visible from the gas-station parking lot. *He was here, watching her, maybe trying to get up the nerve to talk to her.*

I avoid a pothole on the dirt road and pull up on the edge of what passes for a lawn in this brown season. A new gold Camry shines among the glinting rocks of the gravel parking spot in front of her trailer. A tricycle and a wagon sit midway across the yard of the next trailer. A swing set stands rusting in the backyard. A tool shed, its door gone, gapes beside it, sheltering a push mower, rakes, shovels, and a stack of cardboard boxes that hide whatever lurks in the back corners. I climb five wooden steps and stand beside a green ceramic frog to knock on the door.

I'd only seen her from the distance, but as the door opens, I know I have the right address because I see a reflection of my not-too-distant self in her round face — grief and depression fed by anger and resentment. I imagine her in party attire with her blond tresses falling around her face in place of the simple ponytail and bulky green sweatsuit she's wearing, and know she must have been gorgeous in her youth.

"Hello. My name is Rachel Winters, and I'm looking for Brenda Leed."

"Am I supposed to remember you from somewhere?"

"No, we've never met, but we do have something in common."

She props a hand on one hip and scowls at me. "Am I supposed to guess?"

I feel contrite, trying to formulate my words. I know what it is to have the loss of a child reduced to a frivolous statement. My comment, however graciously executed, will be a knife in her heart. I struggle to put that understanding into my introduction. "I suffered the loss of a child this summer on the same day as you."

Her eyes are cold. "And this is supposed to make us blood-brothers, or what?"

I have to get an edge into her darkness. I see it smoldering in her. I know the key: blame. "I know the man who killed your son."

She eyes me warily a moment, then eases the door open and lets me in. *Please let me into her heart as easily.*

It doesn't take much to get her talking. She shows me his room, his baseball mitt, his Pokemon cards, his collection of Star Wars action figures proudly displayed on a shelf in his room.

I tell her about Caroline and how I allowed her death to destroy my marriage. Her downcast eyes tell me she's done the same.

"I have a son," I tell her, "but I only get to see him every other weekend. It's hard."

"I had a daughter, but it's the same deal. I lost custody. I don't get to see her at all. There's a restraining order."

We sit in silence a moment, mourning what's happened to our lives, before I open a window in her mind, an escape from the darkness. I tell her about a man who helped me understand the power of forgiveness and how much it's helped heal me and restored my life.

Hours later, when night has settled over the land and the cold creeps through the thin walls of the trailer, she fixes us steaming cups of coffee, and I tell her who that man is.

She cries in my arms before we're done. The wall around her heart opens and light seeps back into her.

We are kindred spirits — friends.

Now she needs something concrete to grasp.

"Tell me about your daughter," I say.

She wipes away her tears and smiles in a sad, forlorn way. "I haven't had custody of her since the day she was born, so I don't really know her. I'm not allowed near her, you understand. Not even in the same state for the first five years. But I finally moved back here last year, hoping her father still lived in the area, and that maybe we could work out a more congenial agreement, but his wife won't let me near him or my daughter. I've been volunteering at her school so that I can watch her from a distance. She's a tiny thing with long blond hair and the prettiest blue eyes I've ever seen."

"What's her name?" I hold my breath.

"Lilly. Lilly Gordin."

Thank you, God.

Wednesday, I'm setting the puppets back in order and getting a drink of water. I'm bracing myself for Seth's arrival, all the words of our weekend running through my head like a mantra to my ineptness, my failure as a mother.

When his class arrives, Marley, the sweet little redhead, runs to my side and hugs me. "Hello, Miss Rachel. What story do we get to hear today?"

"If I tell you, it won't be a surprise."

Seth is watching, walking closer than before. Other children clamor around me and sit as I take my seat. Marley is still seated with one arm around my leg. Seth steps up. He doesn't come right to me, but he sits on the front row and scowls at Marley. He doesn't say anything. The children are as rambunctious as usual, jumping up to answer Pudgy's questions. Some yell out comments, but Seth says nothing.

At the end, Marley hugs me again. "Thank you, Miss Rachel. I loved that story. Can I check that book out? I want my mommy to read it."

"Sure, sweetie. Here you go. I can pick out another for tomorrow's group."

"Thank you. I love you!" she says, hugging me again.

"You can't love her. She's my mother, not yours," Seth says, giving her a push away.

"Don't push her, Seth."

"Are you really his mommy?" asks the little girl.

I pat him on the head. "Yes, I really am."

"How come he doesn't sit in your lap?"

" 'Cause the teacher said to sit on the floor, dummy," says Seth.

"I think maybe next Wednesday he may sit on a stool right here beside me and help me with the puppets."

"Really?" Marley asks. "He gets to help with the puppets?"

"Sure I do," Seth says. "She's my mother."

I lean down and hug him. "That's right. I'm his mother."

He hugs me back.

I talk to Seth every afternoon that week. He tells me about putting clouds on the weather chart, but no rain, and how much he hopes it will rain on his next turn. He tells me he's been invited to a pirate birthday party and that he'll get to wear a real eye patch like Captain Hook. He doesn't mention the library, and neither do I.

Wednesday, Seth is plodding along in the center of the line as usual, his eyes darting over his classmates.

Marley, front and center, runs to my side. "Hello, Miss Rachel. Look, I drew a picture for you." I wonder if the bug-eyed lady with stick arms is a rendition of me. At least I'm not a monster in her eyes. "Thank you, Marley."

Seth eases his way through the group and stands at the puppet table.

"Ready to help today?" I ask him.

He nods.

I turn to the group. "Today my son, Seth, is going to help me with the puppets."

Several kids exclaim their jealousy. Seth beams.

I think being my assistant has rated right up there beside charting the weather at preschool.

I try to recall when he stopped hugging me. Was it after Caroline died? Or earlier, after she was first born? Maybe I was too distracted and didn't hug him enough. I didn't intend to neglect him. I always loved him. Even at my worst moments, even when I was frustrated with him and angry, in my heart I still loved him.

When the class is ready to leave, I wait with bated breath. He turns to me, but I don't do anything. I don't want to force it. I want him to do it on his own this time.

He starts to walk away, but then he spies Marley heading my way, and spins around, holds out his arms and jumps at me. He's hugging me, and I'm on top of the world.

It's a moment of joy. *Seth is finally hugging me again; I am his mother.*

My heart leaps with the hope of all that lies before me.

I know there is someone else I need to talk to.

CHAPTER THIRTY-NINE

※※

Sinclair and I meet downtown for lunch. Finding parking isn't easy, so we meet at the street corner and start walking to Cottonwood Café with the sun on our backs and an icy breeze cutting our cheeks.

He broaches the subject almost immediately. "Seth asked me yesterday why you live in the pool house."

"What'd you say?"

"That you went away to heal."

"Good answer."

"He says you have."

"Have what?"

"Healed."

"Seth said that?"

"Yes. Don seems to agree."

"Donald Doc cures the quack."

"What?"

"Nothing. It's a joke between Lilly and me."

"He wants to know when you're coming home."

"Donald asked *you* that?"

"No, Seth asked."

I stop in my tracks and turn to face him. "So what'd you tell him?"

It's a serious question. I know he thinks so, too. He twists his wedding band around his finger. I hadn't noticed before now that he still wears it. He says, "I told him I'd find out and let him know."

"Meaning it's up to me now?"

He doesn't say yes. He doesn't even nod. He just breathes deeply and stares at me.

Suddenly I understand my mother. I understand why she let my father walk away. I don't want Sinclair to invite me home as Seth's mother. I want to be invited as his wife, his love. We have made love, but for a man, that's not always the same as *being* in love.

Unlike my mother, I'm not going to give up without prompting the answer. I step closer. "Tell me why you want me to come back."

"I thought you wanted to come back."

"I do. But I have to reinvent myself here. Now that all the dust is settling, I have to look at myself in the mirror, and this time around, I have to know who I really am. Pretending won't work anymore. When I married you, I loved everything about you, but you didn't really know me. Now you do."

"Are you trying to make a point?"

"I have to know what the terms are. Making love in secret is far different from being seen with me out in public after all that's happened. Do you really want me as your wife again? Can you love the real me now that you know the truth of who I am? Can you love me knowing what everyone else thinks of me? Do you want *me*?"

"If I didn't want you, we wouldn't be having this conversation."

I close my eyes. "Why did you marry me?"

He takes my hand and pulls me along; it's too cold to stand still. "So many reasons, but initially I was intrigued by the fact that although you were an only child like me, you lived a totally opposite life. You could do anything you wanted to do. You had no strings attached to your life, to who you were or what you became. I envied your freedom of being who you wanted to be. I wanted to be a part of that freedom, to touch that through you."

I had never thought of my life in those terms. It's a revelation to think of anyone envying the kind of life I worked desperately to escape. But it's not the answer that I'm seeking. "Tell me why you want me now."

"You're making this too complicated, Rachel. Come back, or make the decision that it's ending permanently. Seth can't live like this, not knowing where we stand."

"What about you? Can you live like this? Do you want me back?"

"How many times do I have to say it?"

He doesn't understand. I stop again and lean into his ear. "Tell me what you miss."

"What I miss?"

"When you think of me in the middle of the day, what comes to mind?"

He caresses my arm and then my hair. "Watching you get dressed."

I lean back, surprised. "Really?"

"Yes. Watching as you sit at the vanity to fix your hair and put on your makeup. Watching you pick out outfits and try them on, twisting and turning and posing in front of the mirror the way you do, then abandoning one and trying another."

I search his eyes and know he's not teasing me; he really does miss that.

He caresses my cheek. "And our long conversations. I could talk to you about anything and everything, not just surface stuff, but things that really matter."

My heart aches with the memory. "There are so many things I've wanted to discuss with you."

"I miss hearing you sing too."

"Actually, I sing in the church choir, now."

"The church choir?"

I nod and laugh at the shock on his face. He doesn't know about my visits to the basilica. I am a different person now, stronger, like steel, for having been through the fire, reshaped into something better.

My mother's words rise up inside of me. *Don't trust him.* "I don't want to go through all this heartache again either, Sinclair. How do I know you're not going to change your mind? I know now why I had to leave; the lamp episode, right?"

Sinclair nods.

"But there had to be more to it. Why couldn't we work our problems out?"

"You'll remember. Don says to let you remember on your own."

I step away from him and walk on. "Donald doesn't know anything."

Sinclair follows. "He's made you better, hasn't he?"

I'm not sure Sinclair is ready to hear what's happened to me, but it's who I'm becoming, so I have to tell him. I can't give up what I've found, not even for him, not even for the security of his house and his arms around me. I've learned they can never shelter me the way the light does. I can't leave the light. I have found God, and I plan to stay in his light. I won't let the darkness back in. "He may have helped, but it wasn't Donald that healed me."

"What then?"

I take his hand. I can't tell him. He'll think it's corny. He won't believe me. He has to feel it like I've felt it. I pull on him. "Come on. I have to show you."

It doesn't take long to get down the hill to the basilica. The noon Mass is underway. The church is full, but that doesn't bother me. I am a part of it now. I genuflect at the seat, having learned why, and I take a seat midway, pulling Sinclair in beside me.

The smell of incense tickles my nose, but after just a few Masses, I've come to associate it with the resonating voices raised up in chanting prayers and the hushed tones of the consecration.

Sinclair is silent as we make our way back up the street afterward. He is thinking. I see it in his face and in the steady pace of his steps. He stops in front of the bookstore halfway up the block. "You've been going there on your own?"

"Lilly took me the first time. But I kept going because of Father Jay." We walk more slowly as I tell him the story. I tell him how Father Jacobsen helped me, and how Lilly helped me, and how I want to help both of them. I tell him about the miracle of Brenda Leed being Lilly's mother, and wanting to reunite them. He listens to it all, accepts it all.

We stop at the top of the road. "I don't have much of a lunch hour left," he says.

"I'm sorry. We can still grab a sandwich together."

He caresses my neck. "I remember what we used to do with my lunch hours."

"Me, too." I rub my hand over his face. "I miss feeling the scruff of your face late at night."

He runs his hand through my hair. "The scent of your perfume lingering in the bathroom."

"The feel of your heart beating next to mine in bed."

"The curve of your body fitting mine while we sleep."

I smile. "Spooning."

"Yes, spooning." He kisses me. "Tonight?"

The kiss sizzles on my lips. "Yes, tonight."

CHAPTER FORTY

Henry has returned home and left again several times, never staying more than a day or two, but he can't stay gone forever. I can't leave without Lilly. I promised myself I would take care of her. I have to save her the way Ricky saved me. *Pay It Forward.* First I'll take her to live with me and Sinclair, and then I'll reunite her with her mother.

I decide to be direct with Colette. "I'm moving back in with Sinclair. I want to take Lilly with me."

"You want to what?"

"You've got to let her go, Colette."

She barely turns her eyes in my direction. "Why might that be?"

"If you don't, I'm going to go to the authorities."

That gets her attention. She sits up. "You don't know who you're dealing with."

"Really? Who am I dealing with, Colette? You have no more power in this town than I do."

"Henry does."

"He won't anymore if I have anything to say about it."

"You dare to throw a threat in my face? I took you in when no one else would speak to you. You would dare smear my family's reputation?"

I stand my ground. "You took me in so you could keep an eye on me. Keep your friends close and your enemies closer. You don't know which I am, do you, Colette? Well, I can tell you this: I wouldn't have Henry on a silver platter."

For some reason, she finds that amusing. "He doesn't come with a silver platter. All the silver, green, and gold are mine. He's nothing without me."

Then it dawns on me, all the innuendoes I've gleaned over the years. "No, he's poor without you, but it's you who are nothing without him."

I see her life story written on her face, and the stress of the past few months playing out; Henry really has found someone new, and she's scared to death. She throws her drink in my face and comes toward me.

A tray drops in the doorway, and we both turn to see Betts staring at us, our lunch lying scattered on the floor amid broken china.

I realize the predicament I've gotten myself in. I need to escape. I shift tactics and hope Colette will give in under Betts' gaze. "I don't care about you and Henry. All I want is Lilly. I *was* Lilly. I've walked in her shoes. It's a lonely road. She doesn't know how to live without Steven. Just give her a break from the stress."

Colette's features shift. Her most cunning smile creeps sideways up her expression. "That's what we're talking about? Stress? She's stressed over missing Steven, is she?"

I know she's not fooled, but maybe Betts is. "What did you think we were talking about?"

"Nothing. Whatever."

"So it's a go?"

"I don't know."

I have to get her out of Henry's grasp. "You and Henry could take a cruise. Relax a while. Get out of town for a while."

She frowns. "Stuck on a boat. If he gets in one of his moods, there's no escaping him."

Betts watches our exchange as she cleans up the mess Colette made, but I persist.

"Well, how about Europe? You've been saying for a year how you've wanted to go back." I get straight to the point. "He'd be away from everyone and everything in Europe."

The idea appeals to her. I see the wheels turning in her mind. Her eyes take on a faraway look. "That's an idea. We had such a wonderful time on our last trip there. We need a trip to clear the air." She snaps back to the present. "But the same rules apply. You don't let her go gallivanting around. You keep her home, hear?"

"Sure. Of course." *At home permanently.* I have no intention of ever letting Lilly fall back into Henry's hands.

I have my bags packed before Lilly gets home from school. I didn't have much in the pool house. My books, my clothes, my shoes. I'll send movers around for the bed and television in a few days.

I'm sitting in my car, waiting for her at the end of the driveway when she gets off the bus. "Go grab some jeans and whatever else you can pack in five minutes and we're out of here."

Her ticked-off school expression falls away to a huge question mark. "What?"

"You and me. We're leaving. Moving in with Sinclair."

"Huh? I don't understand."

"You said we had to get out of here, so we're doing it. Now go, get your stuff. Five minutes."

"You, not me."

I didn't expect her to put up a fight. "I'm not going without you."

She still isn't sure what I am saying. "You mean you're taking me to *live* with you and Sinclair?"

"More or less, yes. I'll explain later." I want to tell her I've found her mother, but not yet. Not until I'm sure things will work out. Neither of them needs more heartbreak. "Just get a few clothes and your toothbrush and a handful of that million-dollar jewelry, and let's get out of here."

She steps back from the car and stares at the house, still absorbing what I'm saying, glances back at me, then toward the garage, presumably looking to see who is home. Colette left an hour earlier; her car is gone. She turns once more, her eyes wide with the first sincere smile I've ever seen cross her face, and then she's gone, sprinting across the pavement to the front door like a gazelle crossing a field.

I sit tapping the steering wheel as the minutes tick by. Seven minutes and thirty-five seconds later, she comes out with a huge suitcase in each hand and a bedraggled Raggedy Ann doll under one arm. She hauls them to the car and throws them in the trunk.

"I hope that's a butt-load of Tiffany jewelry, because *I* can buy you clothes."

She laughs. She laughs!

I shove the car into drive and we race out of the cul-de-sac without looking back.

CHAPTER FORTY-ONE

L illy and I settle into Sinclair's house, at first awkwardly, watching everything we say, conscious of everything we touch, everything we use, but Seth accepts her without question, and Sinclair makes no demands, so we relax. At first, Lilly sleeps a lot, but then finds ways to be useful around the house, something new to a girl who previously had a maid doing everything for her.

A week later, Sinclair's mother asks all four of us to dinner to celebrate our reunion, but I know Lilly isn't ready for that. I'm not sure I'm ready for it, especially not with Lilly watching our every exchange. So I make excuses to Sinclair about Lilly needing some time in the house by herself.

But I can't make an excuse to get myself out of it. As I get ready, I grit my teeth. I can't believe I have to go under her microscope again. It's like starting back at the beginning, having to prove my worthiness.

Sinclair knows what I'm thinking without my saying so. "She's anxious to see us back together, you know."

"She hated me when I first came around, and I'm sure she hates me now."

"On the contrary, she's been your best advocate. She's wanted you back at home all along."

I try to digest that, but it doesn't make sense. Certainly, we'd become friends over the years, but I'd never lost the feeling of being on guard with her, of being mindful of my every movement, knowing a misstep would send me careening out of the social loop. But then it begins to make sense. "She wants to maintain the family image, doesn't she?"

"Of course she does. That's not her only reason, though. She likes you, Rachel. Why do you have such a hard time believing that?"

Because I've learned to be mistrustful. Sinclair wouldn't understand, though, so I go to him and kiss him. We still have much to work out, but we don't have to do it all in a day.

Whether he's right or wrong, I can approach her with a new attitude. It's a small thing. The Little Way.

Stepping into her house is strangely disconcerting. I'm guessing she wants to weigh the solidity of our situation, to see what damage she can do. I find her humming over a sink of sudsy water in the kitchen. She looks up and stops to dry her hands. "Rachel! It's so good to see you. I've missed you."

Said the spider to the fly. "I've missed you, too."

"I can't talk to a soul in the world the way I can you. You're such an easy person to have around."

What am I to say? Sinclair is moping on the far side of the kitchen, poking through the pantry, looking for cookies, no doubt. He knows I'm staring a hole through him, but he won't acknowledge me with more than a glance. Mrs. Winters and I have sidestepped each other ever since the funeral. She hasn't ever said anything bad to me, but I still suspect she has to everyone else in town. I have a sense of her nodding over my breakdown saying, *I told you so* to Sinclair. So why is she being nice to me now?

She drops the towel on the counter as she measures the interaction. "Have I said something wrong?"

"No."

"Then what's all this about? You know I didn't realize how much I wanted a daughter until you quit coming around to visit me. I love Sinclair dearly, but you've shown me what it means to have a daughter."

I've known what it is to have a daughter. Tears well up in my eyes. I try to ward them off, but they come anyway.

"Oh my, not five minutes in my house, and I've put my foot in it, haven't I? I've made you think of Caroline. No wonder you've been avoiding me; I'm so careless with my words. I'm so sorry, Rachel. That was terribly uncouth of me."

Is this a test to see how I'll react? I don't care. I won't pretend her words don't hurt. I'm done pretending. She can take me at face value or not at all.

She slips an arm around my shoulders. "You cry, Rachel. Cry all you want. I know I've told you before that you had to pull yourself together, but I was wrong to do that. A mother ought to cry for her child whenever she needs to, not bottle it up inside. My mother did that." She grips my arm as her voice shakes. "I had a sister who died before I was born. It made my mother afraid to ever take her eyes off me. Other mothers worried their kids would break their arms or legs; my mother constantly feared I was going to die walking down the road. All those stories I told you of frolicking around in the country? I didn't tell you my mother was right there in my shadow. I didn't get out of her eyesight until I was in my teens. It made me near crazy." She lets go of my arm and eases herself into a kitchen chair and stares at the floor. "I guess I aimed that anger at you when you kept carrying on so about Caroline. Accidents happen. We can't go on blaming ourselves forever. But we can cry out our grief whenever need be. My mother, she was still crying when I was ten years old, right in the middle of a sunny day, just because some passerby would say a girl as pretty as me needed a sister to make a matched pair. My mother would set to bawling, and there wasn't a thing that could stop her flow of tears except for me to crawl into her lap and let her get her fill of holding me close."

I grab a napkin from the table and turn away to busy myself stirring a pot.

She's focused on her own memories and doesn't sense my discomfort until she looks up at me. "I resented all that crying," she says. "Now, I'm not sure why. Maybe it seemed as if she loved my dead sister more than me. I don't know. I'm not a deep thinker. But I've been thinking back over my life and your life, and about sweet Caroline, and we need to cry. We need to cry."

Tears are flowing down her cheeks as steadily as mine. Sinclair's, too. He turns and strides from the room.

Oh, Sinclair, I don't blame you. Not anymore. Don't take my tears that way.

I tell him so later, and he takes my words silently and knits them into his heart. He sweeps my hair from my forehead and kisses me. "I cry whenever you cry, Rachel, but sometimes my tears fall inside, where no one can see them. There's not a day that goes by that I don't wish we could replay the whole thing differently. I can't make time go back. I wish I could." He takes a deep breath. "I can't fall apart. I have Seth to think about and a medical practice to run. Don't fault me for trying to be strong."

"I don't. But I can't hide my emotions. Not like I used to."

"I know."

I weave my fingers into his, and he lays his other hand over them. "Mama wants to take you out to lunch next week. Are you up to it?"

"Downtown?"

He nods.

"Then the question is, are *they* up to it?"

"Who?"

"The ladies. I know she'll take me to one of their hangouts. I'm not sure they'll know how to deal with the Revived Rachel Winters."

He laughs. "Don't be too hard on them."

I smile and caress his hair.

My old society friends are seated in the center of the restaurant enjoying a festive luncheon when we enter. I'm guessing Mrs. Winters knew they would be here. She's testing me to see how I'll behave.

She touches my arm and whispers, "Go on, dear, say hello."

I don't disappoint her. I'm not faking anything anymore; I'm stronger than I was. I know how the game works. I can play it. And maybe, just maybe, it will turn out that they are real friends after all, and I haven't given them a chance, any more than I gave Sinclair's mother a chance.

I stop at their table and nod to each one of them. "Hello, Zoe, Maureen, Andrea."

Maureen's fingers play along the stem of her wine glass. The soft light glints off her rings and bracelet, and all I can think is how gaudy the pieces look. I wonder how I ever cared about such useless trinkets. Does she recognize the real treasure in her life — her husband and children? One does not exclude the other, but sometimes one outshines the other.

"Nice to see you again, Rachel. We hear you and Sinclair have gotten back together."

I must be newsworthy again. "We've never been apart, really." Let her puzzle that one out. "Enjoy your lunch," I say and return to my mother-in-law's side. As I open a menu, Amy Bollen walks in and surveys the room. Her gaze pauses on me a second, her face stiff, her smile forced. I think about how she treated me when I dropped off Seth at her son's birthday party — wavering as to how to regard me when her own position in this small social circle remains so tenuous. She moves through the lunch crowd and arrives at their table. Andrea picks up a shopping bag off the floor and places it in the empty seat. Zoe looks away. Maureen is saying something, her words no doubt as coy as her smile.

"What's going on?" I ask Mrs. Winters, motioning toward their table.

"Haven't you heard? Patrick left her yesterday. He moved in with Jocelyn."

"Patrick Bollen and Jocelyn!" *That certainly puts a new twist on Patrick joining Sinclair's practice.*

Amy is turning from the group, floundering. Her world is falling apart.

I have been there. I still have one foot on the crumbling edge of my cavern. *How sweet is the way of love . . .* Yes, Saint Thérèse, how sweet it is. Help me to live for love instead of spite or appearances.

I am whom I've become, strengthened by fire and polished with God's love.

I stride across the room and take Amy's arm. "Amy, it's been ages. I wish you would come join me. We have so much to catch up on."

She turns to me, her wide-eyed shock turning to gratitude, and I escort her back to our table.

CHAPTER FORTY-TWO

Lilly has been with us for two weeks. *Paramore* blares nonstop from the guestroom, where we replaced the fold-out couch with Caroline's bed. Lilly has relaxed and turned it into her space with her odd mixture of *self* imposed on it: a crucifix hangs over the bed directly across the room from a poster of some hunky guy with dark, smoldering eyes. Her dresser is cluttered with random jewelry and makeup, but her tastes are changing. She really didn't pack many of her clothes other than jeans and a couple of shirts; most of her suitcase space was taken up by shoes, so her sloppy half-gothic look has given way to a more stylish persona as she prowls through my closet each evening looking for outfits, and her makeup routine includes less black than it did just a week ago.

Sinclair has come to care for her as much as I have. She's a far different girl from the one I first set eyes on. She still moves silently with the stealth of a cat, but she no longer slumps, and dark circles no longer ring her eyes. Thankfully, the same can be said of me.

It's long past time to introduce her to her mother, Brenda Leed.

Lilly hangs back at first, sizing her up. When she finally steps forward, her face is a cold, expressionless mask. I'm surprised by what she says. "I recognize you. You volunteer at the school. I've seen you watching me."

"It was as close as I could get to you."

She glares at Brenda with eyes that could kill. "Why did you leave me behind?"

"Your father had the power of lawyers behind him. And money and people. I had nothing."

"He's a pervert. You left me in hell."

I put a hand on Lilly's shoulder. "Lilly, she doesn't need this. She didn't know," I say. "I told you she's been trying to get you back."

Tears stream down Brenda's cheeks. "You're right, Lilly. I was a scared kid. I was too young to be married to a cunning man like Henry, not much older than you, and I was defenseless. I tried running away, but he sent men after me. There was no escape."

"So you sacrificed me."

"I thought I was leaving you to a better life. Henry could take care of you. I had nothing, not a dime to my name. He made sure of that." She steps forward. "Marge loved you, didn't she? She wasn't faking it. I would have known. She told me you were the reason she married Henry, because she couldn't have children."

Lilly sniffs and wipes her runny nose with the sleeve of her shirt. I know from the jut of her chin that she wants to say something but can't get it out.

I take a guess. "It was after that, wasn't it?"

She nods.

Brenda bites her lip and swallows something she was going to say, then mutters under her breath. "After the two bimbos?"

Lilly nods.

I'd seen pictures of them. Blond bombshells. Failed relationships one after the other. Further proof that he married Colette for her money.

"I'm so sorry, Lilly." She reaches out and touches her arm. "I'm so sorry. But I'm here now. I won't let anyone hurt you again."

Lilly isn't as tough as she wants to be. Her shoulders begin shaking with sobs. I embrace her. I want so badly to wash the hurt away, but it will take time. She is scarred so deeply. All the heartache of my troubled childhood was worth the cost, knowing I can help Lilly find her way back to normal. It's not too late. I won't let it be too late.

I wave Brenda forward, and she comes into our clasp, and Lilly leans into her, releasing a torrent of tears along with a hoarse whisper, "I still have the doll."

Brenda smiles through her tears. "Raggedy Ann?"

Lilly nods and sobs even louder.

"Cry, my Lilly. Cry," Brenda says. "Mama won't let you go ever again."

It's time for me to make amends with my mother, too.

I go to see her on Holy Thursday with an Easter basket in hand, put together for me by Miss Claire, of course: Italian pasta and sauce, superb garlic bread, a bottle of Vietti Masseria Barbaresco wine, and two crystal wine glasses.

She accepts the basket with a nod, and we share the meal together sitting in front of the television with our plates in our laps.

Mama drinks the wine and licks her lips. "Not bad."

I grin, knowing she would have been just as happy with a grocery-store brand. She would faint if I told her how much I paid for it. "Are you happy, Mama?"

"What's to be happy about? I reckon I'm as happy as you are. I thought I taught you better than to trust a man, and you've done it twice now with the same one. Be on guard, girl. He'll just drop you again."

"Some guys are worth trusting. Some guys are truly capable of love, Mama."

"Nonsense. It's only lust that registers with them. I never yet met one I could trust, and I've knowed more men than most."

We sit in silence for a moment, both of us thinking of all the rotten men who passed through our lives.

"You could have trusted Ricky, Mama. He loved you."

"Bah. Ricky. He only thought he was in love. Soon as things started going sour, he'd a'been gone same as the rest. Better to end things before they get to where they break your heart open. I did that once, and I promised I wouldn't never go there again, and I ain't ever, neither."

"Did you, Mama? Did you love somebody?"

I can tell she doesn't want to say anything. She turns away from me and lights a cigarette. She pulls a heavy drag and slowly blows out smoke rings. She still at her age thinks it makes her glamorous to have a cigarette dangling from her fingertips, but I see the age lines the habit has etched into her face and how it's stained her teeth. I'll change my clothes as soon as I leave to rid myself of the clinging odor, but it's who my mother is, and I've long associated the smell with her.

She puffs away half the cigarette before she turns and crushes it into the ashtray. "I was young, and he was married. He kept saying he was going to divorce his wife, but he never even told her about us. One day she found out, got herself a detective, and built up a whole portfolio on him and me together, and took it to some lawyer. Got her divorce quick as a wink. I figured that was a good thing for me. He was free of her, and he could move in with me, right? We could get married and live happily ever after. But that's not the way it worked out. He was so twisted up at her cutting him loose that he couldn't stand it. He claimed he needed time to get his head sorted out. She'd taken most everything that belonged to them, and he was about broke. Just had his guitar left. Turns out that held more promise for him than a life with me. One day he just didn't come home from his job at the garage. He disappeared in his truck with nothing but the clothes on his back, his paycheck, and his guitar. I never heard from him again. I guess he thought he'd make it in Nashville or somewheres, but I ain't never heard tell of him on the radio, so who knows what happened to him."

The obvious question is battering my brain. I can't ignore it. "Was that my father?"

She stares at me with a slapped look. "You'd like that, wouldn't you? To think the one guy I loved was your daddy, so's you could've been part of the one good thing I ever had. Well, don't figure on ever knowing who your daddy was."

Tears well in my eyes. A choking sensation rises up my throat. I sit a little longer, trying to calm the quivers rising through me, but it's no use. I need to be alone. "I've got to go, Mama. It was good seeing you again." I move to her side and bend to kiss her. The smell of tobacco fills me as she turns her leathery cheek to me. Despite everything, words of love fill my mouth, but I don't want to say it now, even though that's why I came.

As I stand, she reaches out to grab my arm. "I never regretted having you, Rachel. You kept me company on a lot of lonely nights, girl."

And then it pours forth, and I'm saying it once again, maybe for the last time. "I love you, Mama."

Halfway to the door, she stops me with her words. "Yes, he was your daddy."

I don't turn around to look at her. I know there are tears in her eyes she doesn't want me to see. "Maybe he didn't come back, Mama, but I always will. I'll always come back." And I meant it.

CHAPTER FORTY-THREE

I call Sinclair to tell him I'm on my way home. It's a long drive, but when I arrive four hours later, he is sitting on the front porch, waiting for me. I rush to him, and he enfolds me in his arms, his lips meeting mine.

Inside, Seth is sprawled on the floor, putting together the last of a wildlife puzzle on a huge foam board. He wants to frame it for his room. I look over his shoulder at how much he's accomplished while I've been gone.

"What do you think?" he asks.

He's including me in his life again. "Wonderful," I say to him. "You'll be done tomorrow, won't you? We'll take it to the framer right away so it won't get messed up."

That satisfies his need for orderliness, his need to control his surroundings — a need caused by me.

Sinclair has been with Lilly long enough, seen enough of her gradual transformation to know that Henry has been abusing her. We anticipate having to press charges to win Brenda's custody battle, and he knows it will get ugly. She must be willing to tell what's been happening. We finally confront her later that night.

She's on the sofa, reading a book. Sinclair sits on the ottoman in front of her and waits for her to look up. She knows whatever it is, it's serious. She closes the book and grips it with both hands. "What?"

Sinclair doesn't touch her with his hands, but his eyes embrace her. "Tell me about Henry."

Lilly sneers at me, all the trust that's grown between us shredded in ten seconds. "There's nothing to tell," she says to Sinclair. "I just don't like him."

"You're safe now, Lilly. You can tell me the truth."

She clamps her lips together.

"It's wrong, Lilly. Whatever he's doing to you, it's wrong and it needs to stop."

She glares at him a moment more, then at me, and then turns her face away to stare out the window.

I take a seat beside her and lay one hand on her leg. "Lilly, come on. This is it. The moment of truth."

She stands and walks from the room.

Sinclair sits back. I can tell from the set of his expression that he knows she's lying, that she's afraid to state the truth.

I want to run after her and press her to admit everything, but I don't. I've been there. I know why she won't admit it. Fear. Shame. Denial. You just want it all to go away.

Sinclair agrees with me when we whisper about it in bed that night. "I can't make a case for her, though, if she won't make a statement against him. It's not like she's four years old. If questioned, she would have to speak up."

"Maybe she feels like she's safe now, so it's easier to ignore what happened and move on."

So we let it go. He can't be charged with anything until he and Colette are home from Europe anyway.

I'm pretty forgiving of messes, but we've invited Sinclair's mother over for Easter dinner, so Friday afternoon, while she's at school, I decide it's time to clean up the catastrophe of Lilly's room. An hour into the job, I'm working through the stack of mess on her dresser when I come across a sock with something hard inside — a cassette tape.

I turn the tape over in my palm. Could it be the tape from the front-door intercom? The one that went missing? Why would Lilly take it? What could possibly be on it that she was afraid of someone hearing? Something she and I said to each other? Something between her and Steven?

Then it dawns on me. *The murder!*

It's a microtape. I don't have anything to play it in. Do they even sell microcassette players anymore? The easiest option hits me — to go to Colette's house and plug it into the intercom there. There's no one in the house but Betts, and even she might not be there, since Colette and Henry are gone. I glance at the clock. It's two o'clock. Good Friday service is at three, of course. If I run by Colette's house to listen to the tape, I'll be cutting it close, but I have to know.

I don't want Lilly with me when I listen to the tape. I get my cell phone from my pocketbook and punch in a text message to Sinclair: *Please pick up Lilly from school. Seth and I will meet you at church. I'm running by Colette's house on the way. I found a tape in Lilly's room that I think goes in the intercom. It might be something important.*

It's a day in mourning, gray with rain hanging in the clouds, threatening to spill down at any time. The cold air, fifteen degrees cooler than just two days earlier, bites at my face. I tie up the belt of my leather coat and hurry to the car.

Seth doesn't notice where we're going until I pull into the driveway. "What are we doing here?" he asks. "I want to go home."

"I just have to check something. It will only take a minute."

Colette's car is in the driveway, but it's been there all month. I lived there long enough to know that Betts uses it to run errands and moves it around so it looks like someone is home whenever Colette and Henry travel.

I pull down to the pool house, not caring if Betts is staring out the windows.

I climb out and open Seth's door. "Come on."

"I don't want to."

I spot his blue ball in the backseat, left from our visit to the park earlier in the week. "Bring your ball. Come on." It's a temptation he won't refuse. He never liked ball until Lilly started teaching him to play soccer and Sinclair pulled out pictures of himself in the field during high school. Now Seth practices because Sinclair has promised to get him on a team when he turns five.

A gust of wind whips through the trees and flips over a lawn chair set out in the sun by the pool. I zip up Seth's jacket. "Warm enough?" I ask. He nods and pulls away to kick the ball. I glance around the yard. It feels abandoned, unused. There are leaves floating on the surface of the pool and swirling in the depths of the water. The lounge chairs have been stored away. The trash can has rolled on its side into the far corner, where it rocks in the gusts of air sweeping across the yard. I check the gate to the pool: locked.

I turn back to Seth. He's already absorbed in practicing his kicks. He is single-minded and will be totally absorbed until I call him back to the car with the same urging it took to get him out. I leave him there and follow the sidewalk around back. The key is under the brick as usual. I ease the door open, half-expecting the boogey man to jump out at me, but it's empty, silent, and musty. I can't believe I was living there just a month earlier.

I look at the intercom and realize it's only a speaker and microphone. It's the unit at the front door that takes a cassette.

I leave the door open and rush across the yard, pausing as I pass Seth. "I have to run up to the front door."

He ignores me. He's practicing. I leave him with his ball.

Betts peers at me through the front door, her face contorted in the bevels of the opaque oval of glass. Grim face and shifty eyes. She gives me the creeps, but my distance from this house of horrors fills me with bravery and I smile.

She retreats from the door, her footsteps slapping against the slate in the foyer, leaving another figure in the center of the foyer still staring at me — the cable guy. What is he doing in the house? Has he taken up residence with Betts in Colette's absence? Have they been having an affair the whole time?

He leans against the wall and watches me through the beveled glass.

My hands shake so much that it's hard to maneuver the tiny cassette.

A tech-nerd would laugh at the intercom system. It's original to the house, at least thirty years old. The brass plating has chipped away and the lettering on the buttons has almost worn off, but not completely: *Record a message*; *Play a message*. Odd to allow someone to play a message, but presumably better than leaving notes taped to the door. I slip the cassette into the slot and press play.

A terrified scream crackles from the speaker. *"Henry!"* It is Lilly's voice, I'm sure of it; Lilly hollering to Henry. My mind connects the dots with alacrity. The intercom can be set to record only from the front door, so Lilly had to have been right where I am. She said she'd gone to the store to get Henry something. Did she get locked out? Did she holler to him to answer the door? Why did she press record?

The tape is still rolling. Another voice comes on, angry, growling, muffled, and further from a microphone. *"I won't allow you to destroy everything I've worked so hard to create. Don't you see if you turn him in, you'll damage me as much as him?"*

I lean in closer to hear. A different voice. Steven's? *"It's going to stop, and if you don't make him, I will."*

"You would destroy everything I've achieved for her *sake? She's nothing. She's a spoiled brat. She asks for it."*

Flesh meets flesh. A slap to the face. Steven slapping his mother, I'm sure. Steven's voice again, firm, resolute. *"I'm turning him in."*

"I won't let you ruin me." Desperation.

A struggle. Something crashes. A scream, a thud, moaning. *"You shouldn't have pushed me. You never understood what I've suffered to get here."*

I shiver as I listen to the scene unfold. My stomach rises to my throat as the connections in my brain come together. I fit all the pieces into place, and the truth flashes inside my head like the glaring lights of a ballfield coming on at midnight. The evidence is so clear now. Everything Lilly said made sense. The drugs, the flashlight, the intercom. Colette was behind it all. Jealousy, fear, rage. She couldn't have really meant to hurt him, to kill her own son, could she? Anger fed by her drugs. She didn't realize what she was doing. She hit him in anger, and the anger got out of control.

The enormity of it crashes over me. *Colette killed him! She killed her son!* I turn to look at the pool house to see the scene as Lilly must have seen it from where I'm standing. I can't quite see in, but I know if I take a few steps down the driveway, I would be able to see everything. The glass doors that look out on the pool are clearly visible. On this gray day, the interior is dark and empty, but in the black of night with lights on inside, it would be like a television screen.

Lilly said she'd gone up the road to get Henry something — some Advil? She must have heard Colette and Steven arguing when she came back down the driveway. Maybe she pushed the intercom button at the front door, trying to summon Henry, but pushed the record button by mistake. It was her scream at the beginning of the tape, calling for Henry in a panic. She must have removed the tape later when she heard what was on it. That's why there wasn't a tape when I tried to leave a message for Colette: Lilly took it.

Did she stand in the dark and watch Colette bludgeon Steven? Did she watch Colette stab him to death?

I hope Lilly didn't see. I hope she dashed down the road to the phone booth and missed the worst of it. I close my eyes and I'm with her that night, seeing it unfold as it must have been:

Steven had left me in the grove and returned home to Lilly. I'd sent him home to her, to hold her in his arms and remember it was her that he loved, not me. He went ready to gather her in his arms and profess his love for her, I'm sure of it.

He went to the pool house. That's where they always met. He walked through the pool house, calling softly for Lilly, expecting her to be there waiting for him in the dark, and instead his mother was there. He threatened to report Henry to the authorities. Colette probably didn't intend the first blow. She didn't mean to kill him. But fury took over. He fell at her feet, his head bleeding onto the carpet, but still conscious. Colette, crazy with drugs, driven with madness and disbelief, struck him with the knife to silence him. His body bled onto the floor while Lilly ran back from the phone booth.

I had still been driving around town, wasting time, wasting away the hours of my life because my life meant so little to me, while Steven bled away the last of his.

My heart cries out for Steven, and my soul bleeds for Lilly, for the horror she witnessed and will carry with her always. No wonder she was afraid to tell what she knew. Whom could she trust? No one. No one but God.

I turn back to the intercom. There's only one voice now muttering incomprehensibly amid shuffling and moans. I can't bear it. I pull the cassette from the machine and slide it into my pocket. I have to call the police. I have to get Seth and get out of there.

I turn around, ready to run.

Colette is standing behind me.

CHAPTER FORTY-FOUR

W hat a surprise," Colette says around her cigarette. The gray day has sucked the life out of her. Despite the vacation, her skin is pale and blotchy.

Her bloodshot eyes are trained on me, so I suck in air to keep from fainting and act as if I've shown up to see her. "I wasn't sure you were home."

"Obviously." She takes a drag on her cigarette. "Where's Lilly?"

"She and Sinclair are meeting me at church in a just a bit." The half-crazed look in her eyes frightens me. "I just wanted to let you know I'm going to look in the pool house for some earrings I've misplaced, if that's okay."

"Earrings. Sure."

I take a step to go around her. "I'll only be a minute."

Fear tingles up my spine. Did she hear the tape? Does she know that I know she killed her son?

Every step, she's right behind me.

"Seth!" I scream his name, fear rising. I don't see him anywhere.

"Oh where, oh where has that little boy gone?" she sings.

I turn on her. "What have you done with him?"

She laughs.

The tension is too much for me. "You're crazy!" I scream at her. I turn and search the yard with my eyes. Better to think, not just run. Where would he be? "You won't get away with this!"

"I'm not the crazy one, here," she says. "You are. Everyone knows that. They'll assume it was you."

"Lilly will tell."

Colette cackles. "No, she won't. If she was going to tell, you'd have been to the police with her already. You're my only problem, but you're insane, delusional, suicidal."

She doesn't know how much stronger I've become.

There's no sign of Seth. "Seth?" My voice dissipates in the wind. "Seth!"

"He was here a minute ago," she says with a lazy drawl, "I gave him some candy."

Candy? She sees the question on my face and laughs, and I know it wasn't candy. What has she done to my son?

Colette sees my panic and blocks my path as she sneers at me. "You're pathetic. I can't believe you have the guts to stand there and act like you're better than me. At least I had a motive," she says. "Steven turned against me."

"You're crazy. You murdered him in cold blood! How could you do that?"

She grabs my arm and hisses into my face, "Love and hate are but a breath away from each other. Who knows that better than you?"

I try to pull away, but her grip tightens. I assume she is talking about Sinclair. "You're wrong. I don't hate Sinclair. I never stopped loving him. And I would never hurt him!"

As her face twists with anger, a memory flashes in me, but shuts down. I can feel my defenses pushing whatever it is away.

Colette leans closer. "I couldn't let him ruin me after all the effort it took to reach this point. If I lost Henry, they wouldn't accept me anymore. I'd still be rich, but money without respect is nothing. I like who I am in this town, and I'm not going to let anything take that away from me." She crushes her cigarette under the toe of her shoe. "What's your excuse?"

"My excuse? My excuse for what?" I scan the yard. Is he behind the car? "Seth?"

I jerk my arm from her clasp and get far enough from the house to see the pool house clearly. *Where is he?*

She follows me.

"Seth!" I scream, but still no answer.

Don't panic. Think clearly. Where could he be? Behind the pool house? In the woods? Did she lure him inside? I glance back at her house, but I don't want to go in there. I head toward the pool house. He must be behind it, in the narrow area before the woods.

Colette is still laughing, dogging my steps. "Oh, I forgot. You didn't murder your daughter. It was all a tragic accident."

I stop in my tracks to stare at her. *Murder my daughter?* Images flare in my memory. Father Jacobsen's green eyes narrowed at me with that odd consternation of love, worry, and mistrust. Seth's tiny hand pulling out of mine, his little face with its mashed-together lips and sniffling nose displaying fear as he ran to his father and hid behind his legs. The look of disgust tossed at me by old friends. The cold emanating from Sinclair.

And the car. I remember the car.

"Tell me what you remember," Donald Doc would say.

It was the day of my argument with Colette.

My eyes settled on the shopping bags sitting in the entranceway. Like a robot, I carried them down the hall and put everything away.

I passed by Caroline's bedroom, but I didn't go in. She slept through Colette's fit. It was nice she was taking such a good nap. I needed one, too. I was exhausted. And the whiskey had worked its magic. My bones felt like limp noodles. I couldn't keep my eyes open. I dragged myself down the hall to bed.

I relive it in slow motion, every step drawn out, but it is a mere flash in my mind, a coming together of reality.

"Seth!" I scream and take off at a run.

I hear her behind me, standing there, watching me, laughing like a maniac. "I think I kicked his ball into the pool. Oops. Another tragic accident."

I hear the splash and know she's planned this. "Seth!" I rush across the lawn, to the brick pathway that runs along thick shrubbery and the chain-link fence bordering the pool, to the gate. "Seth!" *Please, God, not my son, too. Please God, not my son.*

As I pass through the gate, I hear the squeal of a car in the driveway. Colette leaving? I don't care. I don't look. Seth is floundering in the water, his face contorted with fear and the shock of the cold water. His lips are turning blue. His eyes are wide with horror.

It's the same look I've imagined over and over again, the look I picture on her face at the end.

Caroline was in Sinclair's black Expedition. I remember buckling her in, looking at her cooing in her car seat, sucking on her fingers, little bubbles of spit glossing her lips. She had such long, dark eyelashes for such a tiny thing. The blackness of them stood out against her pale skin. Her little fluff of hair stood in a red barrette to match her new red polkadot jumper and infant-size Mary Janes. Her cheeks were flushed. It had to be Sinclair's fault — it was his car. He forgot! Not me. What did Colette mean? I did not murder my baby girl!

When Sinclair got home, I was still asleep. He asked where Caroline was. I told him she was in her crib. But she wasn't. He yelled at me from her room. I loped down the hall. He was right. She wasn't in her crib. She wasn't in the family room. I remembered buckling her in. I laughed. I *laughed,* thinking he'd forgotten to pick her up from his mother's house. But he hadn't ever taken her to his mother's house. My car had broken down the day before, so he had left me his car for the day, and Jocelyn had picked him up for work.

I remember.

I remember what happened.

I had left Caroline in the car while I unloaded the bags. But then Colette had shown up and started the argument. The stress, the drinks, the frustration, the lack of sleep . . . I had fallen into bed thinking Caroline was napping in her crib.

While I slept, Caroline cried inside the tomb of the car. Sinclair's car. Because *I* left her there, not Sinclair.

We found her there, in the car.

We found her dead.

I forgot to take her out of the car.

I forgot her.

While I slept, Caroline cried.

While I slept, Caroline died.

I killed her. "I didn't mean to! Oh, Caroline!" *It was my fault. All my fault. Not Sinclair's.* Oh, Caroline. I'm so sorry. I'm so sorry."

The shroud of darkness swirls around me, pulling me down, sucking the world from under my feet.

"God forgives," Father Jacobsen said.

Not this!

The memory almost consumes me.

But Seth is there, in the water, floundering, sinking.

Not Seth! Not Seth, too!

Sirens are screaming in the distance.

I dive into the water. The cold envelops me and time stands still, his tiny body sinking slowly in front of me as I struggle in my sodden clothes to reach him, his mouth open in a scream I cannot hear.

My son! I wrap my arms around him and heave him upward, kicking with all my strength. As we break through the surface, I hear voices and sirens. Lights are flashing.

Sinclair is there, running to the edge of the pool, reaching for me, pulling at Seth, heaving him from the water.

I let go of his little body, and the cold sucks me down.

A hand stretches out. It's too far away. It's too hard to reach. I can't be forgiven. I am not worthy.

I killed my baby.

I don't want to remember anything anymore.

Let me die. Let it end.

But there is a light glowing. *Forgiveness is but a breath away.* "O Jesus, forgive me."

Even the tiniest wildflower.

A daisy. He loves me, he loves me not.

A splash beside me. Sinclair's strong arms encircle me and thrust me to the surface. Hands grasp me and pull me out. An officer. In an instant, Sinclair heaves himself up beside me and urges me forward to where Lilly is crouched against the wall with her arms around Seth. Someone lays a blanket around them. I crawl over and join them with Sinclair at my side. Lights flash orange and blue around us. "She gave him something! Some kind of drug!" I scream.

Sinclair bends over him, takes his pulse, checks his eyes and begins peeling the wet clothes off of him. "He's fine. He's going to be fine." Another blanket appears and we rub him down, wrap him up.

"Paramedics are on the way," an officer behind me says.

"Colette killed Steven," I say to Sinclair.

He nods. "They know. When I got your text, Lilly told me everything. They've arrested Colette."

There's more to it than that. I feel my blood rushing through my veins. My head is spinning with disbelief. She drugged Seth. She lured him to the pool. I almost lost Seth.

The loss of Caroline flows over me anew. I turn and bury my head in Sinclair's chest, sobbing so hard I can barely breathe. "It was my fault."

"Shh," he says, patting my back. "You saved him. He's fine. He's fine."

I shake my head and back up from him. "Caroline," I say. "It was my fault. I left her in the car, didn't I? You've known all along and said nothing." The enormity of the realization pours over me. "You've known all along."

He pulls me back into him. "It was an accident." He kisses the top of my head.

I think back over Caroline's death again, the scene plays over and over, a memory zipping by again and again, ten times in as many seconds. Colette was there. We argued. She stormed out to her car. I fell asleep. Caroline died in the car from heat exhaustion. It was my fault. Colette was there. We argued. She stormed out to her car. I fell asleep.

Caroline died in the car. We argued. She stormed outside. Caroline was in the car.

I throw off the blanket and jump to my feet. *Where is she? Where is Colette?*

I see them putting handcuffs on her.

I rush up the yard. "How could you?"

She shrugs. "I didn't tell him to jump in. He was chasing the stupid ball. I just kicked it in."

"Caroline!" I scream. "You must have seen Caroline in the car. You saw her in the car and said nothing, didn't you? You knew I'd left her in there, and you didn't tell me. You were so angry at me that you wanted her to die."

"Not my fault," she says flatly. "A tragedy that ruined you."

The cop nudges her toward the patrol car. She plods forward, her expression bland, devoid of any regrets over what she's done or the mess she's made of our lives.

I want to beat her. I want to scream and pound her with my fists. But I am dying inside. I fall to my knees.

I am being crucified.

CHAPTER FORTY-FIVE

⚜

Friday night, the realization of my part in Caroline's death wed itself to my soul. I felt the nails of my guilt anew as I replayed it in my mind over and over again, all night long. Saturday, I buried myself in living memories of her. I touched her clothes. I caressed her pictures. I cradled her doll.

I watched Sinclair and Seth watching me, and I knew I couldn't do it all again. I couldn't let myself fall apart a second time.

I clutched the small cache of Caroline's hair, stared out at the world, and found the resolve to be strong. Saint Thérèse had armed me, and it was time to live the lesson of accepting pain and trials in the name of love.

I let my guilt build like a snowball, rolling through the caverns of my mind, collecting all the pinpricks of remorse and shame from every hiding place I'd created until it there was no memory, no morsel of that day or any event leading up to it that I hadn't recalled. I let it concentrate in a hard knot at the core of my being, and refined it until it was a glowing black globe, like a ball of onyx.

And then, when the sun crept across our yard this morning, I ventured out to the swing, to the quiet sounds of spring rising in the grass and blooming in the trees, and I offered it up to God.

It is Easter Sunday. The resurrection. The sun is warm upon my face, and the Holy Spirit has filled me with light. Jesus has washed me clean.

Sinclair, spying me from the kitchen window, must see that I am smiling into the rising sun. He joins me and pulls me into his arms for a long kiss. He has loved me through everything. I look into his eyes and know we are going to get through this together.

"It's time to get ready for church," he says.

We all attend Mass together: Sinclair, Seth, Lilly, and I.

As Lilly and I take our places in the choir loft at the back of the church with the choir for the first time, I smile to myself at the irony of how I'd run from this place like a scared rabbit such a short time ago, never dreaming what lay ahead.

I see Brenda in the crowd, sweatsuit replaced with a pale-green Easter dress. I squeeze Lilly's hand so that she follows my gaze and grins. When Brenda heard that Lilly not only attends church but sings in the choir, she had a change of heart. She met with Father Jay. As much as she sought forgiveness from Lilly, she understood she had to extend the same healing to him, especially knowing how much he helped me. I don't know what was said between them — I introduced them, and stepped across the room — but at the end, I saw them embrace, and as Father Jacobsen hugged me goodbye, there was peace in his misty eyes.

And then Brenda insisted on attending Mass to see this church that had embraced her daughter.

She is on the path to finding peace with what happened in her life.

As much as I've learned, as much as I've been overwhelmed with the changes in my outlook and faith, I am washed anew with joy as I sing along with the choir, and even more so when Lilly solos during the Responsorial Psalm. Brenda beams, Sinclair nods and prays, and I sigh with contentment.

Brenda and Lilly are going out for lunch after Mass. Lilly told the police everything after Colette's arrest, and Henry was picked up on rape charges, so we know Brenda will soon gain custody, and she's no longer afraid of violating the restraining order that's kept her at arm's length. Despite that being my goal, my heart aches over the thought of Lilly's room being empty and silent. I'll miss her keeping me in line with her scowling eyes and forthright comments. I pray she'll forever slip in and out of my life like the elusive moonbeam she is.

After Mass, I stand in the thin April air with my eyes clenched shut and clasp Sinclair's hand as Seth places an Easter basket full of flowers in front of the family tombstone. I don't want to cry.

I have lived through what Saint Thérèse was trying to teach me: I am but a daisy beneath towering cedars, as helpless and defenseless as a tiny wildflower, and yet God loves me as much as the ancient oak tree or the perfect rose and forgives my every mistake and every sin.

I have thrown myself *with abandon* into His arms.

I know there are dark valleys ahead. I know there may be more dark than light. But there will be light. He has promised me light, and I must trudge forward with my heart turned to doing the little things that express his love without any thought toward compensation. That is Saint Thérèse's Little Way. To love for the sake of love alone.

Seth pulls at my dress and points to Caroline's little grave. "Look. There are flowers here already."

I open my eyes to see him pointing at a plant sprouting from the grave, a wild rose with pale pink petals and a crown in the center like a dogwood blossom.

Sinclair bends down and touches the delicate flower. "Who do you think planted it?"

Seth answers before I can. "Saint Thérèse."

We both look at him, astonished. Sinclair laughs. "What do you know about Saint Thérèse?"

"Lots," he replies. "Lilly told me."

I sigh and let the joy of the flower fill me as we stand and face each other. He sees the sadness and joy intermingled in me, and takes me into his arms. I am humbled that he loves me so much that he has held my hand throughout this long journey when he could have so easily hated me. He knew Caroline died because of my negligence and yet he never turned his back on me, not even when he had to set me aside for

Seth's sake. He has lived the Little Way without even knowing what it was. I want to show him love in return a hundredfold.

I have a secret I've been holding all day, waiting for the right moment. It scared me at first. Everything in my life has been shaky for so long that I wonder if I can handle any more emotional upheaval. My heart is crying because I don't want anyone or anything to seem like a replacement for Caroline, but as I've thought about everything I've learned from Saint Thérèse, I know this is a gift of joy God is handing me, and any time, especially in the darkest of times, one must cherish rays of light. *O Lord, you have turned my mourning into joy.*

I wrap my arms around Sinclair's neck and kiss him. "I love you," I say.

"I know," he responds.

"And I'm having your baby."

His face is ashen for a moment. "Are you sure?"

I nod.

I see his mind working. Maybe he's worried I'll go insane again and think this baby is Caroline. Maybe he's worried I won't be an attentive mother, that I'll make some horrible misjudgment again. But he's a doctor, so I guess he's thinking about the meds. "It's okay. I've been off them for two months, and I'm just barely pregnant. She's safe."

"She?"

I shrug. "He."

He caresses my face, and then leans into me again with a kiss that says everything I need to hear.

As we walk away, I see a girl in a brown Carmelite habit, black veil lifting behind her in the wind. She looks over at me. Our eyes meet. Warm eyes, wise for her youth. She smiles at me as though we share a secret, raises her hand, and vanishes over the side of the hill.

EPILOGUE

I have now reached a stage in my life when I can glance back at the past, for my soul has matured in a crucible of inner and external trials. Now, like a flower braced by a storm, I can raise my head and see that the words of the Psalmist have been fulfilled in me: "The Lord is my shepherd; I shall not want. He maketh me to lie down in green pastures: he leadeth me beside the still waters. He restoreth my soul . . . Yea, though I walk through the valley of the shadow of death, I will fear no evil: for thou [art] with me."

Saint Thérèse

ACKNOWLEDGMENTS

❧❦

To my husband and children, whose sweet patience made this book possible. A huge thank-you to Wendy Toy, Sylvia Roller, and Larry Jacks for reading early drafts. To Lisa Jackel and Lesa Bethea for their input. To Bucky Bethea for being the hero. To Dan Shine for his legalese. To Jan Null for expertise. To Jeana Ledbetter for giving me confidence. And many thanks to my editor, Regina Doman, for her wonderful enthusiasm and guidance.

As always, all glory be to the Father, and to the Son, and to the Holy Spirit.

Michelle

ABOUT THE AUTHOR

Michelle Buckman lives with her husband and five children near the Carolina coast. Walking the long stretches of sandy beaches is a favorite pastime that provides great writing inspiration. She shares news and welcomes comments from readers through her website at www.MichelleBuckman.com.

Chisel & Cross books are works of popular fiction by contemporary (and sometimes first-time) Catholic authors. Among them are thrillers, mysteries, fantasies, historical novels, teen books, science fiction, and even romance novels. Each is a tale well told, and each has a strong Catholic sensibility.

By means of *Chisel & Cross Books*, we at Sophia Institute Press® seek to help rejuvenate Catholic literature in our day by giving voice to novice writers and a wide readership to veteran Catholic authors more practiced in their art.

Sophia Institute Press®

Sophia Institute® is a nonprofit institution that seeks to restore man's knowledge of eternal truth, including man's knowledge of his own nature, his relation to other persons, and his relation to God. Sophia Institute Press® serves this end in numerous ways: it publishes translations of foreign works to make them accessible for the first time to English-speaking readers; it brings out-of-print books back into print; and it publishes important new books that fulfill the ideals of Sophia Institute®. These books afford readers a rich source of the enduring wisdom of mankind.

For your free catalog, call:
Toll-free: 1-800-888-9344
or write:
Sophia Institute Press®
Box 5284, Manchester, NH 03108
or visit our website:
www.SophiaInstitute.com

Sophia Institute® is a tax-exempt institution as defined by the Internal Revenue Code, Section 501(c)(3). Tax I.D. 22-2548708.